Deep Bay Vengeance

A Christian Mystery Suspense

By Kathleen Morris

Copyright Kathleen Morris 2012

ISBN – 978-1-927828-55-7
2nd edition

ROUGE PUBLISHING

This book is dedicated to my loving husband Barry, who never ceases to give me inspiration for my writing, with his colorful crazy life of adventure that I love so much. It is also dedicated to my three beautiful grown children Renee, Philip, and Brett, who have given me encouragement to write what I love and love what I write. Last but not least, I wish to dedicate this, my very first book, to Jesus Christ, my God and Savior, who brought me through the best and the worst of life, so that I may help others see his light…even through the darkness!

TABLE OF CONTENTS

Prologue

Monday, January 30th - 3:58 p.m.

Screaming customers collapsed against a cold tile floor as the first gunshot ricocheted.

"The kid gets the next bullet if I don't get a key to the vault in five seconds," the masked man shouted as he yanked a teenage boy backward shoving a .357 Magnum to his lower jaw with a white-gloved hand.

All doors to Chicago's largest national bank suddenly locked simultaneously. Three more men appeared with Uzis, wearing black ski masks and white gloves. They shot out security cameras, shattering glass while customers covered their heads with their arms.

Silence.

"One...two...three...," the man shouted again, pushing the .357 Magnum further into the teenager's jaw. "Somebody better give me the key or I swear I'll blow this kid's head right off."

"Stop!" a woman cried with her hands up. "*Please!* Don't hurt my son! Let him go and take *me* instead. *Please!*"

"*What?*" the man retorted. "I don't care about your kid, lady. I'll kill both of you if you don't shut up and get a key to the vault. Got it?"

The boy's mother shook her head, sobbing. "*God help us!*"

"Unless God has a key, you'd better shut up, lady!"

"I'll shut her up," another masked man answered as he hit her on the back of the head from behind. She wailed as she dropped to the floor, holding her bloodied scalp.

"Wise up, people!" the man shouted. "We mean business so don't try anything stupid. Now, get a key to the vault or I swear I'll shoot him!"

Nobody answered.

The masked man eyed the crowd and then the boy as he continued to choke, squeezing harder this time, pulling him backward while he struggled. "You guys are pathetic!"

Sobbing sounds filled the room as the man started counting again. "Let's see, where was I? Two? Three? No, it was four. Now four and a half, four and three quarters...Times up people."

"No...!" the boy's mother cried again. "Wait!"

"...Five!"

The gun pierced against the screaming cries as the teen's lifeless body dropped to the floor, speckling a bloody mess around him.

"Oh God! No!" his mother moaned, sobbing into her hands.

"Get up," the man kicked her head as he pulled her up by her black hair.

Screaming, she surrendered to his tight grip around her neck like a vice. "She's next if I don't get that key in five seconds. One...two..."

"Stop! Wait!" A small bald man from behind the counter rose with his arms up. "I know where the key is. I mean, I can get it for you."

"Well it's about time."

"B-but...I don't have it with me," the man smiled painfully. "I need to call someone first."

"Right, and maybe I just need to skip to five."

"*No*! Really! See, the boss, he left early. He...he's the only one with the key."

The masked man smiled and slowly cocked his head to the side. "Well then, that's too bad for you, now isn't it, baldy?"

The man's smile waned as he suddenly realized his fate. He collapsed immediately as a bullet perforated his sweaty forehead.

"Well, this is your lucky day, lady," the man grinned at the black-haired woman, releasing his chokehold on her. "Seems as though baldy took your place."

She grabbed her throat with both hands and gasped for air, coughing as she crumpled to the ground beside a young woman in a pink business suit. Their eyes locked for a moment, sharing pain until the woman quickly darted hers away.

"On to plan *B,* guys," the masked man grinned to his comrades. "We'll have to use the explosives. Come on, Ruby. We need you, babe."

The young woman in the pink business suit sheepishly looked around and slowly got up. All eyes met hers with shock and disbelief. She blushed against her long blonde hair and flipped it backward as if she didn't care what they thought. "I'm coming, Hun."

Moments seemed like hours as the hostages lay on the bank floor in wait. Suddenly a small explosion illuminated the hallway to the left where the vault was situated. Within minutes, the men ran out carrying bags, jostling machine guns over their shoulders.

"Hurry up, we set the silent alarm off," the woman in the pink business suit warned the others.

"Thanks, Babe."

"What do we do with the hostages?" one asked.

"Shoot em!"

Cries filled the room as the men pulled off their ski masks, rubbing their matted hair. "On the count of five...One...Two...Three..."

The black-haired woman who lost her son lay her body down in surrender.

"Four…Five."

The compact submachine guns peppered the crowd as hostages scrambled on the floor screaming in terror. Some of them foolishly stood trying to run, only to fall like martyrs. The visual horror mirrored itself in the eyes of every victim as they cried for a mercy that would not come.

The grieving mother lay in wait. She peered through an opening between her arm and the floor. All four men wore smiles; their faces clearly etched in her mind forever. With a sudden jolt, a bullet pierced her arm, then her shoulder, then…

Her eyelids fluttered, her breathing laboured until a force beyond her control coaxed her to lay her heavy head down, relinquishing the fight, giving her the right of passage as her eyes glazed into a complete and utter darkness.

Chapter 1

One day earlier – Sunday, January 29th.

Loretta Lancaster hated her life.

If only she could turn the clock back twenty years. Being forty-five stunk. Who enjoyed watching her own body deteriorate anyway? Nothing seemed to fit anymore. Her saggy bulging stomach looked like white bread dough with too much yeast. It did nothing but expand every year, and the crow's feet only made her premature greying black hair appear even more pathetic. *Thank the Lord for black hair dye.* At least she could change that part of her looks without much trouble.

She dried her dripping hair upside down with a towel, her now *jet-black* locks without the grey, and flipped it up, examining herself in the mirror. Her hair fell limp next to her pale dry aging skin, wrinkles creasing her forehead. She scowled at the pathetic reflection. *Lord, I know we're supposed to get old, but why must it be so difficult?*

The phone rang, startling her. "Get the phone, Bob!" she yelled from inside the steamy bathroom. "I'm doing my hair."

Loretta heard her husband pick up. She was relieved because she didn't want to talk to anyone anyway, not yet at least. First, she needed some time alone. After all, it was a special day for her, and she had to manifest a more youthful version of herself.

Sundays usually brought out a more cheery disposition in her, but today she couldn't seem to shake the depression. Today had crept up on her too fast. Ever since her fortieth birthday, time seemed to cheat her. Now at forty-five, Loretta was still stressed, still just a mom with numerous problems. Nothing ever changed. Her kids always needed something. If it wasn't money, it was her time. Everyone demanded her attention but never appreciated it, and her atheist husband was no better. In fact, he was the worst, taking her for granted, putting her faith down, and causing her tremendous suffering.

She wondered if life would ever get better for her. Part of her wished she never met her husband, never gave love away as if it came from an endless source. The fact was she had no more love to give. The well was dry.

For the longest time when the kids were young, she prayed for the day she could just have time for herself. But it didn't work out that way. Trudy started college two years ago and is still living at home, draining the family income. Tammy, the second youngest, is supposed to graduate from grade twelve this June, but wants to stay home too, and Jeremy, the baby of the family, apparently needs to sponge money from his mother even though his part-time job at McDonalds gives him plenty of spending money.

"What do you need twenty bucks for this time Jeremy?" she asked her son last night before he left for work.

"I need it for gas, mom, what do you think? I told you my car is a gas-guzzler. If I had a new one, I wouldn't have to borrow so much money all the time."

"I told you we're not going to get you a new car, Jeremy. It costs too much."

"Dad said I could."

Bob always handed the kids anything they wanted. It was an ongoing problem since birth. He always undermined her authority as a mother. Lately she found herself wishing she were anything but a mother and wife. After all, wasn't slavery against the law? She should be free to call herself, Loretta Lancaster, world-renowned children's book illustrator.

What a joke. She ran her little art business from her home for nearly six years now, and not one decent book contract had come her way. Oh, she could draw beautifully, and the paintings she did were the finest quality, but to try to sell them, that was the problem. Nobody wanted to pay her. She always ended up giving her work away more than selling it. Nobody took her seriously, especially her husband. He told her to get a real job in the heat of an argument once, and he meant it. Everyone means it with their insulting remarks they make about her work being a good *hobby*. Didn't they understand? It *wasn't* supposed to be a hobby; it was supposed to be a job.

Loretta sighed; nobody respected her, not as a mother, a wife, or as an artist. *Lord, when will things ever change for me?*

As the morning lingered on and Loretta got herself dressed and ready for church, she gave herself a half-smile in the foggy mirror before she left the bathroom.

Jeremy complained when she got out, "*Finally*, you were in the bathroom for two hours. Are you going for lunch with the President or something?"

"Don't you talk to me that way, young man, I am your *mother*."

Jeremy ignored her as he sauntered into the empty bathroom, "Whatever."

"I hope you're going to be ready for church on time, young man," Loretta called after him as he slammed the bathroom door, grumbling. "I *can't*, mom!" he yelled from behind the door. "I told you I gotta work at eleven."

Loretta sighed again, backing down like she usually did. *I give up.*

She worried about Jeremy's salvation. She didn't want him to turn out like Bob, even though she was sure of his conversion when he was ten. But ever since he took the job at McDonalds, he missed church too often. At least he went to a good *Christian* school and Friday night Youth Group. She only hoped it was enough.

Maybe she should side with Bob and let him purchase the boy a new car after all, or perhaps one that just looked new. After all, Jeremy's car *was* a money pit, and it did consume most of his pay check. Maybe he wouldn't have to work so much then. Maybe he would be able to come to church more often.

"Bob," Loretta summoned her husband as he sat at the kitchen table eating breakfast. "I was thinking about Jeremy's car…"

Bob sat at the kitchen table still in his pyjamas. He was a balding, fat, unattractive male chauvinist who seemed disconnected from Loretta most of the time. His bifocals sat at the end of his pointy nose as he scoured the paper without a hint of courtesy. He didn't even bother to look up at his wife. "What?"

"Jeremy's car," she said with her hands on her hips.

Loretta hated his blatant disrespect for her. Was she *really* as repulsive to look at as her husband made her out to be? "Bob! Would you look at me please?"

Bob scowled, reluctantly looking sideways at her now. "What on earth do you *want*, woman?"

"I'm speaking to you."

Her husband pulled off his glasses and shockingly looked his wife up and down. "What the heck are you all dressed up for?"

"Church."

Loretta's face grew red. "Not that *you* ever want to go!"

Bob shook his head, "Not on your life! Church is cancelled anyway. Someone called an hour ago to tell you but I wasn't about to interrupt your *spa*."

"What? Since when do they cancel church?" Loretta snapped.

"Since there's a winter storm warning," Bob grumbled and started reading his paper again. "You'd know that if you hadn't been in the bathroom primping for two bloody hours."

"Thanks a lot!"

Bob didn't look up. "Your welcome…By the way…Jeremy's old beater needs a new transmission. We could hunt another one down at the wreckers, but by the time we found one and put it in, it would cost a fortune. What he really needs is a new…"

"I know," Loretta reluctantly completed her husband's sentence, "a new car."

"Yah, I've been looking in the classifieds," he continued to read the paper, "and I found a good one in here for only ten-thousand."

"Ten-thousand?" Loretta shouted a little too loud. "We can't afford a ten- thousand-dollar vehicle!"

Jeremy came out of the bathroom then and casually walked bare-chested into the kitchen, grabbing a banana and peeling it. "Come on mom, don't be such a tightwad," he said, stuffing the fruit in his mouth and mumbling. "Trudy doesn't have to drive an old beater, and neither does Tammy."

Perhaps she *was* being a little stingy. If it would help him out so he didn't have to take so many shifts at McDonalds, it might be worth it. He could come to church more often. What was ten-thousand dollars compared to that? *I'm outnumbered anyway.*

"Fine."

Her husband circled the car advertisement and reached for the portable phone beside him. He punched in a phone number and talked to her before it connected. "You can go to the bank tomorrow and get the money, can't you honey?"

Now you call me honey.

"No, if Jeremy wants a car for ten-thousand dollars, he's going to have to go to the bank with me and see just how much money that really is, *Bob*."

"But mom," Jeremy whined, "I have to work after school, and..."

"Well you're just going to have to take some time out of your busy schedule to go with me to the bank if you want the money."

Bob groaned and rubbed his head. "Do what your mother says, Jeremy."

His statement almost gave her a heart attack. Usually Bob told Jeremy the opposite. It was obvious he wanted to butter her up.

Loretta slumped down on the kitchen chair beside her husband and glared at her spoiled son still chomping on yet another banana. Sometimes she wished he'd get a little taste of reality just to push him to grow up for once. Adversity wouldn't hurt him one bit, it might actually do him some good.

Jeremy stomped away without saying a word.

Bob jabbered on the phone to someone about the vehicle he had found for his son. Loretta wondered why her husband would choose to use all of their savings to buy a car when part of that money was supposed to go for their summer vacation; the other part she assumed was going to be an investment for her art business. Bob had promised.

Why do I always have to give up my dreams for everyone else? And today of all days. Didn't anyone in this family even remember?

"So, I'm gonna run over and take a look at that car with Jeremy before he has to go to work, Loretta," Bob informed her as he folded up the newspaper and pushed his chair away from the breakfast table. "At least Jeremy's beater is good for something: It starts no matter how cold it is, and it's as heavy as a tank on these icy roads."

"Be careful."

Bob rolled his eyes as he stood up. "Why don't you do something constructive instead of worrying about everything, Loretta, like take that getup off?"

Loretta frowned. "Maybe we could go out for lunch when you get back?"

"Are you kidding, I'm not starting up *our* car in this weather."

No, but you'll take your son out in it.

Bob impolitely brushed past his wife. "Oh Loretta, don't pout so much, you'll give yourself more wrinkles. Why would you want to go out when they're forecasting a snowstorm anyway?"

Tears blurred Loretta's vision as she watched her son and husband slip their winter parkas on and slam the door behind them. Sobs turned to heavy weeping. Part of her wished her husband would never come back…and he could take that carbon-copy son of his with him for all she cared.

Oh, how she wished there had been church this morning. It was her *only* release, a time to decompress. At least *God* respected and valued her. He'd never turn his back on her, reject her, or abandon her like Bob and Jeremy always did. *Why did you have to let the weather turn bad today Lord, today of all days?*

What did she expect anyway; winter in Chicago was always like this.

Loretta stopped her pathetic weeping for a moment, sniffling as she listened to the creaking rafters of her empty home. Nothing but the brutal wind howled against her picture-framed walls. Jeremy's school picture hung there in a gold frame like royalty. Oh, how proud she was when she mounted it on the wall at the beginning of the school year. Now, she wondered why she even bothered to pine after his love.

Rejection was the only thing that lingered in the vacuum she lived in, constantly reminding her that her once happy home full of giggling children, noisy toys and bustling schedules, was empty now, just like her heart.

Empty was an understatement today. Trudy wasn't even home, she stayed overnight with a friend, and Tammy was still at a youth retreat. Bob and Jeremy's silly vehicle garbage had hurt her more this time than they even realized. But it didn't matter, nobody remembered anyway. She would just spend the day alone again.

"Well," she sniffled as she raised Bob's half-empty coffee mug as if to make a toast, "Happy birthday to me!"

Chapter 2

Present day, Thursday, June 29th.

Five extremely long and painful months lingered by since the robbery, and Loretta's arm still wasn't feeling up to par. The doctor said it would take a while, but at least the exercises were helping. She kept reminding herself that she really had nothing to complain about compared to the other victims. They were dead.

Loretta had been going to a shrink for a while. He wanted to help her with her *"issues"* as he put it. More like he wanted to take advantage of her situation. Some doctors would do and say almost anything just for a buck. It sickened her. It was bad enough she had to go through what she did, but to lose her son, and have someone make a profit off it: *unbelievable*. So, she gave her shrink the boot. He didn't make much sense anyway. He said she wasn't dealing with things. How could she not be dealing with things? It took her a week just to get up enough courage to talk about it. Did she finally do it? Yes. Did she talk to the police? Yes. She even went as far as working with a sketch artist to identify the four felons responsible for the heist. She never mentioned the bimbo in the pink though. That was *her* secret. Secret. Loretta herself was supposed to be a secret. The media reported that all the hostages had perished in the bank robbery. They didn't want anyone coming after Loretta.

"We know these four guys," the police told her when she was helping the sketch artist. "They're known felons."

But it didn't matter. They were long gone by the time their pictures surfaced on the news. It was her fault. She had taken too long to speak up, to identify them.

"They probably left the country by now, Mrs. Lancaster." The police went on, "If you would have only co-operated sooner."

That statement still made her blood boil. Everybody blamed her, even Bob.

"Tell them what happened!" Bob shouted at her, as she lay wounded and speechless in the hospital bed. "Tell *me* what happened. *I* want to know what happened to my son!" He swore a string of swearwords at her but she didn't bat an eye.

Hospital security had to haul Bob out with his hysterical shouting and ranting. She heard him sobbing by the time the two officers escorted him down the hallway. But she couldn't do anything for the man. She had nothing left inside of her.

Bob never came back to visit her in the hospital again.

Jeremy's entire school had attended his funeral, everyone except his own mother. News excerpts showed distraught friends and family sobbing and hugging each other. Loretta, on the other hand, could not even cry. She still couldn't. She tried to, but for some reason, nothing came out at all.

Trudy moved out of the house the first week after Jeremy's death. Loretta received flowers at the hospital one day with a small white card that simply read, "Sorry mom, I can't deal with this. I moved out."

Tammy apparently graduated last week. Without a word, she took off to Europe with her friends. Her dad gave her money for the trip no doubt. At least she had the decency to send a postcard from Paris. Loretta wished she would have been able to go to the graduation but she knew she wasn't wanted there. Bob would have made a fuss.

Her husband finally got his wish. The divorce came through today. Loretta held the papers in her lap as she sat on her living-room sofa. At least Bob left her the house and Jeremy's old jalopy, though all it does is sit in the garage now, left as a shrine.

She never wanted the blasted divorce in the first place. In the beginning, she fought him tooth and nail. Then when he started dating all those younger women right in front of her nose, she didn't care anymore. He had wounded her heart beyond repair.

He spent most of his time drinking his sorrows away anyway. He moved in with some bimbo named Mandy, or Candy, or something like that. Apparently, she's supposed to be a beautiful twenty-six-year-old, and everything Loretta is not. Bob was old enough to be her father for heaven sake.

No loss though. She could have the old bald fool. Divorcing him was actually a relief. Life would be a lot more enjoyable without his put-downs anyway. But it was lonely. Sitting alone in a big house all day was the hard part. Old church members periodically popped by to visit even though she tried to give them the brush-off many times. She stopped attending church altogether after Jeremy died. Why should she pay homage to a God that seemed to be on vacation when she needed Him the most? How cruel. If He didn't care about her, why should she care about Him?

Loretta set the divorce papers aside and moved over to the computer, her lifeline now, thankful for the second mortgage that helped her pay for the expensive thing. She borrowed against the house right after Bob told her she could have the "hideous thing" as he put it. The deed had never been in Bob's name. It had been her mother's beloved home up until she passed away. It was sixty years old, very small, and in desperate need of renovations, but it was home. She was glad Bob didn't fight her for it. He'd taken almost everything else.

The money from the house would be her soul source of income for a while until she figured something else out. Income. At least she had that now. She remembered her drawings...That silly business, never able to bring in a dime. Burning all her artwork was the best thing she could have ever done for herself. She had no talent anyway. But computers, this she could do, maybe even make a living from.

Playing around on the internet was how it all began, her brilliant idea that is. She typed in the names of the four felons one day, just to see what would pop up on the screen. From that, she obtained numerous amounts of pertinent information about them. Everyday she'd find out more. It was almost like a sickness. Finally, she came up with the perfect plan. If nobody else was going to find her son's murderer, she would. Luring those four goons to the most remote place she could find was easy.

Now she just had to get there.

Chapter 3

Friday, June 30th.

The morning was dreary and overcast when Loretta got up. She could smell the hint of rain in the air, odd for the end of June, yet somehow appropriate for the long over-due retribution that would soon follow.

"Come on," Loretta complained as she surveyed the empty parking space in front of her house. The taxicab she had called over an hour ago was late. Loretta checked her watch impatiently for the umpteenth time. It would be just her luck to miss the flight. She had to be at O'Hare at least two hours early.

Everything was ready, suitcases packed and waiting, every piece of pertinent information like her passport with that hideous photo, tucked away in her wallet. Loretta wished she would have been able to dye her hair already but that wasn't the plan. Her homely grey hair looked like a skunk because she hadn't bothered to dye it in the past five months. The top was grey and the ends were leftover black from January. She couldn't do anything about it now. She'd have to wait until she passed customs. It was very important that she follow her plans precisely. Every detail mattered, especially her hair. This time it would be a different color. She always wanted to be a redhead.

Moments later, a cab honked outside. "Finally!" she rolled her eyes as she glared out of the window. Loretta grabbed her two modest suitcases, and swung her combination laptop case-purse over her shoulder fumbling to open the front door. She set one suitcase down outside to pull the door closed and stood quietly on the step for a moment reflecting on how far she had come, how many pain staking hours of research and planning it had taken her to reach this point. She almost prayed for her plans to succeed. A dog barked in the distance, thankfully, nudging her mind from the thought. She didn't need God, and she was definitely going to prove it.

"Come on lady," the cabbie complained as he stood beside his open trunk.

"I'm coming."

Loretta lowered the two suitcases into the trunk and shimmied her way into the back seat of the cab swinging her laptop bag beside her.

"Where too lady?" the driver asked as he laboured back into the vehicle. Speckles of rain began to dance across the windshield as the driver put the car into gear. She didn't answer him right away. Sadness seemed to linger, a sorrowful moment as she watched the rain dribble unevenly down the window, like mini streams not knowing which way to flow. The reflection troubled her. Perhaps it was last minute jitters, or maybe a little nausea. Whatever it was, Loretta didn't have time for it.

"Come on lady, where too?" the cabbie sighed impatiently.

She gulped hard, it was now or never, "…O'Hare International Airport please.

~~~~

"You've got to be kidding Harvey. Why would *I* want to go on a fishing trip?" the older woman chuckled. "Take one of your friends. You know I don't like to fish."

"Please Bertha! I told you Ben dropped out at the last minute, and he already paid for the non-refundable vacation package. There'll be an empty seat."

Harvey didn't really want to take his sister, but his options were running out. He had taken these sorts of trips with Ben ever since his wife died five years ago. But to face going alone? That was frightening. Lonely idle time meant idle thought, and idle thought meant him feeling sorry for himself, pining after his dead wife's memories. No. He had to find someone to take Ben's place, fast.

Since Harvey took an early retirement from the police force last year, he seemed disconnected from the people he worked with. He couldn't ask any of them to go. And friends were scarce since Rose passed away too. The only ones suiting that description these days happened to be Ben and his sixty-year-old big sister, and for some reason he couldn't picture Bertha roughing it out in the wild. Yet…as a last resort, he'd ask her one more time. "Please Bertha. I have nobody else."

It wasn't going to be a great July long weekend if she didn't say yes.

"No…and that's final." His sister scowled as she continued to stitch one of her monstrous Ladies-Aid quilts for charity. Bertha was a good companion when he needed a little company, but she sure could be cantankerous. His decision to move in with her after Rose passed was a blessing, but sometimes she could really get on his nerves. It wasn't as if he was asking her to give up a kidney. He just wanted a traveling companion. Ben sure left him in a bind.

"Why don't you ask someone from church?"

Harvey rolled his eyes...then contemplated it for a moment, "Maybe." He started leafing through the church directory. "Pastor Bill might want to come."

"Now there you go Harvey. All is not lost."

He picked up the phone with an impish grin and punched in the numbers. "Hi Pastor Bill, its Harvey Strong."

"And what can I do for you sir," the charismatic thirty-five-year-old preacher chided back.

"Well, I have a strange request..." Harvey noticed complete silence on the other end, not a good sign. "I was wondering what you were doing for the next few days."

"Well you know, it's funny you should ask...My wife just twisted my arm to clear my calendar for the weekend. Apparently, she wants to take the *whole* family across to the island for the July long weekend, see Butchart Gardens, Fable Cottage, and Sea Land. You know...the works."

"Is that right," Harvey frowned. "Well...you have a nice trip then."

"Oh, we will. We haven't been on a real family vacation in years, and since it's in our own backyard, we might as well," the pastor said. "But you wanted something?"

"Oh, it's nothing...nothing that can't wait anyway," he lied.

Harvey set down the phone with a sigh.

"Way to go chicken," his sister teased as she sat within earshot of the phone. "You're not going to get anyone that way, and your running out of time. Doesn't your plane leave soon?"

Yes mother, it does!

He had exactly four hours in which to convince someone to go with him on very short notice, and then make it to the Vancouver International Airport on time for his flight. Harvey exhaled through his puckered mouth and punched in another number. "Hi, is this Gale? This is Harvey…Harvey Strong. Your husband wouldn't happen to be home this morning by any chance, would he?"

"Oh…No Harvey," she said, "Martin's out of town this week. Is there something I can help you with?" *Yah, maybe you'd like to go with me?* Harvey scrapped that thought the minute it entered his mind. Now he was just being plain foolish.

"No. Just tell him I called."

Harvey placed the phone back on the receiver and blushed at his sister. She didn't have to be such a hawk, sitting there watching him with those carping eyes. "What?"

"I didn't say anything."

Thank the good Lord.

One more, Harvey thought to himself. He'd try one more number and that would be it. He punched in the numbers, turned his back to his sister, and plugged one ear with his finger. "Hi, is Pete there?"

"Speaking…"

Harvey's stomach started to hurt. "What are you doing this morning?"

The man on the other line answered, "Nothing."

"How would you like to take a vacation with me?"

"What?" the man replied with confusion.

"How would you like to take a fishing trip with me? I have an extra ticket and…"

The man interrupted rather annoyed, "…I can't go anywhere. Didn't you know my back was out again? Margaret put it on the prayer chain yesterday. Where've you been *man*?"

"Oh…I'm sorry…" Harvey blushed, apologising like an idiot. "I didn't…"

Click. The phone hummed in his ear. The guy didn't just hang up on him, did he? If that didn't beet all. Harvey slammed the receiver down, frustrated and enraged. He fingered his crumpled hanky in his pocket, yanked it out, and wiped his sweaty forehead. He didn't dare look at Bertha.

That's it...I'm going alone!

He marched down the hall to his bedroom and slammed the door. *Rosey dear, I wish you were still here. You'd go with me I know you would.* He sobbed, lifting a single dowdy brown leather suitcase to his bed. He popped it open and started heedlessly stuffing things into it. He was going on this vacation one way or the other, even if he had to go alone. And by George, he was going to have the time of his life too.

Bertha waved at him from the door as his taxi rolled away. He nodded at her as if he was about to explode. It wasn't her fault. It was nobody's fault. He would just have to endure this trip alone.

"Vancouver International Airport please," he told the driver, forcing a smile. "I'm going fishing!"

~~~~

Vicki Booth headed North on I-94 racing her vintage Harley Davidson Motor bike against the unfavorable weather. She'd picked a miserable day for riding with the on and off drizzle since this morning, a type of weather that made her think of Brighton England, her home where she grew up, where she and her sister were born.

She only found out that she had a sister when she was fifteen. Her drug-addicted mother had sent her sibling to a different orphanage in Chicago shortly after she was born. She lived there until she was twelve. Then, after a great deal of searching and persuading, Vicki finally managed to bring her sister home to England.

Now, after all those years, she still remembered the pain of watching her nineteen-year-old scrawny sister leave for the very place she rescued her from: Chicago. "It's much better than England," her little sister would boast, threatening to move back as soon as she was old enough, refusing to pick up the British accent like everyone else. "Talk right," she'd scold Vicki, embarrassed of her own heritage. It saddened her now.

Missing her sister more than words could say, Vicki said goodbye to her birthplace and followed her sister five years ago. It seemed as though she'd spent a lifetime tracking her down...and now again. A tear streamed down her already wet face as she thought of the only relative she had in the world.

Thunder cracked above her.

If she had been thinking clearly, she never would have left the motel this morning. But she had to keep going, if she stopped for too long, she might change her mind, and that was definitely not going to happen, not after everything she had been through.

"If your sister is missing Miss Booth, we have no leads at all and we can't spend any more time on the case. Chances are she doesn't want anyone to find her, or she's already dead. Aside from the last place she was, we don't know where else to look. If you want to hire a private detective, he would be more than willing to further the investigation. Other than that, there's nothing more we can do."

Vicki shook her dripping helmet head. *Thanks for nothing!* She had no use for a worthless police force that was too preoccupied to care, and why would she pay a P.I. to do something she could do herself? She knew her sister better than anyone else did, and if there was one thing she was definitely sure of, her sister wasn't dead. *They* were wrong. Her sister *was* alive; she could feel it

They were both women who had been around the block. They were flatmates for five years already, or "roommates" she was supposed to say. She knew her sister well enough to know she could fend for herself. No, if anything, her sister was just lost, wounded maybe, but not dead.

She floored the throttle with her black leather glove, and sped off toward Fargo, North Dakota. With any luck, she would reach the Canadian border by nightfall.

Chapter 4

Loretta was completely exhausted by the time her connecting flight from Minneapolis had arrived at the Saskatoon Airport. She gasped at the high temperatures reported over the intercom as they landed. She didn't know the weather in Saskatchewan could get up to thirty-six degrees Celsius. Actually, she didn't know much about Saskatchewan at all, or Canada for that matter. She never had a reason to until now. Her research informed her somewhat, but before that, she actually believed the rumors that they lived in igloos.

The first matter of utmost importance was to find a decent restroom, she thought to herself as she waited to exit the plane. Her bladder was completely full. She wondered for a moment if they even had modern facilities. Would she have to use an outhouse or something?

The modest contemporary terminal was buzzing with people. Loretta had underestimated what it would be like. She thought it would be old-fashioned and quiet. Instead, it was just like O'Hare, but a lot smaller. The business of the place struck her as a little odd. It was so noisy. Then she remembered the long weekend. This country had a holiday tomorrow. Why didn't they celebrate Independence Day on the forth like everyone else? But then, they did tend to do things a little backward. They celebrated Thanksgiving too early too.

Loretta shrugged her shoulders and headed for the bathroom, thinking how silly she was to assume she'd be using an outhouse. The extremely long line-up filled with women and children from all sorts of ethnic backgrounds. They waited with bags at hand and suitcases propped up against them. The wait was unbearable. For a moment, Loretta considered skipping it, but her bladder told her otherwise. She sighed as she gave into the hullabaloo, setting her own bag down on the floor against her leg to join the endless multitude.

~~~

The plane had been delayed two hours but Harvey didn't seem to mind. He was never one for schedules anyway, that was Rose's department, not his. He would rather be spontaneous anyway. As long as he got to Saskatoon some time tonight, it really didn't make much of a difference.

He ignored the crowd as he sat waiting for his luggage, chomping on the scrumptious baloney sandwich his sister had packed for him. He'd have to thank her after the trip. She must have snuck it in his bag unawares. What a doll.

The weather outside threatened a storm with its foreboding black clouds. Harvey missed that part of his old homeland the most. He hadn't been back in many years but he missed the unpredictable weather, this land of living skies where he grew up. It was like no other place, very different from the mountains. Prairie life always was. It seemed to have a certain charm to it, unlike the hectic fast-paced lifestyle of Vancouver. Yet, British Columbia was the place he met his beloved Rose. He stayed for her, and that was more than worth it. At times, he often thought of coming back here, but then he changed his mind, not bearing to leave her memory behind. He still had distant relatives here, but the last time he took Rose to visit them, she was young, vibrant, and cancer free.

Harvey pondered on that thought as he smeared a tear with his broad course thumb. *No self-pity, remember?* This was supposed to be an enjoyable trip and by golly, he was going to make it so. He checked his watch, wondering if he should bother looking up an old relative for the night or find a motel. He opted for the motel since he was practically a stranger to them now.

~~~~

"Can I please have your attention everyone?" The voice interrupted on the loud speaker. "Environment Canada has just issued a severe weather warning as well as a tornado watch. This includes the city of Saskatoon and areas within a 60 km radius. Please be advised that all planes are grounded until further notice."

Loretta shook her dripping hands without drying them and quickly retreated from the confines of the bathroom. She shifted the weight of her shoulder bag, propelling her way through the crowd to the enormous glass windows facing north. Lightning bedazzled the onlookers, illuminating multi-level shades of ebony and emerald in the sky. It was like some ominous distant galaxy from a science fiction movie come to life. It was, to say the least, incredible, unlike anything Loretta had ever seen before.

It was time to move. Loretta turned around to locate the nearest pay phone. If she didn't hurry and call a cab soon, she might not get one before the storm hit. She'd manoeuvre her way to the luggage ramp first. Hers should be there by now. She'd pick it up first, call a cab, and then be on her way to the Prairie West Motel. It wasn't supposed to be far, just five minutes away, but she had to hustle her butt.

Suddenly…the lights went out.

The crowd began to scream.

Glass shattered and crashed to the ground.

Wind exploded through fragmented windows.

Loretta collapsed to the floor on instinct. The violent whirlwinds seemed to suck the air right out of her lungs. She couldn't breathe. Was she going to die? It was the bank all over again. She couldn't see the shots, but she definitely could hear them. Yes, someone *was* shooting at her. She could feel the bullet penetrate her shoulder again. This time she wouldn't make it. This time she would surely die.

~~~~

Harvey stumbled over a woman lying prostrate on the floor. At least he thought it was a woman. He couldn't really tell in the dark chaotic mayhem that danced around him. He knelt down, gripped her body in his arms, and started shaking her, but she didn't respond, she only palsied in his arms like a rag doll.

"Lady!" he hollered as loud as he could.

What was wrong with her? Did she get hurt? He wondered if the flying debris had pierced her body somewhere…but it was hard to tell in the shadows.

Suddenly…the wind died down as quickly as it started.

Lights flickered back on to a duller imitation, auxiliary lights that seemed to labour just the same. For the first time, Harvey surveyed the damage. Bloody lacerations marked the faces of panic-stricken people as they hobbled aimlessly about. The sight of it sickened him. Flashes of old images from days on the force, perpetuated through his troubled mind. *Focus Harvey! Get a grip.*

He closed his eyes and shook his head, remembering what he was doing in the first place. The woman...she still lay lifeless at his knees. He bent over to check for a pulse. It was pounding like a drum, calming Harvey with its rhythm.

"Wake up dear," he smiled as he patted her cheek, more confident now.

She gradually fluttered her eyelids until they opened. "What happened?"

"We went through a tornado dear." Harvey beamed, glad she was coherent now. "You must have passed out, but you're not hurt. Not like some of these people." He pointed to the destruction around them. "Mostly cuts and bruises, I hope. I don't think anyone got...I mean...I think the damage was minimal. Tornados are quite common in these parts. We're lucky; this one must have just clipped us..." He realized he was jabbering too much and suddenly stopped himself, blushing at the skunk-haired woman with beautiful green eyes. He cleared his throat, "Never mind."

The woman glared suspiciously at him.

"What's your name," Harvey asked her as he guided her to the nearest seat.

"Loretta," she crabbed, yanking an oversize carrying bag to her shoulder as if she was afraid someone was going to steal it.

"Is there something wrong?"

"No, I'm fine now...just leave me alone. Please."

Harvey's smile quickly turned to a frown. *Way to go Romeo.* He had been too forward. It was hard to gear what was appropriate and what was not, this day and age. He was definitely rough and out of practice when it came to women. He scratched his head confused. "I'm sorry…I just wanted to help. I could call you a cab or something."

"I can call my *own* cab."

Strike three…You are out buddy.

"All right then," Harvey mumbled as he walked away. He could take a hint. That's what he gets for being a Good Samaritan.

Chapter 5

Saturday, July 1st.

Loretta inspected her new reflection in the mirror as she wailed at the odd woman in front of her. "What the heck is this?" Something obviously went wrong during the processing. It wasn't supposed to look like...a cartoon orange. Luckily, she decided to dye her hair in her motel room instead of a public washroom, people might have thought she was a freak. She certainly resembled one now.

The sun hadn't even begun to rise when Loretta started dying her hair. Now as it rose, she pulled out the scissors from her bag and attempted to chop enormous chunks of it away. If she was going to look like a freak, she might as well go all out.

Hanks of the feathery orange stuff fell into the sink, clogging up the drain. She didn't care. It wasn't her sink; it just belonged to a dingy motel. If it had been her sink, she never would have permitted one of her girls to do this. But she was liberated now, free from responsibility, at least the old ones she used to have. *Go free and fly...*

Yet, for some reason, Loretta didn't look like a new liberated woman. She looked like something else...a clown, a punk rocker...or perhaps just a big fool. At least the new hairdo would conceal her age...or maybe not. The hideous wrinkles across her forehead that plagued her before were still there, her pasty white complexion with sunken eyes and gauntly cheeks still revealed her age...and those unsightly grey-black eyebrows, against the orange hair, were a clear ridiculous giveaway.

Loretta observed her complete body image as she stood in the mirror. She'd lost a lot of weight in the past five months, now her skin hung in places it shouldn't. And without makeup, she looked like a ghost. If only her skin wasn't so sensitive, she could at least apply some blush. She sighed at her homely appearance. The orange choppy mess didn't help matters much either. Bob would have disowned her had she done this when they were still married. She couldn't help but chuckle. At least she was unrecognizable, and that was a good thing. She'd top her ensemble off with a trendy pair of glasses.

As Loretta glanced at her watch, she realized she was out of time. She had one more stop to make before boarding the Greyhound bus. She hoped she wouldn't have a repeat of yesterday, with the tornado. To come out of it unscathed, was something else. There was no need for that old geezer to dote over her so much. It was embarrassing. Never had anyone fussed over her like that before. It was uncomfortable, odd. She didn't need *anyone* to take care of her.

~~~~

Harvey handed the man his credit card as he waited for him to complete the rental agreement. He had chosen a candy-apple red Toyota Land Cruiser, hoping it was hardy enough for the trip. Ben would call him silly, but why not? He might as well go all out.

"Quite the storm we had last night, hey?" The man from behind the counter smiled, chatting while his back was turned.

Harvey grunted trying not to say much. Somehow, he had to get this fellow to move a little faster, or he wouldn't make it to La Ronge to connect with the floatplane.

"So where are you off too?" the man asked Harvey as he continued to chat.

"North...," Harvey sighed, fidgeting impatiently.

"North is a lot of places...Anywhere specific?"

Be nice Harvey...Do unto others, remember?

"I'm going fishing," Harvey said, hoping that would shut him up. It didn't.

"Oh...I got the perfect place. Tobin Lake, ever heard of it?"

The man droned on and on for fifteen excruciatingly painful minutes telling Harvey every detail about Tobin Lake, and about every trophy winning fish he ever caught: Northern Pike, Lake trout, Walleye, you name it. He went on about the cost of fishing licences, about boat rentals, about how it was highway robbery the prices they charged these days. Apparently, that's why the man purchased his own 16.5-foot aluminium boat with a 30 hp Yamaha motor. Harvey forced a smile trying so hard not to be rude. He only nodded in agreement and hoped the guy would catch his drift and give him the keys some time before Christmas.

"So...are you off to Tobin Lake then?" the man asked again, waiting for the correct answer as if he *needed* confirmation.

"If I tell you will you give me the keys to the Toyota?

The man chuckled, "Oh, sorry about that pal. I get a little carried away when it comes to fishing...but yah. You tell me where you're going, and I'll give you the keys."

"Fine...Ever heard of a place called Reindeer Lake?"

"Have I ever! I haven't been lucky enough to go but that place is legendary. You can actually catch Arctic Grayling up there, and they're sneaky little buggers. You can't find them in most still water, but Reindeer Lake…Had a buddy of mine go up. He says there's this one place that's more than 700 feet deep."

Harvey beamed at the fellow's captivating response. Excitement washed over both their faces. "That's what the brochure says…I bought a vacation package and everything. It's a fly-in-fishing camp, one of the smaller ones on the north end of the lake. It's supposed to be a real secluded place."

"Well…I envy you man…Have fun."

Harvey felt sorry for the jovial car-rental attendant. His enthusiasm moved him with those round saucer eyes, mentally begging him to go along. For a moment, he almost invited him, knowing there was an empty seat available. Rose would have encouraged him to ask. She would have told him Jesus invited strangers. Yet, on this muggy sweltering morning, Harvey smiled; perplexed with his own paradoxical decision…He didn't want a companion. For some reason, as illogical as that sounded, he was looking forward to finishing this quest alone.

~~~~

Last nights storm affected Vicki more than she realized. She'd think twice before sleeping in a tent during a frightening storm next time, even if it did save her a few bucks. The radio announcer informed her this morning that a tornado touched down near the Saskatoon airport last night. No wonder there's nothing left of her tent. She trashed it shortly after the storm began, opting for a cold hard bench at the bus depot instead. Aside from a backache, sleeping there didn't bother her. She figured she could take care of herself if anyone tried to mug her while she slept. Her job at the truck stop prepared her for almost anything. Luckily, nobody bothered her. Aside from an occasional tourist gawking at her as she curled up with her leather jacket, the rest of the night was uneventful.

With morning, a sudden rush of travelers filled the bus depot, coaxing Vicki to move on. She swung her jacket over her shoulder and positioned her helmet under her arm, wrenching her back as she composed herself. With every inch of her body aching, not to mention her butt from the previous days ride, getting on that bike again did not look very appealing.

Vicki left the building with a sudden rush of heat wafting into her face; she realized it was going to be another scorcher. Straddling her mammoth bike, she jumped the motor to life, reminding herself why she was here in the first place. Her sister was missing and she'd never find her if she didn't get a move on. Stuffing her thick red curls into her metallic- black helmet, she tore out of the parking lot with a reverberation so loud it followed her long after she was gone.

Chapter 6

The silver Greyhound bus roared northbound on highway 11 toward Prince Albert. Loretta relaxed her head backward against the headrest of the seat ignoring the overweight man snoring next to her, invading her space. She had no choice but to lean against the window. If another seat was available, she would have taken it, but it wasn't. The entire bus was full of holiday travelers.

The morning beamed with sunshine as she swayed to the motion of the bus. The scenery was different from home. It was so...rural. Farms with tall towering things stood out everywhere...and the cows. She couldn't remember the last time she had actually seen a real cow. Field upon field conjoined every farm, and they looked so pretty with their different colors of yellows and purples and bright pea greens set against the turquoise blue sky. It calmed Loretta.

She coddled her shoulder bag as it sat on her lap, not trusting it down on the floor. It was now a lot heavier than when she left Chicago and for good reason too. Her recent purchase consumed more room than she thought it would, concealed deep in the bowels of her bag where it should be. Lucky thing her contact was on time or the bus would have left without her. The memory was still fresh in her mind.

"You got the money?" the punk with the red bandana whispered to Loretta in the Midtown Plaza parking lot.

"Yah...I got it." Loretta whispered in response as she looked around nervously. "But you better not be hustling me...or...or I'll have my goons shank you."

The brown-skinned teenager screwed up his face, threw his head back, and laughed hysterically. "Who do you think you are lady, some secret agent or something?"

Loretta blushed and shook her head. Tears rolled down her cheeks. "I'm sorry... I...I didn't mean that. I'm a little nervous...I...I've never done this before."

"No kidding."

"Please! Give me another chance."

Look," the punk sighed. "Are you sure you want to do this?"

"Of course, I'm sure," Loretta sniffled as she wiped her tears, "I didn't come all this way for nothing."

The punk shrugged his shoulders and jerked out a gun from his jacket. "She's a nine-millimetre Glock 17, powerful. Here, see if you like it."

Loretta fondled the magnificent boxy thing, flat black and cold. She fingered the peculiar framed evil monstrosity weighing heavily in her hand, "...And the ammo?"

"...Clip...It holds seventeen rounds," the punk grinned taking the gun back and slapping the ammo into the magazine well with one thrust of his hand. "That's a lot of ammo lady. You know what I mean don't you?"

"I think so."

"Lady...I mean you could do a lot of damage with this baby. She even comes fully equipped with a laser."

"That's what I want...I'll take it."

The bus suddenly jolted Loretta's memory back to the confines of the vehicle as it retarded its brakes to a crawl.

"Ladies and gentleman," the driver announced over the intercom, "we'll be making a ten-minute stop in Prince Albert. If you need a smoke or a bathroom break, now would be the time to go."

It appeared they were back in a busy city again. Loretta had just gotten use to the prairie scenery. It seemed to change from one thing to the next here. She yawned, realizing how groggy she was, stretching like a cat into the seat adjoining hers. She was glad the big guy next to her left. This time she would plop her bag in his seat, hoping people would catch the drift and sit somewhere else.

The monitors above her were showing some kind of movie. Some of the passengers still watched, sitting like zombies with those silly headphones to their ears. She never understood how anyone could concentrate on a movie with the bus swaying as it did. And not only that, why would they want to? The scenery outside was much more interesting.

Loretta pulled out a bag of salt-and-vinegar chips and started chomping. She licked her tangy fingers and noticed that people were already starting to board the bus again. An old woman paused by her seat as Loretta fumbled with her bag. *That's right grandma, just keep on walking. I need this seat for my bag, see?* What a relief, she managed to chase her away. The woman scowled and found another seat, shaking her head as she sat. There were plenty of seats available now. The woman didn't need this particular one, she said to herself, grinning as she finished her chips. Her old self would have kindly moved over, even chatted with the stranger. That would have been the Christian thing to do. She missed that side of herself a little, the loving caring Loretta she used to be. But it had to be that way…as cruel as it was. She had no time for remorse. She wiped a tear as the bus came to life, remembering her plans.

As the bus left town, massive evergreens dotted the sides of the highway as they continued north. She checked her watch…only a few more hours to go. Her stomach churned wondering if she was ready to see that monster's face again. If all goes well, he should be there.

~~~~

The deep cavern reeked of earthy dampness, as Ruby lay crumpled within its walls. Her twisted ankle throbbed as she tried to catch her breath, gasping for air. If she weren't careful, he'd hear her. Then he'd kill her just like T.J.

Twigs snapped above her.

If that sound was what she thought it was, she had no chance. She couldn't escape. She could barely breathe. Her chest rose and fell in steady motion, beating profusely as she listened and waited for some sign that he was still there. Looking up, the light at the top of the hole seemed to darken. A figure blocked its path and quietly hovered. Then, as if distracted, it veered off, exposing the light as it disappeared.

Ruby hushed herself, afraid to make a sound. She remained where she was, flexed between the slippery wall and the bottom of the pit. Her body stuck to the muck and twigs, poking into her cold mangled body. Beside her, open wide to the world, was the small suitcase she had stolen. Hers really, for what it was worth. Now, at least *he* wouldn't get it… Nobody would. If she had to take it to her grave, then so be it. Her soul had not been a fair trade for the thousands of dollars worth of diamonds now scattered beneath her contorted body.

No, she had been cheated…deceived like a stupid schoolgirl.

~~~~

"She won't be back," Joe smiled, grinning through his calico colored teeth. "The wolves will chew her up before she can even…"

"Just shut up and keep looking Joe. We have to find her. She has most of the diamonds, remember?"

"Oh right…but at least she doesn't have T. J.'s."

"You did hide them didn't you Joe?

"Don't worry Eddie old pal," Joe slapped his friend on the back as he spit a glob of chewing tobacco on the lush- green forest floor. I hid it in a place where nobody will ever find it."

"Good. Now get going. We don't have much time."

Chapter 7

The shores of Reindeer Lake grew deadly as huge frothy green waves blast against the Precambrian rock that kissed the landscape of one of Saskatchewan's biggest bodies of water. The unusually hot humid air had brought yet another storm to the area, the second one in a two-day period. It reminded Pip of the legend his grandfather had told him, the one about the monsters.

Though winter had long since past, warm temperatures often reminded him of the once frozen lake thawing. He could hear Grandfather's voice in the wind. "Legend has it my boy that herds of barren ground caribou that once inhabited this very lake during their winter migration, fell through the ice because of sudden warm temperatures. But we Chipewyan Indians believe something different. We believe monsters rushed up to the surface to eat them all. You see Pipata; even today, monsters live in the deep. In the unlit parts that cloud judgment and reason. They wait...lurking unnoticed until sanity fades, corrupting, deceiving, destroying mankind, until bit-by-bit...the prey...becomes...the beast." His grandfather always jumped as he shouted *beast*, scaring the wits out of him as he finished the story.

Pip always wanted to know what kind of monsters his grandfather meant. Were they ferocious and green with slime dripping out of their mouths? Did they look like fire breathing dragons like the ones on his favorite movie "Reign of Fire"? What did they look like? But he never asked. He was too embarrassed assuming everyone else knew but him. He just laughed along with his brothers who would tease him terribly for having what they called "bug eyes" whenever Grandfather told the story. Grandfather however, never laughed when he told it. He was very dramatic and creative being such a great storyteller, but he never laughed. Something told Pip that his grandfather knew far more than he let on about Deep Bay. No wonder he forbade him to go there.

Pip disobeyed anyway. He played near Deep Bay almost every day as long as he could get away with it. But lately something new interested him at the Shooting Star Lodge. He saw the men he had seen for the past three weeks return to the lodge located five miles north-east of Deep Bay on a tiny river called Star River. It was so remote most people didn't even know about it. When Pip first set eyes on the strangers, he wondered if they themselves were the monsters. For the things they did to that bald man in the forest were unspeakable.

Pip had been tracking them again today. It had fast become the most interesting thing to do since he couldn't get any of his older brothers to come along. Since he turned thirteen, they had all stopped tagging along on his adventures. *"Why don't you grow up Pipata, you're supposed to be a man now."* Pip assumed they were teasing with the mindless snickering he heard in the background. Yet, a fraction of what they said really was the truth, though he didn't want to admit it. He was supposed to be a man, but he didn't feel like one. He wasn't a child, but he sure felt like one still. Who was he anyway?

For now, Pip would be a mighty warrior. He would rescue the Little Caribou the monsters had frightened into the forest. His grandfather would be proud and his brothers would be jealous. He would show them he was Pipata, Great Warrior Chief of the Chipewyan tribe, conqueror of the monsters from the deep. They would not snatch one more caribou on his watch.

As the rain began to pelt the adolescence's black uncovered head, he took off from behind the pictograph his ancestors had painted on the large moss-covered rock. If his plans were to succeed, he would have to act fast. The day was fading and the moon would not be out tonight.

Chapter 8

"Names George," the flamboyant mid-thirties blonde man with the cowboy hat extended his hand as the scorching wind blew his open shirt around revealing his muscular chest. He seemed a little rough and unorthodox but typically the kind of guide you would want to have around when flying into unknown territory.

"Pleased to meet you," Harvey accepted the man's hand and shook it enthusiastically, squinting against the blowing dust. "Looks like the winds picking up."

"Not to worry pal, this float plane can take it."

Harvey grinned with anticipation as he helped George load his bags. "My friend couldn't come so there will be one less passenger," he informed the man, stepping into the bouncing water plane after him.

"No problem…I can fly with just two."

"Oh, so someone else is coming then?"

"Supposed to be."

Harvey wiped his sweaty brow as he positioned himself carefully next to the rounded passenger window. He yawned, stretching his arms upward and kicked off his shoes. "It's been a long day."

George just grinned as he transported himself to the front seat, boosting the older plane to life. The propeller sputtered and turned, shaking Harvey where he sat when suddenly he heard someone rap at the side door of the plane. For a moment, he thought it was part of the engine noise, and then he realized it must be the other passenger. He opened the dwarfish metal door against the wind to a slight middle-aged woman. She forced a smile at him as if she despised him, and pushed her shoulder bag in first, then her other suitcases, stubbornly doing it herself.

"I could have done that for you lady," George called from the front seat.

"I can do it myself," she grumped, hoisting herself up not wanting to take Harvey's helpful outstretched hand.

Something about her seemed familiar to Harvey, but he just couldn't put his finger on it. He would have remembered someone like her with that…that hair. It was the color of Wilma Flintstone's, cut short into choppy uneven shag. He couldn't believe how ridiculous she looked. What would possess a woman her age to do such a thing to her hair? Even with those tiny spectacles she wore, she still looked like someone who was trying to look years younger than she really was. Harvey wondered what kind of fishing buddy she would turn out to be.

George suddenly shouted, "All aboard folks!" He settled himself into the cockpit and put oversize earphones on. Then suddenly yanked them off, turning backward to talk to the new passenger for a moment, "Oh…and lady, "he said, "just so as you know, you don't need to keep that big bag on your lap the whole trip, you can put it down beside the others. There's plenty of room."

The woman slumped in her seat, holding her head down as if she was trying to hide. She mumbled a low "Forget it!" which startled Harvey immediately.

Looney tunes!

"Suit yourself lady," the big pilot shrugged, shaking his head. He forced his earphones back up attempting to pull the plane away from the dock. He punched some buttons, and then chatted on the radio. "Copy that," he frowned as he manoeuvred the plane back to where they boarded, "Straggler acknowledged and ready for pick-up. Sorry folks," he shouted as he forced a smile, "looks like we got a last-minute passenger."

Harvey peered out of the planes miniature window toward the small parking lot that led to the dock. A shiny chrome and black Harley Davidson motorbike screeched to a halt, turning sideways as it did it. A mammoth-sized woman with copper-red hair straddled off the bike and jogged toward the plane, her scraggly red hair blowing all directions into a fuzz ball mess. The pilot leaned over and opened the door across from him as the big woman boost herself up into the plane.

What is this, clash of the redheaded Titans?

"Sorry I'm late," the woman panted. "I didn't know which plane went to Shooting Star Lodge until the last minute."

"You're forgiven," George winked as she took a seat up front, weighing the side down. Harvey noticed the pilots added over-friendly gestures toward the woman. Perhaps *he* was attracted to big muscular females like that, but Harvey was not. He liked the feminine touch, like his Rose. She was a *real* woman.

Oh, how he missed her right about now. She would have calmed him down, chatted with the other women no matter what they looked like, and still been able to convince him that he was going to have the time of his life. She was truly a good woman. *Why do the good ones always die young Lord?*

Harvey sighed. He was not going to feel sorry for himself now. He was about to take his first ride in a float plane to an exotic local, and by golly, he was going to make the best of it no matter how strange the other passengers were. For all he knew, they probably would think a balding over-weight retired police officer didn't fit the package either.

*Lord, keep us safe...*Harvey prayed as he tensed his face, swaying rhythmically to the motion of the bouncing plane as it laboured through the choppy green and blue waters. The pilot gave a proverbial thumbs-up, and started accelerating toward the colorful waterborne horizon.

"All right people," the pilot hooted like a pro, "let's get this bird in the sky."

~~~~

Loretta's stomach churned but not just from the motion of the plane. She had thrown up twice since they took off, not being able to shake the horrendous reminder, that infamous repugnant face that had haunted her for so long.

As the little plane battered though the turbulent sky, Loretta reflected her mind to more pleasant thoughts. She gulped against the subsiding nausea and leaned against the side window, cooling her sweaty forehead. As her face paled against the brilliant lightning now visible in the distance, images of her life flashed before her. She surrendered to the fond memories that once proved joyous and uplifting, justifying her faith and all that it had stood for...then.

"Pray for me..." the much younger, panic stricken Loretta, sobbed while talking on the phone with her mother. "I don't know what's happening. The doctor says he's going to do a Caesarean Section...Mom... I'm *so* scared. The baby might be in trouble...and..."

"Loretta," her mother spoke firmly, interrupting their phone conversation, "calm down. What have I always taught you?"

"…To trust the Lord."

"Yes…and why must we trust the Lord?"

"…Because He is an ever-present help in times of need, and he won't leave or forsake me."

"That's right," her mother calmed her, "now breathe."

Loretta remembered Jeremy's birth fondly. It was a test of her faith trusting those doctors to cut her open like that. They hooked her up to all kinds of monitors, gave her an epidural so she could be awake to hold her son. They even let Bob in the O.R to view the whole birth, though he wasn't too keen on the idea of seeing blood.

"Congratulations, it's a boy!"

"Thank you, Jesus!" Loretta cried. She nervously waited to hear the screeching raspy sound of her infant son. Pausing for a moment, she heard him, relieved that he had a good set of pipes, grateful to a Savior so divine.

"Babes doing exceptionally well," one of the doctors informed his staff from somewhere across the room. Loretta couldn't tell where. She was behind the confining wall of green sheets they propped up between her breasts and her abdomen. Only Bob could see the details, and by that time, he was sitting pale in the chair next to her.

Loretta's body trembled as if she was chilled, a normal reaction to the shock of childbirth they informed her. Her teeth chattered as she prayed aloud, "Thank you Jesus! Thank you for taking care of our son Jeremy!"

Bob perked his head up now, looking better than a few minutes earlier. "You named him after my Dad. I thought you didn't like that name."

"I changed my mind. Can't a girl change her mind?"

Bob sobbed as he took his wife's clammy hand in his. "Thank you dear! Thank you! I love you sweetheart. Now…where is that son of mine? Can I hold him?"

One of the nurses bundled the baby up tightly and set him in Bob's arms. He cuddled him, kissed him, and propped him up to Loretta. "Want to see your mommy?"

"You know," the nurse smiled, "he's a lucky boy. The doctors couldn't believe it, but they thought they had a very sick baby on their hands. What a miracle. He turned out to be just fine."

Bob carefully placed Jeremy in Loretta's arms as she awkwardly cradled him in a tight embrace, the only way a mother could with a sheeted wall dividing her body in two. The doctors tugged away at her frozen belly on the other side as she absorbed the only thing that mattered: Her baby.

"Hi little guy," she cried softly, kissing his pearly white skin. "You *are* a little miracle, you know that. As God is my witness, I will do everything in my power to make sure your life is never put in danger like that again, I promise. "Lord please help me keep this promise …and thank you for bringing Jeremy into the world."

Bob smirked. "You should be thanking the doctor honey. He's the one that did all the hard work, not God."

"I know you don't believe honey, but I do. Jesus used the doctor's hands. Jeremy truly *is* a miracle, a blessing straight from heaven, a precious gift from God."

Loretta jerked awake with a start, tears streaming down her cheeks. Thunder clashed against the plane reminding her of the painful biting reality of her now empty life. Only one word came to mind.

Indian giver!

Another jolt of lighting tossed the light aircraft about. "Hold on folks," the pilot yelled steadying the plane again, "We're all right."

That's what he thinks.

Loretta didn't trust the man as far as she could spit. But then, that's because she was the only one who knew exactly what kind of a monster he really was. Her plan had worked...so far. He had taken the bait.

At this point, Loretta couldn't care less whether he lived or died. For that matter, she could just as well pull out her gun right now and shoot him. The others would perish too unfortunately, casualties of war, a small price to pay for justice.

The tiny floatplane tossed about in the unforgiving sky, lightning dancing across the three zombie-like faces as they tried to hold on to life. Loretta on the other hand didn't care about hers. She didn't care about the pilot either. She wanted to waste him right where he sat, make him suffer the way *she* had suffered, the way Jeremy had suffered. Sweat dripped from her brow. *Do it Loretta!*

She fumbled with the zipper on her bag and reached inside.

Suddenly the plane veered sharply to the right knocking her bag to the floor. The man next to her picked it up. Him again, always wanting to help her. What was the old geezer doing on *her* plane anyway? Was he following her? Was he on to her?

She made a mental note to stay away from him at any cost.

Loretta grabbed her bag quickly, ripping it from the man's grasp. She steadied it back on her lap and zipped it shut. Luckily, nothing fell out, if he had seen the gun, she would have been forced to use it, and, if she was thinking clearly, she just couldn't do that yet. As much as she wanted to see him taste death, she had to follow through with the plan. It was the only way to punish them all.

~~~~

Vicki raked her hands through her twisted ratty hair, not caring anymore that the wind had ruined it. There were much more important things to worry about…like staying alive. The storm was getting worse, and really starting to give her goose bumps. The rest of the passengers didn't seem to be fairing well either. That freakish woman in the backseat couldn't stop gagging, repulsing Vicki to the point of nausea herself.

The over-friendly pilot next to her even seemed frightened. She could tell he was trying to pick her up. He was cute too, but a little *too* charming. Men with muscles always seemed to have a sort of arrogance to them. It turned her off yet excited her at the same time. She'd rather date someone with bigger muscles than she had. That way she didn't feel so awkward. Once she went out with a short thin guy and felt like she was dating a kid.

Vicki could see why her sister came to Northern Saskatchewan. It was beautiful. From what she could see before the scorching sun started going down and the looming storm clouds took over, it was a gorgeous place with miles of evergreen trees and lakes dotting the horizon. Clearly, one of the most breathtaking places she had ever seen.

An out of the way fishing lodge had been the last place Vicki received her sister's chicken-scratched postcard. She warned her it was dangerous following some guy she barely knew to another country. She told her sister that anything could happen in those circumstances, and now it did, her sister was missing.

The police contacted the lodge where she was supposed to be staying only once. The information they received caused them to give up the search. Apparently, nobody had ever heard of her sister at all. That was it, no follow-up, no nothing. End of trail. Her sister deserved more than that.

Perhaps her sister never made it to the lodge at all. Perhaps Vicki's hasty decision to take off to the airport so fast was a mistake. She could have hung around La Ronge for a few days, shown her sister's picture to the local police force, asked a few questions. It might have helped. The postcard had specifically said Shooting Star Lodge, Saskatchewan on the front cover though. Vicki couldn't help but feel that that should be the place to start her own investigation.

Chapter 9

Ruby's face dripped from the intermittent rain that drizzled down through the mouth of the hole. It made things damp and sticky, especially with the mud pasted up her back, cold and soaking through her clothes. She managed to sit up and squeeze around. The walls were tight. Perhaps it was an old well, or maybe an animal trap of some kind. Whatever it was, she knew she had better at least try to get out. The diamonds could stay. At least she'd know where they were if she ever had the chance to dig in this mud again to find them.

Not likely.

With her hand pulling on a tree root above her left shoulder, she strained to yank herself to a standing position. If she could only use the tree roots to extract herself all the way out, she might have a chance. She could thrust her shoes into the slippery sides of the cavern like Spiderman. It had worked in the movies, but then, not with that ankle of hers. It had inflated itself to the size of a balloon.

Ruby leaned her forehead against the wet mucky sides of the pit, thinking, sighing. Her mud-saturated hair hung in tendrils, pasted against her cheeks right down into her mouth. She spit, tasting the mud. *This is impossible.* There was no way she was getting out by herself...alive.

Come on Ruby, you're tougher than you think. Her big sister taught her how to do everything but this. She taught her how to keep herself safe on the street, how to act tough, how to survive. She even made her practice every foul word in the book.

"If you look like a victim Ruby, you'll be a victim...and sometimes you've got to swear a little, no, not a little, a lot. Promise me you'll swear a lot."

Many times, she had to use her sister's methods. It had worked well, even got her out of an extremely frightening situation once. The problem was this was not the street. What was she supposed to do now, in a hole, an abandoned well or whatever it was she had fallen into? How could she apply her tutelage now?

Why hadn't she introduced her new boyfriend to her big sister? Somewhere deep inside of her Ruby knew what he was like even way back when she first met him, just before the bank heist. Her own denial had cost her so much. His charming ways and good-looking demeanour always seemed to fool her. She melted whenever he spoke, as if she didn't have a backbone at all. He brainwashed her, made her cross those moral boundaries she swore she'd never cross. How could she have been so naïve to let him convince her to be his guinea pig?

"Just get us a detailed map of the bank and all the information you can find about the vault and its shipments baby, will you? That's all I'm asking you to do. We'll do the rest. Just stay on the floor until I need your help. It's not like you'll *really* be doing anything illegal?"

And that was just the start of his chronic deception. *"Not really doing anything illegal."* What a joke. Ruby had been doing nothing but illegal things ever since she met him. He tainted her in such a way as if she could never go back. The man expected her to do anything for him, that con man, that cold-blooded murderer. Condoning murder was just one of them. Even though she didn't agree to kill those people, she was an accomplice, guilty of murder as if she did it herself. It still repulsed her, haunted her every day. How could she live with herself? She was a weak pathetic bimbo, a poor excuse for human life. What was wrong with her? And how could she allow herself to get sucked in twice? She should have known better than to go along with his idiotic plan to steal diamonds this time.

Eddie loved to call her an airhead. So did the others. They said she wasn't worth anything, hadn't earned anything either. Over time, she actually believed it. But not this time, this time they were not going to get away with it. She may not have reaped her cash reward from the bank heist, but they were not going to deny her the diamonds. She earned her share no matter what kind of dumb blonde joke they made, no matter how insecure they made her feel. Eddie would eat his own words.

"Oh, that's funny babe, you and your pretty little hands aren't going to touch the diamonds. Stick to cooking and cleaning like dumb blonde broads are supposed to do."

Threatening wind picked up as dusk weaned itself into the dead of night. Ruby thought she heard something above her again, hovering around the opening of the hole. It could be the rain, pounding now, seeming to tire from its drizzle. Still, as twigs broke above her, debris fell, dusting her already soiled face. As she looked up, heart beating loudly in her chest, she realized the grim reality that there definitely was someone there.

Don't breathe.

Had Eddie and Joe found her?

She panted, trying to calm her heaving body, ready for them to find her out, to shout "Boo" like some practical joke. Her own whimpering sounds escaped against her will as she despondently beat her head against the muddy wall. It was hopeless. They had hunted her down like a helpless animal.

Suddenly, from up above, something hit her square in the middle of her forehead. It was a prickly evergreen branch, and then the sound of a little boy calling out, "Do not fear Little Caribou," he yelled, echoing his angelic voice down the deep hole. "I am a mighty Chipewyan Warrior Chief, and I have come to rescue you."

~~~

Shooting Star Lodge sat nestled in a crop of towering evergreens just off the water's edge. It didn't seem to be well equipped for a fly-in-fishing camp at all. Its two wooden fishing boats tied to the decrepit knotty pine dock that stretched out onto Star River looked unprofessional. The river was virtually an uninhabited sheltered place just north of a huge water-filled crater that made Reindeer Lake famous: A product of a meteorite that struck the area long ago, known as Deep Bay. The locals know its 700-foot depth, estimated to be the deepest part of Reindeer Lake and one of the largest craters in the world is bottomless in some places. It's been said that if a man casts his line into the bottomless pit, he will either never return, or if he does, return without a soul.

Three weeks ago, when Ruby flew out here, she never would have believed the old Indian tale about the bottomless pit. Now, with everything that had gone on, she wasn't so sure. Since the kid had pulled her dishevelled body out of the pit, and was helping her hobble through the stormy darkness, she couldn't believe he just asked her if she knew where the monsters were. The question struck her as odd. If she didn't know any better, she'd swear he was talking about Eddie and Joe. But no, only she considered them to be monsters. Only *she* knew just how horrible they could be.

At one time, before the bank heist, they seemed to be decent guys. Then, after they slaughtered all those innocent people, she was *still* blinded by what she thought was love. But after they got here, things started changing drastically. They became altered somehow...*he* became altered, different.

Early on, in their relationship, her boyfriend was verbally abusive, a fact Ruby accepted since that's all she ever experienced with the kind of men she dated. As they became more involved, the verbal abuse progressed. Then it became physical as if some drug had gotten into the water and changed him overnight. He began to beat her shortly after they arrived. Ruby remembered the first blow she took to the mouth. It wasn't clear why he did it then. Now as Ruby put it all together, it was as clear as day...They...had fished the bottomless pit.

"Unpack the gear will you babe. We want to try our luck fishing. Thought we'd have a go at the deepest part of the lake first. The sun stays up late this time of year so we should be able to see well in the dark. It's the best time to catch the big ones."

"We can fish every day if we want to. Can you believe it? Lucky for us we found that website when we did. Winning this free holiday for five is a total rush. And free use of the bush-plane just blows me away. It's perfect babe, a great place to hideout for a while until we come up with some sort of plan for the diamonds."

"Supposed to be an eighty-year-old guy that owns and runs this place all by himself. His name is Terry, I think. Lucky fart, can you believe it? He doesn't even book regular tours anymore, just once a year, and deals like this one for charity I suppose.

I can't believe he chose me. I played it up like I was really needy and everything. The old coot must have felt sorry for me. Thought we'd thank him by taking him fishing with us. He can show us where all the good fishing spots are."

"Anyway, as soon as T.J gets back with the old man, we'll be heading out. And put a pillow in the boat. T.J isn't fishing; he wants to catch up on his sleep. Actually, that's not such a bad idea because we'll probably be out pretty late…so don't wait up for us."

The men returned shortly after dawn, but not with Terry. Instead, they boasted two gargantuan Lake Trout with crushed in sculls. Joe sheepishly giggled about it later that morning telling her his favorite part of catching the fish was crushing the eyeballs. He beamed those ugly rotten teeth of his at her when he told her the story and explained that the old fart didn't much like it. In fact, he said that he didn't like much of anything they did, not even the fact that they had come to the Shooting Star Lodge in the first place. He grumbled, telling her that the old geezer must have had the Alzheimer's disease or something because he didn't remember giving any free fishing trip away. Joe winked at her then, grinning like a Cheshire cat, "He must have forgotten how to swim too."

Did they actually think she was that dumb? She knew what they did with the old man. She knew very well. After that, everyone changed for the worst, except for T'J that is. He had always been the softy. She caught him sobbing in the bushes that morning and asked him what was wrong.

"I have to get out of here Ruby, and so do you! I can't do this anymore. I'm not like them. I can't do it. I just can't do it anymore!"

She figured she knew what he meant, but she didn't dare ask to make sure. He insisted they come up with a plan and run away with the diamonds. At first, she said no thinking he had gone completely loony. But then, after listening to Joe's lame excuse for what happened to Larry and the steady decline of their behaviors and morals over the course of three weeks, she decided to agree to T. J's impressive plan. He had worked everything out to a tee, even found an abandoned trappers cabin in the woods. They had traveled to it many times before actually heading there with the diamonds. She figured that was where the young boy was taking her now.

"Are you okay lady?" the boy asked her.

"I'm alright. But I just need to sit down a bit."

"The storm will get worse. We have to get out of the rain. I know a place you can hide, but we have to keep going if we're going to get there."

"I can't kid. Just let me take a breath," Ruby panted. She could not move her swollen ankle one more inch without passing out.

"My name is Pip."

"Okay Pip, here's the thing. I gather you know those men are not good men. Now, if they're in these woods following us right now, which they probably aren't in this storm, then I understand the urgency to keep going. But they're not. So, let's just take it easy, okay? I'm going to pass out if we go any further."

"But they will get you Little Caribou."

"Would you stop with the 'Little Caribou' bit already, you're starting to get on my nerves."

"But they will kill you like they did that bald man."

Ruby's heart skipped a beat. The gulp in her throat was hard to swallow. She thought she had been the only one to witness *that*. If anyone had noticed this young Indian boy watching them, *his* life would be in danger too. As tired and sore as she was, she couldn't let that happen. She would not put this boy's life in danger. T.J wasn't the only one that had a conscience.

"Okay...You got me. Let's get going. But when we get there, I want you to go home and never come back here. You're not a warrior chief or whatever you said you were, so cut it out. You can't fight these men. You know that. This is serious stuff Pip." She cupped his elfin brown face in her hands, "you hear me? I don't want you to get hurt. If you saw what you say you saw, you know these men wouldn't hesitate to kill you too."

"I understand," Pip smiled innocently. "But who will take care of my Little Caribou?"

"Pip...I'm warning you."

"Okay!" Pip's smile turned to a disappointed frown. "You're no fun lady."

"No, I'm not, not when I can barely walk; My clothes are soaked; It's pouring rain; And being out here in the middle of the night is really starting to freak me out...not to mention we might be killed at any moment...No... I am definitely *not* any fun!"

"Okay! I got it already." Pip shouted, wrapping his lanky arms around her to support her as she hobbled beside him. "Maybe I shouldn't have saved you after all."

Chapter 10

The computer screen scrolled numerous amounts of information. It was more than Loretta had ever imagined that day she decided to investigate the infamous four on the internet. Keeping copies of their repulsive mugs hadn't been such a bad idea after all. At first, she didn't want them when the computer sketch artist offered copies to her, afraid their sickly faces would haunt her. Then, pausing for a moment, she reconsidered, not wanting to disappoint the woman who had worked so hard with her. She was glad now for the blessing in disguise.

Loretta's head brutally thrust against the window, smacking with force as the plane now rocked and twisted continuously against the frightening storm. It brought her back to reality every now and then throughout the turbulent trip. Not that she wanted it to. Daydreaming was better than the imminent fear that enveloped the cockpit right now. And keeping her mind in one place at a time was not exactly an easy chore, not when so much painstaking research had gone into this scheme of hers so far.

The endless all-nighters she invested chatting on-line hijacked her mind backward realizing how truly incredible it was that she had found George Oxford Williams...a.k.a., Thomas Bates...a.k.a., Peter Bell...a.k.a., Richard Summers...a.k.a., James Butler, known felon. He did ten years in the Chicago State Pen for armed robbery back in 1986, in trouble with the law since he got out in 1996; wanted for murder in two states, along with several armed robberies throughout the U.S. and Canada.

Loretta remembered her research well. His comrades knew the notorious George Oxford

Williams by his string of nicknames rather than aliases. She wondered what would happen if she tried a few out on him now? Wouldn't he be shocked? He might even lose control of the plane in this storm. No, she'd behave. She wouldn't call him Biff, Mr. G., or Wild Bill just yet.

She recalled her first raw encounter in the chat room with him. She had been hunting on-line for hours. For some reason, she figured he would be there. The diamond heist reported on the news three months earlier conveyed George's handiwork, and discovering that he was practically a genius on the computer made her think he was up to something illegal with it. Trying to sell the diamonds, trade them, con somebody with them. That would be typical George Williams's style, defrauding unsuspecting women out of their savings. Then, after hours of tedious digging, her assumptions proved correct.

It was easy. Chat all day until something questionable came up. Then, just like that, after five cups of coffee, half a dozen solicitations, and boring endless conversation, someone very interesting wanted to chat. He called himself Wild Bill Hickok, which perked Loretta up immediately.

It wasn't just his nickname, but the content in which he chatted that made her wonder if this was the notorious George Oxford Williams. He bragged about himself more than any person she had ever met. He went on and on about how smart he was, how handsome. He told her how he spent ten years in the slammer for nothing, that they had convicted the wrong guy. He bragged about prison life, how the inmates were afraid of him because he called himself Wild Bill Hickok. He told her classified information about banking systems, claiming he use to be a loans officer. Right! He was the guy, no doubt about it. She offered to chat privately with him, finding out even more details. Talking to him soon became a sick addiction, one she couldn't stop. He revealed many personal particulars, more than she needed or wanted to know, about his ex-girlfriend, his two buddies, all fitting his M.O. perfectly.

Loretta, known to him only as Calamity Jane, promised to chat with him every night at ten. He never missed and neither did she. She conversed with him for two agonizing months until he revealed an incredible secret. He told her that he became a wealthy man shortly after getting out of prison in the mid-nineties. He had obtained a degree in computers while in jail, making it big in the booming Internet markets, claiming he periodically invested in various software companies. He said that he acquired a major portion of his wealth from a recent investment he made at the end of January.

"What a crock!"

Recently however, he lost everything. He apparently used up every dime he had on his elderly grandmother's hospital bills and was in need of a partner to help him with an investment he wanted to make. He told her it was a sure thing. It was the investment of a lifetime, one any *sane* woman would not pass up: Diamonds.

He wanted her to send him fifty thousand dollars to invest, told her she was lucky to have a heads-up on such an incredible deal. Well, he was smooth, charming, but that didn't fool her. She couldn't understand how people let themselves get bamboozled like that. It didn't take a brain surgeon to figure out what he was trying to do.

Right away she told him no, that she was flat broke, and that all she had to offer him was good old-fashioned conversation. He didn't like that much, and told her he wouldn't be able to chat anymore. He told her that he had no more money for internet charges, and had hoped to take at least one last trip before his landlord evicted him from his apartment for not paying the rent.

Boo...hoo... hoo! Did he really think she was that naive?

That's when it occurred to Loretta that she had the perfect plan. He was hunting for cash, suckers, and quite possibly a place to lay low for a while, probably needing to get out of the country with those hot rocks. She spent the entire next day researching the most desirable spot for him to hide out. A place he would take his other convict buddies to and maybe his girlfriend.

Then she found it: Shooting Star Lodge. It was perfect. She decided to make a bogus web site as if she were the owner of the lodge, searching for the perfect *needy* person who would win an all expense paid vacation for five. *What a plan!*

She propositioned him that very night at ten o'clock sharp hoping that it wasn't too late. If her assumptions were correct and he was conning her into giving him money, he'd be waiting for her...And waiting he was.

She however, had something entirely different to offer him. Right about now, she figured he'd be desperate for anything free. She knew he'd go for it. Assuming he'd blown all the money from the bank heist already, and if he was in fact responsible for the diamond heist, he probably couldn't just cash them in anywhere, it would take a great deal of time to find the right connections. So, in other words, he was broke.

"I have a web site for you instead of cash Wild Bill Hickok. You said you like fishing, and you want to take a trip. Here's one for free. Just go to www.freefishing.com. There's a contest for charity. If you're that broke, all you have to do is beg."

Wild Bill Hickok never even thanked her.

Two days later Loretta scanned her web site for his name amongst a dozen other entries. She unpublished her web page and pin pointed Wild Bill's e-mail address. Bingo. He had used an alias: James Butler. How original. Not only was it his known alias, but it was Wild Bill Hickok's real name. Any history buff would know that.

With the clicking of computer keys, Loretta sent him an e-mail informing him that he had won the all expense paid fly-in-fishing trip for five to Shooting Star Lodge in Northern Saskatchewan Canada. Of course, she pretended it was from the owner of the lodge.

She sent him five International airline tickets from Minneapolis to Saskatoon, as well as bus and bush-plane tickets. Wild Bill even supplied the generic box number in which he wanted the tickets mailed. Loretta left it up to him and his thugs to get passed customs. She assumed they'd disguise themselves well, use forged documents like usual, and smuggle the diamonds. They were good at that. If they got caught, that was their problem. She'd be out the money she coughed up for the plane fare, but it would be worth every penny. And if they did make it to Shooting Star Lodge…all the better.

George Oxford Williams had taken the bait. She had sought him out, conned the con man and plotted to kill her son's murderer. Now, as ironic as it was, *he* was fighting to keep *her* alive, trying to hold the runty floatplane steady in a fierce thunderstorm. Twisting uncontrollably, it pummelled through impenetrable clouds of doom, forever obscured in a base of uncertainty.

~~~~

"I don't care if it *is* raining," Eddie screamed at Joe. "If we're supposed to stay here, then we stay here. It's not my fault you didn't bring a jacket, idiot. Look at you; you look like a wet rat."

"Oh, thank you very much." Joe shivered with chattering teeth.

"You're welcome idiot...It won't be long anyway. Before you know it, you'll be in that warm bunk of yours again."

"Starving no doubt."

"Don't worry bud; we'll have time to look for Ruby later, then she'll be back in the kitchen where she belongs. I have a feeling I know where she went anyway. She thinks she's so smart."

"And then she'll fry some pancakes. Right Eddie?"

"Right...But your stomach will have to wait a while. Other things have to come first. We've been over this before. Let's try to get it right this time. We have no room for error here Joe. I'm counting on you."

~~~~

The dilapidated hunting shack leaked badly.

Instead of staying dry, Ruby remained as wet as when she and Pip arrived over an hour ago. Without light, it was hard to find countless holes in the defective ceiling, but Ruby decided that hobbling while trying to find them, was not what she was going to be doing anyway. If Pip were silly enough to be up on that roof plugging holes in a thunderstorm, then *he* would be the one that would have to suffer the consequences, not her. It was hard enough to manoeuvre her bum ankle.

"Pip!" Ruby yelled to the top of her lungs. "Get down from there. You're going to be hit by lightning or something."

"No Caribou!" the defiant teenager squeaked. It was hardly audible. Ruby had to hone in on it just to hear him. He'd been outside fixing the roof far too long.

"Pip!" She shouted again. "If you don't come down from there, I'm going to…"

"You're going to what?" Pip scoffed as he poked his head in through a massive hole near the chimney, obviously thinking he was funny."

"You fool…Get in here!"

"No Caribou! I *said*…I would fix it. The Chipewyan chief has spoken!"

"Honestly Pip, you are driving me crazy!" Ruby screamed as a crack of thunder opened the skies to a terrific bolt of lightning, thundering, sending her prostrate.

"Did you see that?" Pip awed as he hung upside-down.

"Yes…Now get in here you little brat."

Ruby didn't have much patience when it came to kids. It was the direct result of growing up in Miss. Lily's foster home. She and her sister had witnessed so many brats just like Pip coming and going. Now she had to endure it all over again.

Another crack of thunder pealed, but this time there was no awe. Pip's pitchy adolescent voice shrieked an intolerable cry as he hit the floor with a wallop.

"Pip!" Ruby jumped with a start. "Are you okay?"

Lightning flickered through the massive jagged hole Pip had just ruptured. For a moment, Ruby thought he was dead. His petite immobile carcass lay lifeless in a heap on the old wooded floor with broken jagged pieces of rotten boards littering around him.

"Wake up Pip!" Ruby cried as she slapped his chocolate cheeks, rain trickling over his face like sweat.

"Caribou...," he moaned, "Big chief...not so smart."

"That's for sure...you nincompoop. That had to hurt."

"No way," he cautiously eased himself over, trying to stand. "I'm not a wimp!"

As the native boy muddled to his feet, Ruby shook her head in disbelief. If he had hurt himself, he certainly did not let on. He just hobbled over to a broken chair, sat down, and forced a great big smile.

~~~

Oh...my aching back!

If this was what being a man was about, Pip did not want any part of it. His brothers were wrong. Being grown up wasn't fun. He'd take his mother's kisses and hugs any day next to pretending he was tough. His brothers had no right calling him a wimp. Always teasing, always taunting him, telling him to grow up and be a man. What a bunch of losers. If only he could let out a deafening scream, cry, like the insufferable girl they always called him. Then his brothers wouldn't be so disappointed. It would be better than suffering in silence in front of some weird lady.

"Pip?" Ruby broke the silence. "Do you come here a lot?"

"Yes," he groaned against the pain, tearing up a little. "My brothers and me…we use to play here all the time. That was until they decided they weren't going to play with me anymore."

"That's not nice. Why don't they play with you?"

"They think they're all grown up now. They tell me I shouldn't be *playing*. I should be doing something worthwhile instead of acting like a *baby*."

"That's nonsense! I bet you they just play Nintendo all day."

"They do lady…and they think that's not playing!"

Pip felt the sobs coming on. He wanted to fight it. He struggled with his bottom lip as it started to quiver. Before he knew it, his eyes blurred over with globs of salty liquid, streaming down his cheeks into his half-open mouth. With that, and the ongoing excruciating pain running up and down his back, hopes for being anything but a baby seemed disparaging. Tears flushed down his dewy cheeks like a torrential rain as wails of self-pity soon followed.

"Oh Pip…its okay. Everything will be okay. Does your back hurt?"

Pip shook his head to tell her that it did, bawling like a helpless child as the lady rubbed his sore back. She was not his mother, but she would do.

"Good chief I am," he wailed even louder.

"Pip…you're a sweetheart. That's all you've ever been to me since I met you. You have no idea how much I needed someone like you to come along. If you wouldn't have gotten me out of that pit…I would probably be dead right now. If you hadn't helped me to this cabin, those guys would have probably caught me. You know that. You kept me laughing even when I didn't feel like it. So, do not be so hard on yourself. You're a good kid…in spite of that silly stunt up there on the roof…and who cares if you couldn't fix that stupid big hole."

Ruby mused, busting out to a full-blown giggle. Pip mimicked her, deciding it *was* funny after all. "I guess I should go back up then?"

"Don't push your luck kiddo."

Pip fingered his tears as he smiled at her. "My brothers don't think the same way you do about me."

"That's just too bad for them Pip. They're missing out on a really cool person. I wish I could say the same for myself."

"You're a nice lady Caribou…I mean Ruby."

"No…I'm not Pip."

"Yes, you are. You might be a pain sometimes, but you're a nice lady like my mom."

Ruby erupted into flowing tears.

"It must be contagious," Pip sniffled.

"No Pip," she bawled, "you're so naive. I use to be like you. But I'm not anymore…and I'm not a nice lady either. I've done something unforgivable."

Chapter 11

Harvey felt the plane nosedive again.

The pilot had managed to pull them out of it several times, but now; somehow, he knew it was the point of no return. He gripped the red cushioned seat with his craggy pale fingernails until his hands pulsed with pins and needles. The peculiar woman adjacent to him was frantically screaming. The muscular woman beside the distraught pilot was breathing hard, shouting, "Do something!"

The violent storm battered the helpless floatplane, tossing it about as if it were merely a piece of flimsy paper, crumpling it just for sport. Lightning flickered through it's modest cockpit, shadowing ill-fated passengers while thunder clashed against the torrential rains, slapping it, punishing the rebellious vessel.

If this was the end…Harvey had to face it. He'd finally be with his Rose again, together for all eternity. It seemed wonderful. Yet, for some reason, part of him didn't want to leave this world just yet. Not like this. Not with so much fear…and the pain, it would bring so much pain. He tensed at the thought of it, remembering Rose and the miserable torture she went through at the end. *Oh babe, I am not as brave as you were.*

The bouncing winged beast seemed to take on a mind of her own, swaying this way, bumping with an intense velocity too fierce to bridle. It was as if she were trying to communicate in a way, express herself, and birth an imperative message. Throttled at every turn, she shuddered against the violent bolts of electricity that charged against her, trying to mute her, to terminate her, to shut her up.

Lord…Help!

"I can't hold her folks," the pilot yelled like a crazy man.

The lights on the instrument panel flickered on and off, as the plane surrendered weary. It swooped sharply left and shook steadily as it dove, futile, to a steep decline. Lightning struck the left wing. A loud clash deafened Harvey's ear.

Screams filled the plane.

Jesus save us!

Harvey earnestly prayed, panting and breathing against savage adrenalin. Suddenly, with one final strike, Harvey's window shattered, slicing the inside of the plane apart with a cold unyielding wind. The plane spiralled in the darkness, eerie, humming as it dove.

Screaming hysteria filled the plane. Harvey squeezed his eyes closed and prayed a silent prayer, a familiar Bible verse that he and Rose use to pray together: *"The Lord is my shepherd, I shall not want. He makes me lie down in green pastures, he leads me beside quiet waters, he restores my soul. He guides me in paths of righteousness for his names sake. Even though I walk through the valley of the shadow of death..."*

The plane rattled uncontrollably.

"...I will fear no evil, for you are with me; your rod and staff they comfort me."

Smoke…Fire…

"...You prepare a table before me in the presence of my enemies. You anoint my head with oil; my cup overflows."

The pilot frantically flipped through his instruments. Screaming women coughed in the billowing fumes.

"...Surely goodness and love will follow me all the days of my life, and I will dwell in the house of the Lord forever..."

Take me home Father.

The pilot radioed his final message, "Mayday...Mayday! We're going down!"

Chapter 12

Sunday, July 2nd.

The morning sun rose early along with the annoying boisterous crows.

Through the tall jade evergreens, a glitter of light beamed directly through the cracks in the wall of the hunter's shack. It sharply invaded Ruby's dopey eyes, waking her from a cold slumber. The dewy wet of the morning clung to her aching bones, challenged her numb body.

The fierce storm had finally passed. It had prevented her from sleeping most of the night. With the pounding thunder, she wondered how anyone could sleep. Pip must have been an exception. He seemed to be able to sleep through anything, oblivious to the sounds around him. Kids, they seemed to have that knack.

Ruby yawned, stretching her arms. Her stomach rumbled as she attempted to raise herself from the hard floor she and Pip were forced to sleep on. The boy looked so peaceful. It was difficult to imagine that he, a scrawny kid, had pulled her out of that abysmal pit yesterday, but he did. Using a mature pine branch was ingenious.

If she didn't know better, she'd think Pip had run away. But he swore he hadn't. His family knew where he would run to in a storm, or so he said. The hunter's cabin was obviously a well-known place. Ruby pondered on that thought for a moment. If it was so well known, it wasn't a very good hiding place. It was morning now and the storm had passed. That meant Eddie and Joe were probably on their way. If that was the case, she had to wake Pip up immediately and tell him to go home. She had to leave too.

"Pip," she shook him. "Wake up."

"Oh…," he moaned as he attempted to roll over.

"Sore hey? Me too…But now you have to go. The storms over and the sun is starting to come out. You're in danger if you stay here. You have to go home now."

"I can't leave you Caribou. You're in danger too."

Ruby sighed at the sleepy elfin boy's big brown serious eyes. He was starting to grow on her. But if she didn't do something to make him leave soon, she would be putting his life in jeopardy. She would never forgive herself if that happened. It was hard enough to carry the weight of her past mistakes.

"I'll be fine Pip…now go."

"No!"

"Please Pip! Don't be so stubborn. I don't want you to get hurt." Her heart sank. At this point, she had no more energy to fight with him. She was tired, sore, and hungry, a lethal combination for someone tying to make a teenager understand.

"Pip…!" Ruby shouted. "I don't want you here! Okay. Do you get that? You are a royal pain in the butt. Get it through that brainless skull of yours."

"I am *not* brainless. I am Pipata the great Chipewyan Chief."

"We don't have time for games." Ruby's heart sank. He was not getting the message. "I'm serious Pip. You *are* brainless. And what kind of a chief acts like a baby and bawls like a little girl anyway?" *Ouch! Heart crusher.*

The sulking boy froze in place. His eyes bubbled with tears, shocked, as his bottom lip began to quiver. Oh, the pain inside of her now was excruciating, far greater than her throbbing swollen ankle ever was. She had thrust the verbal knife right into him, twisting the thing slowly, confidently, like a pro. Yes, and it was shameful.

He gawked at her, pausing for a moment. His piercing steel eyes threatened her more than words could say. Tears cascaded down Pip's stained cheeks; bringing one arm across his face, he wiped his runny nose. "I hate you *stupid* Caribou!"

The boy ran toward the door.

"Pip...wait, I'm sorry." Ruby called after him hoping to lessen the blow. But he didn't turn back. He slammed the shabby door hard; leaving her sitting on the floor in her own misery, sickened, that she would choose those words. Why did she have to say *that*?

The smell of betrayal filled the ramshackle cabin for quite some time after Pip took off. Obviously, he was not coming back. Ruby dried the tears that washed across her soiled face, wishing she could take back what she said. Her tongue was a wicked thing. Sighing, she decided it was time to leave.

At least Pip left.

Ruby eased her wounded body through the collapsed doorframe, almost pulling the door from its rusty hinges. Stepping out into the deep coniferous forest, she stopped for a moment, grabbed a discarded branch to make a crutch, and continued.

Two hours had already passed. It felt like years. Without Pip to escort her back to Shooting Star Lodge, she had to rely on the sun, and that was a difficult task since so many trees obstructed the view. At times, she thought she was headed a completely different direction, but every now an then she found herself at the top of a hill catching a glimpse of the river below.

Heading toward the lodge was either the dumbest thing she would ever do, or the smartest. She didn't know which. Whatever it proved to be, she had to do it. It was the only way to set things right. Now that her own plan had been unsuccessful, she would not let those ruthless idiots succeed with theirs…even if it jeopardized her life. After her part in the bank robbery, and then the diamond heist, guilt smothered her, suffocated, until she could barely breathe. "Murderer" seemed to stigmatize her mind, gnaw at her soul, and pollute her. Nothing proved to redeem her heavy conscience. Nothing would ever change what she did.

"Just call in sick babe," her boyfriend told her the day after they robbed the bank. But that wasn't so easy. Lying didn't come easy for Ruby. It never was her strong point. Her sister always told her she had to toughen herself up if she was going to make it in this cruel world. Lying was just part of it. It was supposed to get easier. But for some reason it never did get easier for her.

After the job was finished, after that day, Ruby remembered the lies she told. How could she face her boss again? How could she pretend? One way occurred to her controlling boyfriend. It was supposed to be the perfect plan. "Go on a leave-of-absence. Claim some kind of medical leave, shock or something. Take six months. Who would be the wiser?"

Her boss let her go…completely unaware that she had been an accomplice.

Repeatedly, she heard the guys tell her that it had been a foolproof crime thanks to her. They obtained every detail about the building, every precise bit of information needed to make it in and out before the police arrived. Everyone followed the plans to a tee.

All except Joe, he was the trigger-happy fool. Ruby was ashamed she didn't do something to stop him, sorry for those who were killed. She had been a coward, betrayer of humanity, and Pip had not been her only victim.

How could she fall for a handsome sweet-talking criminal the way she did? It still repulsed her. How could she have been so naïve? All she had to do was say no and walk away, but those big blue eyes of his made her melt every time. She fell hopelessly, automatically into his wicked spell like a marionette puppet. He had an enticing quality about him at first. He was cunning, charming, and witty. Then, after it had been too late, she recognized him for what he was…a sadistic psychotic killer.

This time it would be different. This time she would *not* be naive. She would finally out-smart him, foil the plan and save the day. She knew how to ruin everything. She already had most of the diamonds even if she did leave them in that cruddy hole.

As Ruby neared the edge of the forest, she found the old trail she had taken to the rock pictograph, and carefully manoeuvred her way to it. The rock stood approximately fifty feet from the lodge. Luckily, it was still early morning; they probably hadn't even woken up yet. She'd hide behind the rock, watch the place for a while, scout it out, wait for the right moment to go in.

Pip would have been a good asset right about now. He was very experienced when it came to creeping around. He seemed to know exactly how to do it. Apparently, all she knew how to do was disturb a flock of birds in front of her. Obviously, she had been clumsy enough to scare them away. She held her breath as they nervously retreated, hoping the thumping beat in her chest wasn't as loud as it seemed.

The tranquil lodge occupied bright morning sunshine as it reflected sparkle rays off the pristine blue water. Daybreak had always been Ruby's favorite. It was horrible that her situation had to put a damper on such loveliness.

She had to think. If she could only sneak inside and retrieve T. J's diamonds, she could use them as a lever somehow. Finding them wouldn't be a problem. Joe thought he was so smart hiding the case under the kitchen sink like that. Why would he think she wouldn't look there? After all, she *was* the cook. His simple mind must have thought he was really a genius. Had she taken both diamond cases in the first place, she wouldn't be in this predicament. This time she'd do things differently. She'd use her head.

Ruby crumpled behind the picture rock and waited. It wouldn't be long before somebody stirred, that was, assuming they had *all* arrived. The group would have flown in sometime last night. Eddie and Joe would have seen to that.

As Ruby's droopy eyelids fluttered for a mere taste of momentary sleep, she pasted her butt on the cool wet ground to get comfortable. *Stay awake.* Startled, she awoke to a creaking front door opening. It was Joe all right. What's he doing?

Joe stretched on the front porch raising his arms all the way up over his head. He let out an oversize yawn that sounded like a convincing impression of a grizzly. It reminded her how easily she could have been attacked by one of those things last night. She was very thankful that hadn't happened.

"Eddie...!" Joe shouted, sending Ruby into a panic. "Where are you?"

Ruby cocked her head around surprised. She assumed he was still sleeping. He couldn't be out here, could he? Her survival instincts told her to run, to get out of there. But it was too late. Eddie already had her by the hair.

"You stupid woman!" Eddie spit as he dragged Ruby inside the cabin by her long filthy blonde locks. He let out a mouthful of provocative swear words that seemed to sting like never before. "You think I'm blind or something? Huh? I've been watching you behind that rock for the past half hour. Who do you think you're fooling, you clumsy twit? I heard you coming a mile away."

"Stop it Eddie," she cried. "You're hurting me."

Ruby's head felt the rising bulge in her scalp, throbbing, pulsating, as he continued to pull the clump of hair he held in his obtuse callused hand. Clumps of the tattered hair fell to the floor in a heap.

"Oh?" he gritted through his clenched teeth, turning to Joe, sarcasm rising as he pulled a little harder. "I'm hurting her Joe. Did you hear that?"

Joe giggled like a child and danced around the room. "Kill her Eddie. Kill her!"

"Maybe I should," he grinned, punching her square in the nose, yanking her hair.

The force of the blow sent her into a starry foreign galaxy. The room erupted into a spinning tornado. Lights danced before her eyes until she dropped dizzily backward against the cold tile floor. Blood oozed out of her nose, dripping profusely. It pooled next to her, red, warm, and syrupy.

Fight back Ruby.

All she could do was lay there, pain gripping, woozy, and crippled with nausea. It took everything she had just to lift her shaky bloodied hands to her face for protection. Again, Eddie kicked. This time, he pummelled her gut with his dirty steel-toed boot. It was deliberate, fast, and repetitive. Then when Joe joined in…she could take no more.

"Stop!" she screamed, curled up, bloody on the floor. "If you kill me, you'll never find your stupid diamonds!" *That'll make them think.*

Both men stopped immediately. "Tell us where they are or we *will* kill you." Eddie puffed with exhaustion. Joe seemed fuelled by assault.

"They're in the woods," she groaned. About two hours east of here." Wincing with pain and barely audible, Ruby pleaded one last strategy. "I can take you there."

She oozed through a pool of sticky blood to a sitting position, surprising herself that she could actually move at all. "If you want me to take you, you have to fix me up because I can't show you where the diamonds are like this."

"Just tell us where to go and we'll get them ourselves," Eddie insisted.

"I can't, it's a tricky place to find. I won't really remember unless I see it."

"How convenient."

Eddie staggered over to the bathroom and grabbed an armful of unused toilet paper rolls, throwing them at her. "Fix *yourself* up. You have fifteen minutes or we drag you out to the bush the way you are. Got it?"

Joe clapped with enthusiasm. "You're good Eddie. You're good!"

"Shut up goof! You can help her. Go get her some sheets for bandages. And while you're at it moron, get your jacket this time in case it rains again."

Eddie grabbed a cigarette from the kitchen table and lit it. He glared coldly at Ruby as she fumbled about, inhaling a long breathy drag, shaking the match to discard it. He puffed halos of smoke into the air from his pursed mouth and out through his nostrils. "You're lucky nobody came last night in that storm. You got one more chance to stick to the plan sweet-cakes before they arrive…One more."

Chapter 13

The temperate morning sun glistened over the charred wreck of George's bush plane laying dismembered deep in the heart of an unknown forest. Eruptions of billowy smoke still rose upward, kissing the cerulean sky. Burnt matchstick trees scattered against the crumpled metal debris, left over from the planes abrupt impact. It was foreign in a land with such beauty, mysterious in its foreboding state.

Inside the collapsed fuselage, bodies sprawled prostate. Bloodied faces and twisted limbs proved the stark realization of the visible disaster. Empty silence hovered over the group of stricken passengers that hours earlier had been in route to Shooting Star Lodge. Now, all hope was lost. Everything Harvey had expected this trip would bring, every dream, every joy, had died in the crash. Not even if there were other survivors besides him, would there be a chance to revive what was supposed to be. Gaining consciousness, Harvey lifted his weary aching head to assess his surroundings.

Where are the others?

It took every ounce of strength Harvey had just to pull himself out from underneath the seat that appeared to have saved his life. Gathering from what he saw, it looked as if the seat had taken the brunt of the crash for him. An enormous piece of metal stuck out of the seat merely inches from where his head lay. *Thank you, Lord!*

"Hello...?" he shouted.

Across from him, still inside the plane under a pile of metal, the strange woman lay unconscious. She appeared to have a bleeding gash across her forehead. He wriggled over to her, feeling for a pulse. Thank the Lord he felt it right away. She was still alive.

He peered around for the others. The big woman was still in the front seat, slumped over apparently unconscious too. He couldn't see the pilot.

"Lady..." he said, trying to shake her awake. "Are you okay? She didn't answer. "Hey lady...Wake up!"

The woman moaned, slowly fluttering her eyelids. "Where am I?

"We crashed."

"Where's my bag?" she panicked.

"Look at me," Harvey took charge, grabbing the woman's face. He forced her to look at him. "I need your help. We got people hurt and you and I are the only ones conscious. Now listen..."

"No...I can't. I need to find my bag."

"Ma'am...calm down. Are you hurt anywhere besides that gash on your head?" She touched her forehead, realizing it was her own blood. Shifting her body back and forth under the metal slabs that seemed to have collapsed on top of her like a tepee, she found herself mobile, relaxing just a bit. The metal could have crushed her, but Harvey didn't want to tell her that.

"No. I just hurt all over."

"That just means you're alive dear. Now listen. We have to get the big woman out of the front seat. I can't lift her by myself. Can you help me?" She slowly, but hesitantly shook her head in compliance and started getting up very carefully with Harvey removing sheet after sheet of crumpled metal. Aside from a few scrapes and bruises, the woman seemed to have escaped literally unscathed.

Harvey grabbed the woman's large carcass as he and the other woman pulled her unconscious body from the plane and laid her on the ground next to a dowdy withered pine tree. Her face was badly banged up and bleeding from a gash under her eye.

"She's got a pulse, so leave her here for a minute. We have to find the pilot." Harvey insisted, kneeling, frustrated, that he didn't know his rescuing companions name.

"I see the pilot," the woman shouted unexpectedly, pointing a few feet away.

"Good job ma'am. I mean…What's your name anyway?"

"Loretta."

"Good job Loretta." he smiled at her pretty eyes. For a moment, he thought he knew her. Then, as if a bell had suddenly gone off in his head, he realized he did know her. The airport, the tornado…She was the same Loretta, except, she had died her grey hair, and changed her looks. But she was definitely the same Loretta. He'd recognize those emerald eyes anywhere. He would talk to her about it later. Right now, they needed to focus on the pilot.

Harvey steadied himself as he shifted his weight, standing against a very sore back. Loretta had not waited for him. She darted off toward the pilot, screaming something irrational.

"He's dead!" she cried. "I think he's dead. He has no pulse. I checked."

Harvey carefully eased down to check the pilot… "He doesn't have a pulse." He manoeuvred himself around the man and started chest compressions. Panting and counting. "Hope you know CPR," he said, "cause if you don't, you're about to learn. Now how about getting down here and helping me?"

Loretta stared blankly at him and shook her head, "No!" She backed away as if she was in some kind of trance.

"What do you mean no?" Harvey gasped, annoyed as he counted compressions and did mouth to mouth. Tiring he asked again, "Do you mean no, you don't know CPR? Or no you won't help?"

The woman shook her head, "No I won't help you save that man. I am going over to help the *woman* if that's okay with you."

She backed away slowly as a well of tears filled her green eyes. Harvey couldn't figure the strange woman out. He waved her on, too tired to speak. If he had to do CPR by himself, hopefully, the pilot would revive before his arms gave out.

Suddenly with a gasp of air, the big blonde man came to life. Harvey lifted him upright a bit. "Hey there big guy, are you okay?"

George smiled, "What's all the commotion about?

"We crashed."

"No kidding…and who are you, Jesus?"

"Oh…funny," Harvey was not amused. Insulted, he didn't know whether to kick the man or help him. "I just saved your life; you could at least have some respect."

"Respect? Hey…*you're* the one in *my* face, remember?"

"You didn't have a pulse. I was doing CPR on you."

"Well that better be what you were doing pal, or I might just have to kill you."

Harvey blushed for a moment not knowing what to say.

"Oh…don't take me so seriously, I'm just kidding. I didn't mean anything by what I said. What are you…some religious freak or something?"

Yes, if you must know…now how about shutting up.

Harvey fought to keep his composure, not wanting to respond to his rudeness.

"Okay, so forgive me already, and help me out at least. My mouth goes a mile a minute when I'm in pain. I think I dislocated my shoulder."

Was that an apology? No.

At first, Harvey shook his head, and then he sighed, reluctantly zeroing in on the man's arm. It did look dislocated. Shame crept into his bruised ego. He wondered if he could pop it out by himself. Looking around for Loretta and finding her resting beside the big woman, he somehow knew she would be no help at all.

"All right then…I'll pop it back for you but it's going to be painful."

"I'm ready."

The pilot clenched his teeth and groaned as he attempted to sit upright.

"On the count of three…One…two…three," Harvey forced his body weight against the man's shoulder, hearing the assaulting pop.

George yelled in agony, and then stopped short. "That's better," he smiled as if everything was back to normal. He rolled his muscular shoulder to prove it.

"Are you sure?"

"Positive."

Harvey was reluctant to let go but thought it wise to take the guys word for it if he knew what was good for him. "Are you hurt anywhere else?"

"No...Oh, wait just a minute," he squeezed his left knee. "I think my knee is broken. You'd better make me a splint and hurry up. I don't want to stay here all day."

"Right," Since when did Harvey become the man's slave? It was one thing to have bad manners after a crash like this, and another thing entirely to order someone around, or refuse to do CPR like Loretta had. What was going on with everyone anyway?

As Harvey searched for branches large enough to make the splint, he watched Loretta. She was an odd one. She sat beside the wounded redhead who was now awake. He waved, shouting over to both of them. "You two okay?"

Loretta called back to him, "She's fine!"

Making a splint for the pilot's leg was easy. Harvey had learned the technique in the many first-aide and CPR courses he took while on the force. It was fitting it to the ignorant husky man that was going to be a challenge.

He huffed and sweated through his already blood-stained shirt as he used ripped-up pieces of canvas from the plane to bind the man's splinted leg. Once he was done, he wandered over to check on the big woman.

"So, you're okay?" he asked, breathing heavily, completely exhausted now.

"My name is Vicki," the big redheaded woman with an English accent tried to smile against her wounded face, "and I'm okay. I just got a few scratches."

"Call me Harvey...and don't tell me that's just a scratch under your eye. It looks pretty bad."

"I've had worse."

Harvey wondered how worse. Who was this woman anyway, a wrestler?

Loretta was silent as usual. She sat against the tree and frowned.

"Do you want me to find some sort of bandage for it?"

"Thanks mate, but it stopped bleeding already."

"If you say so," Harvey sighed, reluctant to leave. At least she didn't order him around like George.

Harvey peered over at the guy, the incredible hulk, still lying as if he were just taking a nap. He looked at Loretta the zombie, and Vicki the Neanderthal, and shook his head in disbelief. Perhaps he had died and gone to some strange place, some wacky fairytale land. It wasn't heaven…maybe hell, but definitely not heaven.

He knew then that someone had to take charge, and whether he liked it or not, that was most likely going to be him. "Okay," he informed the group, "Listen up. This is what we're going to do. We can't stay here. It's daytime now but not for long. We don't want any wild animals adding to our injuries. We need to find some help and some shelter. So…Vicki and Loretta, you two can help George walk. I'll scout the area and help us find a clear route. Got it?"

"Got it," George mimicked sarcastically. "But who made you the boss?"

"Shut up George and grab your ladies arms."

"And don't forget to promenade left," George snickered as Harvey turned and glared a good one at him.

"I'm not going to help *him*," Loretta demanded, whispering into Harvey's ear. Vicki already wandered over to George.

Harvey rolled his eyes, too tired to argue with the obstinate woman. She probably had it out for the pilot because he crashed the plane or some nutty thing like that. "Fine! You can come with me then."

"Change of plans guys," he reluctantly shouted back to George and Vicki, "Loretta's coming with me."

"Oh...Yes *sir*!" George mocked, forming a military salute with his hand to his brow. "Would you like us to follow you *sir*?"

Vicki giggled. Did the guy think he was actually being funny?

Harvey sighed, ignoring the mockery. "*Yes*!" He hoped this jerk wasn't going to be a problem for him or anyone else. He'd seen many guys like him before. He'd deal with him if he had to, but for now he'd just proceed through the bush with Loretta in tow. Not that *she'd* be any different.

God help us all.

Chapter 14

Loretta didn't want anything to do with George. Of *that,* she was definitely sure. For all she cared he might as well have perished in the plane wreck. For a moment, when it was just her and the unconscious pilot, she thought of letting him die. How easy it would have been just to walk away. George Oxford Williams would have died and the world would have been better off. Yet somehow, that scenario did little for Loretta's vindictive yearnings. *She* wanted to watch him suffer the way Jeremy had suffered.

Now, without her nine-millimetre, how could she accomplish that? Harvey had set off ahead of her. She had no time to look for anything.

George and Vicki were way behind them, giggling like giddy children. She wondered if she should warn this woman, tell her what kind of bloodthirsty killer she was chumming with. No, she decided. It wasn't *her* fault. That silly woman could flirt with the devil if she wanted to. She appeared as though she could take care of herself anyway.

Letting Harvey guide them wasn't what Loretta had wanted. She thought it much wiser to stay near the wreckage and wait for help. It would have been better for her, and then she could have at least had the time to search for her bag and figure out what to do next. Instead, sauntering behind the only man that knew what she looked like before her orange hair, she realized it was a bittersweet decision. At least it was better than helping a criminal. Yet, she wondered if Harvey had any experience in the wilderness. Could he actually find help?

Her head ached. The scrape across her bruised forehead had stopped bleeding but the crushing pounding pain in her skull was starting to make her feel nauseous. "Wait up Harvey," she called. "Let's stop and rest." They had been crawling along at the speed of a tortoise now for the better part of the afternoon and the humidity was taking its toll.

Loretta observed the balding, overweight, pot-bellied little man stop in his tracks as he did an about-face in front of her, disappointed. Oh, how he looked like her Bob. It repulsed her in a way. Yet, the resemblance somehow warmed her at the same time.

"Fine." Harvey sighed wiping the sweat from his brow with a handkerchief he pulled from his pocket. "But we're not going to get very far if we keep on stopping."

George and Vicki caught up, hobbling, sweating, and gasping for air. "That's easy for you to say buddy." he growled in pain. "You're not the one that's hurt, now are you?"

"No...but at least I'm not the one with the big mouth, jerk!" Harvey snapped.

"Stop it Harvey," Vicki interrupted with her distinct British accent, defending her new best friend. "I don't think that's the least bit polite mate."

"What do you mean? *He's* been asking for it the whole time."

"Because he's the one that saved *our* lives, remember? He flew the bloody plane."

Harvey rolled his eyes. Loretta sided with Harvey but she shut her mouth anyway.

"So there, big shot..." George smiled rubbing it in. "I'd like to see you land a beast like that during a thunderstorm...*and*...keep us all alive."

Harvey fumed as he lunged toward George. "I wouldn't have driven it into a thunderstorm in the first place, idiot!"

"Stop it Harvey!" Vicki shouted, shoving him with both big arms.

This is interesting.

Loretta watched silently on the sidelines as the three of them struggled and shoved each other...Harvey being the smallest, shortest, obviously at an enormous disadvantage, battling between the two "wannabe" wrestlers.

Loretta fidgeted, knowing she had to say something, but not wanting to. In a way, it was entertaining. She admired Harvey's bravery. Or was it stupidity? She wasn't clear which it was. But for some reason, she knew if she didn't stop these fools, she might never get out of the bush.

"Will you guys cut it out," she tried to yell. "I'm too tired to break up fights between a pack of schoolyard bullies, now stop it, all of you. You remind me of my own kids."

Harvey tumbled to the ground, Vicki toppled over him. Only George was standing, staring at Loretta, grinning like a Cheshire cat. "Oh, I'm *so* scared. I wouldn't want to be *your* son."

Loretta felt a chill go up her spine. "Do *not* speak to me...*Ever!*" *Especially about my son.*

"Oh, come on," George continued to grin. "Who do you think you are loony tunes? You don't have to be so serious...Man!"

"Leave her alone George," Harvey interrupted, dusting himself off. "Look, we're all hot, exhausted, and hungry right now. We just need to calm down. We're never going to survive this if we kill each other first."

That's what you think.

"You're right Harvey. We *are* tired." Vicki puffed. "So, let's just take a break."

"I know you're all tired," Harvey sighed, "but we really haven't come very far. We can't keep taking breaks every ten minutes. Now let's try to work together and find some shelter for the night. We'll go for another hour and then stop for the night. Okay?"

George rolled his eyes in disgust. Vicki shook her head, disappointed. Loretta just surveyed Harvey's earnest eyes and forced a smile. "He's right," she had to admit. "Let's get going before it gets dark."

~~~~

"Who does he think he is anyway?" Vicki grumbled to Loretta as they prepared to go again.

"Sorry?"

"Harvey. Didn't you hear me?"

Vicki brushed the dirt from her tattered black leather pants, ripped on the knees, and along one side. She stood there annoyed, waiting for a response from a woman who had a voice like a mouse. She seemed spaced out, confused, on drugs maybe. It was difficult to converse with the woman, her whisper almost inaudible. Vicki just pretended to understand her when she spoke.

Oh, how she disliked women like that. They needed help with everything, and men always favored them. Vicki wouldn't let that happen. George was hers, not Loretta's. She didn't even like him, had some grudge against him. Still, that didn't stop some men. Although, he seemed to click with Vicki, she could tell. And the feeling was mutual.

"I'm sorry; my head is a bit dopey right now. What did you say about Harvey?"

"I said, who does he think he is? You don't go off on an injured man like that."

"Oh…he's probably just tired like the rest of us."

Yah, that's a good one.

Vicki despised women that made excuses for violent men. She saw it repeatedly at the foster home, listening to young mothers, visually seeing their bruises. They would come in with battered children hoping to find safe refuge. She'd always listen to the frightened children telling their horrific stories. Then, a few days later, the husband would show up full of remorse. Usually the mother would make excuses for the husband and the kids would have no choice but to go back home with them. It made her sick. She would have to keep an eye on this Harvey, swing at him again if needed.

"So, what does it feel like lugging a big guy like me around?" George teased both of them as he helplessly grabbed their arms and started walking with the group.

Loretta looked white as a ghost as George flung his cumbersome arm around her petite shoulder. She tried to pull away, but he wouldn't let her.

"Stop teasing her George," Vicki blushed hoping he'd take his arm off her. "If she doesn't want to help you, then that's her problem."

"Whatever." George tugged at her, then let her rip away from him. "The arm is still tender from the dislocation anyway."

Figures someone like her would be all stuck up. She didn't say a word as she speed-walked ahead of them.

"I'm sure you're just being polite," Vicki insulted Loretta. "His sweaty armpits are a little foul."

Vicki smiled at her wounded hero. "...Just kidding babe." She grinned, actually wanting Loretta to feel ashamed of herself. Why wouldn't she help him?

Loretta charged ahead, ignoring them completely.

"So, what brings a beautiful girl like you to these parts anyway Vicki?"

"Oh...you know...this and that."

"Well that just about tells me everything."

She laughed, startled, embarrassed as she continued to flirt with George. She didn't care if Loretta and Harvey didn't like him. She did. "If I told you, then it wouldn't be a secret."

"Oh boy, a girl with secrets, how mysterious."

Loretta suddenly cocked her head backward, glaring at the two of them. Apparently, she overheard their conversation, disapproved for some reason. Or was she jealous? "What?" Vicki spat at Loretta's mute frown. "Mind your own business you old bat." She considered sticking her tongue out but decided against it, fearing immaturity would turn a good-looking man off.

"Let me in on your secret and I'll let you in on one of mine."

Vicki considered it. What harm would it do to tell him now, even if Loretta was eavesdropping? He might even be able to help if they ever find the lodge. "I'm looking for someone."

"You are?"

"My sister...She sent me a postcard from Shooting Star Lodge, and I haven't heard from her since."

"Is that right?" George grinned. He stumbled on a twig in front of him, jarring his leg. "Watch it babe."

"Sorry mate."

George's face went red with pain. "I need to stop."

Vicki stopped for a moment, letting the muscular brute lean on her, resting his splinted leg. Loretta stopped too, apparently interested in the conversation though she pretended not to be. Harvey got further and further ahead of them. "Are you okay now?" she asked him.

"Fine now...Let's go."

Busybody Loretta continued in front of them. If she had to put up with this woman's neurosis much longer, she'd vomit. The lunatic couldn't even catch on to her glaring hints and give them some privacy.

"So, George, I told you my secret, how about yours."

The pain must have gotten to him, because he wasn't his jovial self anymore. Her own clumsiness had taken care of that.

"Oh!" He groaned. "Um...I guess I promised you."

Maybe that will take your mind off the pain.

"Well, my secret is...lets see. I never crashed a plane before."

"That's no secret you nincompoop. You tricked me."

Loretta spun her head over her shoulder again...listening.

"I never trick. I'm a good boy."

"Balderdash, you are not!" Vicki blushed again thinking this man was sweet. She should've met him years ago instead of all those losers she'd dated in the past. She could see herself dating a charming man like him, a pilot. How debonair.

They both grinned, laughing at the same time, gazing into each other's eyes. Vicki didn't care if the old bat didn't like it. She would just have to put up with it or walk somewhere else.

"So...you like Harleys George?"

"Don't tell me you're a biker chick," he said, eyes lit up, grinning wider.

"Well I'm jolly well not wearing these leather frocks for nothing mate."

"What are frocks?" George said as he murdered the word, speaking it back to her, making a bad imitation of her British accent.

"Don't make fun of the way I talk, you buffoon."

"I'm not 'mum'," he teased.

"Oh, you think you're funny," she teased back. "Let's just see how you get on without my help."

"Oh, come on babe, you *know* I'm kidding."

Loretta stopped in her tracks, turned around, and busted out laughing.

"What are *you* laughing at witch?"

"Nothing," the odd little orange-haired woman smiled as she continued to giggle.

"Shut your bloody gob. You can't even help an injured man so buzz off. In fact, you probably aren't even capable of handling him. You might break. You're just a feather weight, now aren't you mum?" *You ugly freak...*

"I can handle a lot more than you think I can."

Silence pierced their conversation for a moment as both women caught each other's eyes.

"Oh boy...It's a cat-fight!" George cheered. "Just what the doctor ordered."

"I didn't realize Vicki was short for vicious," Loretta scoffed.

Oh, she's asking for it. "That's right freak, and you better not forget it. I have claws like a cat and I'll use them if I have to. She exposed her long black-polished gel nails. I'm the last person you want to see in a dark alley. You're lucky I'm not armed."

Loretta's face turned red. She looked like she was going to cry. "I'm sorry Vicki. I didn't mean what I said. Let's not fight. I don't know what got into me."

"Oh, come on, you're ruining the fun," George pouted like a child.

Vicki blew her red tangled curls from her parched lips and paused. *Just like I thought, Wimp!* "Whatever...If that's an apology, I guess you're forgiven...this time."

Loretta's eyes clouded with tears as she looked away. It was sad really, even Vicki felt ashamed of her own juvenile behaviour. She didn't know why the woman enraged her so much. Did she have this affect on everyone?

Maybe they were all going nuts. Maybe they were becoming delusional. She heard of that happening before to others lost in the wilderness. They ended up eating their own flesh. Somehow, Vicki knew she'd rather starve than eat *these* people. No, she shook her head repulsed, she was hungry, but not that hungry.

"So...what's your sister's name?" Loretta sniffled with remorse.

Reluctantly Vicki turned to look at her sorry face. "Her name is Ruby."

"Does she look like you?"

"No. We have different fathers."

"Oh."

Loretta shook her head. Just like that, she lost interest. *That should shut her up for a while.* She's probably some religious prude who takes offence to alternative lifestyles, especially the ones that don't line up to her own self-righteous living. If that were the case, and she knew it was, their conversation was over. Thank goodness, at least she had George to turn to. "George?"

George grinned as if something were incredibly amusing. "What's so funny?"

"Nothing."

"No really. I want to know what you find so hilarious."

"It's just the way you said 'Ruby'," he giggled. "I've never heard anyone pronounce it quite so elegantly, as if she's a real queen or something."

"She *is* a queen, to me anyway, now stop teasing. I warned you before about making fun of my accent. I might just have to use my nails on *you*," she gently clawed her fingers across his bristly jaw, half-smiling, shaking her head, "Now come on love, let's get you up and moving again. I think you're going a little cuckoo sitting here."

Loretta started walking again. She was about six feet in front of them now. Vicki and George hobbled behind her. Harvey was nowhere in sight.

"How much longer must we do this?" Vicki complained.

"Don't look at me," George said with a mocking tone. "Why don't you ask the boss up ahead?"

"Harvey!" she called after him. But there was no Harvey anywhere. "Where did that fool go now?"

Loretta touched Vicki's sweaty back, creeping up on her, startling her like some kind of whispering *sneaky* fairy godmother. "Do you want me to go look for him?"

"No, I'll go."

Vicki guided George back into a sitting position, adjusted her gaze through the dark trees. The sunset had snuck up on them, as did the cool evening air.

"No way," Loretta fumed.

"What do you mean, no way?"

"You're not leaving me with *him*. *I'm* going to find Harvey."

"Suit your self," Vicki shook her head, trying to figure out the weird woman. She was too tired to argue so she just let her go. It would give her and George a chance to be alone anyway.

"Harvey!" Loretta echoed through the bush as she stomped off in the direction he had been traveling.

How could he just take off like that?

Chapter 15

Stately jack pines staged a crowded maze as they hung, arms dangling, clawing at Loretta's weary body, hooking her already torn clothing as she jeered left, then right. Prickles brushed across her face, slapping her, halting her movements, preventing her from a clear passageway. She wondered if going after Harvey had been a smart thing after all. There was no obvious route through the towering branchy evergreens. If he had come this way, she might be able to tell if it wasn't so dark, but not now. What was she thinking? How could she expect to find anyone at night leave alone in the middle of the bush? She should have let Vicki go instead.

Staying alone with George hadn't appealed to her, and for good reason. Yet, as she exhaled against a barbed tree trunk, she thought about that for a moment. What was it about George that threatened her so much? She knew just about everything there was to know about him, researched him for months, chatted with him, and befriended him. She knew intimate details about the man that Vicki would probably never know. Still, something kept her back from the man; something scared her still.

Meeting him in person had overwhelmed her at first, sickened her to the point of nausea. She never imagined she would respond like that. She'd seen his picture many times, thought she could handle it. But then, her reaction was probably similar to the way people react to seeing real blood. You can numb yourself to bloody images on television as much as you like, watch horror movies, think you can handle the real thing, but you're only fooling yourself. When faced with actual reality, one never knows how it will feel. Seeing Jeremy shot in the head…was surreal. It repulsed her, shocked her, numbed her, and made her dizzy and nauseous. It was a… *real*…horror flick.

Jeremy. She hadn't wanted to think of him now. The visions of his dead bloody body haunted her every day. Sometimes minutes, hours would go by when she'd forget…if she was lucky. That phenomenon didn't occur often. On the plane, she had let her mind drift, regretting it now. When she was with the group, in spite of George being there, she honestly hadn't thought much about her baby. Now, by herself again, the memories devoured her like a wild beast eating its prey.

Pain wrenched her gut as it always did when plagued with memories of her only son. She bent to the left and vomited beside a tree root. Wiping her mouth with her soiled torn sleeve, she leaned her head back against the cold thistly tree trunk, breathing in heavily through her nose, fighting the dizziness, the demons.

The stars above her were bright in the midnight sky. Just a hint of the moon peered through bits of cloud. Dancing Aurora Borealis flickered through the sky, waving at her through its endless radiant charm. She'd never seen the northern lights up close before. It almost spoke to her, calmed her, talked to her like God use to. God. She had chosen not to speak to him anymore, yet, for some reason, tonight, she felt like having a long conversation. Tonight, just for one moment, she wanted comfort, needed it to keep her sane. She wanted to call out to God like before when life was simple, when all she had to complain about was middle age and hot flashes.

"Jesus...I need you!" was all she could manage to squeak out of her mouth without completely loosing it. It was hard enough to fight the tears that trickled down her ashen face. She pasted her trembling right palm against her sweaty throbbing forehead, trying to push her headache away. Gulping, sniffling, she closed her eyes and sobbed.

A wolf howled in the distance, startling her, reminding her that she was sitting in the middle of a dangerous wilderness. Within moments, she composed herself, rehashing her anger toward God. No, not this time, she thought to herself. She was not going to fall for it again. She would not trust in a God that couldn't even bother to save her son. No. And to think for a moment, she almost did. She almost decided to give up her quest. With no gun, how could she anyway. Still, George had taken her only son, her marriage, her family, everything that ever mattered to her. She had to avenge him somehow.

Loretta slowly rose from where she was sitting and dusted herself off, sniffled, and moved on through the forest at a creeping gradual pace. In front of her a few feet away, she noticed a small clearing. Steadily, she manoeuvred her way toward it, seeing something reflective in the distance.

Bits of debris lay scattered in front of her, crumpled metal, pieces of plastic, and boxes of something. Loretta widened her eyes. *Is this from the plane?* Her heart started pounding, racing like a ravenous thing in her chest. *My bag!*

She ran to it as if it were a long-lost kitten, fondled it, knelt down next to it and started to unzip the monstrosity. As she pulled everything out and spread it around her, there, deep in the bottom, she felt for the cold steel thing.

Pulling it out and kissing it softly, Loretta held the undamaged, still-loaded, nine-millimetre Glock 17 like some addict who needed a fix. She moaned and caressed it, fuelled by her own evil desire, her passion, her retribution. Yes, even the Bible verse that once bounced through her head telling her that vengeance belonged to the Lord, didn't seem to matter.

She chose to believe something different, something heinous.

"Now…Vengeance is *mine!*"

~~~

The night air tasted good to Harvey. It cooled his thirst as he ran through the bush realizing he had gotten himself lost. He twirled around to look for the others, called out their names, but nobody answered. Trees swayed, owls hooted, wolves howled in the distance, but that was all.

Panic struck him as he stood panting in his solitary tracks, sweaty, itchy, and very hungry. He didn't have to be so stubborn. He should have waited for Loretta to catch up. He should have been more considerate toward George. After all, he suffered the most injuries. Rose always told him he needed to be more compassionate.

If anything happens to them, I will hold myself completely responsible.

A rush of sadness and defeat suddenly washed over Harvey as he slumped to the moss-covered ground and propped himself up against a prickly tree. He'd never felt so alone. Not only did he not want to come on this trip by himself, he had found himself in the most dangerous unimaginable circumstance ever. And he was alone.

Tall dark trees laughed at him crumpled on the ground. They mocked him, toyed with him, and ridiculed him, prancing around his body with a lofty swaying gate. He hadn't felt so helpless since Rose died, remembering the moment he stepped back into their house the morning after. He practically lived at the hospital those last weeks, but he hadn't realized what living in that big empty house without his wife would truly feel like until that moment.

He couldn't find anything, not even the keys. Rose was so particular. Everything was always in it's place. And when he didn't put things away, she would always remind him in that sweet gentle way of hers. It was never harsh. She had a way about her that made you feel so special, even when she reprimanded you.

Rose was the poster girl for organization. Even though she kept things orderly, Harvey still didn't keep track of where she put things, or how she organized the finances. Everything was a blur then. It took him weeks, months to find the simplest things. He was in fact helpless. The feeling consumed him, as it did now.

And the loneliness was just the same.

Father...please help me. You have always been a faithful God. You picked me up when I needed you the most: When you took my beloved home. You comforted me, calmed me. You helped me when I was helpless, and took away my loneliness. You were my shelter in a fierce and turbulent storm.

I need a shelter now. I need you to show me the way. You saved me in the plane crash. I don't know why. Just when I thought I'd finally see my Rose again, you put a stop to it. You took my wife when all I wanted to do was die in her place. Why? You must want an old fart like me around for something.

Please! Help me find the others so we can get out of here alive.

Animal noises echoed more notably now as Harvey wiped away his tears and awaited his answer from God. Nothing came, nothing but the sound of wind whistling through the trees, and an eerie silence that seemed to forewarn humans to go away.

Perhaps he really had died in the crash, Harvey thought to himself. If this was death, then where was he now? Hell?

Suddenly, bushes moved, cracking twigs broke near him. "Get up," an evil voice spit out. "How pathetic is this."

Harvey felt the jab of a gun up against the back of his skull as he started to rise. Someone jerked his hands behind his back and tied them together.

This must be Hell!

Chapter 16

The rustic log cabin at the side of the calm river was dark and dingy except for the cigarette Eddie lit. It exposed the way they left the place this morning, blood still in a sticky mess on the floor, red soiled toilet paper beside it, the smell of blood in the air. He bent over fingering the lighter with his gnarled dirty thumbnail, lighting the kerosene lamp as it sat on a table. His eyes grew wild as the low flame flickered in the room. Folding his hands together in a psychotic manner, he cracked his knuckles one at a time.

"So, either you talk, or I'm going to knock it out of you."

Ruby sat exhausted on the couch, her face so swollen and wrapped with bandages that she could barely see what was going on. But she still knew. She remembered the blows from this morning, felt them, and relived them. Every breath she took felt like an elephant was sitting on her chest.

In some sadistic kind of way, she felt a great sense of relief knowing she wasn't Eddie and Joe's punching bag this time. Now, their attention centered on a poor old man they found wandering in the bush. Thankfully, she hadn't led them to the diamonds yet, but apparently, they think he has something to do with it. Ruby felt bad for him as she watched them beating on him.

"Tell us where the money is freak," Eddie kicked the man out of the kitchen chair where they initially put him.

"I don't know what you're talking about," he answered, blood dripping out of his mouth and nose as he lay sideways on the floor.

He was an older, short, heavyset man, balding with and an unsightly comb-over.

"Oh, look Joe, he's crying like a baby, just like when we found him. Want us to find your mama?" Eddie kicked him in the stomach while Joe kicked him in the head.

"What the...Don't kick him in the head Joe. He won't be any good to us unconscious."

"I thought you said to wail on him."

Eddie glared at Joe and told him to go watch for the plane. Joe pouted, stomping toward the front door of the cabin, slamming the door as he went out.

"Who's your buddy Ruby?"

"I swear I never saw him before in my life."

"Do you actually expect me to believe that? For all I know, he's in on your little screwed up plan."

"No...really Eddie. I don't know who he is," she cringed as he charged over toward her, yanking her long blond hair. "No Eddie..." He hauled her bandaged body upward to stand, threw her on the floor beside the old man, and spit on both of them.

The intense pain surged through her every bone, throbbing, nauseating her stomach. The room started spinning, rotating with double vision as she heaved foul vomit beside the old man's crimson pool of warm blood.

"Thanks Ruby. Now you can clean it up," he growled, kicking the small of her back as she lay on the floor.

"I can't," she sobbed uncontrollably. "I can't."

Eddie fumed as he grabbed his gun and cocked it at the back of her head. This time, Ruby knew it was over. "Just shoot me you pig. Just shoot me."

"Wait!" The old man cried. "Shoot *me*. I did what you said. Just take me outside and kill me, but please, leave her alone."

Eddie rolled his eyes upward in thought, tongue balled inside his cheek as if he actually considered believing him. Slowly, he released the gun from her head and cocked it at the old man's temple. "Stand up Pops!"

Without warning, Joe came charging in. "Eddie! It's the plane...its coming!"

"I'll be there in a minute."

He pulled out two kitchen chairs and put them back to back in the middle of the living room. Then he pushed the old man into one, hands already tied behind his back. He went over to where Ruby lay, made her stand up, pushed her into the other chair and tied her hands behind her back as well.

"And just so you two don't try any funny business," He got another rope.

"I'll make sure you can't get out of this." He laughed as he wound the rope tightly around both back-to-back bodies, knotting it with a sturdy tug.

"Now...when I get back, you both better get your stories straight or I will do more than just shoot you." He grabbed the man's comb-over and tugged his head backward as he whispered in his ear. "And you know what that means now don't you pal."

~~~~

The moonlit lake glistened majestically as the lighted buoys directed the buzzing plane to its makeshift runway. Making a water landing was difficult at night, but as Joe puttered around with his little fishing boat making sure every buoy was in place, the big plane landed on the opposite side of another much older bush plane without a problem.

Eddie jigged up and down on the protruding dock that reached into Reindeer Lake. A freight dock much preferred over the dwarfish one that Star River housed fishing boats on by the lodge. It was simply inadequate compared to this magnificent one. It stretched more than five hundred feet into the deep watered inlet of the big northern Saskatchewan Lake as it narrowed into the mouth of Star River. It was much wider too, more than six feet across from one side to the other, good for loading and unloading.

Joe motored to the dock, threw a rope to the metal support beam, and tied the little aluminium boat to it right beside an old beaten-up wooden rowboat. He heaved his lanky body up, thrust himself onto the dock, and joined his buddy at the end of it, both watching the big plane float toward them.

"Don't screw this up," Eddie mumbled sideways with his cigarette hanging out.

"Oh, I won't boss. You don't have to worry about me. I'll keep my mouth shut."

"Good, because if you don't, I swear I'll kill you," Eddie added with a cool flippant tongue as he stared straight at the plane. He threw his half-smoked cigarette from his mouth and flicked the butt down, listening to the miniature waves smash against the dock, and the sound of loons echoing off the water as the plane crawled toward them.

"Let me talk," Eddie spit as he swished his cigarette butt under his shoe like a bug, slowly, methodically, with a twisting motion.

Joe shook his head in dumbfounded compliance as he took a dirty finger, raked a glob of chewing tobacco from his tin, and pushed it into one cheek. He smiled at Eddie with black gritty teeth, brought the same finger to his mouth and shushed himself.

As the small door to the plane flung open, a tall thin man dressed in a white, out of place three-piece suit, exited the plane with only a black briefcase in his hand.

"Where's my cash?" the pilot from inside the plane shouted out to him.

Turning around, the tall man reached into his pocket without expression and handed him a stack of one hundred-dollar bills in American cash.

"Nice doing business with you pal," he smiled closing the door as he turned the winged monster around and headed back in the same direction he came from. The buzz of the plane echoed in the distant twilight as it slowly disappeared through the stars.

"Pleased to meet you," Eddie stretched out a hand to shake. The tall man stood quiet as he ignored Eddie's friendly gesture and looked into the night. His brown face with tiny round wire framed glasses formed a brilliant contrast to the glow of his attire, eerie yet intriguing at the same time.

The tall man turned his back to the two men as he gazed into a dark mute horizon. The moonlight revealed his long black braded ponytail cascading down his back as he inhaled a deep breath of cool pine air.

"It's good to be home," he smiled calmly, turning around to face the two men who had been eagerly waiting for him to speak.

"Now show me my diamonds."

Chapter 17

"My name is Ruby. What's yours?"

"Harvey."

"Well Harvey…that was stupid. You don't ask to take a bullet for someone you don't even know. Do you have a death wish or something?"

"Sorry."

"No…I mean, thank you. It's not every day I meet a guy who would do that for me. It was stupid…but brave."

Lord, I know I'm still alive…so this can't be hell. But please, tell me what's going on here. I just risked my life for a total stranger and I don't even know why.

"Hello…You're still alive, aren't you?"

Definitely…I can feel pain.

"Oh…Yah, I think it was more stupid than brave, but I'll take the compliment. It's the best I've had all day."

Harvey felt his ego raise just a notch. It reminded him of his glory days on the force even if it did hurt. The pain gripped his head as he licked the blood from the side of his mouth. He looked around the dimly lit room. The kerosene in the lamp would not last much longer.

"So why were you out there anyway? Where did you come from?"

Ignoring her and focusing on their escape plan, he wiggled his chair in place.

"Ouch! Don't do that. It's killing my ribs."

"Ever do the bunny-hop Ruby?"

"Yah, it's a little old-fashioned," she sighed. "Why?"

"Well, I figure we've got a little bit of time before they come back. We'll hear the hum of that four-wheeler they took off with, when they come back. If we don't get out of here before then, we're as good as dead honey."

"Okay. So, what do you have in mind?"

"See the kitchen over there. I figure if we both try to hop together with our chairs, we might be able to get over there and get a knife."

"You're kidding me. You must be at least two hundred and fifty pounds. I'm barely a hundred. How do you suppose we accomplish that feat together? Not to mention I can't feel my ankle, my ribs are broken, and I can hardly even breathe. My head is so dizzy it's making me nauseous again, and you want me to hop across the room like a bunny while tied to a chair with you...and you aren't in great shape. Are you crazy?"

"Well...either we try to do something, or we wait till those goons come back. It's as simple as that."

"I guess...but this is suicide."

"I know...So is the other choice."

"Point taken...Let's move."

"Okay...on three." Harvey counted slowly, "One...two...three."

They both hopped in their chairs as they inched across the floor. Ruby cried in pain with every inch and bump. Harvey hurt as well, but he pushed it aside.

"I see it," Harvey cried out as they reached the counter. A knife sat on the edge of the breadboard to the left of his chair.

"We have to rock sideways now so I can grab it with my mouth." They teetered as he bit against the counter catching the knife between his bloody teeth.

I'm going to need dentures when this is over.

"Hurry up Harvey," Ruby bawled in agony, "I'm going to pass out!"

The chairs rocked back down on the floor again with a thump. "It's okay Ruby," he mumbled through his teeth as he bit the side of the knife, "just a little longer."

He figured he could drop the knife to the side of his chair, twist his body even though Ruby wouldn't like it, and grab it with his fingers if he was lucky.

"I hear something. I hear the hum. Hurry up!"

Harvey worked as fast as he could, grabbed the knife almost dropping it, and started sawing back and forth. First one rope, and then another until his hands were free. He started working on Ruby's rope, sawing one way, then another, carefully trying not to slice her flesh as he did it. "You're free," he shouted as he jerked in his chair. "Hold on and I'll cut this rope off of us."

Slowly, the rope holding both of them released, cascading to the floor. Harvey could hear the four-wheeler coming closer now. They had to go for the door, or the window. *Which one is the safest?*

"Ruby, do you know this place?"

"Yes," she panicked. "...That way, through the bathroom window."

They both laboured down a little hall to what appeared to be the bathroom. Harvey opened the window and cut through the screen.

"Just wait. There's one more thing I have to do."

"No...there's no time." he moaned thinking she was crazy as he pried his overweight body narrowly out of the window, not sure Ruby would make it on time.

Come on girl! What's taking you so long? Harvey jigged up and down, waiting impatiently in the nippy dawn.

"Okay I'm back," she limped toward the window with a miniature dark suitcase. "Let's get out of here."

He eased Ruby's delicate well-beaten body out of the window and over toward the tree line. "I know a place to hide," she said, pointing as she put her arm around his waist. He helped her hobble toward it.

"Behind the rock," she told him.

Harvey aided Ruby into a sitting position, puffing in unison. "We can't stay here long; I'm not the only one who knows about this place."

"Oh great, lets get going then."

"I have to catch my breath first…just wait."

Harvey rested against the rock too. He wished none of this had ever happened. Who were these guys anyway? And what did they want?

"So, what's in the case?"

Ruby looked at him with sorry eyes. "Pictures."

"Pictures of what?"

"I'd rather not say. It's kind of personal."

Great job Harvey…You just stumbled into pornography.

"I couldn't exactly leave without them. They're the whole reason I came back."

"Just wait," Harvey blushed. "I don't want to have anything to do with this."

"Too late."

"Is that what they're after?"

"That among other things."

Harvey started to fume. He didn't know what to do. If he made her leave the case, she might not come with him. She might be willing to risk everything for the pictures, and then he would be in the same predicament.

"Come on sweetheart, we have to get out of here."

"I know a trail. It's over there."

He helped her up, her arm still clutching the case. They both hobbled toward the trail, fog now beginning to rise as they hurried into the mist.

"Now you better tell me how you got yourself into this mess."

~~~~

"I was naive," Ruby sobbed, cringing with pain.

"You're telling me you got sucked into taking these pictures."

"Yes, by one of them, I was in love," she foiled impishly, feeling another bout of nausea coming on with the mere mention of her ex-boyfriend. The very thought of him now repulsed her. If it hadn't been for his enchanting charm, she never would have fallen for him in the first place. What a con man. Why could she never fall for the good guys like Harvey? He was a little old and boring for her tastes but at least he cared enough to risk his life for her. That spoke volumes for his character even though he wasn't the least bit attractive. She figured what the heck; she'd take the risk and flirt with the man since nothing else was working to take her mind off the most excruciating pain her body had ever felt.

"So, Harvey," she masked her discomfort with a grin. "Are you married?"

Chapter 18

The crisp night air felt refreshing to Loretta as she stumbled along a trail she discovered. It appeared well traveled, beaten as if some animal used it regularly. Perhaps Harvey had come this way. She had no other option but to follow it. Luckily, she decided to leave her bag where she found it, figuring it was too cumbersome to lug around. She took the essentials with her like her wallet and passport, stuffed them into her jean-pockets, and left the rest. Her gun on the other hand, was the most important possession. She shoved it in the back of her jeans, hidden underneath the flap of her blue blazer. It was cold against her bare skin now as she walked on the path in the dark, smiling that she had something to protect her from all those howling wolves she kept hearing.

Now, as she thought about her original plan, realizing the crash had changed everything, she wondered how things would come together. Could she really pull this off after all? George was still out in the middle of the wilderness and he was her prime target.

If George was right in his calculations as to where they were, the Shooting Star Lodge should be around somewhere. Her eavesdropping had been worth it. Overhearing his conversation with Vicki had told her that at least one part of her plan would work out. She would still be able to corner the others when she arrived at the lodge.

So far, all she figured she had to do was make sure George would eventually get there. She wondered if she should go back and try to find him and Vicki so they could search for the lodge together. That way she could keep an eye on him and possibly even shoot him there if she had to. She gulped hard at the thought, deciding it was better to continue the direction she was going. Vicki was a strong woman; she didn't need any help with George.

Harvey on the other hand, apparently did need help. He was more than just lost out there. She couldn't hear him or see him or any signs that he had traveled this direction at all. It was almost as if he had disappeared, vanished into the night.

Something gnawed at her stomach, something more than hunger and thirst. It weighed upon her heavily as she considered where Harvey was. For some reason she couldn't help but worry about the odd little bald man even though she hadn't really gotten to know him. In fact, he was a complete stranger to her. Why should she care about him? Perhaps it was because he had cared about her, helped her during the tornado at the airport. He didn't have to. He could have walked away as she would have done to him. Yet he didn't. He had a special endearing quality that seemed to draw her to him. He looked much like Bob, yet he was unmistakably different. His personality was loving and caring. She noticed that right away. It was hard not to.

Now, as she forged on though the forest on the path that had been set before her, she realized she faced a dilemma, a glitch in her plans. What would she do about Harvey? She hadn't expected anyone else to be coming. She had researched Shooting Star Lodge and found that Terry the lodge owner was getting old and decided he wasn't taking scheduled fishing tours anymore. Did she get that wrong? Did Terry change his mind, or had she missed something?

Whatever caused the glitch didn't matter now. Harvey was here whether she liked it or not. She'd have to figure out what to do, especially since she never gave those she considered casualties of war a second thought before, the innocent victims that got in the way of her plan for the greater good. At least she knew why Vicki had tagged along, but then she was one of those expendable people that didn't matter one way or the other. She knew what she would have to do if the big woman prevented her from achieving her goal. But Harvey, he would be harder to deal with. It would take a very cold heart to aim the gun at someone who had just helped her. She honestly didn't know if she had it in her.

~~~

George snored loudly beside Vicki. The handsome man was growing on her. He had kissed her softly several times since Loretta left. In a way, she hoped the wretched woman would never come back, Harvey too. She wished she could forget both of them altogether. Still, nothing could make her forget where she was. Owls hooted... wolves howled, preventing her from sleeping; the sounds of the wilderness were much more frightening to her than the streets of Chicago.

Regardless of her fatigue, she still couldn't manage to close her eyes. The makeshift shelter she had built out of old tree branches for the two of them was private, but not very comfortable. The moss under her back was wet and spongy with a root poking into her side. She shifted her weight, trying not to wake her new man.

A mist seemed to hover around them now. It reminded her of Brighton when the fog rolled in from the English Channel. As a child, she would stow away on many of the docked fishing boats at night. Nobody ever caught her. She'd sneak out the bedroom window many times without Miss Lily ever finding out. It was where she did all her dreaming. She'd watch the fog as it billowed in succession overhead, casting bits of moonlight shadows across her much younger innocent face, dreaming of her future. She would imagine falling in love, marrying a handsome prince like the one Cinderella had. In fairy tales, everyone lived happily ever after. That rarely happened to her.

She was a throwaway child, as she often called herself then. Her mother threw her away at birth because she cared more about getting high than her own infant. When Vicki was five, her mother had a drug overdose and died. She never knew her father. As far as she could find out, he was just some bozo her mother picked up at the local pub, a one-night-stand.

For the longest time, she was alone in the world. No relative had ever claimed her. It was just her and the many kids that called Miss Lily's Foster Home *their* home. Until that day when she broke into Miss Lily's office and found her file. Vicki never would have found information about her sister. Miss Lily probably resented her for that. She caused her so much trouble insisting that she help her find her sister.

Now, she had to find her sister again…out here this time. *Where are you sis?*

Vicki sighed against the starry night. Her intensions were to find her sibling but if she were going to do that, she would have to get out of this bush first. George would surely help her find her way. She trusted him much more than that foolish bald man Harvey who got himself lost, or his sidekick Cruella DeVil. At least George knew from reading the instrument panels on the plane that they were near Shooting Star Lodge. He could guide them in the morning.

~~~

The disturbing night was lingering, taking its time to birth the dawn.

Weird animal noises awakened Ruby again as she and Harvey huddled together against the dirty moist wall of the same cabin she and Pip had stayed. It remained untouched from earlier when Pip fell through the roof. Broken boards littered the rotting floorboards. Cold crept in from the massive hole above. Mist devoured the once twinkling stars that had been out earlier. It was damp and uncomfortable though she was grateful she couldn't feel *all* her injuries. Her ankle was swollen and numb as if amputated. Her ribs and head throbbed, mentally keeping a steady beat.

After asking that silly question earlier in the evening, she wondered if she would ever live it down. She had been such a fool to ask, *"Are you married?"* What possessed her to ask *that*? The fact that he said he *was* married made her feel ashamed for asking in the first place. She should have known better. It made her look desperate. And that was definitely not the case, well maybe a little, but only because she had such a bad track record with men. Just like her sister. The two of them didn't share the same fathers, but they did share *that* quality. *Do not make the same mistakes I did Ruby. You have the brains; I have the brawn, remember that?*

Her sister would be very disappointed with her if she knew what she had done with her life over the last few months. As far as she knew, she was still on an exotic vacation in the Canadian North, though she didn't keep in touch as she said she would. They repeatedly told her not too. She remembered sending that old post-card she found in the lodge. Everyone bawled her out and told her not to send it, but she snuck it by them anyway when the plane that delivered supplies dropped by the first week when the men had gone fishing again. The skinny pilot was more than happy to take her money. He promised to mail it the fastest possible method for her. He was so nice, and she never told anyone about his visit. The men never noticed when they were low in supplies anyway. They must have thought food just fell out of trees or something.

That reminded her, what would she do with these diamonds now that she finally retrieved them? Throw them down the hole with the others, or keep them with her? She opted for dumping them, deciding she would at least know where they were if she ever wanted to find them again.

Slowly she pushed the slumped over, sleeping, snoring man she barely knew, aside without waking him. She grabbed the case and shuffled toward the door, hobbling over each creaking floorboard as she stepped. It was hard not to make noise in a broken-down shack, but she did it. She was off toward the trees and he was none the wiser.

Underneath her feet, the wet forest floor sank two inches with the lush moss she could barely see because of the fog. She was glad it boxed her in, made her feel cozier, not so far away. It did seem like she was entering a spook house at an amusement park though. Caution would have to be her next move.

The hoot of the owl seemed to follow her as she teetered through the muggy dampness of the ominous night. Her foggy breath added to the lingering mist as she wondered which direction the pit was that she fell in.

After a few minutes, she questioned why she had decided on this course of action in the first place. Had she gone nuts? Being out here in the middle of a foggy night was suicide. She didn't know where she was going. She should have woken Harvey, told him everything. What would it hurt; she already told him part of the truth. What if he found out she wasn't being honest with him when she tried to explain where she had gone? And what if he noticed the case was missing?

All she wanted was a little insurance, that's all. She could always go back for the diamonds later. Chances are nobody would find the exact hole anyway. But then again, she might not be able to either, especially if she didn't start looking soon.

After searching for a while, she decided to retrace her steps from before to the exact location. Carefully she stepped to the edge of the hole she once lay helplessly in. The memory made her cringe. If it hadn't been for the large tree stump marking the spot, she never would have found it.

"One...two...three," she counted, closing her eyes as she threw the case of diamonds into the hole. *Parting is such sweet sorrow.* She wondered if she'd ever see them again.

Now, she would have to find her way back to the cabin. It wasn't going to be easy since the fog had become even thicker than when she headed out. It trapped her, confused her, and forced her to push on through unknown territory.

She would give anything to be back in her nice warm bed right now, back in Chicago with the noise, the sirens. Her apartment she shared with her sister use to annoy her because of the traffic sounds. It lay right under the "EL". She wished she could afford something better. Maybe now she could if she retrieved those diamonds later. Now, all she could think of was how much she missed those little annoyances. She recalled the constant banging on the wall from other tenants, the loud music above and below her, and the rodents. She never thought she would miss them. Anything would be better than this place even though she loved it so much at first. Now it just reminded her of her many mistakes, her stupidity. She couldn't even see the beauty in the trees anymore.

Finally, a momentary break in the fog revealed the shabby square box cabin where she had left Harvey to slumber. *See, now that didn't take so long.* She decided to stop for one more break before going for the door. She'd rest her ankle and catch her breath for a moment, fearing her heavy breathing would surely wake Harvey up. Then she would have to tell him another lie.

Suddenly as she turned around, moonlight hit the fangs of a threatening creature as it growled. The low rumbling sound sent chills up her spine, making her breath even heavier as she stood frozen in place. The canine beast appeared ravenous, and it held its yellow glowing eyes on Ruby. Panic thumped her chest as she tried to quiet herself. Should she run for the cabin, or stay where she was? Paralyzed, she decided to wait it out. Even her eyelids didn't blink. Then, as the wolf inched closer, she sweat profusely against the cool summer night mist, noticing something: The mangy animal had blood dripping from its mouth.

Harvey!

Chapter 19

"I trusted you to have everything in order when I arrived," the smooth voice questioned. "Now you're telling me I came for nothing?"

Eddie paced the creaky floor of Shooting Star Lodge, heavily scuffing his boots over the wood plank floor as he walked. "I'm sorry sir, we ran into some trouble."

The tall thin Indian kicked at the two chairs that were lying sideways in the kitchen with cut up rope tangled around the legs. "Yah, it looks like it."

"We still got T. J's diamonds," Joe grinned. "We could give you them."

Eddie eyed the silly man, shaking his displeased head at him, silently warning him to shut up. The Indian's eyes grew wild, annoyed at the apparent games. "Well...get me them then," the Indian grinned like a sly animal, psychotically reaching into his white suit jacket for his stainless steel .357 Smith and Wesson revolver. Slowly, methodically, he pulled it out, fingering it as he flipped open the cylinder and spun it around.

"Right..." Joe fumbled, looking at Eddie as if he needed him to rescue him. "I'll get you the diamonds sir. It will only take a minute. I hid them *really* good!"

Eddie folded his arms as he followed the idiotic bumbling fool over to the bookshelf by the front window.

"Now where did I put them again?"

Eddie's eyes began to bulge, sweat beaded down his forehead as he fidgeted in place. "You'd better find them moron!"

The Indian flung his long braid behind his back and spun the gun cylinder again, this time he emptied three shells from the six-round cylinder leaving three in there. He spun the cylinder again, then smacked it back together and smiled. "I'd say so, or we'll just have to play one of my games."

"Oh, I know where it is." Joe giggled. "Old Joe might be slow, but he aint dumb. I put it under the kitchen sink."

Eddie rolled his eyes as he followed Joe back to the kitchen. The Indian stood and watched while he played with his handgun, smiling, twisting his head to the side.

"What the...Where did it go? It's not here." Joe looked up shocked. His ghost white face frowned as he looked at Eddie from underneath the kitchen sink. "I know I put it in here. Where did it go?"

"Where do you think numskull!"

"Ruby?"

The Indian slowly and deliberately walked toward Joe. His eyes small and beady as he aimed his gun at Joe's temple, finger on the trigger. "Ever play Russian Roulette?"

"No."

"Well...I can teach you."

Joe grinned like a fool, completely unaware of the Indian's intentions. "Okay."

"First you spin the cylinder, and then you aim. You pull the trigger...and if you're lucky, nothing will happen. See, I removed all but three of the bullets. You go first pal."

"Is Eddie playing?" the simple man asked looking back and forth between the Indian and Eddie, grinning and giggling like a child who found a new toy to play with.

"Maybe later...You and I will play first. Now pull the trigger."

The Indian gave Joe the gun, helping him aim it at his right temple. "Pull!" he shouted." The gun went click and Joe started laughing like a psyched-up lunatic.

"Again!" the Indian shouted even louder.

"But I thought it was you're turn next."

"No, not yet...It's still your turn. Now pull."

Click.

"Hey...I'm real lucky. I like this game."

"Pull it again!"

Click. The India looked annoyed now.

"Do it one more time!"

This time Joe's face started turning red. He gulped as he continued to aim at his temple. "But...I thought..."

He looked at Eddie sadly, jaw dropping. Eddie just frowned and said nothing as he looked away. The Indian smiled and shouted, "Come on...you said you're lucky, now pull the trigger on more time."

With sullen emotion, Joe pulled the trigger, blowing his own scull apart. His lifeless body dropped to the ground, blood splatter decorating the Indian's white suit.

Eddie backed away.

"Oops," the Indian mocked. "Guess he wasn't so lucky after all."

Stuttering, Eddie tried to compose himself. "I'll ta...take you to the girl," he said. Her name is Ru...Ruby. She has the diamonds."

The Indian twisted his demented smile. "I should think so...You can take me in the morning though. Cleaning my suit comes first. If you don't catch it right away, stains like this never come out.... And get some more fuel for that lamp, it keeps flickering...better yet, why are we not using electricity? Are we all of a sudden primitive now? Turn the blasted lamp on so you can clean up this mess. I'm going to bed."

~~~~

"Don't move," Harvey whispered to Ruby as he steadied the gun on the wolf. She wasn't going to anyway. He had startled her with his voice at first, and the gun, but not enough to make her jump. Doing that would be a mistake. The wolf stood poised to attack. If she even as much breathed the wrong way, she was sure he would jump at her with that bloody mouth.

As Harvey stood his ground, Ruby noticed something. The wolf had been eating from the ground. *His supper, no wonder he's upset.* "Harvey...Don't shoot. I think if we back off, he won't hurt us."

"Are you crazy?"

Ruby didn't care what he thought, she was not about to be part of the meal that varmint was chewing on if Harvey missed his target. Slowly, she inched backward toward the cabin door. "Be very quiet and just back up with me."

Obviously annoyed, Harvey went along with her but still pointed the gun toward the animal, limping out of sink with Ruby as he did. They continued to back into the cabin, when without warning, the wolf darted the opposite direction. "I told you."

"You *are* crazy," he sneered while he shut the door from inside.

"It runs in the family," she replied, tensing against her injuries and forcing a smile, using the wall of the cabin to support her as she slid down to rest on the floor. "Where did you get the gun anyway?"

"I found it...over there, under the floorboards. I thought you were up to something when you woke me up with all that noise by the way."

"Sorry." Ruby felt her face burn.

"Anyway, I got up to follow you and tripped on this board over hear. I couldn't believe I found a nine millimetre just lying around."

"Well believe it. I think I know where it came from. Let me see it." Cringing, her assumptions proved correct when she spotted the letters "T.J" carved into the back of the frame. He had stashed this gun for *her*. "See this initial here," she showed him. "That was my friend. He's the one they killed."

Harvey gulped hard. "We have to go Ruby."

"But the wolf..."

"He's long gone by now, but he'll be back for his meal. So, let's go."

Ruby wanted to finish out the night here. Moving again was going to be hard on her especially with no sleep. "Alright...Lets go then."

Harvey slowly creaked opened the cabin door again tucking the gun underneath his paunchy belly, digging cold below his belt. Pulling out his soiled grey short-sleeved polo shirt, he concealed the monstrous thing. Then, tiptoeing to the door, he peered to check if the wolf really was gone. "Come on, we're going back to the lodge. Those guys won't be so tough when they see my gun."

"No Harvey. They're experienced gunman."

So am I.

~~~~~

Harvey decided the woman was a real con artist, and not trustworthy at all. Did she really think he hadn't noticed she wasn't carrying the case anymore? What did she do, hid it? She wouldn't have forgotten it; she coddled the thing the whole trip to the cabin. She was using him, tried to flirt with him even. What was she up to? She was a real wolf in sheep's clothing. Still, for some reason, he couldn't help but feel sorry for her in that condition, though she was no innocent thing either. He didn't believe that sob story about her being a victim. She didn't look the part. She got herself involved with a bunch of jerks and now she was crying uncle. He knew the game.

As they made their way through the bush again, Harvey's thoughts focused on George, Vicki, and Loretta. They were still wandering around out there somewhere. He hoped they were together...and safe. They must have found some kind of shelter to spend the night. He wished he hadn't lost them. He'd call for help when he reaches the cabin. They had to have some sort of communication to the outside world. With his gun, he'd be able to apprehend the two men. Call the authorities. If he played his cards right, he'd even get in a little good old-fashioned retribution for the beating they gave *him*. After all, he had more experience. At least he used to. He'd humiliate *them*, he'd hurt *them*, then they'd see how it felt.

Do unto others, as you would have them do unto you.

Thanks for the reminder Lord...I guess you're right.

Harvey re-thought his battle plan. Instead of abusing his authority, he'd conform to God's rules. Things always worked much better that way. He discovered that years ago working his first beat as a rookie cop. He observed many officers needlessly going off on their perps, deciding he'd never stoop to that level. Why break a long-lasting record anyway. He could settle for using his weapon in defence. At least he had something for protection. Regardless, he did feel superior holding a nine millimetre again.

Chapter 20

Monday, July 3rd.

Morning broke against the flaxen dawn with sounds of loudly squawking crows. They seemed to be playing in the fern-like treetops above Loretta's head, jumping from branch to branch. She observed them, amused at their antics, listening to them squabble, scolding each other in their own foreign language. They pecked, pushed, and flapped their wings as if some kind of boxing match was going on. It was comical yet annoying at the same time. At least they had served as a wilderness alarm clock.

Her decision to stop and sleep for a while had come some time early this morning when visibility dropped to zero because of the dense fog. It all seemed a blur to her now. Vivid memories of a wolf growling and whispers in the woods started to come back to her. She had wandered aimlessly after that for a couple more hours before stumbling upon what appeared to her as an old fish-cleaning hut beside a river. Nothing much was left of it, just some broken boards she used as a shelter for the night, and an old foundation half buried in the weedy sand.

In the distance, she could see a narrow reed covered beach, decked with different sizes of rock formations hugging the shores of a turquoise river. She hadn't even noticed its pristine loveliness until now, majestically nestled between a carved-out pathway of pines. To Loretta, it reminded her of one of those pictures travel agencies used to persuade you to buy a lavish exotic holiday you couldn't afford. Though this was no holiday, she did enjoy the breathtaking view. Its picturesque landscape taunted the artist in her to pick up a sketchpad and draw it. Had she not given it up months ago, she probably would have.

Stretching and yawning, she picked herself up, dusted off the sand, and strolled toward the river's edge. There was still a bit of fog left from the night before, so she walked carefully overtop the swishy ground, dodging Precambrian rock formations as she went along. As beautiful as this river was, still the best thing about it was the fact that it was *not* that confining claustrophobic bush. She was relieved to be out of it.

As Loretta strolled along the beach, she wondered about the others. Perhaps they had already made it to Shooting Star Lodge and she was the only one lost now. If she followed the river, would it lead to the Lodge?

A loon echoed its unique noise from somewhere off the misty river that was glowing like a jewel now as the morning sun glistened off its shores. Its waters were calm, radiant, and inviting. Loretta couldn't remember when her eyes last saw such a panoramic view. Her nostrils inhaled the natural aroma. It woke her up, invigorated her, and made her feel alive again. She had been cooped up in her musty, dismal house for so long, she almost forgot what that felt like.

With rumbling stomach and parched mouth, she decided she'd better find nourishment. She looked around wondering if she could find something to use as a spear to catch a fish. A few twigs looked promising, but nothing long enough for her liking.

Scraping that idea, she settled for something easier. Lifting one heavy rock at a time, and reluctantly searching underneath, she squeamishly pulled out long swollen earthworms and gathered them in a pile until she figured she had enough. *If they could eat these things on reality shows, then so could she.*

Repulsed by her decision, she sat down beside the pile of earthworms and picked up a small rock, attempting to crush the long gangly things before eating them. Gagging at the grotesque sight, she shook her head against her queasiness, gulped hard and scooped up the mess with her finger, plunging it into her mouth with eyes squeezed shut.

"Not bad," she said, munching, gagging a bit as it slid down her throat. It was better than starving. Little by little, she continued the process, swallowing slowly, licking her fingers. She imagined eating her mother's ground turkey and pickle pâté, the usual for school lunches in her day. All she needed now was the pickles...and a little mustard.

Water was right at her fingertips too. She only needed to scoop the tasty liquid up. Carefully, she cupped her hands, leaning over the edge of the riverbank to fetch the water. With her mouth, she anxiously slurped like a hungry child eating spaghetti.

Suddenly, from the corner of her eye she noticed a shadow. Letting the water dribble out of her hand, she peered at her frightened reflection in the water. Grunting sounds permeated her eardrums as she slowly lifted her head.

A giant grizzly bear charged toward her.

~~~~

It was all too much.

Vicki decided if the plane crash hadn't killed her, bug bites, dehydration, and hunger surely would.

Her stomach had growled so loudly it finally woke her up. Her mouth was so cracked and dry, and her skin was so itchy she felt like a leaper.

Lucky for George he was still sleeping. She could only imagine what kind of agony he would be in when he woke up. She would have to find something for food. Maybe mushrooms? She'd taken a class on various kinds several years ago?

Sneaking away from George, she wandered a bit until she came upon a rather large pine tree, with a wide trunk. Sage green moss covered the north side of the trunk, just like the ones she remembered from her textbook. Now if she could only find some edible mushrooms growing in the moss. The trick was to identify the poisonous ones and leave them alone. She wondered if she could figure out which ones they were.

Vicki crouched, observing different varieties. Some were brown, white, grey, and some were purplish. She tried to recall which ones were suppose to be the "good color mushrooms". It had been six years since she took the evening class at the University of Brighton. Her brilliant idea was to travel by motorbike for a while, live off the land, and save a bundle of money. However, it did not pan out that way. Distinguishing mushrooms proved to be too difficult. Her teacher told her to be very careful. Unless she was absolutely, positively sure of what she was doing, she should never even try it. "People die of mushroom poisoning every year," he told her. "Most of them think they know what there doing. The problem is both poisonous and edible mushrooms grow side by side."

As much as she wanted to quit looking, Vicki knew she had to try to find the edible ones. It was either try or die, or die trying. One way or the other, she would figure out which ones were safe. Her own hunger drove her beyond the point of sanity, made her press her memory for as many facts as she could.

If her memory served her correctly, she remembered a mushroom family that grew on pine trees called, Inocybe. There were many different varieties in this group. She couldn't remember them all. One specifically stuck out in her mind, something called Caesar's head, Fibre head, or were they from the Amanita family? Whatever the name, she was sure they were the ones in front of her now. They had small brown fibrous caps. The word "corts" popped into her head. They must be the edible ones.

She pulled a handful of the brownish things, next moving to a group of other ones. These she never saw before. She uprooted them anyway, deciding they were too small to do any harm. Putting them in her t-shirt, sagging in front of her like a pouch, she carried them all the way back to George. They would both have a feast for breakfast.

When Vicki returned, she saw George yawning, rubbing his thick blond hair. He had a rough beard forming. It looked adorable.

"I'm back love."

George groaned, mumbling something under his breath. Vicki figured he would be grumpy.

"Not to worry…I come bearing gifts."

"You'd better have something to eat."

"How about mushrooms?"

George shook his head and swore. "I'm not eating them things."

"Why not?"

"I don't want to die…that's why. Those things are poisonous."

Vicki sighed with a pout feeling just a little bit hurt. "I picked the good ones."

"Let's see," George asked, leaning over to peer into Vicki's bowed t-shirt. "Throw them out. They're no good."

"What do you mean? I spent the last hour picking these. I know what I'm doing. I took a class on mushroom picking."

"Well you must have failed then. Those ones there," he pointed to the brown ones, "can kill you in one hour."

"How do you know that?"

"I took a class too, but I actually passed. Anyone with a brain in their head knows that 'good mushrooms' are the purple-browns."

George was grumpy, rude, and obnoxious now. She hadn't seen this side of him before. His leg must really be hurting him.

"So, you're saying that I don't have a brain then?"

"If the shoe fits…"

Vicki gasped as her face went red, boiling like a kettle. "…then you can just find your *own* breakfast…I'm not helping *you* anymore!"

George started to grin, "Oh…come on babe. I was only kidding. I didn't mean it, seriously. Just throw the brown mushrooms out, that's all. You can eat the others…if you like that sort of thing."

"I will…thank you very much," she stuck out her tongue snubbing him, dropping the brown ones to the ground and shovelling the others into her mouth, chewing and swallowing fast. "At least I won't be the hungry one."

"No…but you'll be the doped up one," George giggled uncontrollably.

"What!"

"They're…hallucinogenic mushrooms."

Vicki coughed, gagged, spit. She had swallowed everything already. Why didn't he tell her this earlier? He seemed to think this was hilarious; laughing so hard his face turned scarlet, eyes watering. He could barely speak.

"Just…. Oh, babe I can't stand it," he tried to compose himself, wiping his eyes while she continued to fume. "Babe…Just stick your finger down your throat so you throw it up."

"I *can't*!" she bawled, storming off into the bush.

~~~

"Okay Mr. Eaglefeather, try this phone."

Eddie inspected the old dial phone in his lap, but it hadn't worked since Joe took it apart. The portable was the last one in the house. Besides the broken C.B, they had no way to communicate to the outside world, and nobody else thought to bring a cell phone, not that there would be any service way up here in Northern Saskatchewan. His Nokia cell phone proved to be a dud, always scrolling, "Searching for service". The battery was about to lose its charge anyway, and he hadn't brought an adaptor to plug it in.

"It better work, for your sake." The tall Indian snapped back at him as he lifted it to his ear, sipping on his morning coffee.

"I don't even get a dial tone Ed. Now how am I supposed to get in touch with Mr. Williams?"

"It should work." Eddie grabbed the phone Mr. Eaglefeather handed to him and frantically pushed the talk button repeatedly, listening, banging it into his open hand. Sweat dripped from his forehead as he wiped it, forcing a frustrated smile. "I bet you the idiot screwed up the phone lines when he tried to fix the old man's broken computer."

"So that doesn't work either I suppose," the Indian fumed, not a bit amused. "Okay, just so we're clear. You're telling me I can't send an E-mail. I can't use any landlines, C.B, or your cell phone. Is that right?"

"Right...Joe did that kind of thing. He always fooled around with gadgets, took them apart, put them back together. I told him to stop it, but he never listened. He probably could have fixed it if he was...still alive," Eddie blushed, gulping hard.

"Do I have to waste another bullet again?"

Eddie trembled. "No!"

"Then shut your rotten mouth and let's go find the girl. If I can't contact anyone right now, I might as well get the diamonds back."

Chapter 21

The bear swat at her, slicing the side of her cheek.

He pummelled her with his paws like a lifeless rag doll as she rolled along the edges of the swollen riverbank, teetering between land and water. With her feet, she kicked, fighting the beast with every meagre blow. Her arms flailed in front of her face, protecting herself from his slapping discipline.

Another swipe…this time it tore against her blue blazer.

Panic thrust her into the deep water, splashing.

The bear eased off.

Swim Loretta…swim!

For one small moment, she thought he hadn't followed her, then, as Loretta yanked her soaking wet head around, she saw him sink into the water beside her, floating with open mouth. His fangs were shocking, exposed, displaying vicious anger toward her.

She turned around and continued to swim across the river until she reached the other side. Pulling herself from the water, dripping, heart racing, she stood on the riverbank, surveying the monster as he did a sudden U-turn and headed back to shore.

Breathe…

Wiping the water from her blurry eyes, Loretta flopped to the ground exhausted. She sobbed and gasped for air like never before.

The bear reached shore and pulled his waterlogged body out of the water, dripping fur hanging. He turned around, stood on his hind legs and roared out of his open mouth, warning her, scolding her, telling her…something.

Then, out of the bushes, she saw it, a baby cub. He…the bear, was in fact…a she, a mother just like Loretta. She had been protecting her cub, fighting for it, ready to give her life for it. Hadn't she done the same for Jeremy? Sadly, she eyed the angry beast, connecting with it on some primitive level, sharing the same animal instincts.

If Loretta shot the cub, would the mother bear think twice before killing *her*? No. She even tried to kill her just for being a threat. How was this situation any different form her own?

Because you're not an animal.

She shook her thoughts away, wondering why she didn't use her gun.

The gun…

Loretta felt for it behind her back, hoping it was still there. It was gone along with her wallet and passport, lost at the bottom of the river forever. Lost. She had never felt more lost than now. She hung her head and sobbed, wailed, into her cupped hands.

The beast within her roared, "I *hate* you God!"

~~~~

Hungry savage creatures thrust their bodies toward her.

Vicki could see a scaly purple dragon spitting volcanic fire at her. It moved slowly, reluctantly, inching forward. The head of the dragon looked like someone she knew. Yes, it was Loretta. Her orange hair poked through its purple-ridged skin. Riding on her back was her sister. "No," Vicki screamed, "Get off sis. It's too dangerous."

But she refused to listen, enjoying the evil ride. Her sister's long blond hair stood upright on her head like a wild woman. Her eyes glowed fluorescent yellow bringing attention to her serpent-like tongue. Bit by bit the beastly monster transformed her sister, mutated her thin body into something more repugnant than the dragon itself.

From the side, another monster rose up from the lake. It had six gold horns and a wide girth, lean and mean. His head was familiar too. George. But he was more ferocious than the dragon, swatting its tail, using his weight to force the dragon into submission.

Vicki ran, tumbling through a forest of sharp razor blades. They stung her face, sliced her flesh. She had nowhere to hide from this golden horned monster. He was too smart for her, coning her, manipulating her. And she was defenceless.

Suddenly, a thin black eel-like monster, taller than all the rest, booted the golden horned monster in the stomach, punishing him, reminding him that *he* was the boss. Together, they killed the dragon, and Vicki's sister.

Bloody tears washed down her freshly sliced face. "No," she cried. "Not my sister!" But nobody heard her cries…Nobody cared at all.

"Please! Please! Please!" Vicki cried kneeling before the tall black monster and the golden horned one. "Don't kill me. I beg you. Please!"

But they only laughed.

From behind, someone shouted her name, "Vicki!" She couldn't make out his face. It was too foggy to see. The figure rushed up to her and thrust something into her face. Something cold, something drippy, something wet.

Quickly, she rubbed her eyes, seeing clearly now. It was a man.

"Vicki! Calm down! You're okay babe. It's just me…George."

Water dripped from her hair, her chin. She was all wet. Looking around she realized she had left the other world of monsters behind. She was back in the pine-treed forest again, safe and secure.

"George…I had the scariest dream."

"I know babe, they're called hallucinations. That's why I threw water in your face. I heard you. The entire animal kingdom must have heard you. I decided to go looking for you when I realized you were on a bad 'trip'. I started toward you and saw a flicker of light through the trees, so I headed over to it first. It turned out to be the river, Star River. Now I know where we are for sure. All we have to do is follow the river east, and it will lead us straight to Shooting Star Lodge."

George had a rusty old tin can in his hand still, pointing with it. Apparently, he carried the water back with it. He dropped the empty thing, reaching into his pocket. "I almost forgot, eat this. It will make you feel better."

"What is it?"

"I can't remember the name of it, some old Indian remedy. A friend of mine showed me it a long time ago."

Vicki shrugged and popped it in her mouth, chewing the leafy thing.

"Come on babe. Let's go to the river. If we hurry, we could make it to the lodge by suppertime. Doesn't that sound good?"

"Yes, it does," she admitted, grabbing George's shoulder to help him walk. "You sure seem to be walking better today."

"Yah, can you believe it. It must be your sweetness rubbing off. You're good for me I guess."

Vicki forced a waning smile. For some reason his compliment seemed a little too perfect. It struck her as odd against the vivid memories of his beastly side, the one she dreamed. Even though she knew it was just a hallucination, it stung her anyway.

Locking her arm around his waist, she started to forge through the bush with him in tow, hobbling out of sink. Part of her wanted to tell him every detail of her dream, another part wanted to be cautious and careful.

She decided never to speak of it again.

~~~~

Harvey swat at the black flies buzzing around his head. The huge mosquitoes had already done enough damage to his sticky wet skin. He figured he'd go insane if one more insect tried to attack him. Ruby appeared to be feeling the same way.

The hot afternoon sun was high in the midday sky by the time they finally stopped for a rest. He feared Ruby couldn't really go any further with that ankle and those ribs. His own body didn't want to continue either, but the bugs kept advancing him against his will. They nibbled at his bloody sores until exhaustion finally did him in.

"Maybe you should stay here Ruby?" he panted with short breaths. "I could come back and get you later." *After I take care of those two guys.*

"No way, and get eaten alive? I don't think so. I can make it to the lodge Harvey, really I can."

"Yah but, you're tired." *And I don't want you to get in the way.*

"So are you, and that's not stopping you."

Harvey was frustrated, hot, itchy, and sore, not to mention tired, thirsty, and hungry. He did need a rest, but he had a job to do. He was the only one with experience to handle these kinds of situations. He trained for it all his life. Ruby's life depended on him; the others did too, especially if they made it to the lodge before he did. It would be devastating. They would go into the situation completely unaware of the danger.

"I'm stronger than you, and I'm the one with the gun, remember?" He took it out flashing it in front of her face.

"Give me that." Ruby growled trying to take it away from him.

The two of them pulled at the big handgun back and forth like little squabbling children. "Stop it Ruby. You don't want it to go off do you? Those guys would come running straight for us then."

Ruby reluctantly let go. "Well, what's your problem anyway?"

"I don't have a problem," he put the gun away, "I just have more experience with guns, that's all."

"Oh, is that right. What makes you so sure?"

"I was a cop for most of my life. I'm retired now."

"Well good for you," she mocked, "You must know everything then."

"Yah...now would you *just* listen to me."

They both fell silent then, resting against a tall woody evergreen that looked like it had seen better days, most of it was bare, and the branches only existed at the top of the tree. In fact, Harvey had wondered why most of the trees were like that, sparse, worn, like a balding man.

Ruby pouted as she sat quietly swatting the bugs with her head leaning back against the tree, Harvey did the same. "Why do you think these trees are like this Ruby?"

"I don't know. Why ask me? Aren't you suppose to be the know it all?"

He frowned, recognizing that tone. His wife used it many times when she wanted him to realize she was upset. He had learned a lot about women during his married life. He figured he'd better say something nice before she really gets mad. "Look, I'm sorry I came across as arrogant. Let's bury the hatchet."

"Whatever."

Harvey rolled his eyes. "We should go," he sighed, starting to get up.

"Just hold your horses. I need a longer break than *that*."

Sitting back down like her puppet, he swatted another mosquito on his neck. "Well don't take all day; I'm getting eaten alive here."

Silence lingered between them for a while until Ruby finally spoke, surprising Harvey. "These trees, they actually look like this all the time you know," She informed him, changing her demeanour. "I mean...If you still wanted your question answered."

Harvey smiled. "What Question?" *That should annoy her.*

"You asked me why the trees looked like this."

"I did?"

"Oh, very funny Harvey," she teased. "Did they teach you *that* in cop school?"

Here comes the barb.

"If you're so well trained, what were you doing wandering in the bush? Are you a hunter too, or did you just get lost, Mr. Big shot cop.

Harvey didn't want to trust her but he had to tell her about the others, about them being out here. But was now really the right time?

"I'm not a hunter. Our plane crashed west of here somewhere."

Ruby's smirk vanished, "What?"

He couldn't tell if she was shocked, concerned, or something else. Whatever she felt made her gulp so hard she started to choke. "You…mean to tell me there are three hurt people out there somewhere?"

"Who told you there were three?"

"You did…just now. Didn't you?"

"No…I didn't."

Something set off alarm bells in his head. He knew he shouldn't have trusted her, someone who had a connection with those two jerks at the lodge, someone who'd risk her life and *his* just for a stupid case of porno pictures.

"Well, you did say '*our*' plane crashed so…So I assumed three others."

"Oh…just like that…You came up with the number three out of the blue. Why not five? Why not two? Why did you pick three?"

"I don't know."

Harvey stood fast to his feet. "You liar, you know something!"

"No," she argued, eyes shifting back and forth.

"Are those two guys that wailed on us the *real* owners of the lodge?" Harvey drilled. "Do they run some kind of pornography ring?"

Ruby started to sob. Her whole body began to convulse as Harvey bent toward her, forced her face up with his hand, and squeezed her cheeks so she had to look at him. "Tell me what's going on, and how you knew there were four of us on board that plane. Tell me right now!"

"Eddie and Joe aren't the owners, they're just hiding out. They were expecting you guys the other night…in the storm."

Harvey fumed. "Why?"

"They set the whole thing up. They found out the owner had a pre-booked trip scheduled for the Fourth of July weekend and went ahead with it anyway. They concocted some stupid plan, that's all I know. I swear…and when you didn't show up, I just assumed the flight had been postponed because of the weather…I don't think Eddie and Joe even realize it crashed."

"You'd better hope they don't because one of them is hurt out there, the other two aren't exactly in good shape either, and I need to find them."

Ruby dried her tears. "Is the pilot hurt? I mean, who else is hurt?"

"We're all hurt, but the pilot's the worst. He has a broken leg."

"You should have told me sooner," Ruby sniffled. "I could have helped."

"Help? How, by lying to me?"

Ruby began to sob again. "I don't know, but somehow. You have to believe me, I'm not hiding anything from you. I hate those men. I use to hang with them, but now I can't stand what they're doing."

"What *are* they doing Ruby?" he shouted. "You haven't told anything believable yet. Why are they even hiding at the lodge in the first place? Why was I their punching bag? Tell me that one *please*!"

"They robbed a bank…then a jewellery store."

Harvey's eyes bulged. "Stop lying!" The woman was so full of it she made his head spin. He wished she'd tell him the truth instead of having to piece it all together.

"I'm telling you the truth."

If she was embarrassed about the pictures, he could understand, but why lie? "If they're thieves then why are you worried about your pictures?"

"Because they're not pictures," she sobbed, "they're diamonds."

"You mean you've been lying all along about those blasted pictures? You weren't some innocent forced into pornography? You're just a thief like the rest of them?"

Ruby sobbed harder into her hands without answering him. Harvey's blood was boiling now. "Where'd you put the diamonds? And don't think I didn't notice you're not caring the case anymore."

"I hid them."

"And you're not going to tell me where. Is that right?"

"I can't!"

Sweat dripped from Harvey's brow now. Mosquitoes and black flies hovered around his balding comb-over. "Then tell me this. What happened to the owner of the Lodge? Where is he?"

She fell silent, hanging her head. "Did they kill him Ruby? Answer me!"

Unbelievable! They did.

He spun around with his hands on his head. This was not happening. He can't trust her. Why did he ever think he could? There were a bunch of thieving murderers at the lodge and the others headed straight for them, into a trap of some kind, whatever that meant. He had no idea what kind of trap Ruby meant. All he did know was that he had to warn Vicki, George, and Loretta somehow.

"Stand up!" he commanded, as he pulled his gun out of his pants with a shaking hand and pointed it at her. "You do what *I* say now."

"Harvey, please!" she bawled as she strained to stand. "You don't understand."

"I understand perfectly well, now move!"

"Where are you taking me?"

"Back to the hunter's shack to fend for yourself."

Chapter 22

The shadowy forest cleared for a moment as the sun gleamed brightly against the waters edge. Harvey had found a river. He inched closer, reflecting on his actions hours earlier. He was glad to rid himself of that woman who brought nothing but trouble. Leaving her helpless by herself was what she deserved for repeatedly lying to him, but something didn't sit right. She was female, she was hurt, and she was in trouble. Regardless of what she did or what she was in on, she was still a person and needed help. How could he abandon her like that? He was a Christian. He knew better. Still, he wasn't a doormat, pushover, or some pansy she could manipulate. He couldn't trust a word she said. She could have been using him, setting him up for that unknown trap she mentioned. It was *that* that scared him the most. She had practically confessed to using everyone on board the plane. But what for? Why? How?

The dusky sun was getting old in the sky by the time he made it to the shores of the river. The waters were beginning to get rough. Waves forced against the jagged rock edges, foaming and biting against the sand.

The brisk wind was a welcome change to the hot mugginess of the day. It kept the bugs at bay. From the north, Harvey could see something coming out of the sky, ugly, black, and foreboding. The clouds had formed so quickly that he hadn't even thought of where he would duck for shelter in the event of another storm.

Lord, its Harvey as usual. I need your help. If you could just hold off those storm clouds until I find the others and some shelter, I would be forever grateful. And while you're at it, please protect that young girl Ruby. I may have been a little hasty in leaving her alone. My anger got the best of me.

As he strolled along the sandy shore, he felt the swishy water slowly invade his brown-suede Wal-Mart hushpuppies. They *were* new. Now they felt heavy and waterlogged. He wished his shoes were the only thing destroyed. His fishing trip no longer existed. Not only did he almost die in a plane crash, the Shooting Star Lodge owner was apparently murdered, and in his place, two thugs that almost killed him. He could hardly believe it, it was as if he had walked into a nightmare.

Ahead of him, about five hundred feet on the other side of the river, something caught his eye. It was an object moving around, no, jumping up and down. It was a person. He ran toward it, shouting, and waving his arms in the air.

It was Loretta, drenched from head to toe.

"Am I ever glad to see you," he shouted across the river.

"Me too," she cried.

"What are you doing on that side?"

The strange orange-haired woman jigged around, flailing her arms in the air, frantically trying to tell him something important. All he could make out was the word, swim. "Slow down...I didn't understand what you said."

The woman dropped her arms frustrated. "There's a bear on that side."

"A what?"

"There was a bear over there earlier. It chased me over here."

Harvey's ears weren't playing tricks on him. She did say what he thought she just said. "Okay...I'm coming over there!"

As fast as he could, he jumped in the water. The cold plunge felt good against his itchy sweat covered back, the bear scare did not. He looped arm over arm desperately swimming to the other side.

Loretta reached toward him, trying to pull his heavy wet body to shore. Dripping like a dog, he dragged his own body on to the gritty sand and fell limp. "I'm too old for this," he gasped, trying to catch his breath.

"No, you're not," Loretta smiled sitting next to him, arms crossed, resting on top of her bent upright knees, wiggling her toes in the sand. "You did just fine. You should have seen *me*."

"I can't believe I found you," he said wanting to spill everything he knew, everything about Ruby, about the two men and the lodge. He wanted to warn her, but something told him not to. He'd tell everyone together. He'd wait until they find George and Vicki. There was no need to build anxiety before he had to. The poor woman looked like she had been through enough.

"I wish I wouldn't have gotten lost in the bush Loretta."

"Don't worry about it. At least I had a chance to pay you back."

"What do you mean?"

"For the airport thing…you know, the tornado? I'm sorry I was so rude to you, especially since you were just trying to help me."

Harvey sat up and slid himself over next to her, looking up, squinting in the evening sun. "You're forgiven," he said, pausing for a moment. "What'd you dye your hair for?

"What, you like the skunk look better?"

They both broke out in laughter. It felt good to take his mind off everything. Loretta was different, but right now, different was what he needed. "You're face looks pretty bad Loretta. Did the bear do that?"

"Yah…It will heal. Yours looks bad as well. What happened, did something wild attack you too?"

Harvey grinned, gazing at the distant thunderheads, overshadowing the pumpkin sunset. "Yah…*something* wild."

~~~

The boat was just sitting there, upside-down on the sand. It looked like it had drifted from somewhere. George said it was one of the old wooden boats from Shooting Star Lodge. It must have broken away from the big dock at the mouth of the river a few miles west where he was supposed to land the plane.

"Should we use it George?" she asked, hoping he would say yes. If they could find the oars, and it had no holes, she couldn't see why not. It was better than helping a cripple limp for hours through the sand.

"I hate boats."

"But George, if we walk, we won't beat that storm," she pointed, showing him the looming grey and black puffy clouds that had snuck up on them from behind.

"We have about a half hour before that gets here."

"And we can make it to the lodge in an hour?" Vicki asked, complaining with sarcasm in her voice as she turned the boat over, revealing an oar. The other one lay a few feet away from them, caught in the reeds.

George eyed the sky. "Alright, but I'm not paddling."

"That's fine, I will."

Pushing the boat into the water and helping George into the boat, Vicki decided to kick her black cowboy boots off, peal her sweaty socks off too, and rip off her ragged leather pants just above the knee. "Shorts…see?"

George looked tired and not very amused. "Could we just go please?"

Vicki waded in the water up to her waist, thrusting herself into the boat, almost tipping the thing completely over. George took a fit. "Hey, watch it. I don't want to drown you know."

Giggling, dripping with river water, Vicki sat down amused. "Don't tell me you can't swim?"

"I can't…So what! I didn't grow up on a seaside resort like you."

"Oh, pardon me mate. Where did *you* grow up?"

"You don't want to know."

Vicki teased, flirting as she started to row east along the rocky, waving river, realizing the wind was picking up faster than she had expected it to. "Sure, I do."

"Well, maybe you should mind your own business then."

Startled, she decided to shut her mouth and just row. He was scared, and men that were scared usually acted like babies anyway. She wouldn't let his bad mood bother her, or change her feelings toward him for that matter. Yet something kept gnawing at her, that memory she couldn't seem to shake, those five golden horns.

~~~~

Loretta felt comfortable with him, sitting there on the side of a riverbank. He made her feel safe with his jovial smile and caring demeanour. For a moment, she almost forgot about her quest to punish her son's murderer.

"When I first saw you with your new hair color, I thought you were a punk rocker," Harvey grinned at her. "You seemed so…"

"Weird?" she finished his sentence.

"No."

She knew what he meant. He wasn't the first one that gave her odd glances. "The orange was a mistake, okay," she tried to rub the color off her head. "I was going for Vicki's shade, but I guess I goofed up somehow. I butchered it out of sheer frustration."

"Oh, you should never do that. My wife…"

"Oh," Loretta interrupted, "you're married?"

The man's face fell. "…Was."

"Me too."

"You are?" the sad man asked, looking up again, questioning her.

"I'm divorced, how about you."

At first, Loretta wondered what ever possessed her to ask such personal questions. He was just a stranger to her, yet, they seemed to share some common ground.

"My wife…died five years ago."

I know what that feels like.

"I'm sorry," she sighed, "You must have really loved her. How did it happen?"

Leave the poor man alone. It's none of your business.

"Cancer."

For a moment, she watched the man in silence as he dried his tears. "You never know how much you love someone till their gone you know. I stood by her side right to the end; it was the hardest thing I ever went through. She died in my arms. It's difficult to explain unless you've experienced the loss of a loved one."

"I know...I lost my son." *Why did you tell him you fool?*

"I'm so sorry. Here I am blubbering over my wife, feeling sorry for myself, and *you* lost your *child*. That must be difficult."

"It *was* difficult. I wanted to die."

"When I lost Rose, I wanted to die myself. I didn't think I could go on. Then, I finally realized God has a plan for everything. She always reminded me of that, drilled it into me those last days before she died. I didn't want to hear it then. My life was so scrambled, everything became a blur, even my Christian faith...Are you a believer? I mean, do you follow Jesus Christ?"

Loretta didn't know what to say to such a bold, personal question. She considered lying, but thought he might see through it. He bared his soul to her. How could she not do the same? "Yes...I am, but I feel differently from you. I...think God should take care of his children, be there for them when they need help. Not take a vacation when a poor child gets...his head blow off."

Sobbing, convulsing, she began to cry. Harvey leaned over to put his hand on her shoulder, but she flung it off. Quickly, embarrassed, she lifted her body off the sand and ran away from him. "Loretta," he hollered after her. "Stop! Wait!"

Suddenly she stopped and turned around in a rage, "Why should I!" she screamed and bawled at the same time. "Look at me, I'm a basket case!"

He hurried his chubby body over to her and gently pulled her to his chest. "No, you're not dear. No, you're not." He shushed her as she sobbed violently into his warming embrace. Not even Bob had held her like that.

Together they headed back to the sand to sit again. Loretta had never been more embarrassed of her own behaviour. What had ever possessed her to have a breakdown now? With everything else going on, her emotional stability certainly wasn't a priority.

"I'm sorry Harvey. I barely know you. I shouldn't have…"

"Don't apologize. You lost your son, that's hard enough to deal with. But to lose him like that, that's just wrong."

"So, then you see why I said what I said about God. He just…forgot about me, about Jeremy."

"I don't think so," he said. "I know that's not what you want to hear right now, but It's true. I don't know why God allows what he does, but one thing I do know is that he will avenge whoever did this."

"And what if time flies by, and the guy gets away with it. What would *you* do Harvey? What if your wife had died from a gunshot wound to the head instead of cancer? What if you knew the man who did it? Would you go after him?"

Harvey frowned, "I would fight to the death and hunt him down like a dog."

Thank you! My point exactly. You don't know how long I have waited for someone to agree with me.

"I can understand your rage dear," Harvey continued, "but the police can handle things like this better than we can. They have certain departments for homicides. We would all go after the bad guy if we could, but unfortunately, we would be the ones that end up in jail. Just leave it to the pros honey. Crime scene investigators do it all the time. But sometimes, not even cops can find the bad guy. Sometimes no matter how hard they try, it's impossible to know who the perpetrator is.

"I *know* the perpetrator." *Now you did it. You spilled the beans you fool.*

"You do?"

Chapter 23

The turbulent winds subsided as the storm clouds shifted to the north. Vicki was relieved because rowing against the raging current hade made it almost impossible to advance through the river. Luckily, George had fallen asleep and hadn't even noticed their meandering progress. Now at least the water had reverted to a manageable current once more, and she could finally continue at a more intensive rate.

As the beaming multi-colored sunset glistened through the edges of the dark foreboding thunderheads, the river sparkled like a silver highway. Vicki raised the oars drifting for a moment, taking in the wondrous phenomenon. She had never seen such beautiful breathtaking landscape. With both hands again, she continued on her way, reluctantly forging her oars deeply into in the water, knowing George would be annoyed with her dawdling.

Jumping from the sound of George grunting in slumber, chest rising and falling, Vicki smirked at the sight of the phlegmatic snoring figure. With sore shoulder and broken leg, it was no wonder he was sleeping like a baby. He had done better than she would have done under the circumstances. His tranquil face displayed childlike features with heavy eyelids pasted down; long lashes draped against flushed cheeks like spiders legs. He had one of those attractive profiles that women swooned over, a handsome silhouette. He was the kind of man Vicki never seemed to attract. George however, *had* noticed her. Still, she couldn't believe he had actually fallen for *her*.

Vicki lapped up the vision of loveliness, pleasing to the eye, stimulating her senses. Could it be love? She wondered, heart thumping at the sight of his oversized muscles bulging through his open tattered shirt. Abandoning the attached oars, she scooted forward to steal a silent kiss, noticing something at the corner of her eye. It sparkled, poking out from underneath his dishevelled pant leg. Trying not to wake him, bending over his body, she gently raised the edge of his blue-jean pant that dressed his good leg. On it, she discovered a hidden knife case strapped to his shin. She fiddled with the silver studded case, trying to open it, when suddenly an overpowering hand grasped her wrist with needless force.

"Get your filthy hands off," George growled, squeezing her wrist, digging into her flesh until her hand turned red.

"You're hurting me…"

"Let go!"

Vicki released her grip, but George continued to squeeze, bending her wrist backward until it throbbed with excruciating pain. Her eyes began to water, transforming her face from a lily white to beet red. She locked her astounded eyes with his abusive ones, wondering, questioning his actions as a deep-rooted anger welled up from some unknown abysmal place. "Stop it George!" she screamed. "You're hurting me!"

The two of them wrestled back and forth in the boat, George yanking her down against him, contorting her body, constricting her movements into an unwelcome bear hug. "I don't like this!" she shouted, gritting through her teeth trying to fight his big strong arms. Even with a sore shoulder, he was still about twice her strength. She had no hope but to surrender.

"Now," George smiled, reining her forcibly against her will, "that's better. For a minute, I thought you were going to tip the boat over with all this fussing. Can't a guy cuddle his woman?"

Vicki fumed, shaking her head, refusing to play his obnoxious game. If this was supposed to be funny, she wasn't laughing. If he expected her to believe he was just a big practical joker, she was not buying it. No, he really bruised her wrist, not to mention her ego, and it was definitely not amusing. How could he treat her like this?

George grabbed her cheeks and squeezed, forcing her parched lips to his coarse ones. He kissed her hard, not allowing her to come up for air. She stiffened, fighting him off, trying to pull away, with no success. Then, as he continued, arms closing her in, forcing her against her will, his kiss fell limp and soft…and she fell into his spell.

The two of them cuddled in the boat together, mutually kissing now, Vicki no longer confused or threatened. "Now see," he lifted her chin, pouring on his charm, "that wasn't so bad."

"I still don't like you being rough," she said, still a bit unsure of his delinquent behaviour. "If you wanted a kiss, all you had to do was ask. Why the games?"

"I love games doll. You just have to get use to me."

Vicki wished she could tell him she didn't want to get use to *that*. She wanted to lecture him for twisting her wrist the way he did, wanted to tell him that his game stunk, that it only confused her. But she couldn't. As much as she wanted to, she couldn't break the spell he had on her, the mind-game he played. It was almost as if she were an anesthetised fly caught in a spider's web, aware of the danger, the deception, but helplessly numb to free herself from his clutches.

Contradictions of love and hate tore through her mind. *Five golden horns.*

Pulling away from George, Vicki lifted her body up, thinking she heard voices. Turning, she realized something was in the water ahead of them. It looked like two people in front, wading in the water at the edge of the riverbank. They were waving their arms and yelling something at them.

As the boat drifted near the two people, George bobbed his head up. Vicki waved, recognizing them. "Well what do you know," she smirked, "It's the long-lost duo."

~~~

Eddie had led the Indian in the wrong direction, wasting an entire day. Instead of going west, he had tracked them south on purpose. When they arrived at the shores of Deep Bay, there was no more fooling Leon Eaglefeather. "I may have been away for a while, but I'm not stupid," the Indian grinned. "Why would you take me to Deep Bay?"

Eddie wiped sweat off his brow, squeezing his forehead, pretending to be confused. "This is Deep Bay?"

Suddenly from the Corner of his eye, he noticed a fist coming, ploughing him square in the jaw, toppling him to the ground. "Don't con me, fool," the Indian growled, bending down and scooping him up by the scruff of the neck. "Take me to the girl or you'll join your nitwit friend in hell. Got it?"

"Got it."

Eddie lifted himself from the ground and steadied himself. "Follow me sir," he said, spitting blood from his cracked fat lip. "We'll go north-west this time. I think the girl is hiding at the old hunter's shack. I won't take you any other place, I promise."

"Oh, you had better promise!" the Indian insisted, pulling out his .357 Smith and Wesson. "Maybe this time you might think twice before taking me on a wild goose chase," he shoved the gun firmly into Eddie's back. "Now move it pal."

~~~~

"Ladies and gentlemen, welcome to the lovely Star River, one of Reindeer Lake's most charming arteries," George announced, smiling as he skipped a stone across the serine waterscape. "And to think we're only miles from Deep Bay, home of the giant monsters of the deep," he chuckled, resting on the beach with the others.

The boat sat on shore beside Loretta, Vicki, and Harvey; the four of them perched at the river's edge chatting like long lost relatives. "That's not true!" Vicki insisted, "You're making it up."

"It *is* true," George beamed. "I saw it myself once, ugliest thing you ever did see. It looked eel-like but it was huge, about the size of a dinosaur."

Swatting a swarm of nasty mosquitoes, Vicki challenged him, "If you saw it, how did you live to tell the tail Mr. wise guy?"

Harvey chuckled, amused at their antics. He was enjoying himself listening to the much-needed entertainment. Loretta on the other hand, was quiet, alarming him. He hoped she wasn't still upset from the talk they had earlier.

"Seriously, he tried to bite my head off when I bent over the boat," George grinned wildly. "The only reason I lived to tell the tale was because of my buddy. He jumped in to wrestle the thing...and it killed him. Yup...bit him in the neck like a vampire...ate him for lunch. I wouldn't be surprised to see part of him still floating around out here somewhere. We're not that far from the bottomless pit you know."

"What's the bottomless pit?" Harvey asked, knowing the Bible's version but wanting to here what George meant.

"It's the deepest part of Deep Bay, the place where all the monsters hide. I've been told that there is no bottom there."

"Don't scare us George," Vicki teased, giving him a playful slap, "Behave!" She smiled and pecked him on the cheek as she got herself up from the sand. "Come on you guys, we better get in the boat so we can get to the lodge before it gets dark."

Harvey enjoyed the tale. It kept his mind off what he knew he had to tell them. Without the information, they were sitting ducks. He still had no idea what to do about the situation at the lodge, but perhaps one of them had a thought. "I have something to discuss with you people," he said, "before we all get into the boat."

"I'm afraid it will have to wait, pal," George interrupted, patting him on the back as Vicki helped him in the boat. "Look at the sky. I think those clouds are headed back our way again. If we don't get going, we'll end up in the middle of it. I don't know about you guys but I don't intend to chance an unwanted swim."

"Yah," Vicki chuckled, "the big boy can't swim."

Harvey watched, as the pilot blushed, glaring at the woman he'd been obviously infatuated with until now. "Shut your big mouth…witch!" the pilot shouted, suddenly shocking everyone, all eyes turning toward him.

"Hey now," Harvey interfered, "there's no need to be *that* rude to her."

"Mind your own business and get in the boat."

"It's okay Harvey," Vicki answered in her own defence. "George has been a little cranky because of the pain. Don't hold it against him."

George just glared. "Sorry folks. She's right it *is* the leg. Now, everybody just ignore me and get into the darn boat before I *really* panic."

Once everybody was in, Harvey popped both oars into the clamps on either side of the boat and started rowing. He wondered why he had to do the dirty work all the time while the big ape professed to be aching more than he was. "This river will curve around up ahead there," George pointed, relaxing against Vicki's lap, "then it will go for another hour until we reach Shooting Star Lodge. We're half way home folks."

Harvey stiffened at the mere mention of that, remembering he still hadn't told them about the situation at the lodge. He didn't quite know how to break it to them, wasn't even sure he wanted them to get to the lodge either knowing what was waiting for them there. As he struggled to find words, he rowed through the glass-like river thinking, praying. *Lord, help me tell these people what lay ahead.*

"Look at those clouds everyone," Vicki said, breaking his train of thought. "We need more than just two oars if we're going to beat…"

"I need to say something important!" Harvey interrupted, ignoring her completely, demanding their complete attention.

"Well take a number then," Vicki fumed. "Don't interrupt *me*. I was talking first. And if I'm being honest with you, you're behaving a mite bit ignorantly I might add."

Without warning, the wind shifted, shutting them all up, advancing them sideways. The once calm waters, changed to a choppy violent current in a matter of minutes. Harvey knew this was not good. He held on to the oars and rowed with every ounce of strength he had in his old aching body. "Hold on everyone," he yelled though the howling wind and booming rumbles of thunder, "it's going to get rough!"

Chapter 24

Instead of staying at the old hunter's shack, Ruby decided to head for Shooting Star Lodge shortly after Harvey abandoned her. She would fight her own battle, live with her own consequences. Eddie and Joe would be out looking for her anyway. She might as well head over there and figure out what to do next, contemplating as she traveled.

The lodge was dismal and vacant when she arrived some time in the evening. It smelt of a potent cleanser, almost knocking her out as she inhaled her first breath through the door. The fumes reminded her of the many times she had to clean the bathroom at the foster home. A chore despised by everyone who lived there.

Collapsing on the sofa, Ruby's numb body finally relaxed. She sighed, wondering what she would possibly do if the men came back. She couldn't shoot them without a gun, but she could use something else as a weapon. Better yet, she would hunt for that phone Eddie took apart a few days ago. It was time to call the police anyway, even if that meant she would go to jail too. She'd do the right thing this time. Lives depended on it.

Ruby laboured off the couch and gradually stood up, peering out the large living-room window. Still no signs of Eddie and Joe thank goodness. She almost shouted, "Hallelujah" like Miss Lilly periodically did. It annoyed her then, and shocked her now as she found herself wanting to pronounce the loathed charismatic term.

Spending her teenage years in a Christian foster home had accustomed her to all kinds of so-called Christian dialect. She and her sister heard it every

Sunday when Miss Lilly dragged them off to church against their wills.

At first, Ruby condemned church exactly like her older sister. Then, some of it started to make sense to her. She prayed the sinner's prayer with her Sunday school teacher one day, becoming the thirty fifth student in class to make a commitment. Miss Lilly was so proud. Back then, she remembered how real God was to her. She couldn't stop talking about Jesus, annoying her sister more than anyone else. But her faith was short-lived. Life happened. May things got in the way of her God, and she soon rejected Him and all his ways. Her sister was ecstatic, Miss Lilly was furious.

Now, she almost wished she still had that innocent childlike faith back again, if only just to give her a morsel of much needed comfort. Perhaps God could still hear her after all these years. She never should have turned her back on Him, done her own thing, and left Him behind. She needed someone to save her right now.

As Ruby paced through the lodge poking around for that phone, a sudden rumble of thunder made her jump. Charging to the front window, she peered out frantically looking for Eddie and Joe. It was too dark to see anything except the iridescent flashes illuminating the trees as the distant lightening storm displayed its sceptre-like bolts.

Moving over to the door, she locked the deadbolt and sighed, relieved that she remembered and thankful that she was inside where it was dry. Rain started to clang against the window-pain and pounded on the sheet-metal roof above.

If she couldn't find a phone, she would grab a knife, thinking to herself, hoping that a weapon would at least give her a chance. She fingered a short jagged paring knife, took it from the top left-hand drawer, and laboured back to the couch. If they came back, she would be ready for them.

Without much thought, as her drowsy eyes waned to a close, she whispered a soft prayer for the first time in over ten years. *"Jesus...protect me tonight."*

~~~

The winds became violent as the doddering boat bounced upon the frothy water. Loretta could feel every pounding movement jolt through her body as recurrent waves forced themselves against the boat, shifting and turning the thing as Harvey frantically rowed. "Hold on to the sides everybody!" the old man shouted as a massive wave slapped the boat from a sideways angle. Loretta wiped her eyes, face dripping with lake water as another cold torrent bathed them all. Up and down the motion of the boat danced, making her dizzy, nauseating her stomach beyond what she could bear.

Vicki clung to George and the side of the boat displaying white knuckles as she joined Loretta, wailing with each crack of thunder. "We're going to die!" Loretta screamed, suddenly standing up in the boat as the wooden craft teetered even more.

"SIT DOWN!" they all yelled at once.

Loretta dropped to her seat deciding that the boat idea had not been a wise one after all. They could barely see, and the storm had caught them by surprise. Harvey could no longer control the bouncing cursed vessel. "If you can't do better than that Harvey, give the oars to me!" George yelled at the top of his lungs with yet another clap of boisterous thunder.

"Be my guest, big shot!" Harvey shouted back, handing over his job to the big man with the broken leg. He seemed to have more muscle power than Harvey did yet he still could not bring them back around.

"We're going to die!" Loretta cried again. Vicki put a hand on her shoulder, making sure she didn't stand up this time. Still her sobs grew loud and frantic. Loretta was not stupid. She knew if lightning hit the water, they *didn't* have a chance.

"This way George," Harvey insisted. "We've got to go this way!"

"I know!" George fumed, wet face dripping as he struggled to dig the oar deep into the churning water, trying to turn the tossing vessel as lightning flashed with rumbling thunder, unified like military forces about to attack.

"Give me the oars back!" Harvey yelled again, reaching toward George. "You're just making it worse." The two of them fought for the oars as the women wailed.

"Give it," Harvey demanded compliance.

"No!"

George swore at Harvey, ripping the oar from his sturdy grip losing the thing as it boomeranged back to him. "Look what you made me do!"

"*You* did it you fool!"

Loretta panicked, shivering as she tightly held Vicki's arm. Abandoning the other oar, George wrestled with Harvey, trying to knock him overboard.

"STOP IT!" both women cried, spitting mouthfuls of rainwater as the river deluged the teetering boat, tossing George into the angry river.

"George!" Vicki cried, reaching after him as he toppled into the violent water.

Harvey dove in immediately after him.

The women remained helpless in the crippled boat as it battered against the two men in the water, Harvey with one arm on the boat's edge, the other around George's neck. "Give us a hand," Harvey yelled holding tight to the side. Loretta and Vicki both leaned over the same side, weighting the boat to an extreme disadvantage. Without much warning, a sudden wave hit from the opposite side…capsizing them all.

Chapter 25

Tuesday, July 4th.

Ruby rubbed her eyes, awaking from the uncomfortable couch she had been sleeping on all night, and stretched to peer out the living room window above. So far, Eddie and Joe had not come back. That was a good thing.

Now, as the early morning crows squawked in the dawn outside, already giving her a throbbing headache, she noticed the foggy dismal day, an aftermath of that ferocious storm that pounded down last night. Actually, she had been relieved that it came, hoping it would keep the two men away as long as possible, perhaps even for good. Yet, for some reason that didn't seem likely. With her luck, they'd be coming back at any moment. She had to figure out a plan, before that happened.

Ruby stood on her bad ankle, testing its sturdiness, deciding it felt better than yesterday. It was far from feeling normal again, but at least the swelling had gone down and she could walk better today. She leaned her weight into it, thinking for a moment as she walked around the dimly lit cabin, remembering the ancient computer that sat tucked away in the corner. On the slim chance that it worked, she might be able to get out an E-mail to somebody, or at least she could try.

Straining with painful ribs, Ruby shoved the towering stack of National Geographic magazines off the antique computer desk, watching them slip to the floor with a reiterative clapping noise. Then, she discovered an ancient computer. It belonged to Terry no doubt. Only an old recluse would have one so obsolete, with minimal internet capabilities, slow as molasses. Yet, he probably used it for business purposes only, though it looked like he hadn't dusted it off in ten years. First, she tried to switch it on, crossing her fingers as she gawked at the black screen. Nothing. She hammered it with her fist but still it didn't boot up. Then, peering behind the thing, she discovered all the exposed wires and remembered. Tinker Joe had been working on it, one of his lousy irritating projects that drove her nuts.

With disappointment, Ruby crumpled to the couch, peering through the front window again nervously watching for the two men to return. Scooping up the knife that lay beside her all night, she fondled the cold stainless-steel blade and pledged to use it on both men if they dare return to harass her. But would she be strong enough to take them on? She needed Harvey's help. Why would he just leave her like that?

As she wondered about the survivors from the plane crash, another much greater fear came to mind. If Harvey returned with them *before* Eddie and Joe, she would be in considerable trouble. At least she'd have a heads-up before they neared the lodge if she kept a steady vigil at the window. It would give her time to seek a hiding place at least.

Resting her head against the cold clammy windowpane, Ruby smeared her swollen bruised forehead back and forth against it as if it were a much-needed ice pack. She closed her eyes for a minute as a steamy tear rolled down her cheek, intertwining with the dew dripping down the covered glass. She really messed things up this time. Of all the stupid things she has done, this one takes the cake.

Something Miss Lilly always said in circumstances like this, echoed through her mind now. It was a Bible verse. It was always a Bible verse. Yet, this time, Ruby knew she needed it, knew she had no other recourse. "'God *is my refuge and strength, an ever-present help in trouble. Therefore I will not fear, though the earth give way and the mountains fall into the heart of the sea, though the waters roar and foam and the mountains quake with their surging'...though my body is aching and Eddie and Joe or the others might return and hurt me and I don't have the strength to fight them, or the courage to use this knife...I need your strength God!*"

Ruby felt a sense of phenomenal release as if her burden had lifted somewhat. Could God really hear her cries even after she abandoned Him so long ago, even after the many years she deliberately defied His laws and *chose* to live her life without him? It was strange, but she knew the answer. Of course, He could. He could do anything. He had kept Eddie and Joe away last night. Even now, they hadn't returned. Yet, why would God answer her prayers after all the awful things she had done in her life? She didn't deserve it. Why would He bother to forgive her numerous perpetual sins, her blatant refusal to repent? If the tables were turned, *she* would never be able to forgive like that.

As she lay there on the couch, gazing through the window at the dull sombre morning, mulling over the vastness of God, she realized *He* had been there all along...in each new day He made, in the dew-dripping pine trees outside, the mist that hung low to the ground. This...is *God's* domain and she had polluted it with her sinful desires.

Now that she had done the damage, she would have to clean it up, make amends. It would take a great deal of effort, but it would be worth it.

Waiting around for Eddie and Joe to show up just did not seem like the wisest thing to do anymore. No! It was time to be brave, take action and responsibility for her mistakes. She would start by scouting the perimeter, a much better plan than just gawking out the window like a chicken, waiting for trouble to happen.

Unlocking the deadbolt and slowly creaking open the damp door, she stepped outside with caution, smelling the waft of fresh humid air after a rainstorm. Another time, another place, she would stand and savour it for a while, but not now. With purpose, she took a wavering step almost slipping on the waterlogged ground. She steadied herself, darting her head from side to side looking for any signs of the nefarious twosome. With the snap of twigs, she lifted her foot off the broken pieces and continued on, alert and attentive as she skirted the hip-level bushes that surrounded the lodge. Suddenly something caught her eye along the tree line a few feet away, almost hidden underneath a fallen tree. The wind had taken many tree limbs down last night, but this...

Approaching it carefully, Ruby gasped in horror when she realized the gruesome reality. Joe was dead, shot in the head. His half-eaten body lay crumpled in a heap, bloody, wet, and smelly, with glossed over eyes beaming wide open.

In panic, she frantically rushed back to the lodge cupping her hand over her mouth sobbing. She flung open the door; slamming it closed and dead bolting her horror-stricken body inside once again. She leaned her back against the door, grabbing her stomach, heaving her chest, panting like a dehydrated animal. Nausea consumed her as she tried to erase the disturbing, yet familiar scene from her mind.

I'm next!

~~~~

The early morning fog hung low against the still glass-like waters. Distant loons made their trumpet calls from somewhere Harvey couldn't quite see. It was thick, flocculent, as if he were walking in a cloud except, he wasn't walking; he was laying down, wet and exhausted with his heavy body stuck to the gritty cold sandy beach.

As far as he could remember, or at least the last time he saw the others, they had all been hanging on the edge of the upside-down boat during the thunderstorm last night. In his mind, he could picture it vividly again, panicking with every clash of thunder and bolt of lightening, fierce wind and waves washing over the screams. At one point throughout the night, he had been unable to hang on, thrown about by an angry violent sky, a living sky. He remembered the sinking feeling just before going under. It had been a moment of terror and hopelessness mingled with an unspeakable, horrific taste of death.

Now, as he laid there chilled and soaking wet, he observed his battered body and realized that he had washed ashore. Slowly rolling over in the sand, he thought he saw a break in the fog that revealed something on the beach in front of him. Staggering toward it, dripping and shivering, Harvey wondered if the brown object he saw could be the boat. He stumbled, tripping on bits of wood and petrified log as he tried to step carefully, discovering that he had lost his shoes somewhere, and feeling the prickly cold numbness as he tiptoed through the sandpaper reeds.

When he finally approached what looked like half the wooden boat, he noticed someone laying there face down in the sand next to it. It was the unconscious body of a man, a rather robust man. "George!" he cried, kneeling down to shake him. "Wake up!"

After shaking him for a few minutes without any response at all, Harvey decided to face the inevitable: the man had drowned. The leg splint he had been wearing obviously must have weighted him down like an anchor. It must have fallen off somewhere along the way because it hadn't washed ashore.

With an aching pain inside his heart, Harvey couldn't help but feel responsible. He stood up and looked to heaven, wiping at his tears. "How could this happen? Why Lord? This man did not deserve to die. He was just a pilot," he sobbed, hating this sick cruel adventure, wishing he had never decided to go.

Harvey let out a long sigh as he bent over and ripped his brown waterlogged socks from his sore feet. If he was going to have to endure the ice-cold water and the nasty prickles anyway, he might as well go all out and do it in bare feet. With gentle steps around the body, feeling thick cold sand squishing between his hairy toes, he decided he would have to bury the poor man even though he barely knew him. The truth was, he didn't even like him, but that was irrelevant now.

As he towered over the prone cadaver, looking around for something to use as a shovel, he suddenly felt something tug at his pant-leg. A cool clammy hand wriggled its way around his ankle.

Harvey's gaze immediately dropped, "Jeepers creepers…you *are* alive! You scared me half to death George."

The man slowly turned his head sideways, sand stuck to his beaten face. He let out a wild grin, "Gotcha!"

"Man, you scared the living daylights out of me pal," Harvey fumed; disgusted with the man's sense of humour but still glad he was alive rather than dead. He helped him into a sitting position and reluctantly started to inform him as to what was going on. "We washed up on shore after the storm George. I don't know where we are exactly."

George squinted, looking around mischievously. "I know that. I saw you coming so I played dead," he chuckled. Harvey was still not amused.

"Fine," Harvey replied, gritting his teeth, "now if you can just stop with the games for a minute, you might want to help me figure out where we are."

"Can't see nothing."

"I know, the fog is pretty thick…and creepy."

George suddenly moaned as if he were pining for attention. He made it clear that he *still* had an injury, subliminally reminding Harvey he was suppose to take care of him. It was a childish tactic, one Harvey thought only pre-schoolers were capable of. Obviously, he was wrong. "Okay, okay, let's see the leg."

"Don't touch it. Just help me up."

As Harvey gave in to the man's immature behaviour, he supported him as he helped him up; amazed at George's strength even after everything he had gone through. *You don't even need my help you ox.* "Look at you…I wish I had your strength." *Not.*

"Thanks."

185

Harvey rolled his eyes and tried to change the subject. "Where do you think we are George?"

"My guess is we drifted up river toward the lodge."

"Well then the girls should be around here somewhere. Do you know what happened to them after I couldn't hold onto the boat anymore?"

"Man...Harvey. I hate to tell you this but...they didn't make it."

Harvey shook his head. "No! That's not true. I'm sure they made it. If you made it, they must have too...and they can both swim."

"Seriously," George frowned to the reality Harvey didn't want to face. "Loretta couldn't hang on, she went under, Vicki followed after her, then she went down too."

Harvey refused to believe this lunatic. He had no reason to take him at his word. For all he knew, he was playing another sick joke on him. It didn't make sense anyway. How could he possibly know? "And you just hung there and watched the whole thing."

"What was I suppose to do?" George began to shout now. "My leg weighed me down like a rock. I hurried to rip the splint from my leg so I could go after them."

Sure, you did. Harvey watched the man as he squirmed.

"Seriously, I tried, but when I finally got the splint off, the boat had already split apart and I couldn't even see the girls anymore. I didn't know what to do. All I could do was hang on for dear life myself."

"I hung onto *you*! Remember pal?" Harvey wanted to strangle the obnoxious man, yet he knew he had to compose himself. He couldn't understand how George could have the audacity to say he remembered details that even *he* couldn't remember.

"I remember…and thanks for the reminder…but then I grabbed for the boat myself. I couldn't see *you* anymore, that's when the girls went under."

"They could still be alive."

"Doubt it. We should just move on."

"No! Not without them," Harvey fumed, rubbing the perspiration from his face. "I'm going to make you another splint for your leg and then we're going to look for the girls…And so help me, if we *don't* find them alive, you'll be worrying about more than that broken leg of yours."

~~~~

Eddie huddled in the corner of the shabby dank hunter's cabin they had no choice but to spend the night in, shivering, barely sheltered at all. The miserable violent thunderstorm poured torrential rains until early this morning, dripping, blowing, and seeping right through the ragged leaky roof.

"I can't stand this," Mr. Eaglefeather shouted as he paced the creaky floorboards. "You *are* going to find that girl today. Do you hear me? You and your foolishness the last couple of days has driven me completely up the wall. I don't even care that you *did* bring food and water along. You're an idiot anyway, just like I said you were yesterday when you led me on a wild goose chase to Deep Bay. I should have killed you then."

"But Mr. Eaglefeather, I swear I can find her," Eddie shivered.

"She wasn't *here* yesterday like you said she would be, and then we get stuck in this stinking shack waiting out a storm. No. Eddie my boy, you're going to eat a bullet if you don't find her today. And that's a promise."

"I swear I will. The only other place she could be is back at Shooting Star Lodge. I can even tell you everything about her. She's thin, with long blonde hair and…"

"I get the picture, now shut up before I shut you up. I don't need a retard like you messing things up for me," he growled, flipping his long black braid behind his back.

Eddie munched on some dry bread as he reached out his hand and gave some to Mr. Eaglefeather in a small kind gesture of truce. The Indian automatically slapped the bread from Eddie's hand crumbling it to the floor. Then without warning, he punched Eddie firmly in the jaw. His head flew backward, choking on bread, spitting blood.

"And that's for Mr. Williams. I'm sure he wouldn't be very impressed with the kind of job you've been doing lately."

Eddie spit red again as he held his jaw. "I know where *he* is too."

"Well please, do tell. You seem to have a lot of secrets. Maybe today will be a great day for you after all. We'll have to go back to the cabin and get out those birthday balloons to celebrate. I'll make some cake while you go find the girl and Mr. Williams. We'll have a wonderful family reunion afterward won't we retard?"

Sarcasm pierced through the cool morning air as the big Indian's voice echoed through the damp little cabin. "I keep my word Eddie," Mr. Eaglefeather smiled with an evil grin as he rushed up to Eddie's face with his gun, jabbing and twisting the thing into his temple. "If you don't come through for me this time, if you lead me on another wild goose chase, I swear I'll kill you. I will let this trigger go and fill those balloons with your warm sticky blood. Then we'll have a *real* party. Do you hear me?"

"Yes Mr. Eaglefeather," Eddie cried as blood dripped from his mouth. "I hear you sir. I hear you!"

"On second thought, turn around," the Indian grit his teeth taking a set of handcuffs from his long black overcoat he borrowed from the lodge. "I can't stand your ugly weasel face anymore; it's making me sick to my stomach. You can stay here for the day instead. I need to go somewhere else first. I'll be back for you tonight…if I feel like it. And you better be here when I return if you know what's good for you retard."

Chapter 26

By mid afternoon, the remainder of the lingering fog was completely gone. George said he recognized the area being the far west end of Star River a few miles east of the large boat dock used for private and commercial floatplanes. The storm had made them drift in the wrong direction away from Shooting Star Lodge, but If they stepped up their pace, they could still be at the lodge by nightfall.

As much as Harvey wanted to be somewhere dry with food, water and shoes, getting to the lodge wasn't exactly a safe refuge. He knew what was waiting there for them. The thought made him shiver as he contemplated telling George. Eventually he would have to breach the subject. But for some reason, as he helped the bulky pilot walk the riverbank, searching for the two women, he thought it best to hold off.

They hadn't caught sight of anything washed up on shore for the past few hours since they started walking. This seemed unusual for Harvey. He was sure they would find something by now. He couldn't make sense of it. If the girls *had* made it, why weren't they nearby? Perhaps they were and they just hadn't gone far enough yet, he convinced himself trying to stay positive, hopeful. He feared he would soon go nuts if he didn't find something else to think about, like a conversation about something totally off topic.

"So, George, have you always been a pilot?"

"Why? Don't I look like a pilot?"

Harvey forced himself to smile at the arrogant man, wondering if conversing with him was better than worrying after all. "No, you look like a cowboy."

"What? Even without my hat?" the man grinned, raking his worn fingers through his blonde ragged hair, vainly attempting to comb it.

Harvey pretended not to see. He rolled his eyes and insisted, "Come on, answer the question. Have you always been a pilot?"

"Well...no. I've only been flying for a short time."

"Really...Is the plane yours?"

"Yes."

"That must have cost you a pretty penny. Those things are worth a small fortune. How did someone like you manage to afford that?" Harvey knew the question was too intrusive, but he didn't care. He had worked and saved all his life and still couldn't afford something like that. He wanted to know how he achieved this incredible feat.

"Now come on Harvey, I take offence to that kind of question. It's none of your business. I don't like people knowing about my finances. I don't ask you stuff like that."

Harvey felt his cheeks blush a little. "You're right, I'm sorry." He *was* being a little rude. "Hunger and pain does that to me." *And the fact that I want to expose you for the conniving liar that you are.*

"You're forgiven. Now why don't you tell me what *you* do for a living?"

"Retired."

"Retired from what?"

Harvey ignored the question at first, deciding to focus on his feet instead. He felt every excruciating laggard step as they hobbled along the beach, both barefoot and sore. He didn't really want to share personal details with this man either. But now, after his nosy question, he had no choice but to reveal himself.

"Police force."

George suddenly started to cough, choking on something until his face turned red. Harvey patted him on the back, "You okay man?"

George bent over wheezing as if he had asthma. "Sorry," he sputtered, trying to clear his groggy windpipe. "I caught some bug in my throat when I opened my mouth," He coughed again. "It flew right in." *What a coincidence.*

Harvey lowered the man to the rock beside him and waited for him to regain his composure. "That happened to me a while back. This beach is so bug infested; I've been bitten so much my skin looks like I have the chickenpox."

"Tell me about it," George hacked again.

"But just so we're clear...Are you sure you didn't choke because I told you I was a cop? It *was* a little coincidental."

The man blushed, "No way," he cleared his throat again. "I don't give a hoot what line of work you do buddy. You could be the President for all I care." *Right.*

Harvey squinted up toward the sky in front of him and noticed that the sun was already beginning to set. They had taken too long. They hadn't made it to the lodge and *he* hadn't told him about the two men yet. But now he didn't know if he should.

"George?" he asked. "If this is the west end of Star River and we're travelling east, shouldn't the sun be setting behind us?"

"Yah," George cleared his throat, speaking a lot better now, "so what."

"Well, it's not setting behind us."

"I don't follow."

"Well the sun is setting in front of us, not behind us, and I'm wondering why."

"How should I know?"

And you're a pilot? No wonder we crashed. "Look, aren't you supposed to know your directions better than this? Everyone knows the sun is supposed to set in the west and rise in the east. We must be going the wrong way, don't you think?"

"Okay already. You don't have to rub my nose in it. So, we're heading west, big hairy deal. You're more of a nag than my old lady."

"George!" Harvey shouted, frustrated now more than ever. "I admit I'm a bit directionally impaired sometimes, but I *do* know where the sun is supposed to set. You told me yourself that we were going east toward the lodge. Why did you trick me into going west when I thought we were going east?"

George rubbed his head as his face blushed, appearing to Harvey as if he were a mouse caught in a trap. "I know another way to get to the lodge, that's why…Okay?"

~~~

Uncle Leon was back.

From Pip's elevated vantage point, perched in the old jack-pine tree beside his rustic home, he could see everything. It was hard to sit in the prickly branches, especially at night, but he didn't care, he had nothing better to do. His brothers still didn't care about him. They were in there playing video games again. They wouldn't miss him.

Pip had no friends, at least none that would hang out with him in the bush, especially up in a tree. He would pretend he was a monkey this time, hang upside-down for a while until his head felt like it was going to explode.

He wondered why his uncle had come to visit. It was odd. Uncle Leon had left five years ago after a huge fight with Grandfather. He still remembered even though he was only eight at the time.

Grandfather told him he was no longer welcome if he brought drugs into the house. Uncle Leon punched Grandfather in the jaw, hard, making him fall over. Pip could almost re-enact it all over again in his mind.

At the time, his parents had just died in a fishing accident and Uncle Leon was the only survivor. That's when Pip and his brothers and Uncle Leon came to live with Grandfather. Uncle Leon didn't have any other relatives to stay with except a cousin-in-law down south somewhere that lived on the streets. Grandfather took pity on him, even though he knew what Uncle Leon was like. It didn't matter anyway. He hated Grandfather and left shortly after.

It was a memory that Pip had tried to forget so many times. He hated seeing people fight, hearing them swear, watching them get hurt. Uncle Leon was a fighter, among many other things. Pip never did like him or trust him for that matter. He was always into something illegal.

What was it this time? Pip wondered as he tried to get comfortable in the prickly tree, listening through the open window to the erupting argument now between his wild uncle and elderly enraged Grandfather.

If he had heard correctly, Uncle Leon called Grandfather a foolish old man among other obscene words he wasn't supposed to say. He yelled some more and finally flashed his gun. Pip's brothers paused for a moment, and then continued playing video games.

"Put that away Leon," his grandfather insisted.

"What if I don't old man?

"Then you will leave."

Leon shrugged, quickly grabbing his grandfather around the neck, squeezing like a snake. "Not before I get what I came for."

"Please..." Grandfather choked. "You can't take it."

Leon released his grip, and turned up every cushion on the couch. Then he headed for Pip's brothers, smashing the TV with his gun. "Don't waist your life playing stupid video games. Join a gang and play *real* games."

"Get out of this house!" Grandfather tried to shout, but only squeaks came out. He stood now, pointing to the door. "You're not welcome here anymore. I told you that last time. Now get out, and take your drugs with you!"

"Drugs? You want to see drugs old man?" Leon spit, pulling a little baggie filled with white powder from his pocket, "Here you go boys." He threw the bag of drugs at his nephews, as they stood there dumbfounded. "Enjoy!"

Grandfather picked up a bat and positioned it to strike Leon," Take your devil cocaine away from my boys right now you filthy piece of garbage or I'll..."

"You'll what, old man?"

"I'll use this on you."

Pip wanted to run in and help, but he was still upside-down, and monkeys weren't very fast anyway. He'd stay put for now, watch, wait, and then sneak up on his uncle at the last minute like monkeys were supposed to do.

"Oh, I'm so scared. Tell me where you put the keys to the bush-plane Gramps or I'll use that bat on *you* and crush in your ugly scull."

"No! I told you it's for my business…You can't have it!"

Grandfather swung his bat, but Leon only caught it before it did any damage. Then as the old man teetered, Leon punched him in the face, sending the thin elderly Indian down to the ground like a broken pretzel.

"Now, I'm only going to ask one more time. Where are the keys?"

Grandfather's nose was dripping blood. He slowly lifted a shaky finger and pointed, "Get your uncle the keys Robert…so he can go to *hell*!" he shouted at Leon.

In response, Leon stopped in his tracks, turned around and booted him in the stomach. "Hell is where you'll be going if you don't shut your mouth old man."

As Leon swung his long black jacket on, Robert threw him a set of keys. Leon caught them, grinning back at his relative. "You can come with me you know. The "Indian Head Hunters" need new gang members with good arms."

The teenager cracked a fake smile and shook his head.

"Didn't think you had the guts," Leon winked as he grabbed the baggie of drugs out of Robert's hand and headed out the door into the black of night.

Quickly, Pip tried to dislodge himself from the constricting branches that held him in the large tree. He sat upright now, wanting to attack his Uncle Leon, stop him from taking Grandfather's bush-plane. But timing was everything and he had to wait for the precise moment.

The hooting owl laughed at him and his foolishness, but he didn't care. He would get down before Uncle Leon came near, and then...Then what? He'd have to think about that. What would a Chipewyan warrior do? Grandfather told him that they were direct decedents of the great Matonabee. Surely, that fact alone would give him enough courage to do this deed. But something didn't fit. He wasn't a warrior right now, he was supposed to be a monkey and monkeys did only one thing: Jump.

"Pip, king of the monkeys," he whispered. "One, two, three...jump!"

Flopping like a rag-doll, wiggling his arms, Pip hung upside-down against his will, dangling from caught up shoelaces, arms hanging, shirt draped over his back. *Not such a wise monkey after all.*

He did an upside-down sit-up to reach back up to the tangled balled up laces trying to dislodge them. He tugged, he yanked, and he pulled hard until he could no longer keep himself upright. Panting, breathless, he gave in to the struggle and let himself flop back down in the upside-down position once again. It was useless.

For a moment, Pip just hung there, motionless, swinging like a monkey, swaying and thinking. His head rushed with blood. If this is what monkeys had to go through everyday, he was glad he was not one of them for real.

Suddenly, Pip heard a loud crack. *Oh...no!* The tree limb was apparently not as strong as he thought it had been. The large limb bowed to his weight as sudden jerks dropped him down a few notches. With yet another crack, Pip felt the decent; he plummeted to the ground like a man without a parachute, falling head first to the ground wailing loud enough to wake the dead.

Thump.

Pip lay crumpled in a heap on the ground, shoelaces free at last, aching body sprawled about. Hiding up there had not been worth it after all he decided, fingering his scalp where a gigantic bump began to swell. *Oh, my aching head.*

As he surveyed his injuries with a loud moan, he heard a click behind him.

"Hey runt," the voice with the gun said. "Let's take a walk with Uncle Leon."

Pip's eyes grew wide as his uncle lead him away from his home by the scruff of the neck, gun pointed at him. "What did I say the last time I saw you?" his uncle whispered as he continued to drag the boy into the moonlit bush.

Trembling, Pip shrugged, "I don't remember Uncle Leon," he winced. Uncle Leon waved the gun in his face, taunting him, scaring the living daylights out of him. Tears started to flow down the boys face from the pressure of the gun against the throbbing distended bump on his head. "Owe!"

"Well let me refresh your memory. I told you that I was going to rip your little tongue out for telling your Grandfather about the drugs. Oh yes...*I* remember."

Pip's eyes grew big as his uncle pulled him close to him, "I knew it was you, you little brat."

"Please Uncle Leon," Pip bawled, bottom lip quivering now. "I'm sorry. I'll make it up to you, honest I will."

"That's right you will, because I'm going to cut that little double-crossing tongue out of your mouth once and for all," the tall Indian smiled as he shoved the gun back into his pocket and took out a homemade pocket-knife, flicking it open in front of the boy.

Suddenly, Pip managed to squeeze away from his uncle's grip. He darted through the bush like a trapped rabbit, his uncle running after him. "Leave me alone, you creep!" Pip shouted running until his shoelaces did him in again. Face down in the mossy bush, he tasted defeat as his uncle caught up to him and pressed the knife against his raw throat. He managed to squeak in one last plea, "Please don't Uncle," he whispered against the cold blade, feeling the sting as it pressed in further.

"You're lucky I'm such a nice guy," his uncle grinned. "I'll let you off the hook for now. You can pay me back instead of me cutting your tongue out. I have an assignment for you in the morning."

Pip whimpered when his uncle released the knife-constricting blade. The tall Indian resorted to yanking the boy's shirt, practically carrying him through the bush. "Don't cry like a sissy girl, kid. Be a man for once."

If he could only be as brave as a Chipewyan warrior could, he would punch his stupid uncle right in the face. And if he was as crafty as a monkey, he could show him that he *was* a man, a better man than him. But he wasn't a warrior, and even though his protruding ears made him look like a monkey, he wasn't *that* either. No, it was time to grow up. No more make-believe, no more pretending some young braves would rush in to save him, no more secret missions. It was reality now, his Uncle Leon's reality, *his* demented schemes. And who knew what he was up to this time.

Chapter 27

Wednesday, July 5th.

Morning broke to the heaving sound of someone vomiting. Loretta assumed it was still Vicki. She had been sick to her stomach all through the night and the better part of yesterday. After finding themselves washed to shore with nothing but the broken pieces of boat they clung to during the storm, they decided to stay put for a while because Vicki felt so nauseous. They were cold. They were wet, and could have made it to the lodge by now if they hadn't wasted a whole day because of *her*. And now she was apparently *still* sick.

"I'm sorry," Vicki choked. "I'm so sick. There's nothing more in my stomach but I'm still gagging. I think the wild mushrooms I ate the other day made me sick. Or maybe that stuff George gave me."

Loretta stared at the pale helpless woman, red hair wild and fuzzy, groping her stomach as if she were about to die. "It could be the water you know. They say you should boil lake water before you drink it but I've been drinking it and it doesn't seem to bother me. It really *can* give you the runs though…or make you sick to your stomach."

"Perhaps," Vicki hurled again.

"Maybe you'd better lay down again. I should head off on my own today, find the lodge and get some help. You're not in any shape to go for a hike today anyway."

The fuzzy redheaded woman fell limp against the sand, sweating and sighing, "I wasn't in good shape yesterday either. You can't go alone, and we're not going to waste another day just sitting around. I'll just have to force myself, besides; you need me to help look for George and Harvey. They're probably hurt, or worse. They never showed up yesterday and I really thought they would have found us by now."

"All right," Loretta frowned, not wanting to take the sick woman. "Let's get going then, before the weather turns bad on us. It looks like the sky is overcast again."

The morning gulls laughed overhead as the two women laboured along the foggy riverbank. Loretta shivered, hugging her damp tattered clothes. Vicki moved slowly, pushing her lethargic stocky body beyond what was sensible.

"So, are you a wrestler or something?" Loretta asked, curious as to the woman's physique. Not everyone could force themselves beyond their limit, except perhaps a mother. She remembered her own frustrations as a mother, never able to have a sick day. Bob wouldn't let her. Her kids wouldn't let her. They expected her *always* to be on her toes. Moms were supposed to be superhuman. Maybe she was a mother.

"A wrestler?"

"Yah, you look like a wrestler," Loretta grinned. "You're not a mother by any chance…or pregnant?"

Loretta watched the big woman fight off a wave of queasiness before she responded, annoyed. "*No*…I'm not a mother. And *no,* I'm *not* pregnant lady. I work out…been doing that since…Well, let's just say I work out so I can protect myself."

"From what?"

"From jerks, that's what."

"Did someone hurt you?" Loretta asked, knowing she shouldn't be nosy and remembering the last time she pried into Harvey's business. Yet, she had to do something to pass the time, and the conversation was a good way to keep Vicki's mind off her stomach so they could keep moving. She often used this distraction tactic with her own daughters…even with Jeremy.

"Look," the woman stopped and scolded her. "I know you mean well, but I don't feel like telling you my entire life story right now."

"You're not the easiest person to have a conversation with you know."

"Neither are you."

The two of them walked in silence then, frustrated with each other. Loretta could tell their personalities clashed. They had nothing in common with each other except the fact that they had both been on a plane that crashed. They had both been on a shipwrecked boat. They had both taken a trip to a foreign country for something other than a vacation. But they had nothing in common with each other. Loretta smiled at the irony, squinting sideways at the sick woman as they continued in mute succession.

~~~

Pip didn't like the drizzle any more than his uncle Leon seemed to, but at least his uncle had a long coat with a hood. Pip had no other option but to let the rain dribble down his shaggy damp black hair and down his elfin face. His black T-shirt stuck to him and his arms were wet and exposed, shivering as he walked with a gun to his back.

Uncle Leon had led them all the way from Grandfather's place, down through his favorite bush trail. They had been walking all night long, right by the old hunter's shack, and stopping in for only a moment so Uncle Leon could check on one of the monsters he had locked up in handcuffs there. A sight Pip still didn't quite understand.

Now, continuing into the drab morning overcast, Pip wondered why his uncle didn't go the other way. He could have gone to the freight dock at the mouth of Star River where Grandfather kept his bush plane. Perhaps he had changed his mind and not wanted to take it after all. Somehow, Pip doubted it. His uncle must have some unfinished business to attend to before he takes off with Grandfather's bush plane. Pip figured he knew what that business might be: Uncle Leon was after…Little Caribou.

"Okay stop right here Pip," his uncle demanded once they sighted Shooting Star Lodge almost hidden in the morning mist. "I will wait behind this rock while you sneak up to the window and tell me if there's a woman inside."

Pip knew his uncle meant Little Caribou, but he didn't want to ask questions, he just followed orders, afraid of the gun his uncle pointed at him, knowing he wouldn't hesitate to use it. "What do I do then Uncle?"

"You get your tail back here as fast as you can and tell me what you see, that's what. And keep your head down or someone will see you. If you try anything funny, I'll be waiting. I want you in clear sight the whole time. Remember, I have the gun *Piptata*!"

Pip hated him. He hated how he pronounced his name, as if it were something to make fun of, to scoff. He had always spoiled his name, been the bully. Why do bullies have to hurt people all the time? Why do they always get their way?

"Go!"

Pip crept down the woody embankment toward the lodge fighting the mist that suddenly turned to pounding rain. It hammered upon his very sore bump from the night before, torturing his scalp as he ran. If he saw someone inside, he was supposed to run back and tell Uncle Leon. Or did his uncle tell him to stay where he was and call him? Pip couldn't remember which. He was so nervous. His heart forcibly pounded so rapidly he thought it would jump right out of his chest.

Finally, as he crept up to the side window, dripping with droplets of rain, he wiped a small portion of it dry with his sleeve, peering in to see a familiar face. "Caribou!" he gasped. *You should have run away by now.* Pip wanted to warn his Little Caribou. But how? He ducked back down crouching underneath the window, wondering what to do. Uncle Leon still had the gun pointed at him, so running inside or banging on the window was out of the question. He turned his head backward and forward looking at his uncle as he sat frozen solid in the squatting position. Panicking, he watched his uncle angrily waving one arm in the air, reminding him to come back. But Pip didn't want to.

Suddenly Uncle Leon made his fist into a gun and pointed it at his own temple, gesturing a shooting motion to scare Pip and show him that he had better get back or that was going to happen to him.

Without hesitation, Pip obeyed. He came running back to his uncle as fast as he could, rain pelting every aching inch of him. His uncle greeted him by jamming the gun to his head and pulling him down beside the rock, gritting his teeth in anger as he said, "You took too long you little brat. I should shoot you right here."

"No!" Pip's eyes widened. "I'm sorry uncle." He cringed to the pressure of the guns barrel against his temple. It was hard and cold and felt as if it was about to thrust right through to the other side.

"What did you see?"

Pip didn't want to tell. He couldn't...it was Caribou. He had to protect her from all the monsters, especially the big ugly black-pony-tailed one.

"If you don't tell me, I swear I will not only kill you but I will go after Grandfather as well. I will kill him just like I killed your parents."

Pip's mouth dropped, hanging open in disbelief. "They drowned?"

"They sure did runt...And who do you think did that?"

Pip looked into his uncles beady little eyes. His grin soured to the most evil grin he had ever seen, crooked and foul. He knew he was telling the truth. "Why?"

"They ticked me off...just like you're doing. Now tell me who was inside."

Pip began to sob. "Okay...I'll tell you. But don't you hurt Grandfather."

"Stop your blubbering. I won't have to if you co-operate," he winked.

"I saw a lady."

"She's supposed to have long blond hair. Does she have blond hair?"

Reluctantly, Pip had to tell him about his Little Caribou regardless of what might happen to her. He felt like a traitor. "Yes...she does."

"Good," his uncle gleamed. "Is there anyone else in there?"

"Not that I saw."

His uncle released his grip on him and lowered the gun. "Good! You did well my boy," his uncle smiled and ruffled his hand through Pip's hair, pulling it hard as he did it.

I'm not your boy you murdering monster.

"Now this is what I want you to do: Go back down there, knock on the door. Pretend that your motorboat ran out of gas. Ask her if she could get you some more. Here," he paused giving him a twenty-dollar bill. "Show her you have money to pay for the gas. Get her outside and walk toward the boats. I'll take it from there."

"But why don't you just go in," Pip asked with a shaky voice.

"Hey! You don't ask *me* questions. Just do it if you ever want to see Grandfather alive again. And play along with me when I show up."

Pip couldn't figure out what his plan was. But one thing was certain, he knew it would backfire on him whatever it was. He had already met Caribou. Swallowing hard, he rushed up to the door while his uncle watched him knock. Smoothing his hand through his wet black hair, he slicked it back, shivering in the rain. He wished she would hurry up and answer. Knocking once more, he jigged up and down against the cold pelting rain.

A heavy fog started to settle around the place, making it hard to see his uncle. The tree line was blurring in front of his eyes. Maybe this was his chance. He darted his head back and forth looking for Uncle Leon. As he glanced toward the misty covered river, he seemed to catch his eye on some movement. Uncle Leon was over by the old boats now, in front of the lodge waiting like a vulture ready to eat its prey.

He'd try knocking one more time. *Come on Caribou...answer the door.* Slowly the door eased open to a small crack. "Shhh!" he whispered right away. "Don't say anything Caribou, just let me in quickly." He closed the creaky door behind him, tears bursting the floodgates, sinking to his knees.

"What's the matter Pip?

"My uncle," his words were panicked and broken. "My uncle...he...he hiding...he...like a monster...Pow! Gun!" The words didn't come out the way he had hoped they would. He had too much to say, and not enough time to say it. How could he get her to understand what was going on, to realize the danger she was in?

"Pip, just breathe, and start from the beginning."

She was such a nice sweet lady, a pretty lady. She reminded him of his own mother, except for the blonde hair. His mother's was black but her personality was the same. She was a fighter, stubborn and bull-headed just like Caribou, just like him. Pip missed her so much. Caribou brought back all the fond memories. He knew she didn't really mean those bad things she said the last time he saw her.

"My Uncle Leon, he's back," he tried to speak slowly but his mouth didn't listen. "He's going to kill me if I don't come out that door with you in a few minutes," He said it so fast this time that he wondered if she even caught on. Her face frowned as he said it.

"Are you telling me that some bad guy is out there right now waiting for me?"

Pip cried, *"Yes!"*

"I'm not going out there just to be shot. You think I'm nuts?"

"Caribou please! I won't let him shoot you. Just come outside. If you don't come, he's going to kill Grandfather like he killed Mom and Dad. He killed my *parents* Caribou! He killed them five years ago," Pip howled, fearful and distraught.

Ruby rubbed her bruised forehead. "Stop crying," she patted Pip's shoulder. "We'll just have to outsmart the lunatic then."

"But how?"

"You just leave that up to me."

Suddenly, they heard pounding on the door. Pip jumped to his feet, eyes bulging. Ruby cleared her throat and looked sideways at him. "I'm coming." She motioned for him to stick close beside her and be quiet.

As Ruby slowly pulled the creaky door open, shifting her weight from her swollen ankle, she faked a smile and swallowed hard. "Hello?"

"Excuse me. I don't mean to bother you, but that's my son there. He was supposed to ask you for some gas," Uncle Leon sneered, giving Pip the evil eye while attempting to pour on his charm, forcing his way in.

"You don't mind, do you? I mean, giving us some gas."

"Not at all. I don't live here, but the owner always has some on hand for lost fishermen like yourself. You *are* a fisherman I presume."

"No, but my son here is," he smiled, patting Pip's head and pulling him backward to his chest, hugging him a little too tightly with that bogus grin of his, concealing the gun that was now thrust into his back. "Aren't you Frankie?" *Frankie? Where did he get that name from, a mob movie?*

"Isn't that nice," she winked privately to Pip. "You must really love fishing to be going out there in this rain."

Pip started to perspire. His face felt like it was going to burn right off.

"Actually," Uncle Leon cracked open the door and held out one hand, "it stopped raining. Can you believe it?"

"Well then, I better get that gas for you, shouldn't I? It's just over there in that small shed beside the boats. You can head over there; I have to get the key first. It'll take me a few minutes anyway. My ankle and ribs are sore so I might move a bit too slowly for you two. I fell down the stairs the other day…Clumsy me."

"Oh…we can wait for you miss. We're not in a hurry. Are we Frankie?"

Pip fidgeted. He didn't know what Caribou was up to, but whatever it was, it didn't seem to be working. She looked like she needed some help. "Um…Uncle…I mean Dad," Pip said, cringing from his mistake, feeling the butt of the gun jab into him harder than before while his uncle glared sideways at him. "We *are* in a bit of a hurry. Remember? Maybe we should just get the key from her and go get the gas ourselves. The lady can't walk very well anyway."

"No!" Uncle Leon snapped loudly. Silence pierced the cold air.

"Honestly, I can get around pretty good with this broom handle I use. It'll only take a few minutes to find the key. But the owner *did* tell me not to give it to anyone else though. Sorry kid." Ruby glared at Pip as if she knew what he was up to and didn't want him to interfere with her own plan.

"You really should head down there sir," Ruby politely smiled, putting on a little charm of her own. "No need to wait here. The owner doesn't like strangers in the lodge when he's away. It makes him mad. But the boy could stay and give me a hand walking."

"No!" Uncle Leon fumed again, jabbing the gun. "He's with me."

The door slammed behind the two of them as they started for the shed. "What the heck do you think you're doing? You *want* to eat a bullet runt?"

Pip whimpered, "No," as he tried not to trip while his uncle hauled him to the shed. He yanked his nephew's wet black t-shirt so hard, ripping open the entire underarm on the left side.

"I was just trying to help you uncle," he blubbered.

"Sure, you were you little liar." Uncle Leon cuffed him a good one on the side of his head right on the bump. Fuzzy ringing in his ear penetrated right through his brain to an ache so painful it made his head spin.

"I'm *sorry* Uncle!" Pip screamed an apology out of utter fear.

"Shut up you snivelling little brat. No wonder your parents hated you."

"They did not!"

Uncle Leon beamed his devil grin again. "Shut up or I'll bat you a second time."

~~~

Ruby left the door wide open as she quickly hobbled to the kitchen to find the key and some paper. Panic screamed inside her head as she fumbled for the pen on the counter. With shaky hands, she attempted to scribble something on it. *What now?*

She had to warn Harvey about the uncle especially if she didn't make it. If her plan failed, and it was likely that it would, she was the only one that knew the uncle was in on it. If she was lucky, her plan would work and she could put a stop to him. But it was risky unlocking the shed, knowing what was inside.

Harvey, she scrawled quickly in sloppy panicked handwriting. What should she say? She couldn't even think straight. What was the uncle's name? Ruby checked toward the doorway for Pip and his uncle, they were already down at the shed waiting. She should hurry; she'd taken too long already.

Harvey,
Made it to the lodge okay, but had to take off again.
Watch out for the ponytail.
Love, R.

Not enough information. Harvey would only be confused, but she didn't have any more time to write the details. And her head wasn't thinking straight either. Placing the note on the kitchen table with one hand and grabbing the keys to the shed with the other, she headed for the open front door. The broom handle she used as a crutch leaned against the doorframe waiting for her to use it. *Come on old body...Don't fail me now.*

By the time Ruby finally made it over to the shed, the uncle already looked annoyed. She unlocked it quickly and eyed the mowing and fishing equipment inside.

"The gas is over there," she pointed, walking in with the two of them. "Your uncle can grab it," Ruby said, eyeing Pip and realizing her mistake.

She figured the man had a gun pointed at him and hoped her slip of the tongue would not cost him his life.

She grabbed the sickle that hung on the wall just inside the door as the uncle bent to pick up the jerry can. Pip stepped aside while Ruby backed out of the shed and waited for him. Hiding it behind her back, she motioned Pip to get out of the way as they both backed out of the shed. Suddenly the uncle spun around and threw the jerry can of gas at Pip, knocking him down to the ground, spilling gasoline all over him.

"Uncle? Pip...you disappoint me. You told the lady who I really was. Shame on you. Now, I'm going to have to teach you a lesson," he grinned, pulling a book of matches out of his pocket as his gun fell to the ground beside the boy. Instead of picking it up right away, he lit the match.

"Pip, run!" she screamed. He fumbled to his feet as his uncle was about to throw the match down on him. With one arm, Ruby raised the sickle and chopped at the cruel man, extinguishing the match before it could do any damage, allowing the boy to get up, grab the gun, and run.

Without warning, the Indian grabbed her arm as she swung the sickle at him a second time, halting her advancement. "Give me it...witch!" the man shouted, adding obscenities. His hand was bleeding where she cut him with the sickle, constricting her hold. "Let me go," she struggled, trying to get free.

"Stop...wiggling and get in the shed you stupid broad." He struggled with her forcing her steps backward toward the shed. Pip stopped running, turned around, and headed back to them both. He was not more than a few feet away when Ruby saw him holding the heavy gun up with his shaky wrist, "Stop it or I'll shoot."

"You don't have the guts to shoot me, you little wimp."

Pip trembled, aiming the cumbersome thing, "I *can* do it."

"No Pip...just get out of here," Ruby screamed at the boy. "Run!"

"He doesn't listen very well does he? That's okay runt, come over here and give your Uncle Leon the gun."

"Run...!" she screamed one last time. Instead, he hurled the heavy metal weapon into the air with one swift movement, watching it plunge into the river.

Leon's eyes grew wild. "You're gonna pay for that wimp," he said continuing to drag Ruby backward

Pip picked up the broom handle Ruby used for a crutch, and started poking at his uncle, preventing him from dragging her into the shed. "What do you think you're going to do with that, *wimp*?" he scoffed "You can't even *shoot* me?"

"I...I'll *poke* you!"

"Oh boy! *Poke* me? You sure have turned into a *brave* warrior now *Pipata*. I never would have thought you would grow up so fine. Your father would've been *so* proud of you if he was still alive."

"Be quiet, you murderer!" Pip jabbed. "Now let Caribou...I mean, let her go."

"What was that you said?" the Indian mocked, arms still around Ruby's throat.

He said Caribou you big ugly bully...so what.

"Caribou? I heard you. You're still playing those baby games aren't you. *Oh, my precious Little Caribou.* What's the matter, big brothers don't want to play your silly make-believe with you

213

anymore? Now you're playing baby games with *her*? Grow up!"

Ruby was proud of the elfin teenager. He was just a kid standing up to a very strong man...for *her*, for his Caribou. Suddenly, from nerves of steel she didn't even know he had, he lunged forward jabbing the end of the broom handle hard into the Indian's groin, freeing her from his clutches.

Pip ran as fast as he could while the Indian shrieked in agony. "Get...back...here you little brat," he said, groaning with pain, holding his breath as he doubled over. He swore a line of colorful words and grabbed between his legs as he fell to both knees.

It was her turn to move and she knew it. Ruby wished she could run as fast as Pip but she couldn't. It was all she could do to focus on what had just happened. Guardedly, as if to make sure she was safe, she backed away from the injured Indian down on the ground as he rolled around wallowing in the pain.

"Caribou run!" Pip cried out from the distance, stopping for a moment to catch his breath. She knew what he wanted her to do. He had risked his life to save her, and he wanted her to follow him, half expected her to be already there. But as much as she wanted to, she knew she wouldn't get far with her ankle. She would have to make a run for the lodge. She would have to get the sickle and run, run with all her might to the lodge and lock the door behind her.

Ruby waved an arm at Pip to urge him to go without her. She wanted to say it to him audibly but nothing seemed to come out of her mouth. She picked up the sickle and limped toward the lodge. He flew up his arms as if to show his frustration with her for not running yet. Reluctantly he stood there until she pointed in the direction of the lodge and motioned for him to get out of there. He seemed to understand what she was up to so he took off into the bush. The India still crouched down on the wet ground in pain as she turned around and hobbled up the hill to the lodge.

Ruby's heart beat loudly in her chest as she hobbled the last few feet to the lodge. She hadn't turned around once to look at what the Indian was doing. Maybe she should have, maybe that wasn't smart. All she could do was focus her energy into getting back to the lodge before he did.

Maybe she should have turned around.

Just as she started toward the step, carrying the sickle in her hand, something grabbed her arm from behind and squeezed the tool out. With a twist and a yank, he pulled her backward before she could reach the door. The big Indian spun her around like a rag doll, pulled her close and fondled her long blond hair. He inhaled deeply as he laughed, letting out a wild animalistic yelp. Then as if he was half-mad, he shushed himself and whispered something softly into Ruby's ear. "Look what I caught," he said, "a delicious Little Caribou...Yummy!"

Chapter 28

George and Harvey had been traveling east again now since early this morning. After finding out that they were going the wrong way last night, Harvey insisted they go back toward the lodge and find the girls. He was still a little annoyed even now.

"Stop moping Harvey. You got your way." George huffed as he stopped to rest, setting down the makeshift crutch Harvey had made the man out of a tree branch instead of the splint he wanted to make. But George insisted he didn't need one now. Just a crutch would do. That was okay with him. Why hadn't he thought of making crutches before? The guy weighed a tone, and trying to help him walk up to this point wasn't easy.

"We would have found the girls by now if you hadn't taken us the wrong way. Seriously, George, I don't know what other way you were talking about going, but as far as I can see, only one river leads to the lodge. Doesn't it?"

"I was trying to get us to the freight dock."

"Why, what's at the freight dock?"

"I thought there might be a boat there Harvey. Did you ever think of that? For a cop, you sure aren't too bright."

Harvey wanted to slug the man for cutting him down. "Excuse me, but you're the one that's not too bright. *Maybe* doesn't mean there *is* a boat. Cops don't generally make decisions based upon assumptions, especially when there are two women out there who need our help. You don't save yourself first pal...you help the wounded. Like I'm helping you, you thankless good-for-nothing piece of..."

"Alright! George shouted. "I get your point, now shut up before I really get mad."

"Oh, you're so scary."

"I'm warning you! And get you're arm off me. I don't need your help anymore just like I don't need a splint either. My leg is getting better all by itself."

"Is that right," Harvey pulled away from the obnoxious man who was apparently doing just fine walking on his own now. For some reason, he felt used. If he didn't know any better, he'd think this guy had been faking his injury all along. Broken limbs don't just heal by themselves. At times, he even caught him favoring the wrong leg. Maybe it was his imagination, or perhaps it was his growing dislike for the man. Something about him made him sceptical.

George sat down ahead of him, apparently fuming. Harvey had really struck a nerve. Perhaps he had misjudged the man, he thought, heading over to the ornery man, deciding to call a truce. "Look, he said sighing, trying to make peace. "I'm sorry, okay. I shouldn't have been so snappy." He reached out his hand to shake George's but George didn't even respond. Instead, Harvey just took a seat in the wet moss under a tree beside the man. They both sat in silence, listening to the rain, waiting for it to subside.

"So, got a wife?" Harvey decided to ask, trying to force a conversation after a long stretch of silence.

"Buddy, you have some nerve. You saw Vicki and me. I'm not a cheat. Would I behave like that if I had a wife?"

Harvey darted his eyes away from the man, hoping he hadn't struck another nerve. "I don't know, would you?"

217

"How could you even ask that? I'm not that kind of a guy."

"Well, how am I supposed to know that? You haven't told me much about yourself. I told you *I* use to be a cop."

The man looked annoyed again. All he had to do was open up a bit. It wasn't like Harvey had asked him to be his best friend.

"Okay, let's see," the man toyed with Harvey, "Did I tell you I 'm a pilot?"

"You told me that about a thousand times, but what else do you do?"

George sighed and rubbed his wet forehead. "Look, I'm not good at this male-bonding stuff. I don't talk about my personal life."

"What is your problem?" Harvey fumed not being able to stand it anymore.

"I don't have a problem."

"Well obviously you do. I've done nothing but help you since we met. I make you a splint, a crutch; I help you hobble miles through the wringing wet wilderness, take care of you when you fall into the water..."

"That was your fault. You started fighting with me. Remember?"

Harvey stood to his feet. "I can't believe you. After everything I have done for you, this is the thanks I get. You really are a jerk, you know that."

George was silent again. All Harvey could hear was the sound of his own heartbeat and the trickle of rain.

"You're right," George threw up his hands. "I *am* a jerk. Okay. Is that what you want to hear? I should appreciate what you've done for me. Heck, I'm not even a very friendly guy, except to the women of course. To you, I'm just a jerk."

Harvey felt *really* bad this time. He was supposed to be the Christian. *Lord forgive me.* "I know I said it before, but I'm sorry George. I really am this time. Being hungry and wet hasn't made me the nicest person."

"I accept your apology for the umpteenth time; now let's just get going so we can find the girls. And despite what you think, I *would* like to find Vicki."

"Well now that's something. You showed a little feeling there George. I'm surprised. Do you love her?"

"She's a broad. She's got the right equipment, so I guess so."

Not the answer Harvey was expecting, a shocker really, but it would have to do. At least he was opening up a little, but that answer sure disturbed him. "So, you're a ladies man then," Harvey pried as they crept along the rainy riverbed, "a ladies man, but not a cheat. You probably got woman chasing you all the time."

"Oh, I've had my share of women," George bragged shaking his head in a cocky manner. "I told this chick once that I had my own business in Chicago. She thought I was a millionaire or something. She followed me all the way out here on some quirky vacation of hers. She wouldn't leave me alone until I finally told her I was just a pilot."

You jerk! "You don't say."

"Really," George laughed so hard he had to stop for a moment. "She was a real sucker. I could make her beat a dog over the head if I wanted too. I could make her do just about anything."

"Yah…like what?" Harvey asked, repulsed by his twisted sense of humour.

"Oh shoot," George laughed hysterically, trying to breath, red faced in the rain, "I shouldn't tell you, you know, you being a cop and all. I don't want to incriminal myself you know."

"Incriminate George, the word is incriminate. And I told you I'm retired."

The man was speechless. He hadn't caught his vocabulary mistake, nor did he seem to understand about him being a retired cop. "Come on George," he forced a grin, trying not to show his utter disgust for the man. "Stop laughing and pick up the pace." *Before I beat YOU over the head.*

If he didn't know what kind of a man George was earlier, he certainly knew now.

As they continued to walk, Harvey noticed something in the distance, as the fog began to lift. "Do you see that over there, across the river?" he asked, pointing.

"What, I don't see anything. I think you're seeing things pal. Let's just go."

"No seriously. I saw something across the river," he insisted, wanting to jump into the water and swim across, wishing he could leave this jerk behind and follow his instincts that told him someone or something was over there. Maybe even the girls.

Harvey wiped the leftover rain dribble from his forehead and forced a smile at George. "It's got to be them man. Let's swim across."

"No way, you know I can't swim."

Harvey grabbed the big man's arm and tried to force him into the water. "I won't let you drown. I will help you. Please George! Come on."

"I said I can't!" George shouted as he pulled his arm away from Harvey's grip.

"Come on, your girl might be over there. You say you love her. Don't you want to see if she's all right?

At that moment, something seemed to change in George. He suddenly threw down his crutch, squeezed his beady eyes into a devilish grin, and snickered "You think you're so smart. You don't even know what smart is."

Harvey stepped back from the wild looking man, confused with his demeanour and his senseless words. "You've gone mad George. You don't make sense."

At that moment, George reached down to his good leg, lifted his pant leg, and pulled a pocket-knife from its case. He flicked the blade open toward Harvey and thrust it forward, inching closer with more ease than a man with a broken leg ought to. *I knew the leg wasn't broken, you faker.* "What happened, did your leg suddenly heal?" he fumed as he backed up trying to get away from the knife.

George inched forward. "It's a miracle! Can you believe it? *Jesus* healed me." He said the word Jesus in such a way that seemed to eat away at Harvey. The mockery made him want to punch the man's lights out if he could only get that knife away from him. "Miracle my foot...You wouldn't know a miracle if it hit you in the face."

"Come on," George inched forward trying to egg Harvey on with the knife. "Bet you can't even hit me in the face you old fat pig. No wonder you ain't a cop no more."

That comment seemed to boil Harvey's blood but it wasn't enough to push him into the kind of battle George wanted. It would take more than just words to make him angry this time, especially since he was the one without a knife. Then, as Harvey stared at the weapon edging toward him, he remembered he had a weapon of his own tucked under his shirt. As George advanced the knife, Harvey pulled out his Glock. "Back off."

George was surprised to see the gun, but as Harvey held it at him, his eyes held no fear. "Well, well, well," the man grinned, "the fatso was packing all along? And I had you pegged as some wimpy traffic cop. Boy was I wrong."

"Drop it or I'll shoot," Harvey threatened.

"Okay…but you might want to look behind you first."

Harvey turned his head slightly, wishing he never did. His feet tripped on a large rock as he fell backward fumbling with the gun. George lunged after him, yanking it from his hand in one swift move.

Grinning, George leaned over Harvey's panting body, sprawled out on the wet grassy sand. "Checkmate," he said, aiming the Glock at Harvey's forehead.

The odds were not favorable. *Help me Lord!*

Unexpectedly, in one swift movement, George released the gun, "On second thought, I prefer knives old man. They hurt more," he said, chucking the gun away, smiling with his sharp knife, ready to use it.

Elbowing the man in the face, Harvey knocked him sideways, rolling off his back. "You idiot!" he shouted as George lunged forward again.

"I'm not the idiot," George snorted, struggling, rolling with Harvey as they both fought against the knife, "you are…for…believing…my…lies."

Suddenly, Harvey submitted to the enormity of the brawny man as panic consumed his pliant body. The knife jabbed, piercing, puncturing into his portly flesh as he realized the finality of the situation.

He…had lost the battle.

~~~~

"Why haven't we reached the lodge by now?" Loretta sighed, wiping her forehead, frustrated, tired of this mucky walking…and *she* wasn't even the sick one. Vicki lingered behind her white as a ghost.

"We better find it soon…or you're going to drive me nuts with your whining. Why don't you just shut up for a while before you *really* drive me insane…or this bloody flue bug won't be the only thing that kills me."

"You're *still* not feeling better?"

"What do you think?"

"Right…Well, anyway, the lodge better be around here somewhere or I'm going to…Wait…Did you here that?"

"What?"

"I thought I heard something in the bushes, a noise or something. And a little while ago, I heard a wolf howling. Maybe it's tracking us." Shivers went up Loretta's spine as she shuddered at the thought.

"Oh no…the boogieman might get us too."

"Vicki would you stop fooling around, I'm serious."

"Whatever."

Chapter 29

Ruby gasped for air as the big Indian gripped her throat. He had managed to yank her wounded body through the doorframe as he kicked the door closed with his one foot. She shuddered at the loud slamming sound it made, almost deafening her.

Teeth wide with a filthy grin, the Indian threw her down to the hard wood floor.

Jesus help! Jesus! God! Oh, God help me!

She slithered on the floor like a wounded animal trying to get free from a hunter's trap, clawing at the floor as if it would redeem her. The Indian squatted down beside her, ragged ponytail hanging in her face. "You think you're so smart...*Caribou.*"

Ruby loathed the way he pronounced her nickname, the name only reserved for Pip, *not him,* not a filthy animal like him. "Leave me alone you pig!" she spit at him.

The Indian smacked her pursed defiant lip with the back of his hand, then rose against some obvious pain he still had from Pip's blow to the groin. "You want to see a pig lady?" the Indian growled. "I'll show you what pigs do to women like you." He fumbled with his belt buckle trying to get the thing undone.

This was her chance.

Ruby heard her heart pumping through her ears. *Lord, help me get away from him.* With one swift thrust upward, she forced her throbbing ankle between his legs, adding to the damage Pip has already caused his uncle.

Keeling over in pain, he grasped his private parts and moaned, "You little...witch!" He continued to degrade her, swearing at her, cutting her down with every word as he tried to advance toward her.

Instead, he fell to the ground beside her, throttling her neck with one free hand.

Ruby seized his mammoth hand with her dainty ones trying to disengage his stubborn chokehold. She bent her neck, opened her mouth, and bit into his wrist, blood oozing from her teeth as she squirmed to get away, screaming like never before.

~~~~

"There it is again," Loretta said, cocking her head to listen. "Did you hear it this time Vicki? It came from over there."

"Yup...It sure sounded like the boogieman to me," she replied, smirking against her ghostly pale face, mimicking a facetious scream.

"For Pete sake Vicki...I heard a woman scream! It could be your *sister*!"

"You're right...I'm sorry," Vicki chuckled, shedding her comic grin for a more serious one. "Let's go then." They both hustled in the direction of the sound, Loretta grabbing the big woman's arm and helping her out of the sticky mud they had been standing in. Within moments, they reached a clearing...and there it was...the lodge.

"Loretta....," Vicki panted hard, "I'm stronger than you, so you stay here." "No way...you're sick; you're weaker than me right now."

"If that *is* my sister, not even a truck could stop me, and besides...adrenaline can do wonders for a sick body."

Loretta lowered her head. The truth was she didn't really want to go in first anyway, and arguing with the woman wasn't going to make a difference. "How about we go together...but you go first?"

"Fine."

"Okay then…lead the way."

Approaching the front door, Vicki wiped her damp frizzy dishevelled red hair from her pasty face. She stood on one side of the door, and Loretta stood on the other.

"Are you ready?" Vicki whispered, grabbing a large half-circle grass sickle that lay at the doorstep, raising it above her head.

Loretta's eyes widened, "I am now *Wonder Woman*," she whispered back, glaring at her with a smirk as she heard another scream come from inside.

"I'll kick the door in on three…One…two…three…" The solid door burst its hinges as the athletic woman charged through it toward a tall Indian kneeling beside a blonde woman, choking her as he held her on the floor. Her face flushed a reddish blue color as she floundered about.

The Indian turned his angry head in disgust.

"Get your filthy hands off of her," Vicki shouted, steadying the sickle against the Indian's broad shoulders, "Or I'll decapitate your ugly head right now!

Sobbing sounds pierced the silent room as the Indian slowly released his grip on the woman's throat and raised both hands in the air. "Get up and step away from her," Vicki demanded, pointing the sickle in the direction she wanted the Indian to move. "Lay down on the floor and place your hands on you head."

Vicki cautiously inched toward the man, thrusting the sharp sickle into his shoulder blades and putting her foot on his back. She kicked his side as she stepped harder on his torso.

"Find me something to tie his hands together Loretta."

"How's this?" she smiled, grabbing a half roll of duct tape from the counter, tossing it to her free hand. Vicki caught the tape, steadying the sickle against the guy's back, foot thrusting against him.

"Nice catch," Loretta grinned.

"Thanks – Did I mention I play baseball too?" Vicki bragged while yanking the duct tape with her teeth and stretching it out in one long piece. She ripped it off and gave the piece to Loretta. "Wrap it around his hands."

Loretta grabbed the Indian's hands and wound the duct tape around them. Vicki gave her another piece and she did the same with it, tightening around his bloody bitten up wrists and then went for the ankles. Vicki stepped off the man's back and released the forced sickle as well, tossing it to the floor. She threw Loretta the duct tape and told her to wound the rest of it around his ankles and wrist one more time.

Vicki was already kneeling at the blonde woman's side by the time Loretta finished up with the Indian. She could tell the two of them obviously knew each other. They hugged each other, bawling at their awkward reunion. It was touching; yet discouraging at the same time…Vicki wasn't the only one that knew her.

~~~~

Their reunion was bittersweet.

Finding her sister made Vicki's heart skip a beat, but when she saw what was left of her gorgeous face, she just wanted to scream. "Ruby honey," …Vicki sniffled, smoothing her siblings bloodied blond hair against her forehead. "What did I tell you? What did I *always* tell you?" she sobbed, "You *stupid* girl...you stupid, stupid girl."

Ruby cried "I'm sorry," as her sister drew her into her sturdy arms. "He was a jerk. My boyfriend...he..."

"I know," Vicki turned and scowled at the Indian while embracing her distraught sister, "men are scum!" That was the truth. Most men let *her* down. It was as simple as that. They never came through with their promises, always caused some kind of trouble, and had to have their own way all the time. Vicki knew what could happen if a guy didn't get his way. She had witnessed first hand many a loving boyfriend turn tails and swing at her like a spoiled child who didn't get his way. She wondered if Ruby's boyfriend was like that. Did he act like a gentleman just to get what he wanted and then throw her away like some kind of used up dirty snot-rag? *Probably.*

"Men *are* scum," Ruby sobbed into her sister's oversize arms. "My boyfriend betrayed me. He told me nothing but lies."

"Well he won't be doing that anymore! We bound him up pretty tight with that duck tape," Vicki grinned at Loretta then at the Indian. She turned back to her sister grinning like a court jester.

"*He's* not my boyfriend Vic."

"Then who is this scumbag?"

"I don't really know. I never saw him before in my life. He just started attacking me and then you came in when he was trying to..."

"Did he do all this to you, or was it your boyfriend?"

"You don't want to know."

Her sister had a swollen twisted ankle. Her leg seemed to be inflamed. She had an obvious rib fracture from the amount of pain she appeared to be in as she helped her up. Her right eye was black and blue as well as her cheek. Her lip was cracked and teeth were bleeding, not to mention the bruise marks on her throat. "I *do* want to know Ruby. Look at you. You need medical attention."

"You don't look so hot yourself sis. What happened to *you*?"

"It's a long story."

"Not longer than mine I bet."

Vicki smiled, "We'll see," she said as she eased her sister to the couch. "All I know is that I'm going to kill the guy who did this to you."

"Hey Indian," Loretta all of a sudden butt in, kicking the prostrate man in the side as he lay there silently bound on the floor. "Did you hear that? She said she's going to kill you, you filthy piece of..."

"Shut up Loretta!" Vicki shouted at the stupid woman. If they didn't come up with some sort of plan fast, she decided, *they* would be the ones killed. Even George and Harvey were in the same danger they were, even though they were still missing. But what if they managed to make it back to the lodge soon? What would happen then?

She wondered what her sister got herself into *this* time.

"Ruby..." Vicki whispered so Loretta and the Indian couldn't hear. "What kind of trouble are you in? Seriously, should I be worried?"

"Big trouble Vic...and yes you should be worried."

"*Ruby*...What did you *do*?" Vicki whispered, frustrated with her sister. She had taught her better than that. Still, it seemed likely that she had gotten herself involved in yet another altercation. All she ever did was clean up Ruby's messes.

"Vicki…" Ruby continued to whisper in her sister's ear, sobbing softly. "I helped him rob a bank…and then I even helped him rob some diamonds…And now…"

"Don't tell me anymore," Vicki fumed disappointment. "Not one more word."

"Do you hate me?"

Vicki thought for a minute. How could she hate her sister? She did many stupid things, but she could never hate her sister. "No baby…I don't hate you."

Loretta was getting agitated, clearing her throat, obviously annoyed. "Excuse me," she said. "I hate to interrupt this touching display of affection, but aren't you going to introduce me to your sister? She *is* your sister I assume."

"*Yes*! Sorry…Ruby this is Loretta. Loretta this is my kid sister Ruby."

"Pleased to me you."

Ruby gawked at Loretta for a long moment. "You look familiar. Do I know you?"

Vicki teased Loretta, "Hope not, she's a royal pain in the butt."

"Oh, thanks *Wonder Woman*."

Vicki grinned, ignoring the weird woman's silly platitude, "Thank me when we get out of here. Where's the phone sis?"

"No phone," Ruby scowled.

"Great," she sighed, "Now what? Our plane goes down in the middle of nowhere; we go through some crazy storm and almost drown. I find my sister but apparently, she's in need of medical attention… and we can't call for help. What kind of place *is* this?"

"What plane crash?" the big Indian interrupted, appearing genuinely concerned.

"Shut up scum bag!" Loretta shouted, kicking him again.

Vicki wanted to tell her to cut it out like the last time, to stop kicking and aggravating the Indian, but she felt the same way as Loretta. She wanted to hurt him just as he had hurt her sister. Yet, he might be valuable to them. He might just help them connect the dots; help her understand what was going on here.

"No Loretta, let the jerk talk," Vicki turned sideways as she sat on the couch beside her sister. The Indian eased himself to a sitting position on the floor, hands taped behind his back.

"Do you want to know about the plane crash?" Vicki asked the Indian.

"Yes," he pleaded.

"Then tell us who you are first."

"My name is Leon Eaglefeather. My plane flew in a few nights ago. I was supposed to meet some Eddie guy here, but he didn't show up."

"You filthy liar..." Ruby spit at him.

Vicki admired her sister's spunk but now was not the time. The more she could learn from this Leon, if that's what his real name is, the sooner she could figure out what was going on.

"Just wait Ruby," Vicki said. "You'll have your turn at him, just let me finish first. Now, Leon...Why did you have your hands on my sister?"

"She attacked me first," he answered with a snap.

"Really!"

"Really. I was minding my own business when she came along and tried to rob me. She even tried to kill me with that sharp thing you were using on me."

"I was not!" Ruby spit.

"So…She tried to rob you and kill you with the sickle. Is that right?"

"Yah…"

"…A tiny little thing like my sister?"

"Vicki, come on!" Loretta interrupted. "You don't honestly believe him."

Let me drill him, you foolish woman. I don't believe him any more than you do. "He's lying through his teeth," Loretta shouted, pacing the floor again. "This is getting us nowhere. The guy stinks. He's obviously a criminal *too*," she insisted, pounding toward the door, opening and slamming it shut as she stormed outside.

Vicki shook her head, bewildered as to what just happened. She caught her sister's perplexing glance and shrugged her shoulders. Loretta hadn't heard Ruby tell her about the robberies. How could she have known about any criminals? *Eavesdropper.*

Vicki scowled at the tied up Indian sitting on the floor trying to scoot his way over to them. "Don't even try it, or I'll break your legs off," she said. "If he moves an inch Ruby, scream for me. I want to go see what's eating Miss Loony Tunes."

She rushed outside to stop Loretta, "Wait," she called out. "What are you all fired up about Loretta? I can't do this by myself you know. I need your help."

"Oh…*now* you want my help. I thought you were *Wonder Woman*. You don't need *my* help. You know *everything*. Hey, why don't you try to figure out why *I'm* here while you're at it? You might find a connection."

The crazy woman was in tears, overly distraught. "What's *that* suppose to mean?"

"You tell *me*, since it's your sister that's the common denominator now."

"What? You're nuts lady. You really are a freak, you know that."

"Don't' call *me* a freak Vicki. I'm the one that put up with your awful barfing. I helped you more than you helped me. I helped you even though *she*...is your sister. I wasn't sure at first, but now I am and I'm not going to put up with it. I will not fraternize with the enemy any longer. Don't you understand? I *can't*!"

"Enemy?"

"Yah, you heard me, *enemy*! Figure *that* one out since you're so smart. I have to get out of here. I can't take it anymore. I need to think," the crazy woman shouted even louder, yanking at her cartoon orange choppy hair like a mental patient as she took off the way they had arrived.

"At least go look for George and Harvey while your thinking then," Vicki yelled at her as she stopped and turned one last time before disappearing into the night.

"That's the last thing I want to do right now," Loretta moaned like a tortured animal. She turned and started to run away from Vicki, echoing one last thing. "You're better off without me anyway. You all are...Trust me on that one!"

Self-centered psychopath!

Vicki stood there for a moment, silent, astounded, trembling in the damp chilly night. If the woman was that selfish, and could only think of herself in a situation like this, then she deserved the alienation she so desperately wanted. *She* was definitely *not* going to run after her, *or* feel sorry for her.

Enemy. Nobody called her sister the enemy.

She turned around and headed back to the lodge, shaking her head at the strange woman, thinking the bizarre situation they were facing was even stranger.

In the midnight sky above her, she saw those magnificent Northern Lights again. It sure felt like *The Twilight Zone*, weird, wild, and wacky. That was her trip so far. Tomorrow had to be better than today. She'd think more clearly in the morning.

If George would only get here, he'd know what to do. For now, she'd just go back inside, lock the door, and wait for him. She and Ruby would be safe for the night even if this Leon Eaglefeather was there. After all, what could a taped-up Indian do anyway?

Chapter 30

Thursday, July 6th.

Brian Mackie yawned for the umpteenth time in the past hour. Flying the department's twin-engine floatplane all night had taken a toll on him, despite all that coffee he downed at the airport before he left. Leaving in the wee hours of the morning hadn't exactly been his idea of fun, but hey, when the boss says jump you jump.

Sitting in on that meeting last night was the last thing he'd expected. All he wanted to do was take his son's baseball team out for pizza after the game, and enjoy his two-week holiday. He looked forward to celebrating with the Provincial champions. It was a night to celebrate until that blasted cell phone went off for the second time.

"Mackie here," he frowned. "This better be important." Brian rolled his eyes as he listened for a response. He plugged his ear from the roaring and chanting going on in the background. "I can't here you."

"We need you back at the office," the man on the other line shouted into the miniature phone. "Pronto!"

Brian wished he could just switch his phone off, but his boss would know. He wanted to pretend he didn't have very good reception, but he couldn't use that as an excuse either, not since they issued the whole department these fancy new high-tech cell phones, he still couldn't get use to. They were supposed to be the best, or at least that's what the computer geeks in the office told him. Not that Brian would know. He wasn't very keen on the new technology these days. He liked being a *dinosaur* when it came to electronic mumbo-jumbo. Why did people need computers and phones wherever they went anyway? What was wrong with the way things use to be? A guy could enjoy a good game without being bothered for every little thing.

"Yes, I'm here," Brian groaned. "Yes, I heard you, boss. I'll be right there."

Brian saw the foul look on his teenagers face. He hated disappointing his son. He didn't want to go, but his family was use to it by now. Not that *that* made him feel any better, but at least they would understand. Being an R.C.M.P officer was definitely not a nine- to- five job, and he obviously couldn't take a holiday with interruptions.

At the meeting, Brian sensed the urgency in his boss's voice when he told him to take the plane and check it out. For some reason he sensed this mattered a great deal to him. "I'd go myself Brian," his boss said. "But I have responsibilities here right now. I would consider this a huge favor. I've known this guy for eons Mackie. My dad used to take me fishing up there all the time. The guy is a very old friend, and runs it all by himself. I can't even get a line to the lodge, that's not normal. He always checks in."

If his boss hadn't been a close friend of his, he would have made a bigger fuss, but something in his eyes brought him into loyal submission. "Fine," Brian moaned. "But just so that you know – I'm officially off, and I don't care if I *can* go fishing afterward. I was supposed to go camping with my son's baseball team tomorrow." For that reason, and the fact that it was well after midnight by the time the plane was fuelled and ready to go, made the trip almost unbearable.

Brian focused into the early morning dawn glistening off the crisp water below. He had never seen such a beautiful place before. The tall evergreens scattered the shores of the largest body of water he had ever seen. He would have to take his son up here sometime, make up for all those times he'd disappointed him.

Down below, a small lodge nestled in the tree line at the edge of the river that branched off the enormous lake. He'd circle around the area just to check things over before landing.

As the buzzing sound of the plane echoed into the morning air, Brian circled the plane around and roared above the treetops. He was glad he got his pilots licence early on in his career. Nothing beat the beauty of flying in the clouds. Yet, on this particular morning, there wasn't a cloud in the sky. *Breathtaking!*

For a moment, as he circled the trees to the north of the lodge, he thought he saw something. He'd circle again, this time dipping lower and further north. Yes. He was almost positive. It looked like a big floatplane went down in the middle of the bush. He 'd have to land this thing, check in at the lodge first, then trek over there and check it out before radioing it in. The last thing he wanted to do was jump to conclusions. He'd done that before and paid dearly for it. This time he had to make sure. It might just be a mirage, but he doubted it.

~~~~

Loretta awoke with a start.

Something had disturbed her miserable night's slumber, she grumbled, as she huddled next to a sizable tree trunk nibbling on a bag of peanuts she snatched from the lodge. Shivering, she filled her mouth with the salty things that tasted like a gourmet meal. She would need a drink from that crystal-clear river soon if she could only figure out where it was. As far as she knew, she was somewhere deep in the heart of the northern bush again where she frantically fled to last night.

Wiping her salty dry mouth, and swallowing hard, she stood up to look around. The early morning light speckled through the trees as if stars themselves were trying to burst through. The marvellous lightshow displayed a sudden but extremely welcoming sight. The river was right there in front of her all along. She ran so impulsively last night without even realizing what direction she headed. It was stupid now that the new day revealed her sanity. She should have stayed put, but she had to get out of there. The situation had spiralled out of control.

Seeing the blonde woman again, brought back all those memories from the bank. She had needed the woman's help when their eyes met that day when her son died. *She* was the one that was cold then. Last night, to her sister, she played the victim. But she was no victim. Loretta didn't know how she could pretend that there was no history between her and Vicki's sister when there definitely was.

And this Leon fellow…she hadn't expected a stranger to be there. Who was he anyway? She hadn't invited him. No doubt, he was in on the robberies too. How could she not have known this? It would throw her plans off a great deal.

Plans? What plans? She no longer had a plan. All her work had been for nothing. The information was forever lost in her laptop, smashed from the crash. She couldn't even log on to the internet to research the tall Indian. And with no gun, what use was it. She might as well give up and die.

~~~~

"Pleased to meet you sir," the tall Indian smiled as Brian stepped out of the plane and onto the large dock. "Names Eaglefeather...Leon Eaglefeather, pleased to meet you," he spoke firmly as he stretched out his hand to shake Brian's sweaty tired palm.

Brian looked into the tall Indian's beady eyes. He had a firm handshake, but something about him didn't seem right. He appeared untidy, as if he hadn't bathed in days. His braided hair cascaded down his back into a magnificent ponytail, yet straggles and frizzy pieces of it stuck out everywhere.

"Pardon my appearance sir," the Indian said. "I don't usually look like this, I was on a fishing expedition late last night, fell asleep in my clothes I was so tired. Can you imagine that?"

"You don't say," Brian replied, scanning the Indian from head to toe. For some reason he didn't trust the guy, he seemed dishonest, like he was trying to hide something. His teenager acted the same way when caught in a lie. He'd always know when he attempted to pull a fast one on his old dad. Perhaps it was all the training Brian took for the job...or intuition, sixth sense, who knows. Whatever it was, he had the same uncanny feeling that this guy was *not* on the up and up.

Brian noticed the blood on the Indian's shirt. He would keep that observation to himself for now, he decided, narrowing his eyes on the man's bandaged hands, studying them intently until he pulled them away.

"Cut my hand filleting fish again. I guess I'm just not cut out for this fishing gig."

Brian couldn't believe his ears. The guy had an excuse for everything. He chose not to respond to the man's ridiculous subterfuge. "Can you tell me how to get in touch with a Larry Murphy?"

The Indian cocked his head to the side, "Who?"

Quit playing games.

"Never mind. Maybe you could just take me to the Shooting Star Lodge. He's probably there," Brian snapped back, annoyed at him now. He watched him as he jigged up and down sinking his hands deeply into the pockets of his long black trench coat, dancing to the early morning chill. His nervousness seemed to cause him to babble.

"Look, it's pretty early in the morning you know. Larry probably isn't even up yet. You're lucky I heard the plane and came to meet you with the four-wheeler. Larry has those hearing aides and everything, and he doesn't keep them in when he sleeps either you know."

So, he does know the guy.

"Still, I think I'll go to the lodge anyway if you don't mind. I'm sure Larry won't turn away the R.C.M.P," Brian insisted, trying to use as much professionalism as possible, hoping he hadn't ticked the guy off, spooked him into trying something stupid. He placed his hand on his revolver just in case as he followed the reluctant Indian to the four-wheeler and got into the passenger seat.

The Indian had no choice but to start up the machine and buzz down the path with Brian. He would chum with this Mr. Eaglefeather for a while, make him think he trusted him, and then when the time was right, he'd find out what he was hiding. "So... you from around here?" Brian shouted past the buzz of the machine.

"Yah...I mean...sort of. I help run the place."

Brian rolled his eyes. He knew his boss specifically informed him that Larry runs it all by himself. But what did he know? Perhaps he *did* help the old guy a bit. It didn't seem that way to him, but then, he had nothing to go on but his own intuition. For now, he wouldn't question the man on that topic. It was too risky.

Spiny jade tree branches slapped against Brian's windblown face as he felt the four-wheeler accelerate. Either the guy didn't know how to drive or...? "Slow down," Brian shouted as they nearly missed a stump to his left.

The Indian didn't even turn his head. He completely ignored him as if he were deaf or something. Without warning, he sped up even faster, deliberately letting the machine wobble out of control. It seesawed and teetered, bouncing from tire to tire as Brian held a firm grip on the roll bar with one white-knuckled hand. The other was on his revolver. He fumbled to tug it out.

Suddenly, a jolt of great force halted the machine, sending Brian's body hurling through the air. With a thump, he felt his body hit the forest floor. He lay prostrate, helpless in a heap.

Everything was a blur as he rolled over. Stars flashed before his eyes. The trees spun like a merry-go-round until something tugged at his body. He opened his eyes, beginning to focus on the blurry image standing before him. It was Mr. Eaglefeather, alive and well, towering in front of him... aiming at him with a gun.

Brian gasped, realizing it was *his* gun.

"Oh yes. What will poor Mr. Constable do now without his gun? Let's see," the Indian badgered, grinning in the most evil grotesque manner imaginable. "What should I do now? Should I sing him a lullaby before he goes night, night? Hmmm…I think I will."

Then, the big Indian began to jump around, dancing in a strange spooky fashion while still pointing the gun at Brian. "Oh, I know a perfect song…*There was and old lady who swallowed a fly*. You know the one. It's my favorite," he snickered like a crazed lunatic as he sang. "There was an old *constable* who stuck his nose in my business. Why did this *constable* stick his nose in my business?"

Then he shouted as if he lost his mind. "PERHAPS HE'LL DIE!"

Chapter 31

George relaxed and let his mind drift back to last night.

He remembered slinking past that freak Loretta. It was easy, though he should have stopped to kill her right there. She resembled a weak helpless kitten snoozing next to that pine tree. It would have been so easy to snap her scraggy hen-like neck just like all those kittens he tortured and killed when he was ten. He could still hear the mew...then the distinctive pop sound as if he had snapped their necks yesterday. Just the thought of it put a smile on his coarse, unshaven, masculine face.

He couldn't see Vicki anywhere when he passed freak-lady last night. He assumed she washed up on shore somewhere, but he didn't really care. The Black Snake Root that he gave her the other day was supposed to have killed her. He had only given her a few stems of the poisonous plant, but Leon told him the stuff was so toxic it could kill in one hour depending on body size and approximately how much stayed in the system. The problem was, it didn't stay in her system, but it sure made her sick. That was a good thing. She and freak-lady were going to pay. Soon their time would come.

George knew right away that Eaglefeather would be inside the lodge. He and the big Indian just needed to get their diamonds, tie up a few loose ends, and then they could get out of this God-forsaken hole, this place that witch lured him too. She was smart, he gave her that, but *nobody* got away with conning George Oxford Williams.

When he approached the cabin and peered into the window last night, he was clearly astonished at what he saw. Eaglefeather appeared bound with duct tape, sitting in a corner while the two sisters slumbered like the Queen of Sheba on the couch.

His *plan B*, to play the perfect gentleman, had really worked out for him.

When he tiptoed to the door and knocked, he stood there for a moment and waited for it to open; he remembered the soft words he used, "Baby, it's me," he said, hoping it was the other one. Then when he saw who it was, he was relieved somewhat. "Vicki!"

Vicki flung open the door and wrapped her arms around him. How that repulsed him even now as he hashed it over in his mind. She smothered him with those slobbery lips of hers; He reluctantly kissed her back just as passionately. It was something he told himself he had to put up with just to pull off this scam. He always was an exceptionally good faker, anything to get what he wanted.

The memories flooded back into his mind all at once.

"George!" Vicki glowed, stepping back to look at him. "Boy am I glad to see you. I thought you were dead baby. Look at you. You're a mess," she hugged him again. "Come inside. You'll never guess what's been going on."

Don't be so sure about that one you stupid broad.

Leon silently winked at him as he entered the smelly tattered lodge. The rancid place appeared as though there had been a catfight, the cats obviously the undefeated champions...but not for long.

These two sisters were definitely a handful. He knew that first hand. Oh...how he played the two of them. He recalled all his scheming tactics. And this moment was the pinnacle of his efforts. It made it all worthwhile, crowned him the stud of all studs.

Ruby's eyes almost popped out of their sockets.

"*George!*" Ruby hissed like a venomous snake. "You…filthy…*pig!*"

Vicki looked surprised as she closed the door and locked it behind her. "What?"

"*Vicki*," Ruby's swollen eyes started to tear, washing down her dry bloody face. "George is *my* boyfriend."

"Right," Vicki's face turned red. "You're not thinking straight Ruby. He's the pilot. He crashed with *us* Ruby. Remember I told you…"

"Well he should have *died*!" Ruby shouted.

George absolutely loved this. His Cheshire cat grin beamed the sinful truth all along and they were none the wiser.

"Tell her George!" Vicki insisted. "Tell her who you are."

Leon rolled on the floor. "Hey, this is better than the soaps."

"Shut up jerk!" Vicki shouted, flashing a crimson scowl back and forth between Leon and George. He didn't know what she would do but somehow, he knew she wouldn't be half as ticked-off as her sister would. He knew the blonde a whole lot longer than he knew the redhead anyway.

Like a soldier running for cover in the heat of battle, he chose to sit on the couch as far away from Ruby as possible. He wasn't taking any chances knowing what they did to his poor Indian friend. "Actually…Vicki," George grinned like the devil. "Your sister is right. You're my second choice babe. Why would anyone choose you first? But hey, there's enough of me to go around for the both of you."

The rest of George's memory faded after recalling that part of it. The highlight was the look on the two sister's faces when they realized they both fell for the same ruggedly handsome gentleman. Leon was terribly amused. He laughed so hard, he started to cry. What an Academy Award winning mental image.

He didn't even have to use Harvey's Glock to take the women out. All he had to do was punch Vicki once in that nauseous stomach of hers and she tumbled to the floor with those stunned round eyes. And Ruby, well she was easy, she always was.

He found the roll of *duck* tape the girls used on Leon and wound it around both sisters' hands, feet, and mouth, and shoved them in the bedroom closet. Out of sight, out of mind, he always believed.

"Cut me out of this tape George," Leon insisted. "It's about time you showed up."

"Sorry about that. I had a few problems, but the plan is still a go."

"Good. Just get me out of this tape so I can get Eddie."

"I came up with a delicious plan bro, seriously, you'll never believe it."

"Good...you can tell me later. Right now, just get me out of this. And don't waste the girls yet, I need them alive when I get back. Ruby hid our diamonds somewhere and I intend to get it out of her any way I can.

"Go for it Romeo."

"I hope you have some idea where she put them."

"Don't worry, I'll make her talk. I'm a pro with the ladies remember?" George spit on his hand and slicked his hair back with it, puffing out his chest with pride.

"You *dog*," Leon smirked, as he went for the door, free from his bindings. "I still can't believe you conned them *both*. I haven't laughed that hard in a long time."

George shoved Leon out the door, chuckling to himself, flattered by his friends compliment. "Get out of here."

Now as George stretched his stocky body across the old brown paisley couch, finishing off a bag of Doritos and slurping up the last drop of his Dr. Pepper, he wondered what was taking Leon so long. It had been a while since he left to get Eddie. He wondered why Eddie wasn't already there. That was the plan. And where was Joe? He was probably with Eddie no doubt. They were like two peas in a pod. All three of his buddies would probably be back any minute now, and then they could proceed with his brilliant plan. He would ignore those stupid whimper sounds from the closet and try to take a catnap while he waited. He had definitely earned the rest.

~~~~

Lord, help us. We need you now more than anything!

Ruby's legs were pins and needles in the semi-dark closet lit only by a small night-light stuck into the socket above her head. She could barely breathe with the wide taunt tape stretched across her mouth. At least George wasn't smart enough to wrap the tape completely around her head, only across her mouth. She'd use her tongue to pry the sticky stuff away from her masked lips.

Her poor sister, she had been sucked into George's good looks and charming ways just as she had. He was the best con man she had ever known. Even though she hated him, knew what he was like and what he had done, she still had some feelings for him. It was crazy, sick really, but the pangs of love still felt so real.

Vicki had fallen asleep next to her sister. As big and tough as she was, she looked so vulnerable right now. Her sister had put on this tough guy persona to protect herself from guys like George, and still he got through the barrier.

For as long as Ruby could remember, the both of them had built a wall around themselves, Vicki more so. She always personified a true pillar of strength to Ruby and she tried to teach her all she knew. "Be tough Ruby, at least act that way," she'd say. "Swear as much as you can little sister. Make *them* afraid of *you*!"

But she had tried all her sisters' infallible tactics and still nothing kept her safe. Nothing protected her from the hurtful men of the world...and *nobody* saved her. Nobody except perhaps the one she discarded as a child: God. She knew the truth now. She had heard it all her life, had even believed it at one point, or at least tried to. How could she have turned her back on the Lord? What ever made her think she could do her own thing? She knew *now* that she could not save her own life. Only *Jesus* could save her now. Only Jesus could save the *caribou* from the *monsters*.

"Vicki," Ruby whispered, spitting out the awful glue-tasting duct-tape mush from her mouth. "Wake up."

Her sister slowly and silently opened her eyes.

"Let me grab the edge of the tape with my teeth."

Tears filled Vicki's eyes as she shook her head against the idea.

"Don't give up Vic. I know he hurt you. He hurt me too, but George is like that...he's just a jerk. He always has been and he always will be. You have no idea what kind of things he's done. You don't need a scumbag like that. Trust me."

She shook her head in agreement, as Ruby grabbed the edge of the tape with her teeth and slowly peeled the sticky tape away from her sister's protruding lips.

"Nobody messes with the Booth girls," Vicki spit the moment the tape lifted off, tears flooding her sorrowful eyes. Ruby rested her head against her sister's head and sighed. "Or so we thought sister dear, or so we thought."

"What do you mean?"

"Face it Vic, we've tried everything, and still the *dogs* get in."

"Yah, well I know a *dog* who's going to be *dead meat* in a minute."

"Oh yah, and how do you presume to do that?"

Vicki paused for a moment. Ruby could tell she was really thinking hard.

"Stop pretending you're so tough. It doesn't work anymore."

"You're supposed to listen to your big sister."

"*No*, you listen to *me* now. I know how to get out of here, but you're not going to like it very much. It might sound a little radical."

Vicki looked doubtful.

"No really. Listen. We've tried everything. Right? And I do mean everything. Still nothing has worked. We try to protect ourselves, put up a wall so we don't get hurt, and we can't. Only God can. Only Jesus can save us, the *caribou*, from the *monsters*."

She thought of sweet little Pip out there somewhere, the inventor of this odd but wise caribou verses monster theory. She wondered if he had gotten away.

Vicki rolled her eyes. "Are you completely mad? Don't even mention religion to me. And why are you talking about *caribou* and *monsters?*"

"Listen Vicki, *we*...are the *caribou* that need to be protected, and God can do that. Just give him a chance. He's our last shot against the monsters sis. What can it hurt? Let's pray... Or would you rather *die*?"

"I don't want to die."

"Then stop being so stubborn and pray with me."

At that, both women bowed their heads. Ruby whispered a prayer longer than she ever had before. She asked God to forgive her for turning away from him, and for building a wall around her heart. Vicki sobbed silently as Ruby continued to pray. She helped her sister pray as well while Vicki repeated it word for word.

At that moment, Ruby knew without a doubt that they were finally safe, that their struggles were no longer hopeless, that God...had everything under control. "For their struggles were not against flesh and blood, but against the rulers, against the authorities, against the powers of this dark world and against the spiritual forces of evil in the heavenly realms."

Chapter 32

Brian came too in the midst of an angelic light. Had he died? Was this the light in those near-death experiences? Pain suddenly shot through him. No. If this were heaven, there would be no pain, and he was definitely feeling something right now.

He lifted his hand and placed it on his chest while he lay on the earthy forest floor. He felt around for an injury. No blood. Now he remembered. The vest had saved his life from the Indian's vengeance. The bullet had not penetrated. When he was dressing in his uniform last night before the trip, he remembered his boss's insistence that he wear that uncomfortable bulletproof thing. To appease his good friend, he did just that. But he was tempted to take it off the moment he was airborne, thankful now that he didn't. It had saved his life.

Brian tried to adjust his vision better before getting back to his feet. The sun shone so brightly that his eyes were starting to play tricks on him. Was it actually an angel that he saw standing in front of him? His eyes still weren't focusing.

"Who's there," he called out blindly, clutching his aching chest. The shadow just moved out of the light. "I know you're there," Brian said, fighting the blur, raising one hand over his brow to see as he laboured to sit up.

"I'm Pipata, the great warrior," the animated voice whispered from somewhere to the left of him causing him to twist his head to the side.

"Oh," Brian smiled, now seeing the lanky black-haired Indian boy in his childlike grin. "You're my warrior, are you? I thought you were my angel."

"No angel sir, just warrior chief, smart warrior chief."

Brian was amused at the boy's antics. He was really putting on a show.

"How old are you son?"

"Me thirteen sir," the boy snapped back with pride.

"I have a boy about your age you know," Brian smiled as he let the kid help him to his feet. "He lives in La Ronge. Where do you live?"

"Me live in bush with caribou."

Brian dusted off his uniform as he squinted back at the boy. "You do, do you. Well maybe you could help me then Chief Pipata."

"Call me Pip," the boy replied in his normal voice now as he extended his hand to shake the constable's hand.

"Pleased to meet you Pip. I'm Brian."

Pip looked him up and down. "Are you really a Mounter?"

"What? Oh, you must mean Mounty," Brian chuckled. "Yes, but actually they call me Constable Mackie. I flew in this morning to chat with Larry Murphy. Do you know him?"

Pip lowered his head and said nothing.

"Did something happen to Mr. Murphy?"

Pip lifted his head slowly and shook it up and down. "The monsters got him."

"What monsters?"

Brian looked at the boys face. He was terrified. Perhaps he saw the tall Indian do something to him. "Did you see an Indian with a long braid? Is he one of the monsters?"

Pip started into that animated voice again. "Yes. Chief see *monster...again.*"

By the time Loretta found Harvey sitting on the beach, he had his shirt off and his bare burly-grey chest exposed, twisting and turning the dirty fabric as he wrung the bloody thing out. He had ripped strips of cloth from it and bandaged his wounded bulging belly. "What happened to you?" Loretta asked, startling him.

"Loretta," he said. "Am I ever glad to see you. George did this. He *stabbed* me."

"He what?" she screamed, falling to her knees beside him, distraught at the sight of the injury. "Is it bad?"

"I thought it was at first, but when I cleaned it up; I realized he didn't hit anything major. He just pierced my side. I guess this is how Jesus felt when they did this to him, except probably a hundred times worse. I bandaged it up the best I could. It feels like I'm wearing a girdle...but at least the bleeding stopped. I'll be okay. I've had a lot more injuries than this when I was a cop. Believe me, this is nothing."

Loretta felt sorry for the poor man. He was obviously in pain. "Why do men have to act so tough? If it hurts just say so. And it's *not* nothing Harvey. He could have killed you. He's capable of it you know." *Oops...There goes her big mouth again.*

Harvey threw a confusing glace at her, "How do you know *that* Loretta?"

"I know a lot of things. He...he's just...he seems like that kind of guy."

"Do you know who he is?" Harvey drilled her. "He's no bush pilot, I can tell you that. Now who is he? You know him, don't you?"

"No," she lied. Why should she tell him? It was none of his business. If she told him, she'd just put him in danger. Yet, that apparently had already happened.

"I don't believe you Loretta. You know him!"

"I don't," she lied, insisting he believe her. "I swear."

Loretta sat quietly next to Harvey, arms locked around her bent knees, head hanging low. She knew she could trust him with the truth, yet, if she told him...It would mean the end of her plan. Perhaps that time had already come.

"Loretta," Harvey sighed long and hard, "maybe I should be completely honest with you before I expect the same from you." He paused for a while before speaking again, taking a deep breath, and then continuing. "Look...I should have told you about this before. When I was lost in the bush, I found the Shooting Star Lodge. These two guys were there along with another woman. They beat her, and they beat me and then tied us up. I know this sounds crazy but it happened. They're criminals, and I think George is too. I should have told you sooner. I'm sorry."

It was more than she could bear. Harvey looked like one of those three *naive* little pigs from the old classic story books she used to read her kids when they were little. He just sat there like a fat little pig, pink and helpless...and she was the big bad wolf. How could she tell him that she already knew about the whole thing?

"Well...?" Harvey asked, annoyed that she wasn't responding to his big news.

"Well what?"

"Aren't you going to get upset and ream me out for not telling you sooner? Aren't you shocked?"

Loretta moaned with her head in her knees and silently shook her head.

"What's that supposed to mean?"

She lifted her head and forced a smile as she gazed into his innocent blue eyes that seemed to invite her into his open trusting heart. "I'm not shocked, I'm sad," she said. "I'm sad because what you told me wasn't a surprise at all. I knew about the men and that woman at the lodge, and I know about George…and much, *much* more."

~~~~

Brian knocked on the rustic log cabin that the young Indian boy Pip verified to be the Shooting Star Lodge. Pip had brought him to it but pleaded with him not to go in. He didn't stick around very long to push the matter. At least the kid had enough common sense to know this wasn't wise. He on the other hand, had to do his job regardless, unarmed or not. And without backup, he was really taking a chance. It wasn't the best way to lead an investigation, but if he risked going back to the plane, the tall Indian that tried to kill him might try again. And Pip did assure him that he saw the Indian take off in the other direction. If he was going to do this, now was the time.

He knocked again.

If someone didn't answer soon, he'd assume nobody was home and go in to search the place for any signs of Larry. Maybe the old man was just sick or injured, or died of natural causes, he *was* in his eighties. But then, that pony-tailed Indian put a kybosh to that idea. He was up to no good that was for sure. And not only that, Brian could tell he was a crack-head. His eyes had the tell-tale signs of a junky, red-rimmed and wild. Either that or the guy was a psycho. Regardless, it was his job to investigate.

He knocked one last time, "Larry...you in there?"

Suddenly the door creaked open and a husky young blonde man with dishevelled hair opened the door and yawned, "Sorry...You caught me snoozing."

"I'm Constable Brian Mackie," he said formally. "Are you Larry Murphy?"

"In the flesh...I mean...You got him." *I got you all right pal, and you're not him.*

Brian didn't know what was going on, but he was soon going to find out. The guy looked just as shady as the Indian did, standing there like a rock beside the door, obviously blocking the way in. He beamed a phoney frozen smile with *guilty* written all over his face, baring his completely straight overly pearly white teeth.

"Can I come inside and talk to you for a minute," Brian asked professionally.

He responded nervously, "I guess so."

The man's grin waned as he slowly forced himself into the lodge. He backed away from Brian and shut the door, grabbing the back of his jeans with his right hand, deliberately keeping it there. *He's obviously packing.* "So, you own this place?

"Yah...Why?"

"Just a routine question sir," Brian lied, looking around at the messy place that smelled of rancid body odour, dead animals and bad food. Candy wrappers, empty chip bags and crushed pop cans lay beside a ratty old couch with bits of leftover macaroni and cheese sitting crusty in a cereal bowl on the coffee table beside the living room window.

"I'd like to use your phone if you don't mind," he said, wishing he hadn't forgotten his fancy department issued cell phone in the plane."

"No can do…lines are down, been that way ever since the last storm. We had a string of bad luck with storms this season."

"Is that right?" Brian forced a smile. If that was the truth, he was in serious trouble. "So, tell me then…*Larry*, what about the mobile phone?"

With one swift move, the man drew out his weapon and aimed it at Brian. "Put your hands up *pig*…and stop asking questions."

"Hey now…calm down pal, there's no need to get upset."

The man held his ground, fuming, "Don't come any closer or I'll shoot.

"Brian held his hands up, and tried to figure out his next move. He inched forward, lunging toward him tackling the Neanderthal into the wall, forcing the gun upward with one hand and clawing at the man's face with the other. But the man was too strong for Brian's medium build. He buckled from a knee to the groin, dropping his defences as he fell to the floor, gun to his head.

"Who's the big man now *Mounty*?" the man grinned, panting from exhaustion. "I guess you don't always get your man, hey?"

Chapter 33

"Okay," Vicki whispered her plan to her sister as the two of them huddled in the closet, "as soon as I open the closet door, you start screaming so George comes to check on us. I'll hide somewhere in the bedroom, then at the right moment, I'll jump him before he gets to you."

"I hope your plan will work Vic. George is pretty strong."

"So am I, and besides, I'm counting on *divine* strength anyway."

"Vicki…"

"Oh, don't worry sis, I have a few tricks up my sleeve."

Ruby was getting frustrated now. She hoped her sister didn't think she had superpowers now just because she got saved.

"I just can't help thinking we should stay put."

"But Ruby, you know he's beating somebody up out there. It sounds like its Harvey. Who knows what George will do to him next? And if we don't act now, that Indian guy will come back, and then we're all in for it."

"Fine, let's do it then."

Ruby's injured body ached as she rose from her crumpled position on the closet floor. She grabbed onto her husky sister for support, looking like a pigmy beside her. The sticky residue from the duct tape that once bound her wrists, adhered to everything, and it was itchy and hard to ignore.

Vicky slowly inched open the closet door, scurried around the corner, and hid behind a large rustic armoire. She raised her hand and made the okay sign for her sister to start screaming.

~~~~

Suddenly, Brian heard sounds of muffled screaming coming from a back bedroom. The blonde man cocked his head, stopped duct-taping Brian's hands and feet and groaned as if he were terribly annoyed.

"Sounds like it's for you man," Brian gave a sly grin.

"Shut up *Pig* before I shut you up!" the man grumbled, as he set the tape down. He laboured to get up, lifting his muscular body, rubbing one knee as he teetered to stand, grabbing his back in the process. "On second thought, I'll just tape your mouth," he said, slowly bending over to grab the tape again, unrolling a short strip as he ripped it off with his picture-perfect teeth. He plastered it over Brian's mouth, patting it to make sure it stayed on. "There, now that's finished. I'll be back in a minute so don't try anything."

Count on it scumbag!

As the Neanderthal exited the room, Brian rolled from his stomach to his side. He sat up and wiggled to his knees. Then, rising on them, he managed to force his way up to a standing position, hopping and teetering as he did it. Both hands throbbed behind him, bound too tightly with duct tape. His feet were beginning to feel like pins and needles from the tape that constricted his ankles. His five-o'clock-shadow itched with the added sticky duct-tape pasted from ear to ear across his lips.

He looked around the room for something he could use to free himself, but the luxury of time was not on his side. He decided to wiggle his wrists and pull and yank at the binding tape, hoping that somehow, he would manage to free his hands before the man got back.

After a few moments of wiggling, he realized his hands were beginning to feel numb. The stinging, burning sensation in his wrists made it seem like the tape had literally melted into his skin. Suddenly, it felt slippery back there. Now he couldn't seem to feel *anything* anymore...and the room was beginning to spin. Then, within moments, he heard a dripping sound, and something slapping to the floor. Had someone left a water faucet on? No, it was him. The expanding red puddle underneath his feet grew spherically round, steadily filling with his own blood. The duct-tape was so tight, so constricting, that he had accidentally slit his own wrists with it.

~~~~

"Come out come out wherever you are," George toyed with Vicki. She had now moved from behind the chest of drawers where she hid the first time, to the hallway without him noticing. He had rushed to the closet right away and grabbed her sister faster than she realized he would. Now she waited there for him, sweating and panicky. He held the gun to Ruby's temple and dragged her around.

Jumping him now was completely out of the question.

"You think you're so smart Vicki, but all you are is a dumb ugly broad," George yelled out to Vicki, grinning as he yanked Ruby's helpless body through the bedroom, thrusting the gun even harder into the side of her temple. "Yah Vicki, didn't you know that Ruby's the babe, not you? You're the ugly duckling. I couldn't even stand to look at you.

I only kissed you because I needed you to take me to your sister. Well...not really. Actually, I didn't care if you died. When you almost did yourself in with those magic mushrooms, I couldn't believe you could be so stupid. I actually hoped you'd die then, but you didn't. Then I tried the Black Snakeroot. It should have done the trick, but you're like that old Coppertop Battery commercial...you just keep going and going."

"Then I hoped the storm did you in, but just in case it didn't and you made it to the lodge first, which you did, I figured I might as well use you. I'm good at that. I figured you would be my guarantee that Ruby would stick around. She has a bad habit of taking off on me. See, we fight a lot. Don't we sweetheart?" George grinned through his teeth, beaming them at Ruby and then repulsively licking the side of her face.

Vicki wished she hadn't seen that, but she had to stay at a vantage point where she could still see George's movements. Knowing the exact time to tackle the guy meant life or death to her sister, and Vicki wasn't going to lose her now after she just found her. *God...now that I believe in you, maybe you could help me take this guy out.*

Then she lost sight of them somehow. Where did they go? She could hear the floor creaking. Her sister was whimpering softly, but she couldn't see her. Where were they? Were they behind her...in the room still...or in front of her?

She tiptoed in her stocking feet further down the hall even though she didn't quite know what she was doing. She could see a strange man lying in a pool of blood, bound with duct-tape, motionless on the living room floor. He was wearing a uniform of some kind, police maybe, ranger, or maybe a conservation officer. If she could free him, they could both take George on together...unless he was already dead.

She grabbed a knife from the kitchen counter and started for him. The man turned his head at that exact moment, exposing his taped-up mouth. Obviously, he was still alive. His eyes grew big and wild as she cautiously approached him. He frantically tried to speak but only hysterical muffles came out.

Without warning, Vicki heard something behind her. She turned around and screamed as George thwacked the back of her head with the butt of his gun. She collapsed to the ground and lay there motionless as he laughed hysterically, stars sparkling around her, room spinning...until...everything went dark.

~~~~

George loved this part. Always the winner. Boy, he was good. "That...*Pig*, is what I call lesson number one. Never be stupid enough to think you can outsmart *me*. See, you'll just end up with a very bad headache like Miss Incredible Hulk here, and sleeping beauty in the bedroom."

Brian turned red with anger, grunting through the duct-tape.

"Oh, don't worry *Pig*, I don't mean you. I'd never do that to a fine *Mounty* like yourself," the man chuckled like a madman.

Brian rolled his eyes.

"Oh, and don't think I didn't see that *Pig*, I have eyes in the back of my head. I am *invincible!*" George cried out, never feeling more alive. He was on top of the world. And to think, he would be a very rich man as soon he and Leon could take off with the diamonds. Just the fact that Eaglefeather showed up early meant he must have found a Gem cutter to cut the diamonds. They could finally sell the rocks without a trace.

As for that freak Loretta, he'd save her till last. He knew she had double-crossed him for quite some time now. At one point, he just wanted to slit her throat and get it over with, but he held himself back. She would pay for setting him and the others up like this. She would die a painful torturous death…just like her kid. The others were icing on the cake. He would put them all out of their misery soon enough. The loose ends would tie up perfectly. What a plan!

Chapter 34

Friday, July 7th.

"I told you *no* and I mean it!" Harvey insisted for the umpteenth time as they sat in the big R.C.M.P floatplane arguing again, munching on the bag-lunch they found tucked away beside the seat. Immediately, Harvey had dragged Loretta away from the lodge instead of toward it the moment she told him what she was *really* up too.

"Why not?"

"Because I'm not going to let you throw your life away dear."

Dear...Don't patronize me with your nice-guy innuendo. You're not going to change my mind!

"What life? I don't have a life anymore," she started to bawl. Everyone she cared about had left her, Bob, her two daughter's Trudy and Tammy...even Jeremy. There was nothing to live for anymore, nothing but *this*. She would get her revenge on George if it killed her.

Harvey sat quietly in the pilot's seat of the plane. His eyes were as big as saucers. She hated to manipulate him with her tears, but she had to admit she was good at it, and it was working.

"Come on Loretta, you have a life. Look around you. The sun is shining. You can breathe in and out, and hey, we're finally eating a decent meal even though it's only peanut butter and jam sandwiches."

Loretta gave him a half-hearted smile, and then dumped her emotions on the man again, trying one more time to sway him to her way of thinking. "I don't care," she wailed even harder than the last time. "I don't have *anything* to live for. All I want to do is go to the lodge and you won't let me. You have *no* right! What if I just get out of this plane

264

right now and head back there myself? *I* can do whatever I want. I'm a grown woman and you can't dictate my life…you're not my *husband*."

Harvey sighed, "No Loretta, you're right, I'm *not* your husband. But if I *were*, I *never* would have left you. I would have held you close and never let you go, especially when your son died."

"I would have respected you, given you encouragement, love. I wouldn't have let one minute slip by without telling you how much you mean to me. Life is too short. You think you have a lot of time with the ones you love, but one day they're gone and you miss your chance…You know that as well as I do."

"And if I *were* your husband…I would have made sure I built your confidence up instead of down. I would have told you that you're one of a kind, that you're talented, and that you deserve to be happy."

"You have a *good* soul Loretta; I can see it in your eyes. You're sweet, intelligent and God cares about you…and so do I. If I *were* your husband, I would have told you so a thousand times. I never would have let you think otherwise. I never would have let you get so confused and depressed, or think you didn't have anything to live for. You're a *beautiful* person. You're precious…You were blessed with a *healthy* life…when so many are not. Don't think that's nothing dear. It's everything."

Loretta sat there stunned with her mouth open. Never in all her years of marriage has she ever heard Bob express his feelings to her like *that*.

Harvey hung his head, "I'm sorry dear. I shouldn't have babbled like a fool."

This time Loretta was in tears, not for her own selfish reasons, but for something completely different. "You care about me?"

Harvey cleared his throat. "Of course, I do. Why wouldn't I? That's why I don't want you to go back to the lodge. I've always believed that when tempted by sin...you should distance yourself from it. It works. Then, after you've gotten away from it and can think more clearly, God can work on you...He can change your heart."

Not that again.

"But I don't want God to change my heart."

"Yes, you do."

"No...I *really* don't!" Loretta fumed, wiping her tears away, hoping that he would drop the subject. If he thought he was going to convince her to trust God again, he had another thing coming. *Now she sounded like her ex-husband.*

"You can argue all day with me Loretta," Harvey grinned, "but it's not going to do you any good. You *do* want God to change your heart...You just don't know it yet. Besides, I'm *not* expecting you to break into a lengthy prayer right now or anything. I know praying is the last thing you want to do so I'll just pray *for* you."

"Don't bother; I'm not going to listen."

"Oh, *you* won't be listening, I'll do it silently some other time," the man teased like a smart-aleck. His antics were something else. "Besides, right now we have to figure out how to get some help. We don't have the key to either one of these two planes...and someone cut the wires on both plane radios. We can't even call anyone on this useless cell phone, the batteries are dead."

"So, what are we going to do?

"Well," Harvey sighed, scanning the morning horizon through the cockpit window, "this plane was a good place to spend the night, but unfortunately we can't stay here. We'll be sitting ducks."

"What do you have in mind?"

"Well…since this is a police-issued floatplane, I am betting it's loaded with emergency supplies. We'll find them, take whatever we can, compass, map, medical supplies, matches, provisions, you know, whatever we need."

"The other older plane over there must be local. Look, it says, "Eagle's Flight" on the side door, then "Deep Bay tours," on the bottom. Someone nearby must own it. We'll head along the shore toward Deep Bay until we find them."

"You're not going anywhere Harvey," Loretta piped up. "Look at you, you're weak. Blood is *still* soaking through those bandages. You're in your bare feet and you don't even have a shirt on. You're going to get eaten alive."

"Look in the back…Work boots and overalls for the both of us," Harvey informed her, complacent as ever. "They're even orange dear; they'll match your lovely hair."

"Funny…You're such a comedian…but you're still not going anywhere with that wound of yours. You'll pass out on me within the hour. Then what am I suppose to do, carry you?"

"We'll find the medical supplies. There should be some gauze along with some iodine and other stuff. You're not a nurse, are you?"

"No…Do I look like one?"

Harvey blushed. "I mean…Have you ever stitched anyone up?"

"*No!*"

"Well…You're going to learn."

~~~~

Pip sat at the kitchen table eating the mayonnaise and peanut butter sandwich his grandfather slapped together for him on top of some bannock. It had an unusual taste to it, but then all Grandfathers' creations tasted unusual. At least it was food, and he had become accustomed to it since his parents died. In fact, he was lucky he had a prepared meal this morning. Usually he had to make something for himself, but today, Grandfather was acting weird.

"Mmm," Pip lied; trying to convince the leathery old man that he liked it, even though he didn't. "It's good Grandfather. The bannock is…tasty." *Moldy.*

The old man seemed to be preoccupied, he didn't answer. Pip knew why. He wasn't the only one that sensed the danger they were all in with Uncle Leon being around. It was just that his grandfather didn't know exactly *how* much danger.

He wondered how Little Caribou and the others were doing. If only he had been braver, he could have saved them from his uncle. Now they were his. He would eat them too…just like monsters do.

For a moment, he thought about telling Grandfather everything, and then he realized he couldn't. Grandfather would be furious, he'd go after Uncle Leon, and then…Uncle Leon really would kill him. No, if he were going to help, he would have to steal Grandfather's rifle without him noticing. He'd take a knife or two with him as well, and then head back to the lodge to play the warrior again. Only this time he'd succeed.

If it wasn't for his nasty uncle cutting Grandfather's electricity and phone lines before he left, he could have called his grandfather's friend Grayling who lived at Widow's Peak just south of them. He and Grandfather shared a trap-line years ago before the flying business spoiled all that. Grayling told Grandfather that the idea was stupid. He told him that an old man shouldn't do such a foolish thing. Grandfather never spoke to him again, but Pip did. He'd wander over there at least twice a week. They'd fish the edges of Deep Bay together, catch what Grayling called "*his* monsters", clean, and fry them up. Pip could almost hear the crackling sounds of the fish frying outside on the old man's campfire. He cooked everything outside, traditional, the way he said it should be.

Now, as Pip chewed, he realized what he needed to do. He'd finish eating, take some weapons with him, and sneak the old fishing boat. No, Grandfather would notice. He'd go on foot, south through the bushes as fast as he could. He'd convince Grayling to help him.

Later that morning, Pip knocked on Grayling's modest cabin. It was an old log-type home, rustic from the outside, but fully modern on the inside. It lay hidden in the bush near a rock-cliff that edged Deep Bay. The current was strong there, propelling enormous green frothy waves against its walls. The name "Widow's Peak" fit it well. Pip was very glad he didn't try to take the boat.

When he and Grayling would go fishing, they stayed away from the *Peak* and fished further east. Grayling would tell him stories. He'd tell him that a great spirit called Nanináágóó fell to earth creating an enormous hole known as Deep Bay. The spirit fell against *Widow's Peak* on his way down causing him to curse it. From that day on, any man that tried to cross it died. That's why they call it *Widow's Peak.*

Pip always believed the old Indian's stories even though he had heard different variation of the tale. He never told Grandfather he visited Grayling, nor did he mention the stories. It was a secret he kept well hidden.

Now as he continued to knock, he noticed something lying next to Grayling's smouldering campfire. He ran over to it, labouring with his rifle slung across his shoulder. "Grayling…are you okay?"

The old man lay slumped next to the smouldering campfire, his long scraggly grey-white hair frizzing around his droopy wrinkled face. "I'm alright child," the old Indian insisted, "just fell asleep at the fire again, nearly burnt my foot off this time."

"Grayling!" Pip scolded him. "I thought you were dead."

"Why would you think that boy? I'm old, but I'm still breathing."

Grayling eased to his feet, standing in his worn leather mukluks he made himself, stomping his smoking foot out. He still wore the fringed leather jacket he always wore, just as Pip had last seen him. The old man never changed. Yes, Pip hadn't seen his friend in over a week, and he still probably wore the same clothes underneath all that.

"What you got there boy?"

Pip felt a little foolish with his Grandfather's gun strapped to his shoulder. The two of them never hunted together. He said that was something he had to do with his Grandfather. It was the love of fishing Pip and Grayling both shared, not hunting. "I…I have Grandfather's gun."

"I see that, but why do you have it son?"

Pip stood there, about to cry. His eyes flooded with tears, and his bottom lip quivered. With Grayling, he always had to come clean. The man could always see through him. Of course, he intended to tell Grayling everything, except now, it all seemed...foolish, like one of his games. Could his mind have made everything up?

"I stole it Grayling. I stole it from Grandfather," Pip shamefully admitted.

Grayling sighed, and hobbled over to Pip, resting his fringed leathery arm around the boys shoulder. "Had a bad day hey? Well, let's go inside and have some tea together. I need to check on this old foot of mine, make sure I didn't burn off my big toe. Then you can tell old Grayling all about it."

Chapter 35

Father in heaven, Harvey prayed to himself while he trudged along beside Loretta, both of them sticking out like sore thumbs with their fluorescent orange hunting overalls. *Help Loretta see the error of her ways. Put a stop to this lunacy of hers. Help her understand that revenge is a sin. Change her heart oh God.*

He thought of his own foolish heart. He had rambled on about his feelings toward her and made a terrible mistake. He couldn't fall for Loretta. Rose still lingered in his mind, his heart, in every breath. How could he betray the memory of his beloved wife?

Since Rose died, he swore to himself there would be no other. He could never replace her love. There was no other woman like his Rosey. She was one of a kind.

For five years, he refused even to think of dating again. At his age, it was down right silly. His sister would often harass him, try to set her up with her friends, but he always refused. Now what was he doing? Was he a turncoat?

Loretta was no Rose, but something about her wrenched his heart. At first, he just told himself that he was being very helpful, loving...in a Christ-like way. But it was more than that. Even now, watching her as she trudged along beside him in overalls two sizes too big for her, rolled up at the ankles and wrists, she made his heart skip a beat.

Her ridiculous hairdo just added to her flamboyant character, hidden beneath a troubled exterior. He had to peel away her layers of hurt, bit by bit. In a way, she was very much like him. The pain she carried around with her seemed to preoccupy her, consume her, just like his. She was crying silently…doomed to live a life of self-pity and loneliness. Was that what he was doing hanging onto Rose?

"Why are you so quiet?" Loretta pierced the silence with her question. "Don't tell me you're praying right now."

Harvey didn't answer. His heart just ached.

"I did a good job with the stitches didn't I?"

"What?"

"You must be tired…Should we sit?"

"No. I'm fine."

Loretta scowled sideways at him and stopped talking. The woman was a trooper really. She witnessed the shooting of her own teenage son, along with dozens of other people, and still managed to make it through herself. Her husband disserted her, her children don't speak to her, and still she gets out of bed every morning. That's a trooper, albeit a confused, angry trooper, but a trooper none-the-less. That's more than he can say for himself. As wrong as it is, at least Loretta attempted to fight her son's attacker. *Her* enemy was visible. Harvey on the other hand, couldn't even see his wife's assassin. Cancer just crept up on her like a thief in the night.

Harvey still couldn't believe she had managed to lure all these people she considered her enemies, to this place in the middle of nowhere. It was preposterous, yet brilliant at the same time. If it weren't sinfully wrong and completely unethical, not to mention premeditated murder she was planning, she would have gotten the Nobel Prize just for the idea. But it *was* wrong, and he was going to make sure she would never get a chance to carry it through. It was just a delusional plan made up by a heartsick woman anyway. He was convinced that she really *didn't* want to do it. *Lord please...change her heart. And while you're at it, maybe you could work on mine a bit too.*

Harvey's stitches pulled against his heavy gut bandaged in layers of gauze like a paper-Mache piñata at a birthday party. It weighed him down, not to mention the backpack that he carried with supplies. Loretta carried a pack too, except it wasn't as full. He wanted to be the man and carry the heavier load, but now he was thinking twice about his chauvinist decision. The light-headed feeling he was experiencing, was not going away. "I need to sit."

"I told you," Loretta nagged. "I'm going to end up carrying you, aren't I?"

Harvey collapsed his knees to the sandy shore while Loretta doted over him. She took off his hiking boots exposing the mismatched socks he had found in the plane.

"Just relax. I'll give you something to eat with a drink of water. You need to get your blood sugar back up. By the way, how are the stitches holding out?"

"I could tell you if you wouldn't have bandaged me up like a mummy."

"I told you I wasn't a nurse. I did the best I could."

Harvey wiped his sweaty brow with his orange sleeve. "I'm sorry. I just don't feel very well," he said in between sips of water he chugged from a round black metal canvas-covered canteen with a long strap like a purse. "Water helps."

Loretta fumbled through her backpack and took out a pudding cup. She peeled back the lid and smiled. "Hope you like vanilla? I even have a spoon for you. It's plastic but it'll do."

"You're a kind lady," he said, "I can tell you were a good mother."

"*I* think I was a good mother but I don't think my kids think that."

"Sure, they do. They probably remember every little thing you did for them."

"I hope they do. I use to do *everything* for them, and they needed so much. My youngest daughter Tammy had these awful nosebleeds starting in grade five. Her class took a trip to a swimming pool where one of her classmates kicked her in the nose, and from then on, the nosebleeds became a chronic problem even now, poor thing. Her nose poured blood something awful. Tammy use to cry every time. She was so scared; she'd cry "Mommy" even though she was a teenager. She'd hunch over the open toilet, blood dripping into the bowl. I use to make her hold a frozen ice-pack across the bridge of her nose with one hand while pinching the top of her nose with the other. I would do it for her when she was younger, but I started making her do it by herself when she got older. She had to learn to do it for herself."

"See, I was right," Harvey smiled while spooning a mouthful of creamy vanilla pudding into his mouth. "I knew you were a good mother."

"My son Jeremy…he was the baby, he would put on a big show all the time. He'd stomp his feet to get his way, and of course I always put a stop to it. Bob, my husband, on the other hand thought it was cute. I argued with him until I was blue in the face."

"I bet you did," Harvey interrupted, unable to hold himself back from that one. He chuckled, enjoying the stories she told, wishing he and Rose would have been able to have kids so he could have some stories of his own to tell. Cancer robbed them of that joy. Rose never knew why she was infertile until the cancer showed up years later.

Loretta mused at his teasing. "Yes...I *did* argue, and I'm proud of it. I tried to knock some sense into the man's thick scull. Jeremy's temper tantrums might have been cute up to two years old, though *I* never thought so, but after that...Well, just put it this way: A teenager with a temper tantrum is *not* a good thing."

Harvey could tell the woman was trying to hold back her emotions. She looked as though she was about to cry. "Do you miss him...your son I mean?"

Loretta started to sob. "Yes, I do...But I didn't mean to cry. I'm sorry. I don't know why I'm crying like this. You'd think I bawled enough to fill a river already. It's been six months and I'm still weepy."

"Don't apologize, just listen to your heart, it's obviously not finished grieving yet. Mine still hasn't finished and it's been five years. I don't think we ever get finished grieving. It just mutates into a lesser form."

"Well I'd take that lesser form right about now," Loretta sniffled, "if it didn't mean I'd forget about my boy. I'm trying to keep him in my head. You know, picture him like he was. Sometimes I even forget what he looks like, his smell, the sound of his voice. It scares me. I feel like I'm losing him all over again...in my mind. Or maybe I'm just losing my mind."

Harvey knew that feeling well. It was a hard one to shake. He still hadn't mastered it very well. "You're not losing your mind. *I* feel the same way. It's hard *not* to after you've lost someone you loved.

I guess the way I handle it is to pray when I'm feeling like that. I can honestly say God has helped me through every single low point in my life. When I ask Him for comfort, He always comes through for me no matter what."

Harvey could see Loretta struggling with what he just said. He wished there was a way he could comfort her. He could try, but the one she needed comfort from was God. *"Lord...help her open up her heart to you."*

"Tell me something then Harvey. Why does God play favorites?"

"He *doesn't*."

"Then why does he comfort *you*, and not *me*? When I needed Him the most, He wasn't there. Oh, I prayed too, don't get me wrong. I asked the Lord to save Jeremy from getting shot...but he ignored me. How can you justify that kind of prejudicial behaviour? It's cold and cruel...and I don't want to serve a God who could be so heartless."

Harvey rubbed his brow. "Don't you think I prayed for Rose to get better? I prayed every morning and every evening on my knees until they were as red as tomatoes. At one point, I thought if I believed hard enough, I would surely receive what I asked for. I tried that. I went around like a naïve fool pretending Rose would recover. She didn't get any better she actually got worse. I couldn't understand why."

"I started getting mad at God. Rose could see my attitude changing. I became bitter and sad. I didn't want to pray with her. I made excuses not to go to church."

Tears started streaming down Harvey's face now.

"Your situation was different."

"*No,* it wasn't Loretta. My wife died, it took a while, but she still died. There was absolutely nothing I could do to stop it. Your son died, it didn't take more than a few minutes, but he still died. There was absolutely nothing *you* could do to stop it. The only difference is the time it took to snuff them out."

"Stop it Harvey. I don't want to hear anymore," Loretta shouted, covering her ears like an insolent child."

Harvey reached over and pulled her hands off her ears. The two of them struggled with each other until Harvey finally pulled her to him in a soft loving embrace. She fought it for a moment, stiffening her body against his arms, and then she gave in. She sobbed into his chest, muffling her moans. "It's not fair...It's just not fair."

"I know dear. *I know.* But God didn't say it would be fair. The Bible says, *"Trust the Lord with all your heart and lean not on your own understanding; in all your ways acknowledge him, and he will make your paths straight."*

"I trusted him to help me deal with Rose's death, and he did. When I needed encouragement, He sent others my way to see that I got it. He comforted me with his words too every time I asked. Jesus promised me He'd give rest to my weary soul. He said, *"Come to me all you who are heavy laden and I will give you rest."* He's a man of His word Loretta. He truly is. There's no if, ands, or buts, about it."

"I didn't understand at first, but Rose told me that God would heal her even on her deathbed. Do you know how crazy that made me? I couldn't figure it out. I thought there was only one way to heal a person. I was wrong. In fact, there's a lot of things we don't know a bout God, many we're not meant to understand. But comfort…help… strength…those are the things God wants us to know, to experience, to understand. I have, and you can *too* Loretta if you would only ask. Jesus said, *"Ask and it will be given you; seek and you will find; knock and the door will be opened to you."*

"The door is open to you now Loretta. What are you going to do?"

Harvey held Loretta in silence for a few minutes while she sniffled, wiping her nose with her rolled up orange sleeve. "You sound like an old preacher Harvey. For Pete sake, I don't know what I'm going to do."

"Knock."

"I can't."

"Why?"

At that moment, Harvey realized as much as he pushed, she was not ready. If her heart were to change, if she was going to knock, it would have to be on her own accord. At least he had led her to the door of reconciliation with God. Opening it was up to her. Only the Lord could move the stubborn woman now. "That's all I can do God; the rest is up to you."

Chapter 36

Brian woke up on a bony queen size bed. His head lay face down in a musty pea- green and yellow striped pillowcase; he was apparently still under the covers. He rolled to the side, lifting one hand from beneath the worn sheets, then the other. White gauze bandages covered each wrist individually. He had nothing on but a t-shirt and boxers.

Suddenly a strange voice mumbled something to him from the corner of the bedroom. For a moment, he thought he was dreaming. The voice sounded like his wife Jenny. She probably woke up early, wanted to read like usual.

"Can't sleep?" he asked, trying to focus his eyes in her direction.

The voice said something unrecognizable, frustrating him, so he plopped his weary head back down into his pillow.

Jenny was a good wife, putting up with his work schedule. Sometimes he'd be out all night and sleep all day. Yes, he was a lucky man to have a wife as tolerant as she was. She'd take care of their son Patrick, the house, her job *and* him without much of a fuss.

She was a nurse and a good one too. Maybe he was at the hospital and had an accident of something. Maybe she was taking care of *him* now. But if that *was* the case and his wife *was* at work, how could that be? Jenny worked at the morgue.

Suddenly, Brian jolted upright in bed. *No. I am not dead.* Finally, his eyes began to focus. In the corner of the room sat a husky redheaded woman. It wasn't Jenny at all. It *definitely* wasn't his petite raven-haired wife.

"Well, good morning sleeping beauty. Or should I say good afternoon," the woman spoke with a deep teasing tone.

"Where am I?"

"Shooting Star Lodge...still."

Then, as if all Brian's senses came back at once, he flew off the bed to stand.

"Easy!" the woman warned, standing up and moving toward him, then, catching him as he warbled back down to the bed. "You lost a lot of blood. The cuts are just superficial but you sure bled out. I bandaged them up pretty good. My name is Vicki by the way."

"Thanks Vicki."

"You a cop?"

"R.C.M.P actually."

Brian observed the husky woman. He saw visible bruises and lacerations across her face. Her clothes looked freshly changed as if she just put them on. Her blue t-shirt read "Shooting Star Lodge" on the front of it. She wore a ratty old pair of men's U of S Husky shorts that didn't look like hers. "Are you alright ma'am?"

"Don't I look *purdy*?" she said, showing off her ensemble, apparently trying to make light of the situation. "This was the only thing I could find that fit. I got some new pants for you too. They're at the end of the bed. I hope that's okay. Your uniform was covered in blood and dirt."

"I appreciate it," Brian said, easing off the bed again slowly this time, reaching for his pants, shimmying them on overtop his boxers. "What happened here?"

"What do you remember?"

"I remember getting taped up by somebody."

"Well that somebody is George and his friend Leon. They're some scumbags my sister got mixed up with. They think she has something of theirs and they took her with them this morning to find it. Ruby promised to give them what they want as long as they didn't hurt us and promised to let us clean up and have something to eat. They kept their end of the bargain so far except, of course, they locked us in this bedroom. And don't bother trying the window, as you can see, they boarded it up."

Brian scratched his head. "What do they think your sister has?"

"Her name is Ruby."

"Okay…What do they think Ruby has?"

"Beats me."

Brian tried to make sense of the whole thing. It all seemed bizarre. "I came here looking for a Larry Murphy. He owns this place. Do you know him?"

"Never heard of him."

"Well, why are *you* here?"

"That would be a very long story."

Brian mused at the woman's gruff exterior. Her bedraggled red hair paled her freckled skin as it pulled unevenly into a frizzy ponytail. Her masculine arms and legs contradicted her feminine face, even though she did have a double chin. It made him chuckle a bit. Her mannerisms seemed…almost forced, as if she were putting on an act for him or something. It was strange. Even her voice was louder than it had to be. Maybe she thought he was deaf.

"Well, it appears I have time for a long story," he smirked. "How about you start from the beginning?"

~~~

Grayling flexed his loathsome hairy toes, nails yellow and gnarly. "Well, it looks like I didn't burn the *old boys* after all. What do you think Pipata?"

Pip didn't know what it *was* about his friend Grayling, but he always seemed to make him forget about his problems. He had a way of turning everything into a joke, even those ugly feet of his. "I think you're *crazy* Grayling...but in a *good* way."

"Crazy?" he pouted making a funny face. "I give you my special *hand-picked* tea and you think Grayling is a crazy man."

"I said in a *good* way."

"I know what you said you *Little Caribou*," the jovial man grinned, teasing him through his yellow rotted teeth, reminding Pip where he got that saying from in the first place. Grayling started calling him Little Caribou shortly after his parents died. He'd tease him and tell him he reminded him of the baby fawns that ran beside the mother caribou. They had big ears that jetted out to the sides, just as he did.

Grayling slipped his mukluk back on his foot and tied it up. He reached for a jar on the kitchen counter beside them and opened the jar, taking a whiff of the contents. "I can forgive you for calling me crazy if you take a stick of my jerky. It ain't too old yet. Sort of like me."

Pip slipped his narrow brown hand into the jar as if he were sneaking candy. He clenched his teeth *hard* against the leathery piece trying to take a bite out of it. For some reason he never could chew through the stuff very well, but he sure tried.

"So," Grayling smiled, crewing the jerky as well, "You have some trouble, or did you just bring the gun to give old Grayling a heart attack?"

Pip didn't know what to say. He had almost forgotten his reasons for coming over...Almost. Still, somewhere deep in the pit of his stomach, grew a sick feeling. He knew he had to tell. If he didn't, Grayling would surely drag it out of him.

"I...need your help," Pip whispered.

"Speak up boy; old Grayling don't hear so good you know."

Pip gulped hard and repeated what he said. "I need your help...Uncle Leon..."

Then with eyes as big as the moon, he slapped the table and rose to his feet, "Say no more my boy...Just lead the way."

~~~~

Ruby lay in the familiar deep earthy cavern once again.

When George, Leon, and Eddie realized where she had put the diamonds, they made her go down to fetch them. George was the one who pushed her.

"Make sure you get them all babe," George giggled like a child. "Throw both cases up to us and we'll make sure your friends don't get hurt."

They snickered and laughed above, frustrating her, making her doubt their word. She knew not to trust them, but she had no choice. She had to comply. When she threw the two diamond cases up to them, and called for them to get her out, nothing but silence answered her back.

Ruby shouted one last time, "Come on you guys, you have the cases, now you promised to get me out of here!"

Then...the snickering returned. What were they doing?

Seconds passed.

Suddenly…a gunshot rang out. "How do you like that sweet thing?" George shouted down the hole. "You know I don't keep promises babe, besides, nobody tries to steal from *me*," he spit. "You crossed the line when you did that."

"What can I say…even Leon and Eddie agree with me. We can't let you out. What kind of example would that be? Before you know it…everyone would think they could steal from me. I can't do business that way," he burst out with a giggle, snickering along with his friends like schoolyard bullies. "No…I'm sorry babe, I don't play favorites. You'll just have to pay like everyone else."

Without warning, George and Leon lowered their heads into the opening, aiming their weapons into what she now knew was her very own grave. *God…Oh God!*

Shots penetrated down the dank smelly tomb…piercing her, maiming her slumping perforated body…until finally… she gasped her final breath…collapsing to the dust where once she came.

Chapter 37

Another storm was about to roll in. Loretta could tell. The distant cumulous clouds burst with all shades of greys and blacks mixed together with white puffy tones. It reminded her of an atomic bomb going off...sort of like her emotions these days.

Harvey didn't have a chance against her moodiness. Poor man. She was still angry with him for his continual sanctimonious nagging, she was glad he was snoozing on the beach. She didn't know how much more she could take of his preaching.

The man meant well, he even cared a great deal more than she realized. It was mutual, yet she just couldn't bring herself to do what he was asking.

Loretta grabbed her backpack and hauled it away from Harvey. She needed some time alone. Going for a short walk without the man was just what she needed; maybe it would even give her a heads up on where they were.

Digging deep in her backpack, she finally found the pocket-knife she put in there. She'd found it in the plane along with the medical supplies. It would do in place of scissors. She had to cut the long sleeves and legs off on her overalls before she took one more step. Her body drenched with sweat, and she was starting to attract swarms of mosquitoes and black-flies already. There was no more putting it off.

With the knife, she ripped away the rank orange fabric from around her knees, discarding the knife and tearing it more that cutting it. She threw the pieces behind her and picked up the knife again, this time going for the fabric at her elbows.

Finally, when she was done, her fleshy white legs danced like pale jiggling drumsticks all the way from her knees to her brown cougar hiking boots. *What a beauty queen.* If she didn't know any better, she'd think she was in some kind of punk-rock fashion show with her matching spiky orange hair to boot.

But she sure felt better.

The last time she had a chance to create an outfit was for her daughter Trudy's graduation a few years ago. Normally she wasn't a seamstress, though she knew how to use a sewing machine. Bob had told Trudy he couldn't afford to buy her a dress from the store because as he put it, "Your mother spent too much money on her lousy drawing business, and now we can't afford the dress." Bob became furious and literally ordered Loretta to sew the thing. He yelled at her in a complete fit of rage. "Since it's your fault Trudy can't get the dress she wants...*you're* going to save me money and *make* it."

But she played him at his own game.

The next day she took Trudy to FabricWorld and charged the most expensive rose chiffon and bridal satin that she could find, to his credit card. Trudy was overjoyed with the pattern they picked and the two of them worked on it every day together until it was finished, a beautiful one-of-a-kind grad gown that turned out to be the talk of the town.

Yes, Loretta knew how to turn lemons into lemonade all right, just like now. Jeremy's death had been the worst kind of lemons. It took her a while to turn the tables on that situation, but she did it. She managed to lure everyone out here, make the bad guys pay. She refused to give up on her plan. There had to be a way to make it work still. After all, giving up was not in her vocabulary. Her strong will was what kept her going.

Harvey meant well in telling her she needed to ask God for help. But she'd gotten this far without Him. If she tried hard enough, she could still pull it off somehow. For now though, she'd play it safe, let Harvey think she was softening. Then…at the right moment, she'd do it…kill George and everyone else who had a part in Jeremy's death.

Yes, the door was definitely ready for her to open, but not the one Harvey meant. She'd open her *own* door…It was the only one she trusted.

~~~~

By the time Pip had told Grayling the entire story; he realized they were almost back at Grandfathers. He hadn't expected him to take him in the wrong direction.

"But Grayling, I don't want to stay here."

"It's safer for you, Little Caribou. I'll speak to your grandfather. It's about time we made up with each other anyway. We'll figure out a plan. But you will *not* be coming with us to the *Shooting Star*; you'll stay right here and wait for us. Do you here me?"

Pip frowned, "Yes Grayling."

~~~~

Harvey was back in the hospital room with his wife Rose, reliving the same dream that both haunted and comforted him for the past five years. He knew better than to rehash it all over the again. But telling Loretta about Rose seemed to give his memory the unwanted permission to play it again.

"I love you dear," he whispered softly into her ear while holding her hand. Tears gently rolled down his cheeks as they had for months now with her laying in the same modern hospital bed with fancy electric controls. He was sick of looking at the thing.

"It won't be long now," the doctors said. The family was on their way. Her sister and brother-in-law were flying in from Edmonton this afternoon and soon he wouldn't be alone with his Rose anymore.

It was bittersweet.

Selfishly he wanted these last few hours to himself. Nobody knew her like he did anyway. Why couldn't they just stay away? Why couldn't they let him grieve in peace? Why did he and Rose have to go through this torture at all?

If God had only answered Harvey's prayers, none of this would be happening. *Why God? Why her?*

Harvey couldn't understand anything anymore. Of all the people in the world, why did Rose have to be the one with cancer? He knew so many others that cheated death and they weren't even worthy. So often, before he retired from the police force, he saw drug addicts, child abusers, and murderers...still given a chance to live. They didn't deserve it. Why didn't God take *them*?

Rose lived up to her name. Her sweet gentle spirit drew people to her. She could do wonders with her smile. It was remarkable. Even bedridden with cancer in the hospital, she comforted those beside her. She cheered them up, encouraged them, and even spoke of her faithful loving God to them.

Harvey sobbed into the blanket rumpled beside her as she slept like a living sunken-eyed corpse. *Why are you taking such a wonderful woman God?*

Then, while Rose lay beside him, she squeezed his hand without opening her eyes. Softly she spoke to him for the last time that day, "Don't be angry my love. God has *not* forsaken us. He promised to make me better, and He will."

She smacked her dry lips for a moment while Harvey sobbed some more. She squeezed his hand again and continued. "First…the Lord must transfer me to a better facility," she laboured her breathing, sounding like a delusional woman. "He's already prepared a place for me there. It's the only recovery center that specializes in fixing my kind of pain. The *best* physician is there. He knows *all* things and *never* makes mistakes."

"No Rose…don't"

"*Hush* my love and listen to me now. I don't have much time left," she whispered as she tried to muster up enough breath to continue. "We can't be together there my dear, but we *will* see each other again. Don't cry. I will *finally* be free of this cancer."

Then, as she opened her eyes and turned her frail head toward him, she squeezed his hand and smiled, "Until we meet again…*my love.*"

The monitor hummed death.

"*No!*" Harvey shouted, waking up from his nightmare. The beach was cold on his back. His face burned hot with tears. A looming thunderstorm rumbled in the distance, reflecting the turmoil that twisted in his heart.

He laboured against the stitches in his side as he eased to a sitting position. The sun blurred his vision preventing him from seeing what was hovering over him, perched on a large rock above. He put his hand over his brow and squinted to see.

Was it his *Rose*? Had she come back for him? Maybe this was it. Maybe they could finally be together again.

Excited, he sat up further, smiling like an eager child. "Rose?" he whispered, sticking out his hand to grasps hers. He focused his eyes to make sure he wasn't still dreaming. Instead, he heard something shocking. It *wasn't* Rose at all.

There…right in front of his eyes, an evil chameleon morphed its ugly shape into a threatening mangy timber wolf…growling, bearing its sabre-toothed fangs.

Chapter 38

Grayling really wasn't welcome at Grandfathers' that was for sure. Pip could see the angry look in his eyes the moment he opened the front door. The old man immediately rose from the table, kicked the chair over, crossed his arms in front of his chest, and stubbornly ordered Grayling to leave.

"No!" he said. "I will not leave this time old man. It's been too long."

Pip looked back and forth between Grandfather and Grayling. They reminded him of two headstrong bucks defending their territory.

"This is my home," Grandfather shouted, "and I want you to leave!"

Pip propped the gun against the wall by the door where he had taken it from, and stood there inert, unable to move. Would they both fight the same way his Uncle Leon and Grandfather did? Pip hoped not. He didn't want to be in the middle of it. Why couldn't they get along? Why couldn't people just be happy for once?

Grayling didn't back off. Instead, he lowered his own gun from his shoulder, propped it against the wall, and closed the front door, edging further into the kitchen ignoring Grandfather's temper. "We need to talk," Grayling insisted. "I don't want to fight with you Donald. Actually, it never even crossed my mind to have a fistfight with you. I couldn't even if I tried. These old bones don't move as fast as they use to."

"I don't want to talk to *you*!" Grandfather shouted again.

"Grandfather, *please*!" Pip butt in hoping he could convince him. "It's important. You have to listen. It's about Uncle Leon." *Oops.*

Before he realized it, Pip had spilled the beans. Grayling told him *not* to tell his grandfather anything about Uncle Leon until he had a chance to clear the air between the two of them, then he'd tell him what was going on at the *Shooting Star*. Sometimes Pip wished he had a zipper on his mouth so he could control his tongue better. No matter how badly he wanted to keep his mouth shut, it never failed. The first thing he always seemed to do was open it. Now, he had ruined everything.

Grayling scowled, "Pip...Why don't you go and find your brothers. Your grandfather and I have to talk in private." Grandfather gave him a scowl as well.

Why was he always the one to blame? Every time something went wrong, he would either feel responsible or be told by his brothers that it was his fault. He never seemed to do anything right. Not even this.

"I'm going," Pip grumbled, hanging his head down as he left the cabin, gently closing the door into the mid-afternoon overcast. The rumble in the sky meant he'd have to find his brothers quickly before the downpour.

~~~~

Brian stood on top of the veneer dresser kicking at the boarded-up window. Vicki wondered if he would ever manage to loosen them. He'd been at it now for half an hour and it didn't look like he was making any progress.

Frustrated with him, she slammed her hand down on the dresser, unable to be patient any longer. "Let me try!" she insisted. The guy might be an R.C.M.P officer but he sure wasn't very strong. He had smashed the window with a chair, then thought of moving the dresser over to the window and standing on top of it, but he sure didn't have the strength to carry out his plan. He was already fatigued.

"I guess I *better* stop for a while," he said, puffing from exhaustion. "I'm feeling a little light-headed again.

"Get off the dresser," she ordered. "My legs are bigger than yours. You have to kind of kick at an angle."

Of course, Vicki knew exactly how it was supposing to be done. She hadn't spent two years taking kickboxing lessons for nothing. At first, she watched him be the *cop*, the big shot macho man, the big hero. Now she'd show him how to do it right. Why was it men had to always be the rescuers? She was definitely capable of doing it.

Brian came down from the dresser to watch and direct her. "Okay," he said, annoying her with his know-it-all commands. "Don't turn your foot like that."

"Shut up already," Vicki boiled. "I don't need you to tell me what to do."

At that moment, she kicked the boards off the window frame in only three boots. The blinding daylight glared through at them, filling the room with a breezy warm wind.

"I told you," she boasted. "Why do you men think you can do *everything*?

"Let's just get out of here. Okay?"

The two of them wiggled out of the bedroom window, and jumped to the grass below. Brian held out his hand to grab Vicki's hand. "Come on," he said. "Let's get to those trees over there. Then we'll figure out what to do next."

Vicki pushed his hand away. "I don't need your hand. I'm not some kind of wimpy female you know."

"Suit yourself."

The two of them ran to a rock with painted pictures on the side, trees and bushes concealing both of them. "We have to get back to my plane," Brian whispered, puffing from exhaustion. "I can radio for help."

"There's a four-wheeler somewhere," Vicki said, panting.

"I know…Did they take it?"

"No, they went on foot with my sister. But…I'm not leaving without her. Besides, when they come back and find us gone, what do you think they're going to do to Ruby? She promised to co-operate with them in exchange for *our* safety and co-operation. If we break that…we're all dead."

"Do you actually think these guys will keep their word?"

"No. But what choice do we have?"

"Oh, come on Vicki…You always have a choice. You don't seem like the naïve type to me…you're too bull-headed for that."

"I'll take that as a compliment…but I'm still not leaving without my sister. We find *her* first."

"Alright then…Let's go."

~~~~

By the time Loretta heard the animal growling, she was too far away to do anything about it. The wolf hovered over Harvey like a buzzard about to eat its prey. She couldn't see the man but she knew where she left him. If she could only throw a rock that far, she might be able to distract the wolf. But if she did that, the thing might come after *her* instead, and then what would she do?

Loretta didn't have much time to think. If Harvey were one of her children…if it were Jeremy, she would risk her life. Harvey didn't mean as much as her children did to her, yet, her heart still pounded for him just the same. She would do it.

Within seconds, she found a rock and tossed it toward the wolf…It wasn't nearly far enough. She found another one and tried again. This time the animal turned its mangy head and saw her. He appeared torn between going for Harvey or Loretta.

"Yaaah!" she shouted at the thing to coax it away from Harvey.

It cocked its head and charged.

When Loretta realized it was now going after *her*, she took off toward the forest, sprinting as fast as her legs could carry her. The tree line was only a few feet away, but she had her eye on the wolf instead. The thing came charging at her faster than she anticipated it would. *Jesus…Help me!*

Suddenly, it jumped her from behind, sending her scuffling down to the ground. The beast went for her neck, sinking his teeth deep into her fleshy white skin.

Loretta screamed horrifically as the animal continued to maul her. *"Jesus!"* she bawled in terror. *"Save me!"*

Seconds went by, feeling like hours with the beast on top of her back as she lay face down in the dirt. It ravaged her body, growling, moaning, as it tried to rip her apart.

Then…out of nowhere, one solitary shot rang out.

Chapter 39

The Northern bush was the only home Pip had ever known, and he loved it. He couldn't imagine living anywhere else. His brothers always talked of moving south to the big cities, maybe Saskatoon or Regina, but not him.

His older brother had a friend named Nigel who hitchhiked to Saskatoon a few years back. He received letters from him for the first little while. The guy told him he tried to find a job, but he said nobody wanted to hire an Indian. His last letter said that he had found the perfect job. All he had to do was sell a few things for some people. There was supposed to be big money in it. Then one day, his brother was shocked to see Nigel on the news, arrested for drug trafficking, headed straight for the P.A Penitentiary.

Pip realized then, that the city was no place for *him*. Everyone that went there seemed to fall into drugs and gangs just like Uncle Leon. Grandfather swore the big *monsters* of the south would never get to *his* grandsons.

Pip thought about that for a while. There seemed to be monsters everywhere, the ones that lived in Deep Bay, and the ones that lived in the cities. They had all soiled his land and invaded his home. They had come to kill the Caribou and he was powerless to stop them. Grayling said so himself. He couldn't come along. And there was no sense in hoping Grandfather would let him come either.

His job was to find his brothers. He didn't want to, but he'd look for them anyway. He loved them. Brothers were supposed to love each other, but he didn't have much respect for them. Why should he? They didn't respect *him*. They just teased him, and made him the brunt of their stupid jokes. He actually hoped he *wouldn't* find them.

Suddenly, Pip heard a shot. It startled him, as he turned toward the sound, running full steam the way a warrior should in a moment of need. A warrior is always prepared to fight a battle. Soon he would hear the drums. Grayling was going to be proud of him, so was Grandfather. They would be sorry they never let him come along.

Nearing the edge of the forest, Pip could finally see through the trees. He had an energetic smile on his face as he anticipated the battle he would soon fight. Then as he slowed, heaving his chest to take a breath, he hovered behind a large pine tree and observed the scene.

It was his brothers. *Great!*

Disappointment washed his once excited face to a sombre frown as he saw them both standing over a dead wolf, dancing around while a woman sobbed beside it. He'd seen her before, and he'd seen the fat man too.

~~~

"I *can't* stop crying," Loretta wailed. "He almost killed me!"

"But you're okay now dear," Harvey said, trying to sooth the woman. It was a miracle. Most people don't survive that kind of attack. Blood covered her neck, but that was it. He checked the wound and it wasn't very deep at all. At least it didn't look like the wolf hit any major arteries.

Loretta continued to bawl. She sat there on her knees, sobbing into her soiled hands. *"I can't believe it,"* she wailed, heaving her shoulders, completely distraught.

The two Indian boys gave her strange glances as they kicked at the dead wolf. They were obviously uncomfortable with the woman's endless crying fit.

"Maybe I should use some of the bandages you put on my wound Loretta," he told her, saying anything to calm her down. "I have plenty. You'll be as good as new."

Harvey hoped his words would sooth her, but they didn't. She just wailed even more. "You're okay dear," he said again, trying to console her. He put her arms around her and held her tightly, but even that didn't stop the woman's dither.

"You don't understand. I'm okay!" Loretta cried even harder into Harvey's shoulder. "I can't believe it. *He* helped me."

"Yes...you were lucky these two came along when they did."

"No!" She sobbed again, this time heaving her entire body while Harvey held her tight. "You don't understand. *He* was listening to me. I didn't think He would, but He did Harvey. You were right. I never thought it was possible. Why would He save *me*?"

Harvey mused at her for a moment. If she was talking about what he hoped she was talking about, it all made sense. "Did you pray dear?"

"*I...I did*!" she wailed at the top of her lungs, blubbering like a baby.

"Well...I'll be!"

Harvey tried to calm the emotional woman down. He wiped streams of tears from her cheeks with his hand, shushing her as he grinned much too wildly. It was almost comical. The poor woman was so overwrought she didn't know what to do with herself.

"I told you all you had to do was ask," he teased, continuing to smile, trying his hardest not to burst out with laughter. It really wasn't funny. The woman had made a difficult breakthrough. Her guard was completely down. Harvey had never seen her like this before. She looked so vulnerable, so weak, yet something about the whole situation just made Harvey grin.

"Why didn't God hear me when I asked him to save *Jeremy*?" Loretta squealed, still bawling like a child.

Turning more serious now, and realizing her question was valid; Harvey tried to answer her as best he could. "I don't know dear. Sometimes...I guess God says *no*." He tried not to say too much. He didn't have all the answers, and she was apparently now on an unstoppable emotional rollercoaster. He'd have to tread softly.

"Don't give me that garbage. I want to know why God didn't save my son when I asked him too. Why would he save *me* from a wolf, but not save my sweet son when he needed protecting? I can't take it! *I AM SO ANGRY! WHERE WERE YOU GOD?*"

Silence echoed the heavens.

The woman could hardly breathe. Her nose was stuffy and dripping, her chest heaved until her crying sounded choppy and winded. The two teenage Indian boys must have thought there was something wrong with her. They started dragging the wolf down the beach probably trying to get as far away from her as they could.

Harvey thought the best thing to do was to keep his mouth shut. He couldn't believe how a situation could deteriorate that quickly. *Jesus help her.*

Thunder rumbled in the sombre sky as sprinkles of rain began to drizzle down on the two of them. "We have to follow those two boys dear. It's starting to rain."

Loretta was completely silent now. Her lethargic body just hung there, clutching to Harvey's shoulders as they both sat on the damp grassy reeds. Harvey stroked Loretta's dishevelled orange hairdo with his clumsy hand. He inspected her neck that appeared to have stopped bleeding already. At least *that* was promising.

Thunder rumbled again, suddenly sending torrents of rain pelting down on their weary heads. Still Loretta didn't move. He would carry her if he were physically able. "Come on sweetheart. We have to move," he said, attempting to stand, swinging both backpacks over his one shoulder and reaching his other to help her get up.

Without a word, Loretta laboured to stand, fingering her raw wounded neck in the pouring rain. As they started to walk, hand in hand, they didn't say a word to each other. They let the rain drench them, sooth them, not bothering to hurry even with the cracking thunder. It was almost as if Loretta had depleted her energy source. She slowly inched along like a tortoise, oblivious to everything else.

Harvey tightly gripped the distraught woman's trembling hand. Whether she knew it or not, she had opened the door. It wasn't easy. Her door was heavy, confusing, and painful, but she opened it anyway. Sometimes opening it is a risk in itself. We don't know what we'll find on the other side. Harvey knew that feeling well. But he also knew God's promises: "Behold, I stand at the door and knock: if any man hears my voice, and open the door, I will come in to him, and will sup with him, and he with me."

Chapter 40

Killing Ruby was an incredible high, but not higher than George was right now. He, Leon, and Eddie had snorted the cocaine Leon brought with him to celebrate their riches. It would only be a matter of time now until they could get out of there. Then they would take the diamonds to the diamond cutter and sell them for more money than he ever imagined. He could hardly wait.

His brilliant plan hadn't gone over so well. He didn't expect Leon to react the way he did when he told him what he wanted to do with the people at the lodge. Leon told him to forget it. He told him that the cop might have called in for help before they trashed his radio, so they had to get out of there as soon as possible. Too bad, his plan to torture them and set them on fire inside the lodge with a suicide note that included confessions of all their heists to make people think George Oxford William's and his gang was dead, really would have been a remarkable one-of-a-kind plan. Oh well, another time, another place. *Patience is a virtue.*

Luckily, Leon stole the old man's keys to that ugly floatplane of his or they'd be stuck. The pilot that dropped Leon off probably couldn't come back to pick them up until next week sometime. If he hadn't crashed the other plane, he wouldn't have to fly that piece of junk, but they sure couldn't use the Mounty's plane. Leon was right; they'd stick out like a sore thumb with that R.C.M.P logo on the side. The paint alone would give them away.

As soon as the storm cleared up, they could head back to the lodge and take the four-wheeler out to the plane. In the mean time, he'd enjoy another snort of coke, he decided, grinning to himself, blurry eyed and spacey. He felt as young as a twenty-year-old again, and he knew what he was going to do even though Leon didn't agree. He would kill them anyway just for the heck of it. He'd do it fast, before the three of them headed out on the four-wheeler. Why not? It would be such a hoot.

George leaned against the damp wall inside the shabby hunter's shack where he, Leon, and Eddie came to get high. He daydreamed of all the magnificent ways he could kill the two they left behind at the lodge. He would keep his eyes out for that freak Loretta too. Leon didn't know about her yet. He'd keep that to himself for now. She was all *his*. Her death was going to be gruesome and painful whether he found her now or later on after she returns home to Chicago and he hunts her down like a dog.

~~~~

The storm wasn't as bad as the last one but at least they could take shelter in a cabin this time. The two teenagers who shot the wolf reluctantly let them in when they knocked on the door in the pouring rain.

The cabin appeared dark and rustic, but well lived in. Furs hung on the paneling walls and decorated the old wooden floors. Except for a broken TV, the place appeared to have modern conveniences like a DVD player, Game Cube, and a state-of-the-art Apple computer, giving Harvey the assumption that the boys probably didn't live here alone.

"Where are your parents?" Harvey asked the two boys who rummaged through the dark putrid smelling refrigerator and barely spoke a word to them.

"We don't have any," the taller boy spoke up. "Grandfather is out."

"Perhaps your grandfather has some bandages for this woman's neck...and we could use a decent meal if it's not much trouble."

Then, as if Harvey had offended him, the tall boy slapped some bannock down on the table and gave them both a disgusted glare. The shorter one grabbed some old white sheets and plopped them on the table in a heap. "That's all we have," he said. "Grandfather doesn't like strangers so you have to go."

The two boys co-ordinated their baited glances.

"Thank you for shooting the wolf," Loretta all of a sudden piped up, surprising Harvey that she had finally come out of her trance and joined the conversation. The older boy grunted, "We were tracking it anyway," as he ripped his teeth into an oversize piece of bannock. "When the rain stops you have to go."

Harvey washed the blood off Loretta's neck as she chewed the dry bannock. He surveyed the expanse of her wound and ripped strips of cloth from the sheet, wrapping it around her neck. He wished she hadn't used up all the supplies on him, though he still seriously thought of taking some bandages off his wound and putting them on hers. The sheets were clean though, so he didn't have a problem using them.

"Most of the bite marks are okay dear, but there *is* one here that should have stitches," Harvey said. "I have another sterile needle, and some fishing line left in my pack. Do you want stitches Loretta?"

"*No!*"

"Didn't think so."

For now, he would just bandage the wound as best as he could. Loretta had calmed down somewhat, but he didn't want to get her started again. Perhaps stitches weren't the best idea after all.

"Do you have a radio or a phone?" Harvey asked the boys while tying the last bandage around Loretta's neck, feeling the cabin shudder with another peal of thunder.

"We don't have any power," the older boy grumbled.

"We use to, but someone cut the lines," the younger boy blurted out, annoying his brother. "It's not fixed yet."

"Shut up dweeb," the older one scolded. "Now you sound like Pip."

Harvey didn't interfere with the two boys as they squabbled, nor did he question them as to who Pip was or about the power. It was none of his business. The chaotic events of the past few days had obviously spread all the way out here.

Loretta on the other hand, apparently didn't understand that keeping her mouth shut was the wisest thing to do right now. "Do you know a George Oxford Williams?"

The boys looked at each other annoyed. "No lady," one of them said, "we don't know any George."

"Maybe we better not pry Loretta," Harvey whispered to her. "They don't look too friendly."

Loretta ignored him. "Who cut your power?"

Harvey wished she would keep her mouth shut. The more questions she asked these boys, the more irritable they became.

"None of your beeswax lady," the elder one growled.

"Come on Loretta," Harvey stood, grabbing the defiant woman's arm, "let's just go. I can't hear the rain anymore anyway, so we should just…"

"I'm not leaving until they answer my question."

Harvey wished she would realize she couldn't get her way all the time. Some things just weren't worth it. *A little help here Lord.*

"*Tell me!*" Loretta insisted.

Suddenly the older boy grabbed a butcher knife from the kitchen drawer and charged toward her as she sat at the table. Harvey positioned himself in front of her. "We don't mean any harm. We're leaving. Just let us leave."

Harvey eyed Loretta and motioned for the door. They backed toward it and opened it, stumbling over the dead wet wolf as they exited the cabin and closed the door behind them, into the remains of a distant thunderstorm.

"*Now* what are we going to do?" Loretta complained.

"Pray," Harvey said, hurrying away, "like never before."

~~~~

Pip couldn't hear much from his favorite vantage point up in the treetop beside the cabin. He wished someone had opened the window so he could figure out what was going on. It probably wouldn't have mattered anyway because the thunder was too loud.

He didn't mind staying up in the tree during the storm, even though it was wet. If Grandfather had caught him though, he would have been angry. He always told him to stay out of the trees when there was lightning in the sky.

He gently climbed down, and started to follow the two strangers. His brothers probably refused to help them, but he wasn't as rude. He was a warrior. It was his duty to help those in need.

Quietly he rambled through the trees as the wet branches slapped him across his brown elfin face. He managed to stay within earshot, yet far enough away that they couldn't spot him. Now as they stopped, he could hear their conversation.

"Look," the fat man said, "the map says there should be a ranger station right about here. If we can make it there, we can use the radio. Every watchtower is equipped with one. It's the best shot we've got Loretta."

"I'm tired," the funny orange looking woman complained, "and I'm sick of this. I just want this miserable nightmare to be over already. My neck is killing me."

Pip could tell these people were in trouble, just like the others. It was his chance to shine. It was his duty to fight the wicked monsters again and be the mighty warrior.

"If we get moving," the fat man continued, "we'll probably make it there before it gets dark. I don't know about you dear, but I sure don't want to be out here when it gets dark. Who knows what kind of friends that wolf left behind?"

Suddenly, the dead tree Pip was leaning against to eavesdrop on the stranger's conversation, cracked. The sound echoed through the bush as if a lumberjack had just swung his axe at it. "*Look out!*" the fat man yelled, shoving the woman out of the way. The two of them fell to the ground in a pile.

Pip jumped out from behind another tree. "Hi there!" he beamed.

Both strangers jumped as they clutched each other, screaming hysterically.

"Me warrior," Pip smiled impishly, pounding both fists on his chest like Tarzan. "No fear...I come to rescue you."

Pip knew his antics were a little overdramatic, but he liked that part the best. He didn't want to scare them, though he feared he already had. The tree wasn't supposed to fall, but it made a grand entrance anyway.

"What on earth," the fat man spoke first.

The woman moaned. "You scared us half to death young man."

Pip stuck out his hand as a truce and reached down to help the strangers up. "Sorry, "he squeaked, helping them brush the wet leaves and twigs from their backs, making sure they were both unharmed by the falling tree. "Warrior no mean to make you fright. Me Pipata, great chief, want to help."

Pip could see by the confusion written all over their faces that he wasn't getting through to them. He would have to drop the façade. "I'm Pip," he said in his normal voice now. "I'm sorry for jumping out at you. I didn't know the tree was going to fall. I just wanted to help you. I like to pretend I'm a warrior sometimes. Grandfather says that our ancestors use to be great chiefs."

"Do you live over there with those boys?" the fat man asked.

"Yes. Unfortunately, they're my brothers. I hope they didn't hurt you. They don't like strangers. They're usually *very* rude."

The funny woman screwed up her face and rolled her eyes. "That's an understatement. One of them came at me with a knife."

"I'm sorry."

"Don't apologize Pip, it's not your fault they have bad manners," the fat man smiled extending his arm for a handshake. "Call me Harvey...and this is Loretta."

Pip shook Harvey's hand firmly. He reminded him of his father, warm and friendly. Loretta on the other hand seemed very angry. He'd keep his distance from her.

"So...How old are you Pip?" Harvey asked while he folded up the map.

"I just turned thirteen."

"Well, you're sure small for your age. Not like me," Harvey gently patted his protruding tummy, "I'm big for my age."

Pip giggled, grinning at the jovial man. The woman snorted at Harvey's gestures without saying a word. She started walking away.

"I can show you the way to the ranger station," Pip said. "I go there all the time."

Chapter 41

All Brian wanted to do was get somewhere dry and warm. In hindsight, his idea to take the four-wheeler had been a better idea than what they were doing now. They had been searching on foot for this woman's sister for the last two hours in the pouring rain.

The last time he'd been out in this kind of weather was last year at Districts. Patrick had placed second in hurdles at his school track meet. He was so proud of himself for getting to go to districts in Prince Albert. Brian was more than proud of his athletic son. He made sure he could be there just to see him run.

It turned out to be a major disappointment. They cancelled the track meet before Patrick could do his hurdles. Apparently, the track was too wet. They were afraid the athletes would slip and fall. Kind of like the slipping and falling he was doing right now in this rain, except he couldn't just cancel *this* event.

He knew better than to listen to Vicki. She was adamant about finding her sister, but he should have insisted they go for help first. All he had to do was get to the plane, then he could use the radio, but he couldn't leave this woman. He was responsible for her whether she wanted him to be or not. He just wished she would give up the search and head back to the four-wheeler soon.

Suddenly, Brian noticed an old shack straight ahead through the trees. He shushed Vicki with his finger to his lips. She stopped in her tracks and crouched down beside him, dripping wet, wiping her brow. "What?"

"Did you hear that?" he whispered.

Brian could hear wild yelping sounds coming from the shack. It didn't sound like an animal cry, more like a human. Then, he heard the voices. Vicki recognized them immediately. "It's them," she whispered to Brian, trying to remain in a squatting position but losing her balance, teetering over instead. "I'm going in."

"*No!* They sound like they're drunk and that might make the situation more dangerous. Who knows what they might do. I'll take a closer look. You stay here."

"No way! Vicki blurted out too loudly, and then remembered to whisper. "Why should *you* go? She's *my* sister."

Brian wished the woman would at least try to co-operate with him. "Fine, but stay behind me. We're not going in if we don't have to. If we see your sister we'll fall back and figure out how to get her out."

The woman rolled her eyes. She stepped out in front of him, pushing her weight, bulldozing him out of her way. "Wait!" he warned. Then, the insubordinate woman charged right in through the front door of the shack as if she were invincible. Brian panicked and moved forward. *Crazy fool!*

He could see her standing there with her hands on her hips like a fool, ready to take on the world. If he only had his gun, he could cover her, but he didn't and that made his stomach nauseous. He would never let any partner of his walk into something unarmed and alone. It was pure suicide.

"*WHERE'S MY SISTER!*" he heard her scream at the top of her lungs.

The male voices inside chuckled and yelped calling her some obnoxious names, shouting, "We killed her you stupid broad, just like were gonna kill you!"

Brian jumped up immediately. *Run!* He could reach her before they...But the shots peppered the bulky redhead before she even had a chance. She toppled down the rotted step to the soggy ground below...executed with a gunshot wound to the forehead.

This isn't happening. Beads of sweat trickled down Brain's brow. His soggy bandages across his wrist suddenly felt heavier than they ever had before. His back throbbed as he crouched down again, hiding from the three men that rushed out to congratulate themselves on their kill, kicking the dead woman's body as she lay stagnant in her own pool of crimson blood.

"Come out come out wherever you are," one of them shouted, laughing like a hyena. "We know you're out there Mr. Constable so you better show your face." The last thing he was going to do was come out so they could shoot him too. *Think!*

He'd have to make a run for it. They would head in his direction soon and he didn't think much of the odds. He would have to do better than three against one if he was going to get out of there alive. But he was at a disadvantage with no weapon.

He tried to crouch down and move around at the same time, except he didn't see the twig. His foot snapped the thing in two, exposing himself to his assailants.

"He's over there, boss!" the skinny short one shouted, pointing his finger.

Brian stuck his head up like a frightened gopher trapped in a hole. He bolted through the trees, adrenaline driving his nervous body.

Gunfire popped at him from all directions.

~~~~

Loretta surveyed the damage to her neck as they walked. She fingered the bandages Harvey had put on, more sloppily than she liked, but acceptable. At least something covered the stinging, burning wound.

The early evening air gave her goose bumps now, a change from the hot muggy sun earlier in the day before the storm came. Now, as the wind picked up, she shivered, wishing she hadn't chopped her overalls to pieces. Harvey hadn't said anything about her new fashion statement yet. He probably thought she was as crazy as she looked.

As the boy walked in unison beside Harvey, chatting up a storm with him, it reminded her of Bob and Jeremy. Tears of regret formed in her yearning eyes as she considered all she had lost. Jeremy use to be so small. He would hang on his dads every word. She always told Bob that Jeremy worshiped the ground he walked on.

Now, as she observed the young boy skipping beside Harvey, she had to smile. He and Jeremy could've been friends. They both had the same mannerisms. When Jeremy was his age, the bullies teased him at school for acting like a baby. He always was a late bloomer, just as Pip appeared to be. His elfin body looked gangly and miniature for a thirteen-year-old boy.

She remembered the time Jeremy came home from school with a bloody lip. The others boys in his class had harassed him again. Loretta was furious when she found out the *whole* story. The boys had held him up by the neck against the lockers until his feet couldn't touch the ground. And the teachers were *conveniently* not around.

A mother can't handle that kind of thing.

Loretta went into protection mode right away. She stormed down to the school and found the culprits who had harassed her son. They were outside playing basketball. Jeremy had run along behind her frantically sobbing, "No Mom, don't!" but she didn't let him sway her maternal retaliation. They hurt her baby boy and they were going to pay.

Right or wrong, she grabbed them one at a time by the scruff of the neck like a raving lunatic, trying to shake some sense into them. Looking back on it now, she wished she hadn't done it in front of her son. Jeremy sure wished she hadn't. He bawled all the way home after that, moaning that they were going to wail on him even worse tomorrow.

She couldn't explain it, that uncontrollable drive to defend her son. It really was remarkable. She felt that way toward her daughters somewhat, though they never seemed to need her help fighting any of their battles. But her son, he was the baby, *her* baby.

He needed her protection and it was a mother's duty to give it.

"Hell, hath no fury like a mother scorned," she would always say. And it was true right down to the bone for Loretta. She lived and breathed it.

The women in her Bible study class never seemed to agree with her jumping in to save Jeremy from the bullies. They would tell her she had to let him grow up and fight his own battles. They'd tell her it wasn't right to step into God's avenging shoes. Well they were wrong. How could a mother walk away from a needy child?

It turned out that Jeremy was beat up again the following day, and that made Loretta even more furious. She got a phone call from the principal that morning, so she came in to see him. She was outraged when she realized he was accusing Jeremy off egging the bullies on. He lumped them all together saying, "Jeremy is just as guilty as the rest of them." Well that was the final straw. She lost all control of her emotions, took her purse, and whacked it over the principal's head while he sat their stunned. He wasn't a good principal anyway. You don't blame the victim for the crime.

Her obsessive behaviour fuelled even more when she stormed out of his office to see the smirking bullies that were responsible sitting right next to Jeremy in the waiting room as if the principal branded them *all* as troublemakers.

She stopped in front of the boys and slapped each one across the face in front of the secretary, whose slack jaw dropped out the words, "You can't do that." Loretta turned and retorted, "Wanna bet," as she grabbed Jeremy's petite hand and hauled him out of that good-for- nothing school for good. It was the best thing she ever did for Jeremy. Even against Bob's wishes, she made sure she withdrew him the next day, enrolling him in a private Christian school, the school he should have been in, in the first place.

A mother has to protect her son.

Loretta would do anything to ensure her son's safety, and that is what she did. She had to pay dearly for the months of ridicule that followed however, not to mention the assault suits both the principal and the parents of the students threatened. She was worried at first, but they never followed through with any charges.

The only thing she lost in all of that was Jeremy's respect for her. After the incident, he just seemed to withdraw from her and spend most of his time with his dad. It hurt her, especially since she had been the one to go to battle for him.

Bob never earned his son's respect. He didn't involve himself with Jeremy's bully problem, even though it had been going on for years. No, he'd just say, "Leave the poor boy alone. He doesn't want his *mommy* fighting his battles for him." But she never listened to that. What did *he* know anyway? Had *he* invested every living breathing ounce of energy into nurturing his children like she did? No. He was much too *busy* for anything that had to do with *them*.

Even now, it pained her to remember Jeremy's attitude toward her after that. As she watched Harvey and Pip chat, her heart silently ached for that kinship she lost with her own son. Yes, she had paid the ultimate price to defend Jeremy but it had *still* been worth it. If someone asked her if she'd do it all over again today, she wouldn't hesitate to give the only answer that made sense to a mother: "*You bet your life I would.*"

It didn't matter how much she lost in the process, she'd lay down her own life for her child if she had to. A mother just keeps on giving regardless of what she might or might not get in return. It's a selfless act…motherhood. That's what she thought she was doing preparing for this trip, setting up all the necessary information and schedules. It was selfless. It was her being a mother. She put every ounce of energy into her plans to "slap" the ones responsible for hurting her little boy. How could she not? How could any mother turn her back on her own needy child? The only problem was…he wasn't exactly the needy one anymore…he was dead.

Chapter 42

The streetlights gradually illuminated the pavement in front of the modern white vinyl sided bungalow in the middle of the best cul-de-sac in La Ronge, Saskatchewan where Jenny and Brian had made their home for the last seven years since Brian transferred from North Battleford.

Jenny grew up near a small town about forty-five minutes southeast of North Battelford called Sonningdale, a remote little farming community known for its impressive hunting opportunities. She swore she would raise her children in the beautiful rolling hills of Sonningdale one day, but that day never came.

She met Brian while she was still training as a nurse at the University of Regina. It was the last day of her clinical rotation in the emergency ward at the hospital when a dashing young recruit from the R.C.M.P academy came in on a stretcher. His buddies carried him in, fusing about the rambunctious football game they just played. Apparently, the young Brian Mackie lost consciousness while at the bottom of a dog pile.

Jenny snickered at that now. It wasn't very funny at the time, even though she always thought so. He really didn't have anything wrong with him. He was alert enough to ask her out on a date.

After their wedding, Brian got his first posting in North Battleford where Patrick was born. He took that posting because it was so close to her parents who still farm just outside of Sonningdale. Oh, how she missed the close commute.

Now, in La Ronge, she felt a world away from the wheat fields and rolling hills she played on as a child. Nothing but trees and lakes formed her scenery now. It really was beautiful, but she still found it hard to get use to the change even after seven years.

Her friendship with many of the R.C.M.P wives made her transition easier. Now she and Cally did everything together. Cally's husband was the boss, and a good friend of Brian's. He's the one that interrupted their vacation time and sent her husband out in the middle of the night to a remote lake way up north. She still didn't like the idea of him being up there alone.

Jenny watched the streetlights intensifying their glow as the sunset horizon weaned to dusk. She thought of her man out there somewhere. Was he safe? Where was he right now? Maybe John would know. She'd give him a quick call.

After punching in the numbers, she waited impatiently for someone to pick up. Finally, after five rings her friend Cally answered the phone. "Hi Cally," Jenny said, recognizing her friends voice right away. "Did I catch you in the middle of something?"

"Yah, sorry Jen, the twins were in the bathtub. I've been scrubbing them for the past half hour. They got into Johns paint in the garage. Can you believe it? John's going to freak when he gets home."

Jenny frowned, "Oh...so John isn't home yet?"

"No, he's not. Why?"

"Oh...It's nothing. I just thought he might have heard from Brian. John sent him to Reindeer Lake a couple days ago and I haven't heard a thing."

Jenny could hear six-year-old twins screaming in the background. She knew she was bothering her friend. "I should let you go. You sound busy."

"Benjamin...don't you dare hit your brother with that!" Jenny heard her friend scream through the phone at her children.

Silence choked their conversation. "Cally?"

All she could hear was a bunch of screaming and banging going on in the background as the phone dropped. Jenny considered hanging up but thought it might be rude if her friend did come back to the phone.

After a few minutes, she heard someone pick up the receiver, and whimpering sounds echoed the background this time. "Jenny?"

"Yah I'm here. I'm so sorry. Benjamin tried to...Oh never mind."

"Should I let you go?"

"No...No. Don't mind them. They're brats when their father isn't home. I tell John that but he doesn't believe me. He thinks they're little angels. Angels my foot...*I SAID STOP IT!* Anyway, what were we talking about?"

"Brian...Going to Reindeer Lake."

"Oh yah, I'm sure he's fine Jen. John said he might be gone as long as a week, I think. He's playing big brother for him again. John's worried about his friend Larry. I guess he didn't check in or something. The guys too old to be running a fly-in-fishing camp alone and John thinks it's his business to keep an eye on him. You know John."

Jenny tried to butt in. One thing about Cally was her ability to hog the conversation. Usually Jenny didn't mind, but this time it was starting to annoy her.

"Brian told me he was only going to be gone a couple days," Jenny blurted out.

"Oh…" Cally stopped short. "I thought John said a week. Oh well, you know the R.C.M.P…anyway. I'm sure he's alright Jen."

"You're right. It's just…"

Suddenly Jenny heard the twins screaming again. "I'm sorry Jen," her friend apologized, sounding frustrated. "I've got to go. The twins are at it again. I wish John would get home already. I don't know what's taking him so long."

Violent screaming fits drained their conversation. "Call me tomorrow," her friend sighed as the phone went dead on the other end, leaving Jenny stunned, but not completely surprised.

John and Cally got married late in life, and then the first year she and Brian arrived here, the twins were born. From what she could see from the couple's parenting skills, they were not exactly up to par. Either that or raising twins is a stressful hair-raising experience. She thought a little of both was more likely.

Boy was she glad Brian only wanted one child. Patrick was a good kid.

Cally just made her worry about Brian more. Why would he tell her that he'd be gone a couple days when John told Cally a week? Was there something she didn't know? It angered her that wives seemed out-of-the-loop when it came to matters like this. What ever happened to good old-fashioned communication?

She tried Brian's cell phone several time, and he wasn't answering. That wasn't unusual. He didn't really know how to use the thing properly anyway. She always had to show him. He hated the thing. He was such a dinosaur when it came to technology but she loved his old-fashioned quirks anyway.

She would give John a call, and clear up her doubts.

"La Ronge R.C.M.P...Constable Mackenzie speaking. How may I help you?" the female voice on the other line informed her when Jenny finally got through to the detachment.

"Hi Cheryl, Can I speak to John?"

"Hey boss," the woman snickered talking to her boss in the background, "the wife's hunting you down again."

"No Cheryl," Jenny corrected the woman, "I'm not Cally, I'm Jenny. I just wanted to talk to John about Brian."

"Oh...sorry, no problem," the jovial woman said. "Just a minute."

Jenny waited for a while hearing muffled voices in the background again. It sounded like John was annoyed. *I should just hang up.*

"Hi Jenny," a deep male voice finally got on the line, "how are you?"

"I'm worried about Brian. Have you heard anything?"

"Not yet."

Jenny knew she was stepping over the line asking about the case, but she just had to know the details if she was going to sleep tonight. "Cally tells me you don't expect him back for a week. Is that true?"

Jenny could hear sighing sounds on the other end. "Cally...has a big mouth," he said, sounding annoyed. "We only expected him to be gone a couple days, but sometimes you run into...complications when you're on the job. You know...storms...that kind of thing. Lately there's been a cluster of bad storms up there, so it might take him longer than expected."

"Do you think he's okay?"

"Of course, he is. He hasn't even been gone forty-eight hours yet. Give him some time to do his job. I gave him a week at the most. If he doesn't contact us by then, I'll send someone to look for him. This is precisely why I didn't tell you the details. I didn't want you to worry."

Jenny's eyes were turning to tears. "Well I *am* worried John. I can't even reach him on his cell phone."

"Now that doesn't surprise me seeing as how he hates the thing. Look Jen, he's okay. I just sent him to check on a friend, that's all. I'm worried about an old guy who runs a fishing camp up there. I wish I could have gone myself, but I couldn't get away."

"He's not working some secretive undercover operation if that's what you're thinking. I would tell you if he was Jen. Really, he isn't in any danger. He's a good pilot and a good Constable. I even made him put the vest on with his full uniform when he left so his little "wife" wouldn't worry."

"I made sure he had enough provisions, medical supplies and all that. And Jen…you know he's armed so don't worry. Consider it a free holiday in exchange for me taking him during his vacation, even though I sent him up there to do a job. Technically, it's not even anything that falls under our jurisdiction, so I can't officially call it a job. It's personal. He's doing it as a favor to me. I told him to take his time, so relax."

"Then I shouldn't worry?"

"No…and I'm gonna give that wife of mine a talking to when I get home too. She shouldn't have worried you. She shouldn't have told you anything."

Jenny boiled. She wished she could be rude to the man and tell him a piece of her mind, but he was her husband's boss. "It wasn't Cally's fault," she insisted. "I made her tell me what she knew. And please don't bawl her out John. She's been having a hard time with the twins tonight."

"I'll keep that in mind. You just make sure you stop your worrying. Brian is just fine. He's probably doing a little fishing while he's out there. He's officially off the clock so he can do practically whatever he wants up there. Within reason, I mean. He'll probably bring you home some Artic Grayling for supper."

"If you say so," Jenny sighed, ending the awkward conversation. Maybe he *was* all right. But why didn't Brian tell her the details, or that he might be gone longer? It wasn't like him. But then, his job required him to conceal a great amount of detail whether she liked it or not. All she did was make a fool out of herself. She was worried for nothing. Knowing her, probably loneliness was the real thing that was eating away at her. With Patrick still away camping with his baseball team, and Brian away, she didn't know what to do with herself. The house was so silent.

Maybe she should call her mother and find out what was going on in Sonningdale these days. She needed something to take her mind off her worries anyway.

Chapter 43

Brian dodged the bullets narrowly missing his head as he ran full speed through the rain-saturated pine forest in the dark. Large wet prickly branches slapped his body as he rambled his way toward a clearing.

Are they gone?

He couldn't hear them anymore. Nothing but his own heartbeat pounded in his chest as he stopped to listen. Crows cawed and fluttered about, but he could neither hear nor see his stalkers anymore.

Brian breathed a sigh of relief as he slumped against a large tree for support. His chest rose up and down as he tried to catch his breath, wishing he had some kind of weapon, or at least his dreaded cell phone.

As the evening drew dark, Brian shivered with his damp T-shirt on. The wind had picked up, giving him an awful chill. This wasn't exactly where he thought he'd end up for his summer vacation. And to think Patrick was having fun camping with his team right now in a similar environment, except *his* life wasn't in jeopardy like he was.

When Brian was sure that the men had gone in another direction, he decided to take off again. This time he would be ever so quiet as he wandered through the shadowy wilderness. If he were lucky, he'd be able to make it all the way back to his plane and radio for help, except, for some reason, he wasn't quite sure which way to go now.

An owl hooted in the distant trees, startling him, sending beads of sweat dripping down his forehead. He wiped his brow, spinning around in paranoia. Did he hear something? Was it them?

Panicking, he began to run again, this time squinting in the pitch dark. The tall evergreens reminded him of lanky evil monsters towering over him, laughing at his fear, mocking his feeble attempts to find his way. Did the monsters know which way to go? Were they pointing him in the right direction with their swaying arms, or were they just teasing him?

Suddenly a bullet ricocheted off the tree in front of him. *They're back.*

"I found him boss," a voice echoed from somewhere behind him.

Brian still couldn't see anybody. He wondered if they were as close as he thought, but he wasn't going to stick around long enough to find out.

Another shot whizzed by his head. "You might as well give up Mr. Constable," one of them shouted into the eerie night. "We know this bush better than you do."

"Not a chance!" Brian shouted out, knowing it was stupid to give up his location, but doubtful that he could physically outrun them anyway. He feared his only hope now was to outsmart them. "I'm not afraid of you, you cowards."

Positioning himself behind a wide tree, he heard the bullets fly by again. *Yes, waste your bullets boys.* If one of them was using *his* gun, he knew it had a full clip, and it would take a while to empty it, but it was worth a try. These guys didn't seem like they were very smart anyway. Maybe if he kept them talking, they would keep on shooting. It was dark so he could run from tree to tree, dodging bullets without them realizing it.

"Missed me," Brian called out, darting to the next tree as they peppered their weapons through the darkness.

"Funny man, Mr. Constable," one of them said in between firing. "You think you're so smart, but we know what you're doing. You want us to use up our ammo."

Rats.

"No, I don't," he lied, trying to buy time. "I just want to talk. Maybe we can work something out."

"And I'm a monkey's uncle," the guy shouted, sounded less than impressed with him. "You don't want to play games with us."

Brian cocked his head around, thinking he heard something. "And who *are* you?" He darted to another tree; hoping one of them hadn't found him out.

"None of your business wise guy," one of them shouted.

This time, Brian crawled on his knees, shuffling toward the next tree when he suddenly met up with another set of illuminated eyes, small, innocent, yet hostile. He focused his eyes on the furry lounging shape, as it lay there stunned. For a moment, the shape did nothing. The two of them locked eyes as if they understood each other. Then, as if the spell had been broken, the thing came to life.

An awful bawling sound penetrated the eerie silence.

~~~~

Pip led the two strangers to the tall wooden watchtower situated on an outcropping of Precambrian rock that edged the forest they had just come through. He'd played there for many years, climbing to the top, pretending he was in great danger from the monsters below. He never realized his make-believe would actually come true.

"Well," he informed them proudly, "this is it."

Pip could barely see the faces of the two strangers it was so dark. He imagined that they looked surprised, especially the fat man Harvey. He was the nicest.

"So…" Loretta, the odd woman asked him, "You think I'm actually going to climb this thing?"

A wolf howled in the distance. "Well dear," Harvey said, "It's either *that* or stay down here with your canine friends."

"No thank you. I'm coming."

The two of them followed Pip up the structure. Pip could tell they were out of shape with their panting and lollygagging. He wondered if he would have to pull them up with a rope because they took so long.

Harvey helped Loretta for a moment when she lost her footing. Pip wondered why he would bother. Her attitude was so mean-spirited; she didn't deserve his warm friendly gestures. But the man seemed to have a calming effect on her for some reason.

"Come on you guys," Pip complained. "My grandfather could climb faster than both of you put together."

"Just hold your horses young man," Harvey chuckled. "We're not all monkeys like you are, you know."

"And you might try having a little respect for your elders too," Loretta added, like a grumpy old mother. He rolled his eyes, grateful she couldn't see his disgusted face.

Pip approached the top, climbed around to open the door, and scrambled inside. "This is the ranger station," he said, "Isn't it cool?"

Harvey laboured through the door next, and then he turned around to help Loretta inside. They both sat there, panting with their deep breathing. "We made it dear," Harvey huffed, coughing all of a sudden.

"Are you okay?" Loretta asked, sounding concerned for the man, confusing Pip because he couldn't imagine the woman caring for anyone but herself. "We need some light so we can see."

"Oh, I'll get it," Pip chided. "I know where a flashlight is. I was just up here last week. I found a big one along with some cool glow sticks. You just have to break them and shake them to make them light up."

Pip rummaged around in some boxes, taking out a handful of glow sticks and a flashlight. He clicked the flashlight on first and shone it toward Harvey revealing a large round blood spot seeping through his orange overalls. "Your side is bleeding mister."

"Oh, good grief," the woman panicked, "it really is."

Chapter 44

The mother bear didn't have a chance.

She came up from behind the men, apparently on her way back to her cub, ready to defend her offspring at any cost. The moment she stood up on her hind legs, a lone rifle shot penetrated the massive bulky animal until it collapsed to the forest floor in a heap.

The cub bawled, scampering away from Brian and toward its mother.

"Get the cub," one of them yelled, the others snickering like ravenous monsters.

This was Brian's chance to make a run for it while the three of them focused on the two beasts. They wouldn't notice him if he took off in another direction.

As he ran, Brian could hear them behind him, torturing the cub. They exploded with laughter at each whimper the poor thing made. He thought of running back just to save the small cub, to beat those three men the way he could hear them beating it, but he couldn't. The shame and guilt he carried with him for that decision was almost unbearable. Never in all his life did he encounter a situation like this where he had to turn his back on innocent life. It sickened him.

The cub sounded so much like a child bawling. He thought of his own son. Would he turn his back on *him* if he were being tortured? No. He would fight to the death.

Brian stopped to catch his breath. And for a moment, he almost turned his heels and went back. *Save the cub,* his conscience told him. But his face cringed at the common sense that told him otherwise. It was his life or the cub's life and he knew it.

Jenny popped into his mind then as he keeled over from exhaustion, grabbing his muscle-constricted stomach. He wasn't going to make her into a widow just yet. No. He and Patrick needed him alive. He would run for his dear life…for his family.

~~~

George grinned at the sight of the blood. His glowing eyes beamed madness as he and Leon hoisted the dead cub over his head, forcing it up like a dumbbell. The shoulder pain disappeared completely. It didn't even feel like he had sustained a dislocated shoulder from the plane crash earlier in the week. The Coke numbed everything just like it always did. His muscles flexed as he let out a wild yelp. The euphoric high he was feeling was unbelievable.

"All right man!" Eddie yelped too, "You the man."

George envisioned mounting the cub on the wall back home, but he wasn't about to haul it all the way back. He plopped it down on the ground, bending to view his glorious kill.

He lifted his pant leg, took his knife from his leg holster and jabbed it into the belly of the beast, exposing its haemorrhaging sausage intestines. *"Yes!"* he roared, smearing the red dripping blood in horizontal lines across his cheekbones and vertically up and down his forehead and chin. Eddie and Leon did the same.

"What are you going to do with the mother bear you killed Leon?" Eddie asked.

"I'm cutting the head off and carving it out to wear it as a trophy," Leon beamed. "What do you think moron?"

"Are you serious man?"

"Deadly!"

George chuckled at Leon's haunting demeanour. Eddie was so gullible. He'd believe anything Leon said. But then, if he knew his friend Leon, he'd do it just to prove he could. Leon was a man after his own heart. He was glad the two of them were buddies.

"But what about the constable?" Eddie asked. "Aren't we going after him?"

"The man's a joke Ed," Leon sniffled. "We'll catch up to him. He's so clumsy anyway, I can track him with my eyes closed. Besides, I'm not leaving until I clean up my bear head. I wanna wear it for the hunt."

~~~~

Brian could see a light in the distance. He followed it like a hawk.

After running for an hour, he realized the men weren't following him anymore, at least not for now. He was free to explore the light that appeared high enough above the treetops that he thought it might be a star. But for some reason, he was sure it was not.

He hoped Jenny wouldn't be worried. He really didn't think he'd be gone long at all. Even though it *was* his summer vacation, he was not about to take his boss up on the offer to stay out and fish for the week, not without his family. What kind of husband and father would do that? He felt bad enough bailing out on his son's camping trip.

As he neared the light, he thought of the many things that it could be. It was so far away, it could be almost anything: another lodge, a comet, or just a figment of his imagination. Yes, he was good at jumping to conclusions. It didn't mean he was right. At this point, he didn't trust anything to be what it seemed.

One time, he jumped to a conclusion when he was a rookie posted in North Battleford. It could have cost him his career. The memory still stung.

He and Thomas were on a routine traffic stop east of the city on Highway 16 just passed the statue of the Mounty on horseback. They had pulled a late model Ford ¾-ton extend-a-cab truck over for inspection because it had a broken tail light.

Thomas went to talk to the guy, while Brian ran the plates. If he hadn't been so sleepy, he probably wouldn't have had such poor judgement. But his eyes were blurry and the passenger was already out of the vehicle on the other side of Thomas. He thought his partner was in serious trouble.

It was a stupid mistake. Brian saw his partner draw his gun and crouch down. He assumed he wanted him to call for back up so he lay down in the front seat and grabbed the radio to call it in. When he looked up, the situation was resolved.

It turned out that the guy who jumped out was just a ten-year-old kid with a giant water gun. Thomas was still scolding the kid when three squad cars roared up to assist.

Brian still flushed whenever he remembered that moment. It was so embarrassing. He never lived it down until the day he transferred to La Ronge. Even then, his superiors from North Battleford thought it was a big joke when they called the guys in La Ronge and told them that they had the famous *Jump to Conclusion Constable* on staff. He tried to explain, but they roared with laughter anyway. At least they forgot about it after a while. But he sure learned his lesson: No matter what, never assume *anything* before checking it out thoroughly.

Now, as he tried to focus his eyes in the dark. He thought he saw a tower illuminated by that light in the sky. *Yes, of course.* The light was coming from a ranger station. But he wouldn't believe it until he actually touched the thing. He wouldn't jump to conclusions this time.

Chapter 45

The flashlight made it easier to see what Loretta was doing, but Harvey almost wished he couldn't see. "Ow," he cried, "that hurts."

"Don't be such a baby Harvey," Loretta snickered. "For Pete sake it can't hurt that much. Try delivering three babies, then you'll know what *real* pain is."

Harvey's face cringed at every tug, every stitch she sewed. "This *is* real pain Loretta. You try not having anything to numb the pain. Give me a stick to put between my teeth or something, or I'm going to pass out."

Pip sat bug-eyed beside Harvey as Loretta attempted to fix the stitches in his side that had ripped out from the climb up there. "I'll get you a stick," Pip eagerly volunteered, "but I think I have to climb back down to get one."

"Go," Harvey grit his teeth, knowing the boy probably just wanted to get out of there for a while. Why wouldn't he? Seeing blood wasn't exactly number one on a person's most favorite thing to do list. He would run too if he had the chance.

As Pip took off through the door to climb down the tower, Harvey could take no more of this. His head was dizzy and his stomach felt nauseous. "You're killin' me dear," he moaned. "Just stop poking."

"Hush up for a minute," Loretta focused, tongue pursed between her teeth in complete concentration.

"Ow," he complained again. "Why does it hurt more *this* time than the first time you did it?"

"Probably because the stitches ripped out...and the wound is getting a little infected too."

"Infected?"

"Yes," she said, "*infected*. The whole thing looks worse than the last time I looked at it. You really have to rest Harvey. I did what I could. I told you I'm not a nurse but I am a mother and that gives me *some* credibility, but apparently not the right kind. You need a doctor. Do you have a fever?"

Harvey took a breath, relieved that she had finished with the needle. "No, I don't have a fever. I feel fine now that you stopped poking me."

"Why are men such babies?"

Her question that he assumed she meant as a statement, a sexist statement, annoyed him, so he chose not to answer her. He rested his sweaty head back against the wall, pursing his lips to avoid the confrontation. The shadowy clubhouse-style room was no bigger than a bathroom but all four walls had a large glass window that looked out over the treetops.

"Look what I found," Loretta piped up while she dug through some of the boxes, "Some pretzels. I love pretzels." She rattled the bag ripping it open. "Want some?"

"No thanks," he pouted, "babies can't eat pretzels."

"Oh, come on. You're not mad about *that?*"

Harvey looked away, trying to burn off his anger toward her. Perhaps it was more fear and pain than anger, but right about now he didn't really care what it was. All he wanted to do was rest his weary old body.

"Well I'm sorry," she grinned, munching noisily on the pretzels. "It's just that...you see, well...mmm, these are good. You should try them."

Will she ever be quiet?

"I accept your apology," he sighed, *even if you don't really mean it.* "Why don't you try to find the

337

radio? Every ranger station should have one somewhere."

"You mean this thing over here?"

"Yes," Harvey beamed, attempting to force his body up but unable to make it do what he wanted. "Ohhh!"

"You can't do that. Just lay there and don't do a thing. I can play around with it."

That's what worried him. "Don't," he moaned, "Just find the power switch and turn it on. If you mess up all the buttons, we might never figure out how to work it."

"I got it."

The thing came to life with the glowing red switch on the bottom as Loretta picked up the receiver. She pressed the button on the side of it and talked into it. "Come in, come in, this is Loretta Lancaster...Over."

The radio hummed and crackled without answering back.

"Try it again," Harvey insisted, wishing he could manage to move his body over there to try it himself. Maybe she was doing something wrong.

"Mayday, mayday," she said again. "Is anyone listening? We need help...Over."

The radio crackled to a wild unpredictable whine.

"Forget it," Harvey sighed. "Maybe it needs some time to warm up. Try it again in a little while."

Loretta set the receiver down and picked up her bag of pretzels again, crunching them in her mouth as she sat down beside Harvey. "Do you think we'll ever get out of here?" she grumbled with her mouth full.

"I hope so dear."

"What if we don't?"

"Then...If this is my last night...If I die here, I know where I'm going."

Harvey watched the woman hang her head. Either she was worried about them getting out of there, or she wasn't sure where she was going if she died.

"How do you know?" Loretta asked. "I mean, how are you so sure?"

The conversation was headed somewhere Harvey didn't think he had the energy to go. His eyelids were heavy, his body was weak, and the last thing he wanted to do was debate Christianity with this woman when he was in pain. Yet, what he said to her the last time seemed to sink in. It was just that he was so tired. Couldn't she just be quiet for a while, so he could rest his eyes? After all, it *was* the middle of the night.

Lord, give me strength.

"I'm sure because God promised me Salvation the moment I believed. There's a verse," he said scratching his head. "Let me think now. What was it? Oh, yes, it's not as well known as John 3:16 but it's more appropriate under the circumstances. It's John 3:36, *"Whoever believes in the Son has eternal life, but whoever rejects the Son will not see life, for God's wrath remains in him."*"

"Aren't you the memory verse champion. What did you do, memorize the entire Bible cover to cover?"

If she only knew how inadequate he felt sprouting off these Bible verses to her, she might not think the same way. He was no champion at all. In fact, Rose was the Bible scholar; he was just some undisciplined goofball who didn't find much point in memorizing scripture. It took his wife's death to force him to see the point.

"No...I didn't memorize the Bible cover to cover," Harvey answered her question, "but I should have. The comfort I get from knowing God's word is the only thing that helps me...when I'm down."

"Well, isn't that just great. It didn't help me out one little bit. It felt more like a slap in the face to me."

"A slap in the face?" Harvey boiled. "What do you mean a slap in the face?"

Loretta stopped munching on the pretzels. "Well, how can that verse comfort me? I consider myself...well; I use to consider myself a believer until Jeremy died. Where does that leave me when it comes to eternal life?"

Harvey knew the answer but he wondered if he should say it. It was clear and she knew it. Perhaps she just wanted to hear it from him so she could pick a fight, now, when he was weak and she knew she had the upper hand.

Why skirt the issue? If she wanted the truth, she was going to get it. "You rejected God Loretta," he sighed, "That verse clearly says if you reject Him, you won't see eternal life; in fact, it says that you will see the wrath of God instead."

Harvey watched the poor woman tear up; he wished he hadn't said it.

"*This*...is God's wrath isn't it?"

"I don't know," Harvey whispered, not wanting to say anything else. The woman was fragile and he knew she could easily lose it like before. Yet, he felt the Lord nudging him to continue the conversation.

"But I *did* believe...Once," she started sobbing into her pretzel bag. "Doesn't that count for something?"

"I don't have all the answers Loretta," he said. "I just know what the Bible says."

"But if we *do* die here...*You* will have eternal life and *I* will be punished and go to hell for rejecting God and trying to defend my little boy. Won't I?"

"I'm not the judge dear," Harvey whispered again, putting his arm around the sobbing woman.

"But it's true though isn't it?" she sniffled. "I never should have turned my back on God. I never should have tried to defend my baby. But how can a mother turn her back on her only Son?"

Harvey moaned from deep within. He didn't know what to tell the distraught woman, for the pain she felt inside was so similar to his own; his thoughts were bias, so much so, that his only clear realization was to pray for her. *Help me find the words to say to this confused woman, and don't let my own emotional baggage get in the way.*

Then, as if a celestial light bulb went on in his head, he knew exactly what he was supposed to say. "How could God turn his back on *His* only son?" he blurted out.

"What?" she stopped sobbing and looked at him with a confused frown.

"Well, think about it for a minute. You asked me how you could turn your back on your only son. God turned His back on Jesus when he hung on the cross."

"No, he didn't"

"Yes, Loretta, he *did*. Jesus died for everyone, you and me, yellow, red, and black and white...just like the Sunday school song. He took every sin that we ever committed and every sin that we ever *will* commit, and took the punishment *for* us. He had to go to hell to do it. What do you think his father felt like when that happened? What would you feel like if Jeremy came home and told you he'd done what George had done?"

"I don't know," she sniffled again, this time perking up to listen. "All I know is that I would never *ever* turn my back on him no matter what he did."

"But could you stand it if he became a psychopath and killed innocent people. That would be an awful load of sin *any* mother would find hard to bear."

Loretta wiped her eyes. "Yah...It would be hard to accept as a mother. I'd want him to get help, but I would *never* turn my back on my son."

"But how could you help someone like that Loretta. If he was so sick with sin, what could you do? What could any parent do? It would break your heart to see it happen, to see your child so filthy. The only thing left to do; the only rational thing that could break the cycle of sin would be *tough love.* Right?"

"I've seen it a thousand times as a police officer Loretta. One time, a teenage girl I knew from church started using Crystal Meth. It was so sad. I'd catch her hooking on the street just to support her habit. After a few years, it got so bad; she became so filthy with sin, it became her entire life. Her parents didn't know what to do. They disciplined her at first, tried to lock her in her room, but nothing kept her off the street. Sure, they loved her, but they couldn't stand the crazy things she did when she was high."

"One day, her parents caught her dealing to *other* kids from church, right there in their home during a Bible study. They brought her in to the precinct and did the hardest thing I have ever seen. They asked me to book her and charge her with drug trafficking. They went to court and testified against their own daughter, helping us to infiltrate a major drug ring and arrest the top ring leader in the process."

"They had to turn their backs on their own child."

"Instead of serving time, they made a deal to get her into the best drug rehabilitation center in Canada, and to this day, their daughter is drug free. Now she works at a youth center in the worst drug infested part of Vancouver…all because her parents loved her so much, they were willing to turn their backs on her."

"Amazing story isn't it Loretta?" Harvey beamed, hoping she hadn't fallen asleep. She was so quiet he wondered if she got anything out of it at all."

Suddenly Loretta broke the silence, sniffling as she wiped her nose with the back of her hand. "You just made that up to teach me a lesson," she forced a smile through her tears, "Didn't you?"

"I didn't," he insisted, realizing that the woman was trying to make light of the fact that she was actually learning something. At least she found the lesson in it all. He was awe-struck at the wisdom in the story, knowing that it had *not* come from him.

"So, you're saying God *did* turn his back on Jesus…so in turn He can identify with my pain. Right?"

"Yes. He knows the pain…but he also knows the gain."

"I know all this stuff Harvey. I spent many years in church too."

Harvey smiled. "I know, but you've forgotten some things. See, God the father was so hurt; it pained him to see His only Son *filthy* with *our* sin.

God loved Him so much; He had no other alternative but to turn His back until He was clean again. That's why Jesus cried, 'Father why have you forsaken me,' just before he died."

"And my loss…is nothing compared to *that*. Right?" Loretta started to sob again.

"No!" he blurted out. "Your loss hurts just like mine does, just like God's does. That part doesn't change. We all lose part of ourselves when someone we love dies. I'm sure God lost more than we can ever imagine when Jesus took on the sins of the world and died for us. Jesus himself bore the brunt of it. He lost his innocence because of us. But God restored Him, gave Him new life, just like He wants to do for you."

"Oh, stop the preaching Harvey," Loretta sobbed and snickered at the same time. "Really, you should be a preacher or something."

Very funny.

"I don't mean to preach dear. I just want you to know something," he smiled softly, raising her chin with his hand as he looked into her eyes. "Jesus took your punishment already. He knew you were going to avenge your son's death. He knew the sin before it happened. He can restore you. Look how much he loves you. He saved you from that wolf just because you asked. Why not let him restore you completely so you can shed the sin that keeps you from Him. He wants his child back."

"*I* want *my* child back." Loretta wailed again, pulling away from him.

"Well I want my *wife* back," Harvey retorted, being just as stubborn as she was.

They both had walked into a stalemate this time, unable to move foreword. Okay, if this is the way you want it. Be stubborn you silly woman. Yet even as that thought crossed his mind, he knew he wasn't really mad at her. He was just tired and miserably uncomfortable with the pain that was shooting through his belly...and he was suddenly feeling very feverish.

Chapter 46

Brian neared the monstrous tower in front of him. This time his assumptions were correct. It *was* in fact a ranger station. Way up at the top shone a faint light against a dark nebulous sky.

Someone was up there.

For a moment, Brian pondered whether to go up. Could he take a chance that it might be someone who could help? The three men chasing him couldn't possibly have arrived already. If they *were* up there, he would be walking straight into their trap.

Against his better judgement, he approached the old wooden structure and began to climb despite his reservations. If they were waiting up there, he would be a goner, but if not, it was his only hope. He had no choice but to take the risk.

Suddenly an angelic voice spoke to him as if he had some supernatural help this time. For a moment, he truly thought he only imagined the soft cherub voice, but then he realized he had heard it before. "Hi there Mr. Constable. Remember me?"

Brian's pounding heart was soothed at the sound of the welcome voice. "Pip, you scared me half to death. What on earth are you doing here?"

"I came to help."

"Like last time, right?" Brian smirked at the impish boy. "You sure do get around. You must live around here."

"I do."

"Do you know who's up there?"

"The monsters are *not* up there, that I *do* know," the young boy informed him, calming him, proving to Brian that he was wise beyond his years.

"Who *is* up there?"

"The caribou."

Brian grinned, "Oh that again. You sure like talking in riddles. Could you be more specific please?"

"Okay Mr. Constable," Pip sighed, "I guess so. I found two people in the bush. The monsters were after them just like they're after you. They're hiding up there. You want to hide up there too?"

"Is there a radio?"

"Well...yes Mr. Constable, but I think I played with it too much. It might not work exactly the way it's supposed to."

"I'd like to try it anyway."

"Okay then, follow me."

~~~~

Loretta paced the floor, fuming at the conversation she and Harvey just had. He thought he was so smart. She sat through church services for years hearing the same sermons he did, probably even the same Sunday school lessons. What gave him the right to speak to her as if he were more superior?

Yet, he did sound more convincing than any preacher she ever listened too. Perhaps she never thought you could use scripture to solve modern problems. His story was interesting, made her think of the Bible in a completely different way.

She had to admit he almost convinced her to see it his way if he only hadn't made that dumb comment about God wanting His child back. She knew he meant her, but something inside her just burst. How many nights had she sat up longing for her *own* son back? It just wasn't fair.

As she fixated on Harvey now in the dim shadowy flashlight, she realized she'd been too hard on the man. All he was doing was trying to help her, and she was too miserable to appreciate it.

"Harvey?" she whined, apprehensive about their severed conversation, hoping he would listen to her after she argued with him the way she did. If there were any way she could make up for her bad behaviour, she would definitely try. "I'm sorry for reacting the way I did. I shouldn't have snapped back at you like that."

Harvey didn't respond.

"Harvey?" she said, annoyed at his obvious stubbornness. "I said I'm sorry. Don't just ignore me when I'm…Harvey?"

Loretta rushed over to the man's side, as he lay there sweaty and lethargic. She felt his burning forehead. "Harvey?" she shouted, shaking him frantically. *"Lord, please help this man like You helped me when I asked You to save me from the wolf. I know I don't deserve anything. I turned my back on You. I've taken things into my own hands. I thought I could do it all by myself…but I can't. I realize that now. I'm sorry Lord. I want to trust You now; I want to turn back to You if it's not too late. Please…save my friend."*

Harvey slowly opened his eyes and gave Loretta a strained smile. "So…I'm your friend, am I?" he teased.

"Harvey!" she scolded him. "I thought you were…"

"Dead?"

"Yes," she pouted, annoyed that he would joke about such a thing. Really, she was relieved the old fool was still breathing, but she wouldn't tell him that.

Loretta felt his forehead again. It still felt like it was on fire. "You're burning up you know. Let me take your bandages off so I can see what the wound looks like."

"Leave it," he stopped her hand from touching the bandages. "I can't bear the pain again. I already know I'm burning up because of infection. You can't do anything about it dear. I thought if I closed my eyes and rested for a bit, I could save my energy."

"And *I* thought you were dead."

"Well at least you got over your mad…and you prayed dear. You actually prayed the prayer I wanted you to pray. Do you know what this means?"

As Loretta knelt over him, she shook her head, tears flooding her eyes. "I think so, "she sniffled.

"You *think* so? You came back to God dear," he said, pulling her body down to his own and holding her tightly.

"I *did*," she sobbed, sounding as though she were trying to convince herself, turning her head away from him.

"Don't hide your tears," he smiled, lifting her face up to his. "You're beautiful, you know that? You are God's child. Right now, He is celebrating up there with a million angels. He is celebrating because the prodigal has finally found her way home."

At that moment, Loretta's heart beat loudly through her breast; goose bumps erupted from her bare skin. Her breathing was unsteady, laboured, to a point where she could barely breathe. She wondered if Harvey could feel her shaking, shivering against his own chest. She wondered so many things as she swallowed hard against her nervous stomach. She moved her lips forward, hoping she wasn't just imagining the sudden feelings that seemed to enveloped her. Finally, as she pressed her cold lips against his hot ones, she realized she cared for this man, this man who had opened her eyes much more than she thought was possible.

The kiss lingered…long and mutual.

"Hi guys! What ya doin'?" the juvenile voice interrupted as he burst through the door, spoiling the passionate moment.

Loretta abruptly pulled herself from the lengthy kiss and teetered to her feet, dusting herself off in a hurry. Embarrassment flushed across her face. "Pip!" she flipped. "You don't just sneak up on people. You almost gave me a heart attack!"

From behind the boy, Loretta heard another voice clearing his throat. "Who's with you?" she snapped, backing up toward Harvey again, "Show yourself!"

"Calm down ma'am," the voice said shuffling through the door. His voice was pleasant and enlightening as he attempted to inch further in. "I'm not going to hurt you. I'm Constable Brian Mackie."

Like a breath of fresh air, Loretta felt her shoulders relax at the mention of who he was. "Boy are we glad to see you. My friend is hurt and I…" Then she looked at the constables bandaged wrists. "You're hurt too. Don't tell me they already got to you."

The constable acted as though he hadn't even heard her. He just robotically charged straight for the window in a hurry, frantically peering out of each one. "Please! Can you shut that flashlight off, and hide those glow sticks under a box or something? They were right on my tail about an hour ago. I hope they didn't see the light like I did."

"I presume we're talking about the same thugs here," Harvey butt in as he waved an arm in the air from his position on the floor. "I'm Harvey Strong, retired police officer, not R.C.M.P, but Vancouver P.D. How do you do."

"Pleased to meet a fellow officer," the constable smiled, rushing over to shake Harvey's hand. "And yes, it sounds like you met the perps already."

"Yes unfortunately," Loretta added herself into the conversation, frowning, still being able to see faces from the glow of the Northern lights that danced in the sky overhead. "I'm Loretta Lancaster. Did you hear me on the radio? I tried to call the authorities but I couldn't…"

"Where's the radio?" he interrupted, ignoring her again. Pip pointed to it. "Thanks bud. Why don't you stand at the window and tell me if you see anybody? Loretta, you can keep watch too. I'll try the radio."

"I'm not leaving Harvey's side," she demanded, fuming at the fact that he just cut her off mid-sentence. "He has a fever and I'm afraid there's an infection settling into his knife wound." *Oh, that got your attention, didn't it?*

The constable spun around and headed for Harvey as he lay there on the floor. "Who stabbed you?"

"One of the goons…George," Harvey grunted as Brian observed the bandages. "Don't take the…" Before he could get the words out, the constable had the bandages off. "Hand me one of those glow sticks Loretta. Just one…and Pip, come back over here for a minute, Loretta, you two shelter your bodies around me so the light isn't visible. I need to see the wound. I have some medical training and my wife is a nurse."

This time Loretta was more than willing to co-operate. "Just hang on Harvey," she soothed, trying to comfort him as he groaned in pain. She kissed his sweaty steaming forehead. "You'll be okay."

Tears formed in her eyes as she watched Harvey's body convulse to the pain. "What do you think Brian?" she sniffled. "Is there anything you can do?"

"Well," he replied. "It doesn't really look that bad. I mean, gangrene hasn't set in anyway. You need some antibiotics though. There should be a medical kit in here somewhere; otherwise, I have to get to my plane. I have medical supplies in there."

"Guess what," Loretta chided. "*I* have your medical supplies. We spent a night in your plane and looted just about everything we could."

"Great, I think," Brian grinned. "Now find a bottle with a syringe taped to it."

"This?"

"Yes."

Brian took the bottle, quickly unwrapped the sealed syringe, sucking up the entire liquid antibiotic with the needle. He tapped it slightly before he injected it into Harvey's side. "There, now I should have another bottle. We'll give it to him in a few hours if nobody else needs it. Loretta?" he peered at her neck. "What kind of wound in under those bandages?"

"A wolf bit me," she said, "but I'm fine. Really. Save the stuff for him. He needs it more than I do. I don't have a fever anyway."

"Great," Brian stood up, dusting himself off. "Now everyone, get back to your posts. We're going to get out of here as soon as I look at that radio."

Loretta watched Pip and Brian make eye contact. Brian winked at the boy for some unknown reason and started fiddling around with some buttons on the radio. "I tried it earlier," she informed him, hoping she hadn't broken it. "I couldn't hear anyone the first time. I don't know if what I transmitted came through to anyone."

"Probably not," Brian eyed Pip again, lifting the receiver to his mouth as he spoke into it. "This is Constable Brian Mackie; we need help immediately," he spoke into it, "Over." Nothing but crackles returned to him. "I repeat. This is Constable Brian Mackie. We have a situation at Shooting Star Lodge with multiple casualties, armed felons in pursuit, location west of lodge at Deep Bay Ranger Station. Over." Brian paused for an answer that didn't come. "Is anyone listening? Please respond. Over."

Loretta tried to keep one eye on the ground below, while watching Brian fiddle with the radio. He turned some knobs and tried again. "Is there anyone out there? Over."

Still nothing but squeals and static echoed back.

"It's not working," he turned around and frowned at them, specifically at Pip. "I have to get to my plane. I have a good radio in there."

"No, you don't," Harvey spoke impulsively, appearing to Loretta as though he was feeling better. "When we spent the night in your plane, the radio had been destroyed. Someone got to it before we could. And they destroyed the radio in the other plane too; they cut the phone lines in the whole area. There's no way to call for help. This *was* our last shot."

"Great!"

Suddenly Loretta cocked her head, straining her ears to an unusual sound. "Do you guys hear that? I hear some kind of buzzing sound."

Brian threw himself to the window, scanning the perimeter down below. Pip ran from window to window. Loretta's heart pounded in her chest once more. "What is it?"

Then, shrieking like a banshee, Pip wailed something horrible. "They're here! They're on the four-wheeler!"

Chapter 47

Jenny woke from a drippy sweat just after midnight. Her nightmares were getting worse. She had the same recurring dream every night since Brian left. The dream always started with ravenous bears attacking her husband, then, as always, it ended with Brian plummeting to his death, except now he had a bullet through his forehead. It turned her stomach to the point of vomiting.

This time she made it to the bathroom on time.

With moist dark hair hanging into the toilet, she dry-heaved again. She had nothing left in her stomach, she decided, groping her abdomen against the pain. With a cool wet face cloth gripped in her trembling hand, she rubbed it across her brow, then down her one cheek and around to her parched cracking lips.

Jenny struggled to get off her knees, teetering to stand as a sudden dizziness overcame her. She grabbed the side of the bathroom sink while the room spun and swallowed hard. *I have to call John again, something is definitely wrong with Brian.*

Steadying herself, she opened the medicine cabinet and rummaged around for something to settle her stomach. She found some Tums and popped two of them into her mouth, chewing against the chalky tablets that seemed to make her even more nauseous.

The telephone was beside the bed. She was glad that Brian had put another jack in so he didn't have to stumble out of bed when work called in the middle of the night. She grasped the phone and slid under the covers, burping as she lay her head down.

She punched in the numbers hearing the line almost connect, and then hung up quickly so it didn't go through. No. She couldn't call John again. She had just spoken to him earlier in the evening, and besides, it was the middle of the night.

Closing her long dark eyelashes, she moaned, cupping her pale face with her tiny fingernail-polished hands. What was she going to do? If she *was* over-reacting, she would feel like a fool...again. And she couldn't wake her mother up, not with her Fibromyalgia. She would never get back to sleep. She talked to her in the evening too, told her how worried she was about Brian, but not about the dreams. She hadn't told a soul about that.

Jenny sighed. She decided to phone John anyway. What else could she do?

The phone rang and rang until finally a female picked up and said hello in a weary voice. Jenny was glad her friend had answered first instead of John.

"Cally? It's me Jenny."

"Jen...What's wrong?"

She could barely keep it together with the first words that came out of her mouth. Hearing her friend's voice seemed to push her over the edge. "I had a bad dream," she bawled, feeling like a fool for even breaching the subject. As if it wasn't bad enough that she had called earlier, worrying about her husband, now she appeared childish, telling her friend about a silly dream in the middle of the night.

"Calm down baby," Cally attempted to sooth her through the phone. *Baby. Yah, that was exactly right.* Her friend didn't need another child keeping her up all hours of the night.

"I'm worried about Brian," she sniffled, hiccupping from the nasty chalk tablets she wished she wouldn't have taken. "I keep having this bad dream about Brian, Cally. I know something's wrong. I need to talk to John."

"Oh baby," her friend cooed at her, sounding like she was talking to one of the twins. Jenny wished she would stop it. "I wish you could, but John just got called out on an…emergency a half hour ago."

"What kind of emergency?"

A long pause lulled the conversation for a moment until her friend spoke up again. "I'm not supposed to tell…I mean. It's not about Brian Jen. I promise."

"How do you know?" Jenny wiped away the tears that steadily streamed down her checks. Her nose started plugging making her sound as if she had a cold.

"I know! Now stop jumping to conclusions dear or you'll really start living up to your husband's nickname. You don't want to be known as *Jump to Conclusion Jen.*"

If her friend thought she was cheering her up, she was sadly mistaken. She knew John didn't tell her about his job most of the time, especially not after the conversation she had with him last night about Cally having a big mouth. So how would she know the emergency *didn't* involve Brian?

"Okay, so that wasn't funny. I'm just trying to cheer you up baby. Do you want to come over here and sleep? That's what the twins do when they have nightmares. They cuddle up with me."

I am not cuddling up with you. I'm not one of your babies.

This was going nowhere. She would have to think of something else, some other way to find out what was going on. "No thanks, Cally. I think it's best if I stay here. Brian might call me."

"Okay. Suit yourself, but you're welcome to spend the…"

"No!" Jenny interrupted too abruptly. She hoped she didn't offend her best friend. She hated hurting people. It wasn't in her nature. She was a people pleaser through and through. "I mean…really Cal, I'm fine now. I'm sorry for waking you. I'll just try to go back to sleep," she lied, hanging up the phone.

If John was at the detachment, then she was going there too.

~~~~

George tried to scratch his forehead, annoyed at Leon's bright idea to wear the bear cub's head as a cap. He chopped it off under the top jaw and around underneath the ears like Leon did his, so it would fit atop the crown of his head without the lower jaw. His was too small really, but it felt wonderful squishing against his scalp. It got in the way, and it would've kept falling off if he hadn't tied it securely around his chin for extra support like Leon told him *he* did.

The blood he smeared on his face earlier was cracking, drying, and itching beyond what he could stand. It didn't seem to bother Leon. He just strutted around like Daniel Boon with his bear head mounted on top of his head as if it belonged there.

They didn't take very long cutting the animals heads off, chucking the lower jaw, and cleaning the upper heads out. Leon was an old pro at it, said he's been doing it for years. By the time Eddie returned with the four-wheeler, they were already done and waiting for him. They even had time to snort some more Coke.

Now, as they approached the watchtower, they were ready for the hunt to begin. Leon was right about this being a hoot. The stupid constable trapped himself up there like a rabbit caught in a trap...a bear trap ...and the bears were coming to eat him.

~~~~

Jenny jumped out of her car into the warm night breeze with nothing on but her sheer nightgown and fuzzy pink slippers. She had forgotten to change before driving to the detachment. *What a fool.* With her arms crossed in front of her chest, she stormed in through the double doors grabbing a long overcoat that hung on a hook on her way in. She struggled to put the oversize thing on and tied the belt tightly around her petite waist.

Feeling warm now with the coat on, she strode passed the empty reception desk consumed with nausea again. Coffee, she smelt coffee. That is exactly what she needed. Her nose led her down a hall and around a corner, where she suddenly bumped into the newest member of the detachment. "Jenny," the thin woman squawked, obviously startled by her presence. Hot coffee spilled all over her freshly pressed uniform.

"I'm *so* sorry Donna," Jenny fussed, fumbling with the coffee cup, causing the whole thing to flop to the floor. Jenny covered her face with her hands and burst into tears.

"What on earth is going on?" Donna fumed, still exasperated from the coffee being dumped on her. "Are you in your *nightgown*?"

"*Yes*," she sobbed hysterically.

The woman snickered, shaking her head. "Come with me." She led Jenny down the hall the same way Donna had come from. Jenny knew the detachment well, but this early in the morning, she seemed to have lost her bearings. "Where are you taking me?"

"You'll see."

"I have to talk to John."

Suddenly, Donna burst through some large swinging doors with Jenny in tow. "Look what *I* found," she interrupted the meeting sounding like she was about to tell the joke of the year.

"*Sit down*," John sighed rolling his eyes, smiling as he pushed a chair out with his foot. "You can go now Donna. I'll take it from here."

Donna chuckled as she left.

Jenny flushed with embarrassment, hunching in the chair beside the boss. "Don't tell me," he said, "My wife opened her big mouth again, right?"

Jenny wanted to say no, she had to tell him what made her come here in her nightgown in the middle of the night like a lunatic, but she just couldn't. She couldn't tell him what had really pushed her to come here. He would think she really *was* crazy.

Instead of refuting him, she didn't say a thing; she just let him think what he wanted to about his wife. It wasn't right, but it was easier that way.

Feeling guilty and nauseous again, she pushed herself passed her embarrassment and played along with the game he had started. "So, what are you going to do John? I know everything." The bluff was bold, but now she was in over her head. He hoped he couldn't see right through her like Brian always could.

"Okay! So, you know the grim details Jen."

What did he mean by that? She wanted him to tell her Brian was okay, but in her gut, she knew he wasn't. *Good grief, was he dead?* A thready pounding heartbeat enveloped her chest. She was about to vomit.

Instead, she swallowed hard playing along even further. "And what are you going to do about it?"

"Well," John said, turning his head to address the four other constables at the table. "This is what we know. Someone picked up the first transmission about an hour ago. Then Brian identified himself as the caller thirty minutes later. All distress calls."

So, he wasn't dead.

Jenny's stomach started to settle. She breathed in through her flared nostrils and out through her mouth, relieved that her husband was alive. Now, she had to deal with reality. Brian *was* in danger, and these people were discussing what to do. Her dream might not be that far off the mark

As she tuned in again to what they were talking about, she listened intently to the conversation. "We tried to send a message back," John informed, "but there was no response. So…we have no other alternative but to expect the worst. *The worst? No!*

"Mrs. Mackie?" John addressed her now. "I know you're upset, but I was intending to call you in the morning. My wife didn't have to wake you in the middle of the night. There's really nothing you can do but wait."

Again, she didn't refute his accusations about his wife. Guilt consumed her every bone. Should she set him straight now, after she had let the ruse go on so long? "John," she sighed, ready to confess her lies. "I know you think your wife…"

The phone rang, interrupting her attempted admission of guilt. John held up a finger for her to wait. "Excuse me," he said, screeching his chair out and leaving the table. "I have to get that Jen. Men…I'll be right back."

As Jenny watched the middle-aged man leave the room, a quiet hush crept over the room. The four constables sat silently watching her. They must have thought she was a real idiot.

She knew all of them quite well. She even knew their wives…and now she would be the talk of the town. Would they have to leave La Ronge like they had to leave North Battleford? Not now, she couldn't do that again, not with Patrick and his baseball team. No. She wouldn't let her son suffer through another move. It had been too hard on him last time. Yet, she wouldn't let Brian be the brunt of their jokes either.

Finally, John returned with something in his hand. He cleared his throat. "Okay people, the Medi-Vac is ready along with our chopper. We take off in thirty minutes."

"Chopper?" she spurted out. "You're going now?"

"I thought that's what Cally told you." Jenny gulped hard squeaking out a whimpering, "No."

John had confusion written all over his face, and a guilty blush rushed to her cheeks. "Go home Jenny. There's nothing you can do."

"Oh yes there is," she blurted out; surprised at herself for the courage it took to speak up against her husbands boss. "I'm coming with you."

John guffawed, almost choking as he eyed her long and hard while she stood there in her silly nightgown and slippers with the oversize coat, she knew belonged to him. He ran his fingers through his hair, sighing, "You're serious, aren't you?"

She wiped her nose with his coat-sleeve, sniffling as she stood at attention. "You bet your life I am."

John looked around the room at the other officers rolling their eyes. "Well, you heard the lady," he shouted the order. "She's coming with us, but only because you're a nurse Jenny. I expect you to do your job. You can ride in the Medi-Vac."

Jenny jumped in the air, forgetting where she was. She stopped herself the moment she realized they were all gawking at her and grumbling to each other. She hoped she had the skills needed; she hadn't treated trauma cases in a long time. Working in the morgue wasn't the same thing but she was sure she could do it anyway.

"Well, if you're coming with us you better go find Donna. She'll give you something to wear. And hurry up, we're taking off in…" he paused to look at his watch strapped to his hairy wrist, checking the exact time, "…twenty-five minutes now."

Chapter 48

"What are we going to do?" Loretta screamed in a panic, hoping the constable could protect them. "Do you have a gun Brian?"

"No," he answered, "they have it."

"What?"

"Don't panic honey," Harvey attempted to sooth her with his soft voice, but it wouldn't work this time. This time they had nowhere to run.

"I can't stay here," Pip squealed while trying to squirm passed Brian.

"You're not going anywhere young man," Brian blocked his way in front of the door. "Do you know what they'll do to you when you get to the bottom?"

"But I'm a monkey," Pip burst out, pleading with terror in his eyes. "I can sneak around, honest I can."

"Hogwash!" Brian argued back. "You've been sneaking around for a long time, following them, playing games, pretending. Don't tell me you don't know what kind of men they are. *They kill people Pip!*"

Pip's eyes flooded when Brian said that. He hung his head weeping, "I know."

"So, what are we going to do then?!" Loretta shouted, hoping Brian had some sort of plan besides scolding Pip.

Brian took Pip by the arm and led him over to Harvey, making him sit in place, eyeing him so he wouldn't try to run. "Look everyone," he said, "we won't be any good to each other if we panic. Let's just try to work together. Okay?"

Loretta gulped hard, forcing herself to agree with him. She continued to stand guard at the window, looking for the men below. "I can't see them anymore," she squealed, "that could only mean one thing Brian. They're coming up!"

"Okay," Brian ran his fingers through his hair. "We're safe as long as we don't let them get through the door." He looked around the shadowy dark structure. "Help me move this bench in front of the door."

Together, Pip, Loretta, and Brian heaved the large wooden workbench in front of the door, blocking the entrance. Loretta gave Harvey a sober glance, as she looked his way. The man was visibly praying with his hands folded in front of him. "Keep praying dear," she called out to him. "We need all the help we can get."

All three sat on top of the counter in front of the door when they finished. "That should stop them from coming in," Brian panted, "Remember; we got the advantage up here. We have a secure place inside, they don't. Let's try to keep it that way."

"Could I help?" Harvey asked, attempting to manoeuvre himself up.

"Harvey don't," Loretta sighed, "you're not up to it. Just stay where you are."

"No," Brian butt in, "If your husband wants to help, let him help."

Loretta felt her cheeks burn. Her eyes locked with Harvey's bemused ones as she tried to correct the assumption. "He's *not* my husband," she blurted out, watching Harvey's dancing eyes fill with disappointment. *Well he wasn't.*

"My mistake," Brian apologized, continuing with what he had started saying. "Harvey, you can stand guard at one of the windows. Tell me if you see anything at all. If we're lucky folks, they might not even know we're up here. We're not sure they saw the light. We're not sure of anything. They could just be passing by."

Not likely, Loretta wanted to say. She knew that George was capable of killing them all. If they were hovering around the base of the tower, she was sure the only reason was to get at them, no question about it.

Loretta watched as Pip's elfin body trembled beside her. She knew that fear. It was cold, dark, and lonely. Part of her wanted to shrug her shoulders and tell herself, *so what.* The other part of her, the *mother* part, wanted to comfort him, protect him, as if he were her own son.

Her arm started to twitch. *I will not put my arm around him. Everything I love either dies or leaves,* she argued with the inward voice. Still she felt drawn to do it. *I can't, he reminds me of my son too much...and I failed him.*

You didn't fail him, the voice answered from somewhere deep inside of her.

I did, I couldn't protect him, she shook her head, tears flooding this time.

But my sweet child, the voice said again, *it is I who protects.*

Then why didn't you!

I did my child, but in a better way than man can imagine. He is safe now, right here with me. I am his hiding place. I protected him from trouble. I surrounded him with songs of deliverance.

Loretta sniffled, alerting everyone that she was crying. "What?" she shrugged her shoulders, fighting off their wondering glances. "This is stressful. Do you mind?" But even as she said it, her soul moaned the real reason for her tears.

"I don't hear anything," Harvey said, "Maybe they left."

Loretta sniffled, "I doubt it."

Suddenly glass shattered. A scrawny figure burst through the jagged window- opening, pulling Harvey backward in a chokehold against the glass.

~~~~

"What's our ETA," Jenny asked the pilot flying the Medi-Vac. The earphones made it easier to communicate with the crew as the helicopter chopped through the air, mid-flight in route to Reindeer Lake.

"Thirty minutes," the pilot answered back, chewing gum and smiling.

They were over water now, she could tell. The reflection of the magnificent Northern lights illuminated the glistening water even though the sun wasn't up yet.

The swishing sound from the helicopter blades kept her awake, that and the sickly elevator feeling that weighed heavily on her weary stomach as they flew through the air, meandering behind the much larger R.C.M.P helicopter. In it, sat John and four other constables, ready with their weaponry and full armour to go into battle the moment they set down their craft.

She gave a faint smile at the paramedic and nurse on board seated next to her. Their medical equipment swung around, oscillating rhythmically to the motion of the chopper. She didn't dare look at it for long. Her stomach turned at the sight of it.

Jenny force herself to focus on Brian instead of herself. *Hold on honey.* She hoped he wasn't one of the injured ones, but she had to prepare herself if he was.

One thing she was good at was her job. When she had to be professional, she was. She seemed to have the ability to cast all things aside when setting her nursing skills into action, but she never had to work on her own loved one, or frankly, anyone that was still living. Could she really hold it together?

~~~~

Brian jumped up from his seat and flew over to Harvey.

Loretta huddled with Pip, hugging him tightly with both arms around him. "I got you honey," she mothered him, turning her body to shield him from the mayhem as Brian repeatedly pummelled the man choking Harvey.

Harvey grabbed the man's arms as he yanked him through the broken window. His body flopped to the floor, bloody lacerations across his cheekbones. He immediately stood up and pulled out a knife, thrusting it forward into Brian's face. "Come on!" he grinned. "You ain't so tuff now are ya?"

Harvey got out of the way, as the two men danced around the tiny room. Loretta lifted her feet that dangled from the workbench she and Pip sat on. She saw the flashlight just sitting there, deciding to pick it up. "Hey Harvey," she shouted. "Catch."

Loretta hurtled the heavy flashlight through the air, while Harvey caught it with both hands. "Thanks," he grinned, turning it on, apparently waiting for the right moment to shine it in the intruder's eyes, either that or he didn't know what to do with it.

Then, as Brain collapsed to the floor, Loretta knew they were in trouble. Blood speckled the floor around the constable as the man charged toward Harvey with his bloody knife. "You are next old man," he grinned, kneeing him in the gut.

Harvey moaned, clenching his teeth, "That's what *you* think," he sucked in air, forcing a foot to the other guy's groin, causing him to keel over. "I remember *you* scumbag. This is for the first beating you gave me." He kicked him again.

Loretta jumped to her feet realizing the opportunity. She picked up the flashlight, and swung it overtop the man's head, sending him careening down to the ground. His hand still held the knife.

"Grab the knife Harvey," Loretta yelled.

Harvey bent to take the knife, but the guy stood up again like a cat with nine lives. "Oh *no* you don't," he fumed at Harvey, forcing him hard against the wall. They both struggled with the knife as it lowered to a point where Loretta couldn't see it anymore.

"Be careful Harvey," Loretta warned, backing up to comfort Pip again. She grabbed his trembling body and held him tightly to her. "Don't watch," she warned.

Suddenly, both men separated, stunned as they hovered and glared at each other in a slow motion. Harvey collapsed on one knee. Then the other guy collapsed against the bloody wall, crumbling down to his knees with the knife sticking out of his chest. The blank stare the intruder gave Harvey, told Loretta all she needed to know.

"Are you okay?" she screamed, rushing up to Harvey.

"I'm fine," he grunted, obviously in a great deal of pain. "Check the constable."

Loretta knelt down beside Brian. "He's not moving."

Chapter 49

It was still dark. Harvey wondered if the sun would ever come up.

He felt for a pulse but there was nothing. The intruder was dead. He looked over to Loretta who was still checking on Brian. "What's the matter?" he called to her.

"I can't find a pulse," she panicked

Harvey pushed himself over to her, bending against his pain. He felt for the man's pulse, "There. Can't you feel it?"

Loretta put her hands on the spot Harvey showed her. "I feel it. Brian?" she called out, shaking him, "Brian?"

Brian moaned, grabbing his slashed shoulder, blood visible from the wound. "Did I hit my head?"

"No...he cut you," Loretta said, helping him get up.

"Are you okay?" Harvey asked the constable, hoping his answer would be yes.

"Yah," Brian said, holding the ball of paper towel that Loretta gave him to his shoulder wound. His head spun around a bit as he steadied himself, "just barely."

"I was thinking," Harvey said. "There's still two more out there somewhere. If we stay up here, we're just waiting for them to come and get us like this guy did. Well, what if we found a way down without them seeing us?"

"What do you have in mind?" the constable asked.

Loretta looked interested too. "Yah, how do we pull that one off?"

"We use that rope over there in the corner. Look how much there is. I figure there must be enough for four lengths of the tower at least. We cut four equal pieces. We each get our own rope. We tie the ends to something up here, use those work gloves in that box over there, and slide down the rope to the bottom. You know, propel down like rock climbers."

Harvey paused for their reaction.

"But what if we can't," Loretta said, biting her nails.

"Look dear," he continued, "we either try it, or wait for the next guy to show up, and that might be sooner than we think."

"He's right Loretta," Brian added, going for the rope already, plopping it in front of her along with the over piled box of work gloves. "But we've got to move fast."

Harvey started cutting the rope with the knife he pulled from the dead guy's chest. Within a few moments, they were ready to find a place to tie them on. Loretta slipped her gloves over her hands; suddenly spinning on her heels in a panic.

"Where's Pip?" she gasped.

Brian moved over toward the broken window. "He couldn't have gone out that way, we would have seen him."

Harvey laboured over to the door. "He must have crawled under the table and squeezed out the door. Look, he forced it open enough to slide through."

"Well I have to find him," Loretta insisted. "I can't turn my back on him."

Harvey watched the poor woman fall apart again. He knew exactly what she meant. "We'll find him dear. Right now, we have to get out of here. Wait," he paused to listen. "Do you guys hear that buzzing sound? They all rushed to the broken window where the noise became much louder.

"Could they be leaving?" Harvey said, wondering if they had given up.

Loretta sniffled, brightening up. She peered out the side window that wasn't broken and saw nothing at all. "Maybe. I hope so."

Then, as if the earth had shifted, the top of the ranger station fell to a lean. Harvey lost his balance and toppled over, Brian and Loretta held on to the windowsill. The whole thing reminded him of the Tilt-a Whirl at the amusement park.

Brian grabbed the ropes and tied them to a structural beam, "Come on. We have to go *now*. They have a chainsaw. They're trying to cut us down."

~~~

Both choppers set down in the early morning sunrise, beside a place called Shooting Star Lodge. It looked rustic and serine, hardly the place for mischief. Jenny knew they were in the right area though. She'd seen the R.C.M.P floatplane her husband brought out as they flew over the dock before they landed.

The moment they touched down, John came running over knocking on the door of the chopper. "Nobody leaves this aircraft until I say so," he shouted overtop the propellers that were whirring to a stop. "You understand? We have to secure the perimeter first."

Jenny wished he'd hurry up. Brian might need medical attention.

For a moment, a devious thought crossed her mind. *Could she disobey the orders, and look for Brian herself?*

Pip clung to the large tower as it leaned to one side. He knew what his uncle was up to and he wasn't fooling anyone with that bear head he was wearing like a hat. Ever since he knew him, Uncle Leon cut the heads off the animals Grandfather trapped, and wore them as a trophy. Grandfather said it was disrespectful to the spirits, but he did it anyway.

Now, as Pip watched the two men giggling, manoeuvring that chainsaw in the air, he knew they were attempting to cut again.

Above him, he heard voices. The people were coming out.

Like a monkey, Pip swung from post to post, unnoticed by his Uncle and his friend. He managed to swing to the leaning side where the people were lowering ropes. If they thought Uncle Leon didn't see them, they were wrong. He saw them chuckling and pointing to it already. He had to warn them.

Silently, Pip slipped over to the first rope, grabbing it and tugging. He shushed the lady when she looked down at him, hoping she wouldn't scream. He climbed up to them until he reached them.

"Pip," the lady whispered, "you're still here."

"They saw you," he said. "They know you're getting down."

Harvey poked his head out. "We're going anyway. They'll cut us down if we don't. Just hold on to that rope Pip." They lowered some gloves to him so he put them on and started propelling down, sliding his gloves along the rope just like a monkey.

Without warning, the other three started propelling beside Pip. Shots ricocheted off the beams around them, while the chainsaw buzzed away. Then, the structure fell again, giving them a fast decent until they hung in mid-air from the ends of their ropes. They swung in place unable to reach any footing at all.

Pip could hear his uncle laughing with his friend. He caught what the little bear head said, "I'm going to do some more target practice while you cut the next one." Then he yelped, "Ye…ha!"

Pip's eyes widened at the realization of what was about to happen. "Swing," he shouted. "They're gonna shoot at us again."

Gunfire peppered the air as all four ropes swung back and fourth, narrowly missing the bullets. The chainsaw revved up again, this time cutting the third beam that barely held the decrepit tower together.

Everyone screamed as the ranger station collapsed, ropes attached, hurtling to the ground. Harvey, Loretta, Brian, and Pip, hung to their ropes like yo-yo's.

With a jolt, they came to an abrupt stop. The ranger station was stuck on something. It hinged like a broken twig on the last uncut beam. Pip hung there like a puppet, waiting for his uncle to pull the strings, just like always.

"I can't hang on," Loretta shouted. Harvey and Brian looked like they were having a tough time too, each of them grunting to fight the pain.

Pip looked down. "Jump," he shouted, "Look where we are. The ground is only a few feet away."

The others yelled, "No," but he didn't listen. He had an idea but he didn't want to yell it aloud or his uncle would hear him. But it was a good idea. They could take the four-wheeler. It was sitting over to the left of them.

Pip let go of the rope, listening to screaming as he plummeted down to the ground. The other three watched as he landed safely and motioned for them to follow. They dropped to the ground, landing one at a time, tumbling and limping a little harder than he did, but at least they were down.

Pip scurried to the four-wheeler and started it up. Uncle Leon turned his animal head to the sound. So did the other guy. *"Come on!"* Pip shouted, trying to coax the three slow moving adults to move faster. Maybe he could go get them.

He turned the machine around and headed toward his friends, straight into the line of fire. Gunshots ricocheted off the metal frame of the ATV, dancing across the seat as he stood and drove it at the same time.

Then, just as he reached them, the bullets hit the tires, deflating the two on the right front and back. Pip heard his uncle yelp like a wild man. "Now I got you...*Sucker!*" he yelled climbing down from the tower, dropping the chainsaw as he did it. The other guy, Baby Bear, was already behind him.

"Don't move!" Baby Bear shouted, aiming a gun at Pip. He took him by the scruff of the neck and pulled him backward off the four-wheeler. Leon was nowhere in sight yet.

Harvey, Brian, and Loretta, froze.

"Put your hands up," Baby Bear ordered the three adults as he forced the gun to Pip's temple grabbing him from behind in a chokehold. "Now, look what we have here. Calamity Jane and her crew, isn't that something."

The lady started to sob. "Oh yes, you remember, don't you?" Pretending you're someone you're not isn't a nice thing to do to someone. Is it *Loretta*?

"Right back at ya!" Loretta spit.

"Now, that ain't nice either," Baby Bear mused, "especially since I'm the one with the gun. And you don't want to get *me* mad. You know what I'm like when I'm mad. I might start counting. You don't want me to count do you?" Remember what happened the last time? It was so *freakin'* great! Your kid wet his pants before I could even count to three. What a *sissy!*"

"Shut up!" The woman screamed to the top of her lungs, turning red as a beet to match her hair. She charged at baby bear, while he laughed at her.

Pip could barely breathe when he broke free from the man.

Uncle Leon, with a rifle strapped to his back, showed up just in time to grab Pip again pressing a small pistol to his temple, warning the others to stay out of the fight.

Baby Bear slapped the woman, but she just kept coming back for more. The man giggled at her, swatting her, kicking at her as she flopped around in her orange suit. "Look at the orange pumpkin dance Leon," the man grinned. "And it's not even Halloween. "Maybe we aught to drop her from the tower to watch her go splat?"

Uncle Leon chuckled, but still kept a tight grip on Pip.

"You're a monster!" she screamed, stumbling to the ground as she attempted to punch him, but punched the air instead when he moved aside laughing.

She got back up, just like a boxer would, and started swinging again. This time, baby bear dropped his gun, sending both of them down to the ground to fight for it.

"This is hilarious!" Uncle Leon grinned as he tugged at Pip. "I should just shoot her now and get it over with. What do you think geek?"

Apparently, Uncle Leon was amused with what was happening, allowing them to fight in front of them as if they were spectators at a wrestling match.

Remarkably, Loretta was the first one up. She stood with the gun in her hands, pointing it at the guy. Pip couldn't believe *she* had won the battle. Baby Bear was still on his knees in front of her. Pip was impressed with her ability, but he wondered what she would do next, especially with Uncle Leon's weapon aimed at his head.

"Get up Pig!" Loretta spit blood as she gave the order.

Baby Bear rose with his hands up. "Do something Leon!" He huffed in annoyance.

Loretta backed up and dodged the gun back and forth between Leon and his friend. She snorted, wiping her dirty nose with her forearm. "Don't try it Indian or I'll shoot Mr. Wild Bill here, I swear I will."

"And I'll shoot you...*and* the boy!" Leon grinned back, cold as ice.

"She set me up Leon!" Baby Bear whined. "Tell your friends how you lured us all out here to kill us. Tell them you're no better than we are. Tell them you plotted to kill me all along."

The woman sobbed, and turned to look at Harvey, then back at Baby Bear. "I *will* kill you...for killing my son! You took him away from me forever you evil creep! You're nothing but a sick monster!"

"Look who's talking," Baby Bear snickered. "You turned into a monster yourself. Look at you.

You're the one pointing the gun now. Feels good doesn't it?"

Loretta sniffled and said nothing.

"Loretta…don't do it dear!" Harvey yelled out.

"Yah," Baby Bear mimicked. *"Don't do it dear.* You better listen to your boyfriend. Harvey has supernatural powers. He's risen from the dead you know."

Harvey glared at him long and hard.

"Wow…If looks could kill."

Pip caught someone moving in the corner of his eye. The constable had snuck up behind them during all of this and nobody seemed to notice but him.

All of a sudden, Uncle Leon's knees buckled underneath him. Pip pulled away and grabbed the rifle from his back. His pistol flew in the air.

Before he knew it, the constable was on top of his uncle, forcing him down to the ground. "Harvey, give me something to tie his hands."

Harvey rushed up, ripping a strip of ragged orange fabric from the pant leg of his overalls. "That'll do for now."

The two of them bound Pip's uncle, tugging tightly on the knot. Loretta still held the gun on Baby Bear as the constable got up. He snatched the pistol from the ground with his good arm and took the stance of a trained officer. "Now give me the gun Loretta. I can take it from here."

"No!" she argued.

"Please!"

Loretta looked like a confused wild cat, bobbing her head back and forth between them all. She sobbed, "I can't. I have to kill him like he killed my Jeremy." She turned, defying him as she started counting down, "One…. two…."

Baby Bear pulled a knife from his leg holster and inched toward Loretta.

"Ma'am," the constable pleaded, aiming the pistol at her now. "I'll have to insist you co-operate, or I *will* shoot you!"

"…three…four," she bawled, completely distraught, "…five!"

One single solitary shot rang out.

Chapter 50

John had been gone for a while now. Jenny was getting impatient. She looked around at the other members of the medical team and sighed. "I hate this waiting. I wish we could do something. I don't suppose any of you want to go with me to see what's taking them so long?"

The other three people on board shook their heads adamantly against the idea. *Great!* They were no help at all. She would just have to sit tight like the rest of them while her husband was out there somewhere, possibly injured.

She bit her nails and sighed.

As she laid her head back, closing her eyes, she heard a faint rap on the door again. The pilot opened it up to John. *Finally!* "Okay people. Let's move. We're heading to the tower now."

~~~~

"I didn't do it!" Loretta screamed, dropping the gun to the ground, raising her hands in the air. Harvey didn't know if he believed her. George hit the ground like a dead fly.

Brian steadied his aim on Loretta, looking more confused than Harvey did. If Loretta didn't shoot George, and Brian didn't shoot, then who did?

"I wasn't going to shoot," Loretta kept insisting. "Really! I just wanted to scare him. I decided not to do it Harvey. You have to believe me."

Harvey sighed and moved toward the weeping woman, putting his arms around her. "I believe you dear. I believe you."

Brian rushed up to George's dead body laying prostate on the earthy ground and observed the large gunshot wound to his back. He looked up to see the strangers coming at them.

"Grandfather!" Pip cried out, running after two old men with rifles in their arms. "It's my grandfather and Grayling. They came."

Harvey heard the big Indian groaning on the ground, still lying on his stomach, arms tied behind his back. He lifted his face from the dirt, wearing a cumbersome grizzly head like a baseball cap. Harvey thought it was disgraceful. George wore a cubs head. Their faces were dirty from blood smear, sickening Harvey more than words could say.

As the two old Indian men approached, Pip jumped into their arms. They hugged the boy together. "I'm sorry I didn't stay home," Pip said sobbing.

"Oh, Little Caribou," the man he called Grayling answered him, messing Pip's hair, "for some reason, your grandfather and I didn't really think you would."

The two men introduced themselves, shaking Brian's hand, then Harvey's and Loretta's. Pip's grandfather walked over to the thin Indian tied up on the ground. He kicked him hard in the side as he lay there. "You're a fool Leon," he said, bending over, ripping the Grizzly head from him. "You're not of my blood *anymore*. You have no soul." Then he spit on Leon, turning his back and walking away. He charged over to George and yanked the cub's head from him as well.

Then the old man raised both bear heads in the air, closed his eyes as he looked up to the sky, chanting something that sounded like a prayer in his own language.

Loretta stepped over to Harvey, reaching down to hold his hand. "I'm sorry," she said, not looking at him, only squeezing his hand.

"I know," he whispered, squeezing her hand right back.

Then as the early morning sun glistened brightly through the trees, they both squinted to see the two choppers hovering above them.

Chapter 51

During the Medi-Vac ride to the hospital, Jenny patched Brian's shoulder and wrists up and took his vitals. He was surprised to see his wife on board, but glad she had come along. She didn't know how much she had moved him by being there for him.

She was a breath of fresh air.

His wife's nightmares she had every night since he left, puzzled him. She said that's what alerted her to his situation, claiming God gave her the dreams. If he was a religious man, and he wasn't, he might just think the same thing. But it made more sense to him, to write it off as a coincidence.

But what did he know anyway?

She told him she woke up sick to her stomach every night with nightmares. This made him chuckle. She insisted it was because of the dreams, but when she continued waking up sick the fist week home, and he forced her to go to the doctor; he knew the reason long before she did: They were going to have another baby.

She bawled when she found out the results, afraid he wouldn't approve. But even though he demanded for years that they only have one child, it didn't seem to matter now.

After all that had happened, he realized life was more precious then he ever imagined, and vowed to never let his job take priority over his family again.

He'd have to make up for lost time with his son and his wife and take them on a very long vacation…*without* that blasted cell phone.

~~~

Loretta was back at her home, alone in her little house in Chicago again. The mildew smell almost knocked her off her feet when she came through the door. Everything was as she left it, except for her.

She had *definitely* changed.

When she looked at Jeremy's picture on the wall, she actually smiled at her boy, confident that she hadn't failed him, that God had him in His hands. For she truly knew he was safe now, safe from the storms of life.

As she walked over to the dusty Bible that she once carried to church so long ago, she blew off the puff of grey and opened it to Psalms, finding a verse at random. She read the passage that her fingertip pointed too. *"The righteous cry out, and the Lord hears them; He delivers them from all their troubles. The Lord is close to the broken-hearted and saves those who are crushed in spirit."*

Tears flooded her eyes as a droplet dripped down on the thin page, seeping through immediately. She sobbed, calling out to her savior, *"I cried out to you Lord and you delivered me from my trouble, you fixed my broken heart and my crushed spirit and restored my soul. You are love...and You proved it all along even though I thought you abandoned me. You didn't, you carried me though my sorrow like a faithful friend. Thank you, Jesus, with all my heart."*

She wished Harvey were here. He'd be so proud of her for finding a verse of comfort for herself. She didn't have the memorization down pat like he did, but she was definitely going to work on it.

She missed his jolly antics...but then, as soon as she settled with the realtor, she'd hop on the first plane to Vancouver.

After all, life was too short to run from love.

###

If you loved Deep Bay Vengeance, you will love its sequel, Deep Bay Relic. A sample is available on the next page. (Book three, Deep Bay Legacy, is also available to purchase on Amazon.com)

Prologue - Deep Bay Relic

In the beginning...a flaming meteorite sliced through the heavens, leaving a smoky passageway to the waters below, inseminating the surface of the deep, infecting life with a foul ancient creature.

For years, it's been hiding in the 700-foot water-filled crater, waiting, lurking, and feeding on anything just to stay alive, never staying topside for long.

Until now.

Through the creatures small slits that served as its eyes, it saw the blurry mass floating above, waiting, hoping to catch a glimpse.

But the creature was not afraid, it roused at the movement in the shadows above, hopeful for a meal or two, ready to torpedo when least expected.

With the thrust of the creature's body, it quickly headed toward the surface, gaining speed as it neared the top. Then, as it broke through the water, freeing itself from the bondage it once knew, it birthed its ugly head.

The mass was no longer blurry but brilliant with color...and the creature was pleased with its efforts, thrilled to do it again and again until there was nothing left but a pool of crimson blood.

Deep Bay Relic - Chapter 1

Carla Reece took her scuba gear and headed for the boat with Mike, hoping that today wouldn't be as long as yesterday. They had been out all day and all evening and hadn't found anything that resembled treasure.

Being invited to go on a treasure hunt by her boyfriend was one thing, but Mike and his buddies seemed to be more interested in the Loch Ness Monster theories they kept talking about.

The word was, there were supposed to be monsters living in Deep Bay, or at least that's what the guys kept telling her, but she didn't believe that kind of thing. Why should she? She was older and wiser than all of them and knew a tale when she heard one.

Not even a child would believe it. When her kids were young, they always laughed whenever she told them about Santa Claus or the Tooth Fairy. Whenever Christmas came around, they teased her claiming *she* was both the Tooth Fairy and Santa.

What killjoys.

Carla had no one to blame but herself. She had taught her children to be sceptical, and now they didn't even believe in God.

Sometimes *she* even had trouble with that one. There were times when she would sit in church and just laugh under her breath at the Pastor. His sermons were so judgemental. In fact, most of the churches she had been to were full of judgemental hypocrites. That's why she stopped going to church altogether even though she had been a Christian ever since childhood.

Leaving church wasn't a decision she came upon lightly though, she'd prayed about it for a long time until the Lord revealed to her that she would be better off listening to Sunday services on Television instead.

Now, at the age of 49, Carla never missed a televised Sunday morning service, and she still considered herself to be a Christian even though her good-for-nothing husband John, called her a heathen every time he left for church and she stayed at home.

He was the heathen with his judgmental attitude and his self-righteous phoney baloney persona he put on. Christian's were supposed to love each other.

Their marriage had been falling apart for years, but more now since Casey, the youngest had moved out to go to College last year. They were practically divorced but still lived in the same house.

Actually, it all really started when she had an affair twenty years ago. She got pregnant with Casey. It wasn't something she was proud of, but what could she do? John was being a jerk as usual, and she was starving for love…just like now.

"Hey! Wake up Carla!" a voice rang out. "Are you daydreaming or something?"

Carla hadn't realized she was off in another world. They had already arrived at the diving point.

"Are you coming down or not?" Mike asked Carla rather rudely.

"I am!"

"Then move your butt *Grandma!*"

"*Oh thanks!*" she laughed it off, wanting to say more but refraining because, after all, she *was* old enough to be a grandma. What was a 49-year-old woman doing with a 25-year-old guy anyway? She couldn't expect him to be respectful like older men, he was just a kid. The only thing she had going for her in this relationship was the *great* fringe benefits and the fact that he *wasn't* John.

Actually, she should count herself lucky, most women her age couldn't even find a man, leave alone one that still had hair on his head. But she *made* herself attractive, not like the average dowdy 49-year-old. She died her hair sandy blonde to cover the grey and spent a fortune on highlights every month. She always made sure she wore the latest styles as well, and the tanning salons gave her skin a healthy bronze glow. The liposuction and breast implants were a huge success, and the money spent on her face-lift last May was well worth it.

Carla made sure she was beautiful, in fact, she looked and felt twenty years younger. What man could pass her by without winking. Actually, that wasn't really the problem. She'd cheated on John for more than twenty years with anyone that wanted her, always telling herself that it was okay. The Bible said that husbands should love their wives like Christ loved the Church – John failed at that so many times – so it wasn't *her* fault she strayed from him. How was she supposed to get the love she needed?

John's churchy friends had a lot of names for her. None of them nice. That was okay with her though, God knew her struggles and she was *sure* he accepted her anyway.

As Carla slipped her wet suit over her tiny pink bikini and zipped it over her large implants, she sighed at the realization that Mike had already dove down with his four buddies. Why did she feel like the fifth wheel here? Hadn't they had enough treasure hunting for one week?

She spit into her mask like Mike had showed her, rubbing it around the glass so it wouldn't fog up, and slipped it over her tanned face, climbing down the ladder on the side of the boat, submerging her black flippers into the cold dark water.

As she lowered her entire body, put her breathing apparatus over her mouth and took one last look around her before going all the way underwater, something startled her. She ripped her gear off her face immediately and climbed back up the ladder, breathing hard. *There's something in the water!*

Carla didn't know if she was seeing things or if the water actually had turned a different color. She looked again, squinting in the sun, cupping a hand over her brow so that she could see a little better.

She *was* right, her mind confirmed. The water *is* red!

~~~~

It was mid morning and Sadie Long was frying eggs for the two guests that still hadn't gotten up yet. The five divers with the boat had taken off early again with nothing for breakfast but a case of beer. It bothered her that they even brought it along with them since they were told that this was a dry resort. She'd have to call in for reinforcements to deal with the issue. It happened every now and then.

Shining Star Lodge was a Christian establishment, it had been since it opened for business four years ago. Everybody knew it, or at least she thought they did. It even said so on their brochure.

Sadie inhaled the aroma from the crackling eggs in the frying pan. Oh, how she loved the smell of fried eggs in the morning. It reminded her of her days as a school teacher. She'd make breakfast every morning for the children who came to school hungry. It was her own little outreach program that meant so much to her at the time.

She still missed that part of her life, but she was glad she wasn't teaching anymore. It was getting so difficult to do her job properly in an ungodly school system these days. The kids were becoming so unruly and it was hard to enforce discipline on them especially when their parents thought they were angels.

Teaching in a Christian school appealed to her but Sadie couldn't seem to acquire a permanent position. All she could manage to get were substitute positions, and she couldn't pay the bills doing that.

Never marrying didn't help matters either. Perhaps if she had a husband, she wouldn't have had to struggle with money all her life. At least that's what her friends always told her. But Sadie never had the desire to get married. Sure, she liked men, but she invested her time into her teaching career when she was young, and then all the *good* ones were snatched away before she even had a chance. The ones she did date, always seemed to want one thing, and she wouldn't give them *that*. She would not compromise her faith for a roll in the hay. It just wasn't worth it.

In return for her obedience, Sadie always felt blessed. She was content just being single, doing God's work – and when the opportunity arose for her to take on The Shining Star Ministries it was an honour.

Leading Bible Study classes at a wilderness retreat fit her like a glove. God knew all along what He wanted Sadie Long to do with her life. She may not have a husband, but those who came to Shining Star always provided her with enough love and companionship to last a lifetime.

Except the five divers that is.

Sadie wondered why they were here. They weren't like the usual guests who would come to the resort. They seemed to be after something. And the older woman who tagged along with them didn't quite fit, with her Barbie looking physique and her long pink gel nails. It was clear she was trying to fool everyone into thinking she wasn't aging, but Sadie saw it in her eyes. She was old and worn, probably almost as old as she was. No makeup and hairdo could cover up *that*. She wondered why some women fought aging so much. Sadie just accepted her plain Jane looks. God made her just the way He wanted, and that's the way she would stay.

Perhaps the woman needed to hear the same thing, but Sadie hadn't had the opportunity to say much of anything to her since her arrival a week ago. She would always run out early with those boys and return late at night. But that didn't matter, they were supposed to be staying another week. If God wanted her to reach out to this woman, He would give her the opportunity. He always did.

Sadie put the last-minute touches on the two breakfast platters that were now ready to eat. All she had to do was ring the bell and her two guests would come running like they always did.

Eunice had been at Shining Star now for the last two months. Life was hard for her. She had been sponsored by her church to come and stay as long as she needed, but Sadie wondered if she was making any progress at all.

It wasn't her place to judge, just teach God's word, but she'd hoped for more progress by now. Each evening they had a Bible Study together and it was only last week that Eunice finally shared with the group about her problems.

One of her problems was beginning to show long before the woman ever spoke a word. Even though Sadie had never had children of her own, she knew when someone was pregnant. Eunice couldn't hide it any longer, in fact, that was the straw that broke the camel's back so to speak. She must have realized people weren't blind.

At first, Sadie just listened. Eunice had quite a story. She actually *was* a believer, a very strong believer, but like so many women, she got caught up with the wrong man. Now, after ten years of common-law marriage to a Catholic man, and four kids later, she was stuck in a sinful situation.

"But I *can't* leave him!" she would cry over and over. "I tried *many* times. My church even tried to help me get out of the relationship, but I couldn't leave my children. Sin is sin, I know that, but what about the innocent children? They didn't ask to be part of this. Should I punish them for *my* sins?"

Sadie never knew how to answer her. All she could ever think of was Eve, and her sin of taking the apple. Hadn't her children had to pay for *her* sins? Even now, all the sons and daughters of Eve were still paying for her sins.

But Sadie couldn't tell her that. For some reason, her mouth wouldn't open whenever she tried to explain it. She prayed for wisdom everyday for this situation with Eunice. It was definitely a tuff one.

And now she was pregnant with a fifth child. Sadie's heart broke for her especially when she told her of her journey to the abortion clinic one day. It must have been tough on the woman but she was glad she decided to keep the child. Life is precious to God. That advice she did give her, but advice about her family situation was not so easy.

Sadie wondered just how far along Eunice was in her pregnancy, she told her six months or so, but over the past three weeks, it looked more like nine. Maybe that's because of her cooking.

That reminded her of the eggs, they were getting cold.

"Eunice says she isn't hungry Sadie," a voice shot out from around the corner. It was Dinah, a teenage girl sent to Shining Star from another church. She was only seventeen and had already been through the ringer.

At the tender age of thirteen, she was raped by her mothers boyfriend. Her home environment wasn't exactly stable. After that, she fell into prostitution and got hooked on Crystal Meth. If it hadn't been for the local church and their street ministry, she wouldn't have had a chance. They sent her to a drug rehabilitation facility, and then they sent her to Shining Star Lodge.

Sadie led her to the Lord the first week she arrived, and now after setting her up with a Christian group home called Broken Wing, she was almost ready to go.

A tear came to her eye. How could she let her little butterfly go? That's what she called the pixie faced blond with freckles each time she hugged her…just like now.

"You're squeezing me too tight again," Dinah groaned, locked in Sadie's bear-hug, smiling through her tears as she kissed the girl on the top of her head.

"My butterfly."

"Okay already, *I'm your butterfly*," Dinah groaned again, "but didn't you hear me? I said Eunice isn't coming for breakfast, she says she isn't hungry but I know she has to be, you saw how many snacks she had last night before bed."

"Maybe that's *why* she isn't hungry dear."

"I don't think so. I heard her bawling last night. I couldn't sleep a wink."

"I know sweetheart," Sadie frowned, "I heard her too. We just have to keep praying for her. God will help her in his own gentle way. Just like you. Now bow your head with me so we can eat these eggs before they get too cold."

As Dinah prayed for the meal, Sadie opened one eye and peered through the large kitchen window toward the Star River in front of the lodge. A boat was coming in.

"Eat up dear," Sadie said, excusing herself from the table. "I'll be right back. I just have to go see who that is coming in with the boat."

"It's probably those strange diver people."

Sadie just shook her head, hearing the girl but not turning to respond, focussing more on the strangeness of the situation.

"Oh, and by the way," Dinah shouted with a mouthful of eggs. "Those four guys have been flirting with me like crazy."

Sadie stopped then, turned to Dinah with a great big frown.

Giggling, the girl blurted out with laughter, "Just kidding. You looked so serious I had to do something."

"You just finish eating young lady," Sadie scolded her. "Just don't joke about that kind of thing. It's not funny."

Dinah was still grinning when she turned to finish her meal. The girl was such a tease. But right now, Sadie wasn't in the mood. Something was wrong, she could feel it.

As the boat neared the small dock, Sadie rushed over to it, wiping her sweaty hands in her full apron that was still tied around her from cooking breakfast.

"Hello," she shouted, waving her arms to the lone occupant. As she got closer, she realized it was the diving woman. But where were the others?

The woman jumped out of the boat and tied it up to the dock. She flopped like a rag doll down to the grass beside the dock and moaned, "Help me! Please!"

"What is it?" Sadie rushed up to the woman, bending down beside her.

The woman looked a mess. Her black wet-suit was shiny and wet, and her bare feet were all bloody. The black smudged eyeliner under her eyes made her tanned face look like a zombie.

"What happened?" Sadie asked, lowering her voice to a soothing tone, stroking the woman's bushy hair. The woman relaxed a bit but was obviously still upset.

"They're dead," she sobbed against Sadie's shoulder. "They're *all* dead!"

Keep reading (DEEP BAY RELIC) by purchasing it on Amazon.com

ABOUT THE AUTHOR

Award-winning author Kathleen Morris, writes Christian fiction, mystery, suspense, and thrillers, to spread Biblical truths around the world through her many flawed characters she creates. Her hope is to show that we all deserve God's unconditional love. Kathleen's debut novel titled *Deep Bay Vengeance* is her first in the *Deep Bay Series,* with *Deep Bay Relic,* and finally, *Deep Bay Legacy,* to complete the series. Her next two-book series, is called, The Blood War series, consisting of book one called, *The Prion Attachment,* and book two called, *Blood Purge.* Book two in the series, *Blood Purge.*

When she's not writing, she enjoys spending time with her husband Barry and their three grown children at her home in Saskatchewan, Canada. For more on Kathleen Morris please check out her Amazon Author page: Kathleen Morris author page.

BOOKS BY KATHLEEN MORRIS

- Deep Bay Relic
- Deep Bay Legacy

Try the new (Blood War) series
- The Prion Attachment
- Blood Purge

####